EKATERINA

a novel by

DONALD HARINGTON

EKATERINA

HARCOURT
BRACE &
COMPANY
New York San Diego London

Grateful acknowledgment is made to Doubleday to reprint an excerpt from
"The Lost Son," copyright 1947 by Theodore Roethke, from *The Collected Poems of Theodore Roethke*
by Theodore Roethke. Used by permission of Doubleday, a division of
Bantam Doubleday Dell Publishing Group, Inc.

Library of Congress Cataloging-in-Publication Data
Harington, Donald.
Ekaterina: a novel/by Donald Harington.—1st ed.
p.   cm.
ISBN 0-15-128122-X
I. Title.
PS3558.A6242E38   1993
813'.54—dc20   92-37830

Designed by Lisa Peters
Printed in the United States of America
First edition
A B C D E

To Kim

PART ONE

BEGINNING
winter

SHORTLY AFTER THE SECOND WORLD WAR, or the Great
Patriotic War, as Ekaterina was taught to call it, the fabulous
American poet Theodore Roethke wrote a long poem called
"The Lost Son," the conclusion to a volume of the same title.
Critic Lawrence Brace said of it, "No poem in the English
language has better light." The fifth section, last section, is
entitled "It Was Beginning Winter," and it concludes:

> *A lively understandable spirit*
> *Once entertained you.*
> *It will come again.*
> *Be still.*
> *Wait.*

EKATERINA YOU WERE, and you were not at all. You were from a land far away, once upon a time and upon no time at all, where stories always begin, "There was, and there was not at all . . . ," as if to confute truth or affirm invention, in celebration of the imagination's freedom to transcend the stubborn facts of "reality": you were, and still are, Ekaterina: all of this is real, and not a word of it is true: you escaped the clutches of a sadist named Bolshakov (a real name) who could not separate truth from fiction, and you came to America.

There was and there was not at all a great city in an eastern state, a city devoted to the manufacture of a hard but malleable metal commonly used in straight pins, a hilly city at the confluence of two rivers of Indian names and the beginning of a third, a city that, like you and I, gave up smoking—oh, why do I have to shield its name? You did not choose the city, except to whatever extent it may have been chosen for you by your guardian angel, Anangka, and you suspected that Anangka was still half-asleep from jet lag or, at best, becoming frustrated and grim in her efforts to provide a destiny for you.

No, you were sent to this city involuntarily, under the aegis of the Fund for the Relief of Russian Writers and Scientists in Exile, whose New York (a real name) office had met your plane, had interviewed you (in both Russian and English, noting that you were not sufficiently fluent in the latter, and, making you a gift of a purse-size paperback,

Akhmanova's Russian–English Dictionary), had given you in dollars the equivalent of 176 rubles, enough to last out that month of December, and had put you and your pasteboard suitcase (containing one change of clothes, basic toiletries, and a few souvenirs from "camp") on a bus for the ride of 365 miles to the city of your referral. "Wait," you'd said in English to your agent from the Fund, before he put you on the bus. "Am I Writer, or am I Scientist?" He had laughed, thinking your question in jest, and had made no move to answer it.

The bus ride took you through some snow-covered farm country where the people, called Amish (a real name), still wore old-fashioned clothing and the women wore black bonnets. You were wearing a black scarf wrapped around your head like a bonnet, or babushka, knotted into a bow beneath your chin. It covered all of your hair—or rather, your lack of hair, which was just beginning to grow back from the last time it had been shaved in camp. None of your fellow passengers seemed to make anything of your headgear; maybe they thought you were some kind of Amish.

You were, and you were not at all, at least not any longer, Svanetian. It was nothing like Amish: rural and old-fashioned, yes, but not deliberately so, and not particularly religious. Just as the county in which I spent my last years, and our ultimate destination in this story, was and is the most remote of all the seventy-five counties in that (unnamed) state, Svanetia is the most remote district, formerly a principality, of the rugged mountains of the Southern Caucasus in Georgia, once part of a Communist confederation called the Soviet Union, now independent again but anxiously so. You had not been home for three years, not since they sent you to camp at the age of twenty-four, and that was a dozen years ago from now, and you still have not been home . . . except in some of your splendid writings.

Just the other year, and not any year at all, the people of Georgia, making a bold move to assert their independence from the still-existing Soviet Union, established as their president the selfsame Zviad Gamsakhurdia who had been your mentor and friend and whose arrest as a political prisoner by the Communists had led to your arrest. Zviad (your stringing of consonants is going to give me some trouble, although we ghosts are multilingual) was not a Svanetian but a native of Tbilisi, or Tiflis, the capital, and a son of the writer Konstantine Gamsakhurdia, whose work you admired; and Zviad was a lecturer in English (American literature) at Tbilisi University when you taught there (not, alas, in English). He had published your first poems in his *samizdat* journal *Okros Sacmisi,* which means in Georgian "Golden Fleece," and you can remember when you fantasied being Medea to his Jason—you were twenty-three and he was thirty-six—and in his fifties he became president of the whole country, something you couldn't have comprehended in those days when the Kremlin still had all of you under its iron fist.

But you hadn't gone to jail for Zviady. You had gone to jail for Georgia, and for Svanetia, and for the honor of the royal name you carried, Dadeshkeliani, and for human rights everywhere: after Zviady's arrest you became co-chair of the Tbilisi Watch Committee, to observe and protest the violations of human rights that were occurring all around you. By then you had stopped writing poetry. No one, as I discovered myself some years ago, reads poetry.

STANDING ON THE SIDEWALK below the mansion, you studied again the slip of paper in your hand, to verify the address. You had expected perhaps one of those singular dwellings you had seen so often from the bus, what we call "suburban ranch style": one-story, low or flat roof, cozy, convenient, conventional. But this was urban, and miles from the nearest vestigial ranch. This was a castle, nearly, larger than the ancestral manors of the Dadeshkelianis in Etseri and your own village of Lisedi, manors that had been broken up into apartments when Svanetia, along with all of Georgia, was collectivized by the Communist Soviets. This castle had no tower looming over it, but it was made largely of dark stone, with enough busy classical details in wood to decorate it like certain town houses of Tbilisi. You looked up and down the avenue to see that there were other mansions of similar size if not similar style in the neighborhood, and, in the distance, the soaring gothic tower of the city's university.

"*Im, imte, imetchu, Anangka?*" you addressed in Svani your unseen purveyor of Providence. "Have you got in mind for me to live *here?*" Surely these Elmores were very wealthy capitalists, with servants.

The door was answered not by a servant but by a comely youth: a smiling lad of twelve years who instantly struck you as a synthesis of your Islamber and your Dzhordzha: he was tall for his age and skinny, like Islamber, with the Svane's slightly hood-lidded eyes that made him look sleepy or sly or Oriental, depending upon whether he looked straight at you or sidelong; but he seemed to possess Dzhordzha's quality—aura or emanation—of *makap,* precocious sexuality, of being what your fellow writer and near-compatriot, Nabokov (a very real name, of whom you had not yet heard), called (coined and minted) a *faunlet:* the male equivalent, if there is one, of his immortal nymphet.

"*Ivasu khari, Anangka!*" you said aloud, which is to say, Thank thee, Anangka. The boy stared at you, and his smile was uncertain. You were tempted to give him his first lesson in elementary Svani on the spot, or even to introduce him to your invisible companion, but instead you announced, "I am Ekaterina Vladimirovna Dadeshkeliani."

The boy made a sound like "Whew," and then he said, "How do you, like, *spell* all of that?" but he giggled (Islamber's vulgar giggle!) to let you know he didn't really require you to spell it for him. And then he said, "You must be the die sinner."

You attempted to repeat the words, "Die sinner?" and your hand instinctively reached for the dictionary in your purse.

"What Mom calls you," he said. "I'll go get her." He turned to leave you on the doorstep but turned back, remembering what little manners he had: "Hey, come on in." And he motioned to a spot in the spacious foyer where you could stand and wait for Mrs. Elmore.

But in Svanetia one never crosses a threshold without express invitation from the male head of the house, and, unless this pubertal youth was already as mature as you hoped, he was probably not the head of the house. So you remained standing outside the door, the cold air at your back (mild, even balmy by Svanetian standards) rushing through the open door.

You brought out the dictionary. You were sure of *die,* but checked it anyway for other meanings: singular of *dice;* to desire greatly, as if pining away; stamping device; but also possibly just *di-,* prefix meaning twice, double, or two, as in *dicotyledon.* Of course! *Sinner* you did not know at all, and you found it quickly: one who sins. *Sin:* any offense, violation, fault, or error.

You were meditating upon the idea of being a double sinner and the fantastic chance that these people already knew about *both* Islamber and Dzhordzha, when the hobbledehoy returned, saying first, "Don't you understand 'Come in'?" and then, "Mom's upstairs trying to, like, help Professor Ogden. I think that old sinner is *dying!* Anyhow, she says for me to, like, fix you a drink and she'll be down in a minute. I hope you don't drink, though. Do you?"

Still you hesitated outside the door, searching for the English word for *baba* (Svanetian), *mama* (*sic,* Georgian), *otyets* (Russian), and remembering it without having to look it up: "Your fadder. Is home?"

"Dad? No, he's at the Hillman." (I ought to shade the library's name, as I'm taking pains to shade so much else, but I like the real name, being a hillman myself.) "Hey, if you're not coming in, we'd better shut the door." The faunlet put one hand on the doorknob and the other on your coat sleeve, and began tugging each, to see which would move first. You reluctantly entered the house.

The entrance hall was enormous, with a floor of marble, and all the walls were covered with mirrors. Throughout the house, you would discover, there were mirrors everywhere, as if the original builder of the house were either extremely vain (he was) or inspired by Louis XIV. In Leningrad you had seen buildings that had many mirrors, but not like this, and in Svanetia there were several houses that had no mirrors at all.

You glanced at yourself in one. At a rest stop on the bus route, because you had noticed that some of the other women on the bus had been wearing them, you had taken the one good pair of *dzhinsy* out of your suitcase and had put them on: they were comfortable and kept your legs warm, and you saw now how they matched almost identically the pair of *dzhinsy* that the boy was wearing, just as faded. But your coat, the prison-issue *palto,* was shabby, grimy, and patched, and, with the black babushka around your head, it made you look like a peasant.

Reading your thoughts, the boy held his hands as if to pinch your shoulders and invited, "You wanta take that off?" and helped you out of your crummy coat. Then he gestured to the left: "This is our apartment," and led you through some slid-open sliding doors into a suite of rooms, one flowing from the other, each layered with more mirrors, and with shelves and antique furniture festooned with bric-a-brac and lace.

He led you to a polished buffet truly covered with bottles of all sizes and shapes. " 'Name your poison,' " he said and giggled again, and you knew he was quoting his elders, so you did not bring out the paperback to look up *poison*. His fingers began to hop from bottle to bottle: "Rye . . . Scotch . . . rum . . . bourbon . . . gin . . ." His hand stopped and lifted a bottle. "I guess you'd want this one. Vodka. There's hundred-proof Smirnoff and eighty-six-proof Popov."

You thirsted. The night of your leavetaking from camp, the other women had pooled their rations of tea to brew a quantity of *chifir,* a powerful drink, black and thick, invented by inmates, that requires fifty grams of tea leaves; and, in flagrant violation of regulations, they had toasted you with it and helped you consume it, enough of it to make all of you quite tipsy. The *chifir* had given you your first real high since your arrest and your last one until the possibility that now lay before you.

"But like I say," the boy was saying, setting the Smirnoff back down, "I hope you don't drink. You're, like, too pretty to drink. I could give you a soft drink, I mean, you know, some pop, Coke or stuff." Your fingers were groping for your purse, for your paperback. But you did not resort to it, waiting, and trying to understand him: one of his strange words had seemed familiar: *Coke.*

"Coke?" you said.

"Oh, cool!" he exclaimed. "I'll get you a Coke from the fridge." He turned to go but turned back. "Because, you know, everybody in this house, and I mean everybody, is, like, getting fried all the time, you know?"

While he was out of the room you looked up *fried,* without much success.

"THAT *KENNY!*" the woman said, flapping her hand in dismissal, then snatching the aluminum can out of your hand. "He doesn't have the manners of a billy goat! I'm Loretta Elmore, and I'll bet you'd like some vodka, right?"

"Mayest thou be victorious," you said in a fairly good English rendering of the common Svanetian greeting.

"Do what?" said Loretta Elmore. She held the bottle of Smirnoff above a crystal glass, raising one eyebrow in expectation of your approval, and when you nodded she splashed a couple of jiggers into the glass. "Ice?" she said.

It sounded nothing like the Svanetian *kvarmal* nor the Russian *lyod.* "I am having much problems with the English," you said. "How spells 'ice'?"

She took the lid off the ice bucket and lifted out a palmful of cubes. "I-see-ee," she said. She dropped the cubes into another glass, into which she poured some of the amber liquid from another bottle, as if in demonstration. She held it up, said, "Bourbon and branch on the rocks. Can you say that?"

You were always good at mimicry, at repetition. You repeated her exactly, with just a slight misinflection.

"Very good," she said, and pointed her glass at you and said, "Cheers," and drank most of it in one swallow.

You drank your vodka, without ice, in one swallow. It was the real stuff, as we say, and the first you'd had since the days in Tbilisi when you spent too much of your university salary on a daily dose of it.

Loretta refilled your glass and asked, "Don't you want to take that scarf off your head and sit down?" When you hesitated, she pantomimed removing the scarf and sitting.

"Sit, ya," you agreed. "But 'scarf,' no. I am having no hair."

"You don't mean to tell me!" she said. "Now that's terrible. Is that what they did to you? Did they cut it all off?" She scissored together her first and second fingers and you nodded, and she said, "That really sucks! How long were you in the die sinner's slammer?"

"Pardon. What means 'die sinner'?"

"What you were. Weren't you?" She spelled the word for you and it did not spell exactly as she and her son had spoken it.

You brought out your paperback, showed her the cover, and apologized, "I am having to use."

"Use," she said. "Go right ahead."

You looked it up: one who dissents, as one who refuses to accept a religious doctrine. Your finger moved a short distance down the page, to another, better word. You tried not to sound didactic, let alone superior. "I think," you told her, "thou want other word, *dissident,* not *dissenter.*"

"Yeah, that's right!" she said. "That's the word Kenneth—Big Kenny, who's Pa—that's the word he uses. I just got it mixed up. You're not a die sinner. You're a dissident!"

You smiled. And that was your first awareness, dear Kat, that all of us have problems with English.

BIG KENNY, OR PA, came home from the Hillman in time for supper and was delighted to find that you had arrived safely, since it had been his idea in the first place: in the course of the evening, and with much help from your paperback dictionary, you were able to determine that your host, or rather your landlord, or perhaps a little of both, Dr. Kenneth L. Elmore, Sr., 71, was a retired professor of anthropology at the university who, in his superannuation and idle hours, espoused several worthy social causes, including Save-a-Child and Urban League and Amnesty International, and had somehow got his name on the mailing list of the Fund for the Relief of Russian Writers and Scientists in Exile. He had not contributed any cash to the Fund, and he did not now intend to contribute anything at all to your welfare, other than excusing you from paying your first month's rent, or rather what remained of the month of December, and it was to be hoped that you would be able to pay your January rent out of your salary from the university, assuming that his efforts to help you find employment there were successful. Thus far, his efforts had been limited to sending interdepartmental memos to his colleagues in Biological Sciences and Slavic Languages and Literature; he was prevented from phoning or visiting them by an advanced hearing impairment that, in addition to what problems you already had with the English language, rendered communication between the two of you almost impossible. ("The stubborn old gomer refuses to try a hearing aid," Loretta said in the presence of the nonhearing old gomer, a word not in your dictionary.) Dr. Elmore had received, in reply to his memos, an offer to have you interviewed by Dr. Schvann of Slavic and Dr. Dalrymple of Biological Sciences, and, as soon as you got settled into your apartment upstairs (adjacent to, on one side, Dr. Edith Koeppe of Sociology and, on the other side, Dr. Knox Ogden of English), you would be expected to appear for your interviews. ("I'll loan you the borrow of one of my dresses," Loretta offered generously. "I think we're about the same size. And you really ought to wear some of my jewelry, at least a necklace.")

But Dr. Elmore had very little to say to you, that evening or later. At the supper table (Kenneth, Jr., "Little" Kenny, the only sober person at that late hour, cooked and served a supper of cheeseburgers and french fries), Dr. Elmore casually remarked, not looking at you, "I have the greatest respect for dissidents, particularly those against the Bolshevik ideology," but in a voice so hoarse and weak that Loretta had to repeat the words for you, slowly, and yell at her husband, "SHE HAS TO LOOK 'EM UP!" while you successfully found *ideology,* which sounded pretty much the same in Russian, with a different accent. Then the three Elmores, including smiling Kenny, waited for your response to that remark.

"Dissidents," you said, "are being . . . Excuse"—you looked up a couple of words—"successful only if famous. Like Solzhenitsyn. I not famous dissident. I, nobody know."

Loretta yelled this at her husband, and he smiled politely and shook his head in sympathy, or in disavowal of having heard; you could not tell which.

You were not drunk, and neither, precisely, were Dr. and Mrs. Elmore, although all three of you had consumed large quantities of, respectively, vodka, Scotch, and bourbon. You were out of practice, and a quantity of vodka that would have given you only a pleasant buzz in Tbilisi or Leningrad now rendered you a bit stuporous and stuttering and inattentive. Each time Loretta got up to refill your glass, her son would whine, "*Mom!*" and roll his eyes in disgust and give you assorted facial contortions of disappointment, pity, concern, and beseechment.

At one point during the evening, Loretta observed that your unusual name was difficult, to put it mildly, and she delivered herself of the opinion that you ought to pick one of the many American translations, Cathy, perhaps, or Katy, or Cassie, or Kitty, or perhaps just Kay. At the very least, Catherine. "What can we *call* you?" she wondered aloud. Without wishing to be unfriendly or in the least aloof, you announced, "Ekaterina Vladimirovna," dropping, at least, your unwieldy surname.

Finally, when Dr. Elmore seemed to have withdrawn entirely into himself and was making no effort to respond to his wife's shouts of "SHE WANTS US TO CALL HER EE COTTERINA VLAH DEEMER ROV NAH!" Kenny said to his mother, "Can't you see she's *tired?*" and Loretta suggested that maybe it was time that Kenny showed you up to your room, and the boy leapt at the chance.

YOUR ROOM, on the second floor of the mansion, west side, was large enough to house, by Soviet standards, an entire family, but you had it all to yourself, and even a bathroom! You could not believe, at first, that you would not be sharing the bath with Professors Koeppe and Ogden, who, Kenny tried to convince you, both had separate bathrooms. The mansion contained a total of ten apartments, each with its own bathroom, each populated by a single faculty member or graduate student, the latter on the third floor. Each apartment even had its own small cooking niche (Kenny gave you the word: *kitchenette.*) Yours had a gas stove, a small refrigerator, and a sink, but there were no pots, pans, dishes, or cutlery. ("I could, like, snitch you some stuff from downstairs just to get you started," Kenny offered.)

Kenny had already taken from his parents' apartment a table lamp and a reading lamp, which he now put upon your desk and plugged in and turned on. Then he struck a match and lit the gas heater embedded in the exterior wall, and he showed you how to adjust it. The same exterior wall had five tall windows interspersed with mirrors, four of the windows with a view of the busy avenue, now traversed by many car lights; one of the windows (as Kenny, pulling aside the heavy drapes, showed you) had an oblique view of the illuminated window of your neighbor Professor Ogden. He had not drawn his blinds, and his undraped window revealed a dim glimpse of his person, supine upon his couch, one arm flung over his face to shield his eyes or comfort his head. ("That old nerd's really, really sick," Kenny said. "I mean he's, like, barfy and gross, you know? He oughta be in the hospital, but Mom can't make him go.")

The furniture of your room consisted of a small circular dining table with three simple dining chairs (two for company, said our Thoreau, and a third for society); a sofa like the one Ogden was confined upon; a spacious desk with desk chair; a comfortable stuffed armchair; two empty bookcases waiting for you to fill them up (you possessed at this point only three volumes, including the Russian–English dictionary: the other two were a fragment [less than half] of a coverless, torn, much-used Chaucer's *Canterbury Tales,* the only thing you'd been able to read in camp, where books were forbidden and this fragment had served several inmates as a toilet-paper supply before falling into your possession, as if Anangka wanted you to learn a little about the language you would be using for the rest of your life, even in its Middle form, and even without any help from a Russian–English dictionary; and a slim hardbound of Günter von Büren's *Protomycetaceae of Switzerland,* which the KGB man had permitted you to browse for and purchase cheaply under his suspicious eye at a Zurich bookshop before driving you on to the airport); a chest of drawers waiting for your undies and socks and such, once you acquired some; and a pair of what we call "occasional tables": good for ashtrays, magazines, clocks, spare change, TV dinners (your room had no TV). In fact, there was a clean crystal ashtray already upon one of them, and you looked wistfully at it and asked your boy guide: "Thou do not objection if I take . . . *papirosa,* cigarette, no?"

"It's *your* room," Kenny pointed out and, looking around him, noticed the door was still ajar and closed it. "Can I have one too?"

It's ironic, my Kat, that you, who had already throughout the long dull course of exchanging civilities with the Elmores amused yourself with elaborate plans for a soon seduction of this lad, now scrupled against "corrupting" him by letting him have a cigarette. You studied him and his eager face for a long moment before shaking your head. His face fell. His face, you realized, was much more mobile, expressive, mercurial, than Islamber's. But you hadn't shaken your head in denial of his request, only in the realization of your corrupting him. *A cigarette is as nothing compared to what I am going to give you,* you thought, but in Svanetian, not English. You held out the pack of Virginia Slims (its colors had attracted you, and you'd smoked two entire packs since leaving New York, thinking of the coarse shag *makhorka* that you'd only occasionally been able to smoke in camp), and his face brightened all over again, and the two of you lit up and smoked.

There was one essential piece of furniture missing from the room, and you wanted to ask about it but did not know how for the simple reason that the tiny word for it eluded you, that basic appurtenance that is *laqvra* in Svanetian, *logini* in Georgian, *postyel* in Russian, but less than half as many letters in English. You could have tried to look it up, but you would have felt a certain embarrassment in mentioning it, so soon, to Kenny. Staring at the sofa, you supposed that either that was it, or even perhaps the sofa was convertible for sleeping . . . and seduction.

And then—it was so uncanny the way he seemed to read your thoughts, or perhaps Anangka, bless her, was on the job and sending messages to him—Kenny hit himself on the brow (not with the hand holding the Virginia Slim) and said, "Hey, I almost forgot!" He moved to the wall and grasped two of the tall mirrors by crystal knobs attached to them, and the mirrors swung out like doors, revealing a recess in the wall containing a contraption that you recognized even in the instant that he began to pull it out and down. "Your Murphy bed!" he said when he had it fully in place on the floor. It was almost a double bed, you realized, as you filed the word *murphybed* into your vocabulary, but the mattress was bare. Again, as if reading your thoughts, he declared, "I guess you'll have to buy some sheets and stuff, but I could, like, snitch you a pillow and some stuff from downstairs, just for tonight. Soon as I finish this." He indicated his cigarette. Suddenly he laughed uproariously at some thought—you hoped not the same thought you were teasing—and he said, "Listen, have you ever heard of Murphy's Law?"

You knew *coleslaw* but not *murphyslaw.* You shook your head.

He said, "It goes, like, 'Anything that can possibly go wrong is sure enough going to go wrong.' " He studied you. "Get it?" You nodded, although you were not certain of the connection between the murphyslaw and the murphybed. Or was he insinuating something, subtly? Perhaps that your attempt to love him would go wrong. He said, "I'll be right back," and put out his cigarette and left the room.

Within minutes he was back, bringing a pillow, blankets, sheets, and a pillowcase. "Oh, *ivasu khari!*" you said. "Thank thee!"

"I nearly got caught," he declared proudly. "But if you ever need *any*thing, hear, I'm your man." You smiled, enjoying that expression, and thinking in English, *Thou art my man,* and you wondered how you could possibly tell him at this point, with your limited language, what you most needed. He began to make the murphybed for you, and you searched for words to protest but could not find any. There are no good words to tell somebody to permit one to make one's own bed. Finished, he looked around the room, as if searching for other hidden doors behind the mirrors to show you anything else he had neglected to show you. "Well, I guess that's it," he declared at last. "I hope you're comfy and all. I hope old Professor Ogden doesn't bother you. Sometimes he, like, makes a lot of noises in the night, coughing and stuff." The boy made facial expressions of both wonderment and annoyance. "But," he said, "maybe his noises will, like, keep you from hearing the *other* noises." He waited to see if this had registered with you before he went on, "I hate to tell you, but this place is haunted."

"Excuse," you said, and took up your paperback. "*H,*" you said, "*O, N . . .*"

"*A, U, N,*" he corrected you, and you found it quickly, your fingers getting better and nimbler in their constant turning of the pages.

Finding it, learning it, you closed your eyes for a moment in ecstasy. "*O sakvrel Anangka!*" you uttered, which is to say, O marvelous Fate-Thing. The boy's announcement was, as we like to say, too good to be true. But it was true. I, who am a ghost of sorts myself, and have to be, to get this strange story told, can tell you: Lawren Carnegie, the cousin of Andrew, and the man who built this mansion in 1893, a man who had made his fortune supplying his cousin with coal from mining interests in West Virginia, on the night in 1901 when the Titusville mine disaster took the lives of 187 of his employees, tried to put himself to sleep with cognac but, being a corpulent man, required two whole bottles just to make himself drowsy, drowsy enough to consume a third, which deprived his physical entity of its involuntary functions, such as respiration and heartbeat, and his "spiritual" entity has been vacationing behind these mirrors ever since, sometimes clumsily causing scrapes and screeches and an occasional clank to echo between the glass and the wall.

"You hear what I'm saying?" Kenny wanted to know, his eyes big and his eyebrows high. "There are *ghosts* around."

You did not need to look the word up, it was so close to the Germanic *Geist,* even if far removed from your Svanetian *lanchal.* In Svanland you had known many a splendid *lanchal.* "I love ghost," you told Kenny.

He stared at you in disbelief, his stare slowly shading into one of tentative dislike, as if, smitten with you but reluctant to give you his heart wholly, he had had to search for a flaw, which he had found at last. He did not know what to say. At length he said, "Well, if you're not jacking me around, you'll sure be happy here, I guess. If you meet the ghost, just tell him to stay away from me, okay?"

You smiled and said, "I tell him," and then, suddenly, you were overpoweringly weary and wanting to sleep. How does one bid farewell best in the English? *Lishdobe, lishdobe.* You tried a bit of sign language: You touched your hands together as if in prayer and laid them beside your cheek as if in slumber. "I am needing rest," you said.

"Oh, yeah, sure!" he exclaimed, and made to leave. "I'll see you tomorrow."

"Night, tomorrow," you promised, "we talk. We play game. I tell thee stories. Thou like story?"

"I'm kind of old for that," he said, thinking perhaps you had in mind the bedtime tales he hadn't heard since his old father stopped telling them seven years before. "But yeah, we could, like, play games. Do you know chess? Aren't all Russians real good at chess?"

"Am not Russian," you declared firmly. "*Mushwan.* Shvan. Can thou say 'Svan'?" He tried. It was not easy, and sounded more like *Swan* than *Svan,* which was all right. You told him, "But I play chess, ya. So we play chess. Thou have . . . ?" Your fingers pantomimed the pieces: pawns, royalty, clergy, horsemen, crenelated mansions.

"No, but I know where I could snitch some," he declared, and turned again to go. "Well, good night, I guess." But he hesitated. "Could I—?" he tried. "Could I stay and watch you take off that scarf?"

You gave him your very best smile, and, dear Kat, even your middling-to-fair smiles are a wonder to behold, but you slowly shook your head. How did you tell him, Not yet? Or, It is too soon? Or, Comfort yourself with the thought that soon you'll see all of me, but not tonight. But you knew a word, *ugly,* without looking it up. "With no scarf," you said, "I am looking very ugly."

"You couldn't," he said. "You couldn't if you tried. You are the prettiest lady I ever saw."

You blushed, knowing that adjective too. You had learned from him a farewell: "Good night," you said.

"What color is your hair? I mean, what color *was* it?"

You touched your eyebrows, which were still all there, perhaps too much so, because you would never pluck them. "This color," you said.

"Sorta like mine," he said, and his hair was, in truth, very like yours had been: an ordinary brown, a common brown, the color of mice, or of nuts, or, according to your Chaucer at least, "broun as a berye," or, best of all, of the forest floor that nurtured the mushrooms that were your singular overriding interest in this life. "Good night," he said again, and reached out and took your hand and shook it. The handshake was the first time you had been touched since Bolshakov let go of you.

Before putting out your lights and climbing into the murphybed, you spent a good hour in the cozy, easy company of your paperback book, looking up *poison, bourbon, dope, billy goat, cheers, borrow, wrong,* etc., etc. Some of the words, e.g., *sucks* and *gross,* did not have the meaning that apparently had been intended, whereas other words, *slammer, snitch, nerd, barfy, jacking around,* could not be found at all.

And one simple word gave you the most difficulty. You were still thinking about its possible multiple meanings or usages when you drifted off to sleep: *like.*

THE GHOST OF LAWREN CARNEGIE would not make contact with you that night. If he made any sounds at all to indicate his stale and bumbling residue in the physical world, you did not hear them. You slept well, not even wakened when your next-door neighbor, Professor Ogden, had one of his fits of coughing. If your sleep was troubled at all, it was not by Carnegie or Ogden or Kenny Elmore but by the sinister Bolshakov in his trench coat, walking constantly toward you. But the only dream you'd remember when you woke did not feature Bolshakov at all; rather, it was your old familiar dream of climbing and descending an endless sequence of stone steps, concrete steps, iron steps, and wooden steps, staircases that led up or down to significant places whose significance always eluded you.

The next day, bright and sunny but cold enough to remind you of winters in frozen Svanetia—even the distant snow-clad hills that surrounded this city suggested the topography of the purlieus of Lisedi—was, you realized with a pang of nostalgia, appropriately December 10: International Human Rights Day, the day that the women in camp fasted in solidarity. So you did not need breakfast. You dressed, and rewrapped the black scarf around your head, and counted your money, and went out to explore the town. You walked the short distance, less than a *verst* (two-thirds of a mile), past other mansions; past the modern building housing WQED, whose FM station was going to serenade you on many a sentient occasion; past the first of the three churches you came to, Saint Paul's, which was Irish Catholic and where you were tempted, despite being neither Catholic nor even Eastern Orthodox any longer, to go inside and cross yourself and say to Saint George a prayer of thanks for your deliverance; past an institution that even more than the church was unknown in Russia, a bank, Mellon's, where it was to be hoped you would one day have an account; past the second of the churches, the Heinz Memorial Chapel, with its enormous stained-glass windows, where on any Saturday afternoon three to five happy couples were joined in matrimony; past this to the third and grandest and tallest of the churches, a Gothic skyscraper really, with over forty stories, much taller than the central tower of Moscow University, which you had visited on several occasions without ever being a student or a teacher there. Its central shaft, if you squinted your eyes, could pass for a Svanetian tower, much magnified.

This building, you discovered upon entering it, was called the "Cathedral of Learning," and indeed this morning it was already crowded with students on their way to their eight o'clock classes, some of which were meeting in opulent classrooms off the central high-vaulted nave, where there were not pews or altars but tables for study. The students hurrying past you did not stare at you or take any note of your appearance, your black kerchief shrouding a lovely face. Strange for a cathedral, there were two rows of elevators, and the students were rushing into the cars of these, and you followed and rode, because you did not know where to get off, all the way up to the forty-second floor, where you stood in a hallway and stared out a window at the city sprawling in every direction out and out and onward: the distant steel-and-glass skyscrapers of the downtown, crowded together, made a technological phantasmagoria of the towers of Svanetia, those battlemented columns that, poking up all over the landscape (but a mere six or seven stories tall), may have inspired, even subliminally, your initial interest in mushrooms.

This city spread out beneath you was less than half as populous as Tbilisi, where you had taught and worked, and not even one-eighth the size of Leningrad, where you had studied for your advanced degrees, but somehow it seemed bigger and busier than both. For the nonce, it could suitably prompt you into recollections of Tbilisi: There were those two rivers, bigeminal tributaries like the Kura and the Vera of Tbilisi (these were called longer, more poetic, and more romantic names, Monongahela and Allegheny, words from languages that truly fascinated you, the Indians'). And in the distance, you could see the tallest of the surrounding hills (Mount Washington), which, even if its height was no match for Tbilisi's Mount Mtatsminda, miraculously had an important feature in common with the latter: a funicular railway running up its slope (in fact, it had *two* of them, but from your vantage you could see only one, the Duquesne Incline), and you decided to make the fun of that funicular your immediate objective, if you could learn how to get to it.

But you would not reach it on this day. Other things would divert you from your destination. Coming down from the top of the Cathedral of Learning, you spent some time exploring its International Rooms: There was no Georgian Room, but there were, among many others, each donated and decorated by people of that nationality living in this city, a Russian Room, a Greek Room, a Yugoslav Room, and a Polish Room, each containing objects familiar to you. But the room that most attracted you was the Scottish Room, an especially elegant result of careful planning in imitation of seventeenth-century Scottish workmanship: each of the students' tablet armchairs was elaborately carved of imported oak; there was an elegant fireplace (nonfunctional) surmounted by a portrait of Robert Burns, and carved thistles everywhere; each of the four large windows facing the avenue was emblazoned with the symbols and devices of the four great ancient Scottish universities, Glasgow, Saint Andrews, Aberdeen, and Edinburgh; and innumerable little details made me sorry my ghosthood wouldn't allow me to point them out to you, such as the rear window bearing the arms and emblems of the Clan Montrose, my ancestors.

Leaving the Cathedral of Learning, you sought out the closest book-shop, where you might find a city map that would have transportation routes on it, so you could find out, without the embarrassment of stopping someone on the street to ask, how to get to the funicular railway. The bookshop you entered happened to be the chief bookstore for the university, and you could not resist, while there, browsing. You spent two entire hours in that bookshop, enchanted, and only your sense of the need to protect what little cash you possessed kept you from going on a spree and buying volumes right and left. You even resisted an exceptionally attractive book, a Penguin paperback of a modern English "translation" of the Middle English Chaucer of which you already owned a fragment. But there was one book you did buy—or perhaps, as we shall see, it was Anangka who bought it for you: Roaming through the shelves of student textbooks, taking note that "Winter Term" books had already been arranged in neat heaps by academic department, and searching until you found the section on biological sciences, you discovered that there was only one course, apparently, in mycology, as such, and you snatched up its textbook, J. W. Deacon's *Introduction to Modern Mycology,* and you paid at the front desk a price that, like all textbook prices, was exorbitant.

You would carry the heavy book in its paper bag with you for the rest of the long day, but carrying things in bags was a way of life where you had come from.

You did not find a map with transportation routes on it, so, at the first bus stop you reached, you tried a combination of sign language and bad English on a waiting passenger, female, middle-aged, large, very dark complexion: "Where catching bus for ramp train?"

The woman said, "Sugar, where you from?"

"Georgia," you said.

"Shit," said the woman. "I'm from Alabama myself. You don't sound like no Georgia to me. And I don't study no 'ramp train' neither." She turned away from you.

You waited, watching several buses arrive and depart, reading their destinations on their crowns, finding no words that meant anything to you. Finally, you simply boarded one of them, paid the driver, and asked him, with inclined motions of your hand, "Ramp train? Slope rails?"

Without taking his eyes from the road, he tore off a slip of paper from a pad, a transfer, and said, "You want twenty-seven."

Seated, you attempted to read the transfer, but it offered no clue
as to where you should make the switch. The bus took you down from
the heights of the university and into the heart of the so-called "Golden
Triangle," with its dazzle of commercial, financial, and mercantile es-
tablishments. When most of the rest of the passengers got off, you went
with them, and you found yourself face to face with an enormous
department store, Kaufmann's, which would hold you captive for at least
another hour. Noontime came, and Kaufmann's even had an appealing
little café inside it, but you remembered it was Human Rights Day, and
you ate no lunch. Kaufmann's let you go, reluctantly, but only to hand
you over for the rest of the afternoon to Saks Fifth Avenue, to Horne's,
to more. You bought nothing, could afford nothing, but you wandered
up and down the aisles, touching nothing, just looking, looking, looking.

In one of the stores, you finally touched something: There was an
entire department devoted to artificial hairpieces, or rather, actual hair
made into headdresses. In every conceivable color. Your fingers almost
touched one adorning a simple mannequin head; it was a lustrous auburn,
with a reddish cast you'd always wished you'd had. Your fingers could
not resist touching one, not attached to a dummy, that was exactly the
color your lost hair had been, Chaucer's berye. You picked it up, fondled
it, lifted it as if to place it upon your head. You looked around to see
if you were observed. You realized you'd have to remove your scarf for
a moment in order to place the wig upon your head. You found a mirror
nearby and, first setting down your book bag, attempted to summon the
courage to remove your scarf. You summoned it.

A floorwalker accosted you, a nattily attired gentleman of very erect
carriage who lifted his eyebrows at the sight of your bare head as if it
were crawling with worms and said, "Perhaps madam would rather try
another store." Quickly you re-covered your head with the scarf, blushing
furiously, more than you had blushed when Dr. Bolshakov had forced
you to remove your scarf. Indeed, this floorwalker (a word you didn't
know, but you knew he was in charge of this store) reminded you in
other ways of Bolshakov, although he was not wearing Bolshakov's trench
coat: the same tightness of facial skin and pucker of lips and point of

widow's peak typical of the habitual onanist. He lifted the wig out of your hands, returned it to its place on the counter, and, when you made no move to depart, said to you, "Go." When that failed to provide the impetus he intended, he took you by the arm and said, "Take a hike, lady," and propelled you out of the hair department.

For his rudeness, I, who restrain myself whenever possible from intervention in the affairs of mortal, earthbound organisms, decided on the spot to punish him, and I hit him instantly with a maximum dose of *alopecia areata,* which would leave the son of a bitch scratching his scalp before nightfall and would have him pulling out tufts of hair in the next morning's shower, and would render him totally bald within a fortnight. Can your Anangka do things like that? I got carried away, I'm sorry, but nobody can treat my Kat in that fashion.

Oblivious to my thunderbolt, you left the store and wandered north-ward through the Golden Triangle to an area where the triangle was no longer gold but brass, or just brass plated: there were several movie theaters whose marquees each contained the letter X in triplicate. In Georgian, as in Svanetian, the X is pronounced "kh," almost the way some of us, privileged few, begin the sound of your nickname, Kat. The meaning of the triple X eluded you but piqued your curiosity, and you realized that perhaps the best way to practice your English skills would be to listen to the spoken word in the cinema. These particular films, however, had you sat through one of them, would have disappointed you with their paucity of actual spoken words; at the same time they would have totally captivated you with their bold images. You read the various titles, *Hot Prom Girls, Wild West Wild Women, Peek-a-Boo Pals,* and *The World According to Gwyn,* and, on impulse, picked the last. You ap-proached the ticket booth, saw that the price was affordable, and tendered a five to the ticket seller, a middle-aged, morose, pinched woman who reminded you of some of the hardworking peasant women of Svanetia who become old before they're thirty.

She would not take your money. She studied your face long enough to see it and to perceive that even though you'd attempted to hood it with that black kerchief you had a surpassingly gorgeous combination of sparkling, innocent eyes, a perfect nose, delicate cheeks, silken skin, and the sweetest mouth this side of the celestial cherubim. "Hon," she said, "you don't wanna go in there by yourself. Come back with your boyfriend."

Twice today you were turned away! But this woman was not being rude, like that bastard floorwalker, and I felt kindly toward her, even grateful, because the time wasn't ripe, yet, for you to be watching pornography all alone.

"WELL, WHERE HAVE YOU *BEEN?*" exclaimed Loretta Elmore when you used your key to let yourself into the mansion's foyer.

"To main city. Shopping," you told her, and began to count the places on your fingers, "Kaufmann's, Saks, Horne's . . ."

"In *that* coat?" Loretta said, and reached out to finger your threadbare *shinel.* "It's a wonder they didn't throw you out."

"They did," you said.

"Huh?" she said. "We didn't know where you were, and we're holding supper for you. Kenny fixed it himself. He got off his paper route early so he could come home and fix supper for you." You were abashed, even more so because you would have to find some way to explain, in this difficult language, that you were fasting (a word you didn't know in English) because it was International Human Rights Day. "Of course we're not going to feed you every day," Loretta went on, "and I expect you'll find the supermarket pretty soon, but Kenny wanted to fix you a little something just for tonight."

"I talk to him," you declared. "I tell him why no thank thee." You followed Loretta into her apartment, into her kitchen, where Kenny was stirring something in a pot. His face went wild at the sight of you. "Mayest thou be victorious," you said to him, and then you touched him lightly on the arm (your second touch) and said, "I am much sorry.

But today I not eat. Today being Human Rights. Thou understand?"

He looked at first crestfallen, dismayed, but then stoic and even moved. "You're not hungry?" he asked.

"Much hungry," you said, and patted your stomach, then you thrust your nose over the pot he was stirring, a sauce for something. "Smell good. Look good," you complimented the sauce. "But today . . . everywhere . . . all over Russia, all over Georgia . . . many people not eat. People go hungry to say, 'We know how it feels for prisoners to go hungry.' "

Kenny seemed to understand, and he quit stirring. "I hear you," he said. "Rats, it's only gravy for the mashed potatoes."

"After thou eat," you told him, "thou come up. We talk, tell story, play game, something."

"Sure," he said.

As you were leaving, Loretta said, "Hey, next time you go out, you better let me give you a decent coat to wear. And some jewelry."

In place of supper, you had a pleasant hour at your desk with your new book and your dictionary, looking up *decent* along with *mashed potatoes, boyfriend,* and *hike.* You attempted to look up simply *X* but only found, among many other things, that it was a symbol for Christ or *Christian,* and you wondered if those movies were restricted to religious people accompanied by their sweethearts. But why three *X*'s?

When the knock came at your door, you assumed it was Kenny, and you called out, "Coming in!" But he did not come in. "Door is open!" you called. Actually the door was closed, but you had not locked it, something you hadn't yet learned the absolute necessity of doing. A man entered. A stranger. It could have been Bolshakov wearing a disguise of beard and mustache, even though the beard and mustache were grayed, and the man was shorter and fatter than bony Bolshakov and not wearing a trench coat or any coat at all but a cardigan sweater with elbow patches, and he looked old and stooped compared with your malefactor, and he was attempting a smile that would been entirely beyond Bolshakov's ability or inclination, and he was holding in one hand a slim book and in the other hand a glass containing a liquid of the same amber color as that preferred by Loretta, called . . . yes: "Bourbon and branch on the rocks," you observed, aloud, but rising to defend yourself.

"Indeed!" he exclaimed. "And may I offer you one? But forgive me, perhaps I should first offer to introduce myself. Knox Ogden, your neighbor and, I hope, your friend." He offered his hand unsteadily, and you realized from his movements and his speech that he was well along the way to intoxication. You did not take his hand. In Svanetia, one never touches someone without having known them for at least two hours. "Well," he said, withdrawing his hand and sitting abruptly on your sofa. "Excuse me, I'm not feeling too fit." Clearly he wasn't: pallid, his eyes hollow and dark, his movements feeble or jerky. He took a deep but spasmodic breath and said, "You don't have to tell me your name, Ekaterina Vladimirovna; I know it. It is a beautiful name, like that of a heroine out of Tolstoy, although your Georgian surname is not at all familiar to me. Dadiankeliani? Is that royal?"

"Dadeshkeliani," you corrected him. "Very royal."

"You are a princess?" He was the first person in America to know it, unless you include me, and to say I'm either a "person" or "in America" would be misleading. You nodded your head, feeling grateful; Bolshakov had consistently refused to acknowledge that you had been a princess. "I am honored, Your Highness," Knoxogden said, and from his cupped position in the sofa attempted a bow. No one had bowed to you for a very long time, and no one had ever called you "Highness," not in English. You were no longer frightened of him and you were not entirely annoyed with him. "Did you know," he asked, "that Edgar Allan Poe had a cat he called Caterina? It was a tortoiseshell and would sit on his shoulder while he was writing, and when Poe was away from home he would write to Caterina as if she were family. But I suppose you don't know the poet Poe?"

"Ya, in Russian I read Poetpoe." Actually you were more familiar with translations of his short stories than with his poems, but you knew him well and admired his *gad,* weirdness, although you had never learned of his Caterina.

"I am a poet myself," declared Knoxogden. He held up the volume he was carrying, a very slim green book, and passed it to you. You read the gold letters on the thin spine: KNOX OGDEN, *THE FINAL MEADOW*, DOUBLEDAY. You opened it and found handwriting on the flyleaf, a palsied scrawl just barely legible, *For Ekaterina Vladimirovna Dadiankeliani, With the warmest regards of—* The palsy suddenly became a controlled but unreadable arabesque in which you could make out only one letter: *X.* You were embarrassed at the gift of the book but only mildly annoyed at his misspelling of your surname. What most disturbed you was the thought that he had inscribed it without ever having met you; how could he have the warmest regards for you? You searched for proper words of thanks and had difficulty. But there was one word of English you knew well, one of the first English words you had ever learned, when you were young: *kind.*

"Thou art much kind," you said. "*Ivasu khari.* Thank thee."

He laughed, or made a coughing sound that resembled a laugh. "I teach English at the university," he said. "And it looks like I'm just the man you need. We'll start with your use of the archaic second-person pronouns. We don't say *thou* and *thee* in modern English. *You* replaces both, and, alas, is used ubiquitously, without regard to the addressee's intimate familiarity. English doesn't have any equivalent of the German *du,* the French *tu,* or the Georgian *shen.*"

Your sweet, reserved face became unusually expressive. "Thou—you—are knowing Georgian???"

He made a pinch of his thumb and forefinger. "A tiny bit," he said, then used his other hand to lift his drink and lustily swallow most of it. "I once was required to translate some stanzas of Rustavelli, and I had to pick up the rudiments."

You were overwhelmed, as if meeting an old acquaintance in a faraway place. "You know Shota Rustavelli? *The Man in the Skin of . . . Big Cat?*"

"*Panther,*" he said. "Sometimes *Tiger,* but I think the beast Shota intended was the panther."

That great epic is to Georgia what *The Canterbury Tales* is to England, but not even most educated Russians have ever heard of it. Most

Georgians know it virtually by heart, and you could recite it backward in your sleep . . . but not in English. Here was a man, your next-door neighbor, who could probably recite parts of *The Man in the Panther's Skin* in English. Abruptly you were aware again of Anangka, that she was taking care of things for you, that she had "arranged" to give you an erudite neighbor who could help you with your new language. What a pity she could not have found a more attractive person, a more sober person, a healthier person.

The door, which Knox Ogden had left partly open behind him, opened fully, and there was Kenny. He was carrying a folded chessboard and a box of chess pieces. The youth glowered like a panther at Professor Ogden, then looked at you and pouted.

"Coming in," you invited Kenny.

"Most Russian speakers tend to overuse the participle," said Knox Ogden. "That's simply 'Come in,' not 'Coming.' "

Kenny said to him, "You know you're not supposed to be drinking."

"Now there's an awful participle," Knox Ogden observed. He returned Kenny's fierce glower and said, "I'm not drinking. I'm just bringing it to her." And he thrust his glass into your hands.

You were not able to hold it as if it belonged to you, and Kenny observed, "She drinks vodka, not bourbon."

"Oh, my mistake!" said Knox Ogden, and he lifted himself slowly up out of the sofa, took your glass, and said, "I'll be right back with your Stolichnaya. No ice, right?"

"No ice," you said.

"No *dice*," said Kenny. "You just stay away from her, you leem!"

" 'Leem'?" said the professor. "That's a new one. Is it anything like 'geek'?"

"Worse," said Kenny.

"I've been promoted," the professor said to you. "I used to be a mere geek. Before that, a nerd. Before that, a dork." He turned to Kenny. The two males were almost the same height, but the professor was much heavier. "Listen, punk, you spoiled my friendship with Edith. Damned if I'll let you drive me away from this beautiful princess, who needs my help as much as I need hers." He bowed to you.

"She doesn't need anything from you," Kenny said. "Why don't you go play with yourself?"

"Why don't I smack you one upside your insolent face?" said the professor, drawing back his hand.

"Try it," Kenny challenged him. "I'm not afraid of you. Don't fuck with me."

"Watch your language," the professor said to him, then he said to you, "You don't want to expose yourself to this punk's disgusting English. He'll infect you with his contagious slang and vulgarities."

Kenny said to you, "Yeah, so you want me to take a hike?"

You had just recently learned the word, and you said, "No, I am not wanting . . . I do not want for you to hike." You were a little flattered, dear Kat, to have two men (three, if you could've counted invisible me) fighting over you. But you were distressed that they did not get along with each other. You were abashed to be thrust into the position of having to choose between them. If you'd had to choose, of course there would have been no choice: simply as a desirable male, Kenny had it all over the professor. But wouldn't you antagonize Anangka if you chose him? Didn't Anangka want you to choose the professor, so that you could learn good English as soon as possible? And perhaps Anangka wanted the professor to divert you from your lust for Kenny. As gently and politely as you could, you said to the professor, "Kenneth and me, we have plan to play chess." As if on cue, Kenny unfolded the chessboard on your dining table and began arranging the pieces.

" 'Kenneth and I,' " Knox Ogden corrected you. "Okay, I know when I'm not wanted." He made to leave but turned at the door. "But you haven't seen the last of me, either of you!" He went out.

Kenny continued setting up the chessboard. "What a total jerk," he said. " 'Eye-ther!' It's pronounced 'ee-ther'—don't you ever let him tell you different. 'Eye-ther' is the way that stuck-up goody-goodies say it. That's stuffy and chicken shit."

Kenny was going too fast for you. "Wait," you requested. "One word at time. What means 'jerk'?"

Kenny giggled, and the sound of his giggle brought him down from the tough grown-up that he'd been trying to be and made him into your adorable twelve-year-old all over again. "That's just short for 'jerk-off,' and I can't tell you what that means. But a jerk is sort of, like, like a dork, only it's kind of, like, 'jerk' is what you do with your dork, your prick, like, you know? I mean, I don't mean you, because ladies don't have pricks." Kenny was blushing.

You and Kenny sat at the dining table with the chessboard between you, and first you corrected his misplacement of the black king and queen, transposing them. You wished you had something to offer him in the way of refreshment. Your little refrigerator was still empty. You wished you had something to drink yourself, for although you fasted on Human Rights Day you were not required to thirst. As if in response to your thought, the door opened and Professor Ogden returned, briefly, carrying a tumbler with clear liquid in it. "Your Stolichnaya, Your Highness," he said, and bowed and made his exit backwards without turning his back to you. You did not even have time to remember how to say thank-you.

"Shit," said Kenny. "I wish you wouldn't drink that."

"But I have thirst," you protested.

"I put a six-pack of Cokes in your fridge," he said. "I guess you didn't notice." He jumped up and fetched one, popping open its top.

"Thank thee—thank you much," you said. "But you drink it. Please, I drink this." A thought occurred to you. Although you were touched and grateful for his gesture (you would discover later, when you looked in your fridge, that he had also put there a dozen eggs, a carton of milk, and a package of margarine, none of these items "snitched" from downstairs but all purchased at the store with his own money from his newspaper route), you wondered how he had gained admission to your apartment while you were out. For even if you were careless about leaving your door unlocked while you were in the apartment, you still retained your habit, from Tbilisi and from Leningrad, of locking your room when you went out. Hesitantly, searching for the words, you asked him, "How did you come in room while I am out? You have key?"

"Oh, sure," Kenny said, and reached into his *dzhinsy* pocket and fished out a whole ring of many keys and showed them to you. "I guess nobody told you. I'm the super."

" 'Super'?"

"Superintendent," he elaborated. "Of this building. I'm, like, in charge of the whole place." When you looked surprised, he added, "With all of these lushes on every floor, somebody's got to stay sober enough to, like, watch out for everything and stuff. You know?"

KENNY COULD NOT PLAY CHESS. Oh, he knew the rules, and the rudiments, and even some of the refinements, but he had no grasp whatsoever of such instruments as the gambit, the knight fork, or the defrocked bishop, and while he was all too eager to demonstrate he knew how to castle, he castled kingside when he should have castled queenside, and he castled either side when he did not need to castle at all. The first game ended in eleven quick moves, interrupted when you had to hush him, his talkativeness, his trying to explain that although he had access to your apartment and to everyone else's, he would never "snoop" (a new word you loved) or "mess around with your stuff." The second game lasted a bit longer because you relaxed your defense and let him explore. By the fifth game, because you'd finished your drink (on an empty stomach), you were almost tempted to let him mate you, just to keep up his interest and confidence; you were walking him through the steps of the Winawer Variation of the French Defense, trying to explain why he should be patient, not take pawns just because they were there to be taken, hold back and wait for the chance to let his queen pounce, hold back, now pounce, now retreat, stay back, be patient, control himself, wait, watch for the right moment, respond to your movements, not cause them; and for a time he did exercise remarkable endurance, but then impetuously he plunged forward and lost his rook and thus his strategic advantage, and the game.

You doubted he could ever mate you, but you were determined to teach him how, and thus disappointed when he sat back and said, "Shit, I can't put it together. I guess I'm not, like, old enough for you yet. Let's do something else." You told him of the chess players who had already been masters at the age of twelve: Capablanca, Alekhine, Reshevsky, and of course those great precocious American kids Paul Morphy and Bobby Fischer; and you assured him that all he needed was practice, and more practice. You almost told him about Islamber and how Islamber had become very good in chess at the age of only eleven. But you were not ready yet to tell him about Islamber. You asked Kenny what he would like to do, what game, or maybe he would like to hear you tell a story? Maybe you would like to take off *dzhinsy?* you wanted to ask.

"Wanna see my telescope?" he asked. You caught your breath, uncertain about the word: Maybe it was another slang word, like *prick,* for the private part. When you smiled but looked puzzled, he tried a pantomime that didn't help: one fist held to his eye, the other fist stretching slowly out from it, swelling, expanding outward. You nodded your head eagerly. He told you you'd need to put on your coat, and, mystified, you did. He ran downstairs to get his own jacket, then took you up to the third floor of the mansion and to a door to another stairway, that led upward to a shed on the roof.

Climbing to the shed reminded you so much of climbing to the top of the Dadeshkelianis' tower in Lisedi, where you had first made love to Islamber. The shed was very cold, thus your coats. It was also very private, but with windows on three sides. Kenny showed you his telescope. It was a big thing, hard, shiny, pointing toward the stars. It was mounted upon a tripod, and you had to stand on a box to put your eye to its hole and look into it. You did not know astronomy, and he took an almost prideful revenge, considering your superiority in chess, in pointing out to you, eastward, away from the interfering lights of the city's downtown, the constellations of "Little Dog" and "Big Dog," naming the stars of each and telling you how many light-years it had taken for their light to reach the earth. Awesome. You reflected upon, but could not tell him yet, this contrast between your interests: That his was upon the faraway, the unreachable, the unknown, while yours was upon the close-up, smellable, touchable, woods-musky growths of this earth.

You stayed in the shed on the roof for quite a while, until even you with your immunity to cold grew chilled, and then you returned to your room. Did you like the stars? he was eager to know. They were fine, you said.

He looked doubtful and asked, "What do you like to study?"

"Mushrooms," you said.

"Really?" he said. "To collect, or just to eat?"

"Not to collect nor to eat," you said, but to watch, to examine, to learn the growth of, to wonder at how and why and upon what they lived, to measure the way they took the air, to ponder the brevity and urgency of their lives, to look closely at the way they created their spores and spread them to perpetuate themselves.

He wanted to know, "Can you tell the difference between the ones that are poisonous and the ones that aren't?"

You laughed, and you laughed, and then you said, "Oh, I am much sorry for the laughing but, you see, I can even tell the chemistry of each poison they use, and why, and how much, and toward what other creatures the poison is intended as a defense."

"Sunday," said Kenny, "let's you and me go to the museum." Before he left you that night, he gave you four things: a quick, spontaneous (but carefully prefantasized) peck on the cheek and three magazines that he had obtained at the same store where he got the stuff he left in your refrigerator. They surprised you: *Glamour, Ladies Home Journal,* and *Playgirl.* The first two would keep you for hours, for days, showing you a foretaste of all the things you should be and do, what you should wear and put upon your face, what you should cook and how, what you should smell like, what you should say; but the third would keep you for weeks, because it sanctioned the proposition that all women are sexual creatures bent upon the celebration of their sensuality. You thought aloud in English, "Is okay for woman in America to be like this," and you wondered if his gift of it was some message from Kenny that he found you desirable or had at least thought about it. You stayed up very late that night with your magazines and your dictionary, and that was the beginning of your concentrated study of our complicated tongue.

And early on Sunday afternoon (Loretta lent you a decent coat, a very nice one, better than any you'd ever had, and some costume jewelry, a necklace, earrings, a bracelet), you and Kenny walked the not-considerable distance to the museum of natural history that was part of the institute named after the cousin of the man who'd built the mansion and still haunted it. You spent an hour pointing out and trying to explain items in the small but impressive mycology section of the museum, and then Kenny returned the favor in the astronomy section, and then almost by accident you turned a corner and stumbled upon the section devoted to the American Indian, which thrilled you, and you had to spend more time there than in either (ee-ther) mycology or astronomy. Had Kenny ever seen Indians? you wanted to know. Only on TV, he said. After you'd read, or tried to read, every label in the Indian section, you suggested to Kenny that, because it was just next door, you might drop by the institute's museum of art, where you found a collection of modern paintings almost as good as in Leningrad's Hermitage; you had spent many weekends at the Hermitage and thus could tell Kenny without reading the labels which were the van Goghs and which the Cézannes, which the Picassos and which the Matisses, but Kenny was very quickly bored with art, and, since darkness was still an hour or so away, you asked him if he knew how to get to the ramp trains, slope rails, whatever, and he said, "Oh, you mean the inclines?" and he got the two of you onto a bus, paying the fare himself, that took you to the Duquesne Incline, where you had some fun at last on the funicular, from the top of which Kenny could point out all the landmarks of the city: Three Rivers Stadium, Point State Park, and each of the tallest skyscrapers by name. Twilight came while you were up there, and all the lights of the town came on like Kenny's stars.

Weekdays, when Kenny was in school (at Schenley Junior High, where he was in the seventh grade) and when Professor Ogden, who had apparently been required to cancel the remainder of his classes for the term, came knocking at your door, you had a series of intensive private lessons in English grammar. Many years before, when he was a mere assistant professor and overworked, Knox Ogden had "moon-lighted" by teaching evening classes in Fundamentals of English for Foreign Students, of which there were thousands in this city, and he could regale you with stories of malapropisms, blunders, and solecisms committed in the speech and writing of his students that made your own mistakes seem trivial and not ludicrous. Ogden always began each session by bringing you a generous tumbler of Stolichnaya (although by this time you'd acquired your own bottle of less expensive Popov, as well as some County Fair bourbon to offer him in return) and then asking you, "Have you had a chance to sneak a glance at my poems?" In truth, you'd sneaked more than a glance at them, you'd applied your dictionary substantially to them, from the opening piece, "The Yearning," to the concluding and terminal, "Again, the Dance," but Knox Ogden's late (and last) poems, as his critics have since pointed out, verged on the mystical, the metaphysical, the entranced; as if, wrote the critic Lawrence Brace, "he attained not an ultimate serenity but a dark and hesitant glimpse of some grandiose and terrible truth," and you were never able to tell him what you honestly thought, or were unable to feel, about his poems.

One day (or not any day at all) when Loretta was picking you up to give you a ride to the supermarket (an experience that, in contrast to your market shopping in Georgia or Russia, was so fabulous that I've got time to mention only the most fantastic difference: that you had to wait in line for only five minutes), she remarked, "He sure has got a powerful crush on you!" and you replied, "Yes, he certainly has. But he writes such strange poetry."

She looked at you strangely and then said, "Oh, I didn't mean *him!* I meant Kenny."

YOUR CRASH COURSE in English lasted only six days, albeit every day for two hours or more, and on the seventh day two things interrupted it: Professor Ogden was simply too weak to get out of his murphybed and meet you, and you had appointments to be interviewed at the university. The night before, Loretta reminded you that Dr. Elmore had reminded her to remind you, since you obviously found the whole thought terrifying and were seeking to forget it. Loretta urged you to help yourself to her wardrobe, and she gave her advice on picking out a smart dress and shoes for the interview, and which jewelry was most tasteful, and she even tried to persuade you to wear one of her blond wigs—but you declined, accepting instead the loan of a bright Paisley silk scarf to replace the black cotton one. "Well," she observed encouragingly, at the end of your dressing session, "You sure have caught on fast! Your talk and all, I mean."

But perhaps not fast enough to land you a job that required good English. Your first interview was early in the morning in the Cathedral of Learning with Dr. Hector Schvann of the Department of Slavic Languages and Literature. Professor Schvann, whose Ph.D. was from prestigious Berkeley, first exchanged polite chitchat with you in Russian. How did you like America so far? Which part of town were you living in? Did you miss Leningrad? In which politicals' camp were you interned? Really? A terrible reputation, that place. And obviously they have depilated you, Yekaterina Vladimirovna. But an attractive scarf. Professor Schvann spoke excellent Russian, with an American accent, and while it was good for you to listen comfortably to someone whose every word you understood, his language reminded you of people you wanted to forget.

He opened a folder and switched abruptly from Russian to English, and pointed out that according to your curriculum vitae your advanced degrees were apparently in botany, not in languages, and did you feel qualified to be teaching elementary Russian to young Americans? Certainly, you said, with synthetic bluster. Well, perhaps, Yekaterina Vladimirovna, he said; and as a matter of fact there was an opening for a teacher of two sections of Intro, but it also required teaching a literature course, in English: The Comic Spirit in Russian Literature. Think you could handle that? No problem, you said. Which writers and works would you include? he wanted to know. Well, you said, I would start with Gogol, of course, his *Dead Souls.* And I'd probably want to include Dostoyevski's *Idiot,* because he saw Prince Myshkin as somewhat like Don Quixote, did he not? Yes, but, Yekaterina Vladimirovna, he said, but what else? Let me think, you said: And yes, something by Turgenev, because it was Turgenev who said, "Whom you laugh at you forgive and are ready to love." You had always liked that line. *Whom you laugh at you forgive and are ready to love.* The professor nodded and wrote something down; perhaps he was writing this quotation. Finally he asked you, But wouldn't you include something by Nabokov? Alas, sweet Kat, you didn't yet know the man's work (it would be a gift on a saint's day, a favorite American saint, Valentine, when someone would give you your first novel by V. N.), but you knew enough to say:

"No. Is not his funny stuff written in English, not Russian?"

Professor Schvann laughed and agreed, but he said that, quite frankly, he didn't think they could use you. There were other applicants for the position, some with Ph.D.'s in Russian from prestigious American schools like Berkeley. Thank you for your interest, however, Yekaterina Vladimirovna, and thank you for dropping by to chat. Give my regards to Professor Elmore.

I was tempted for a moment to punish the guy, to afflict him with something, ideally some disease with a Russian name, but he was only doing his job, after all, and he wasn't unkind to you. I let him alone.

For your second interview, you were required to enter a building elsewhere on the campus, away from the Cathedral of Learning, a drab and forbidding building that unfortunately reminded you very precisely of the Serbsky Institute in Moscow, that infamous psychiatric hospital where you first fell into the snares and pillories of Dr. Bolshakov and were saved from utter madness by the boy Dzhordzha. Your knees failed you, and you were able to force yourself up the steps and into the building only by concentrating upon your awareness that there were not two swinish KGB men holding you by either arm. You were unescorted. You were free. If this Dr. Dalrymple turned out to be wearing a trench coat, you could simply turn around and run, and nobody would stop you.

But Leonard Dalrymple was (and is) a very nice guy. He offered you coffee and a doughnut, and he told you to smoke if you wanted to (you did), and he put you completely at ease. "Ken's told me where you came from," he said, "and why you have to wear that scarf. No doubt, you'll have your own hair grown back in before we know it, right? No problem." He opened his folder and made some appreciative murmurs, like a gourmet settling down to a feast. "Hey, did you know I saw your paper on the mutant spores of the *phallales* last year in the summer issue of *Mycotaxon?* I read the English translation, of course. Also your paper on the *Geastrum fornicatum* in the recent *Mycologia.* Very impressive stuff."

You assumed he was being polite, that he had seen the articles mentioned in your curriculum vitae, that he had not actually read them. But it was nice of him, all the same. You smiled modestly and said, simply, "Thank you."

"You've been stateside how long now?" he asked.

Alas, Knox Ogden had not taught you *stateside,* but he had taught you how to show ignorance gracefully. "I am sorry," you said, laughing, "but I haven't been here long enough to learn the word *stateside.*"

Len Dalrymple laughed. "Well, that's not very long at all!" he said.

"I expect you'll have to learn a lot of words. But you already know the scientific terminology pretty well, don't you? And that's what counts." Then he told you that Bill Turner, their mycologist, had received a sudden call to London for a six-week symposium and thus had been required to take an unexpected "off-campus duty assignment" for the winter term. He winked at you and said, "Lucky for you." Filling in for Turner would require teaching two sections of Intro Bot, plus the Intro Mike. Think you could handle it? Certainly, you said, without having to manufacture any bluster.

"What text d'you think you'd want to use for the Intro Mike?" he wanted to know.

It was a test question, not conversational, a key part of your interview, but you were ready for it, thanks to Anangka and that previous morning in the campus bookstore. Correctly you guessed that "Intro Mike" was campus slang, and you said, "I'd like to use, if I may, Deacon's *Introduction to Modern Mycology.*"

"*Lucky* for you!" he said, beaming. "That's what Turner has already ordered for next term, so you won't have any problems with the bookstore."

"Excellent," you said, smiling with approval.

"Of course, you understand, the appointment's only for the one term, January through April, while Turner's away?"

"Good enough." You smiled again.

He stood up and offered you his hand, and even though you hadn't known him for two hours yet, you permitted yourself to take it. "Well, glad to have you aboard, Katherine. First classes are January eighth. Marilyn will show you—you met Marilyn, our secretary, out there— she'll show you where your office is and give you the university faculty packet and stuff. Merry Christmas."

Knox Ogden hadn't taught you that expression, but it sounded familiar enough for you to repeat it, "Merry Christmas to you, Dr. Dalrymple."

"Please," he said, "just call me Len." And there, on the spot, I made three of his wishes start coming true: I arranged for his promotion from associate professor to full professor to be cleared through the dean's office that very afternoon, I made airplane reservations for his daughter to fly home from the West Coast for the holidays, and I nudged the editors of *Cytologia* into accepting for publication his article "Mitotic Chromosome Pairing in Allopolypoids of the *Atylosia.*" The next time you saw him, Len Dalrymple would be a most happy fellow.

IN FROZEN SVANETIA, December 25 is just another winter's day. Not that Svanetians permitted their Russian rulers to make them into atheists, but traditionally they follow the Julian calendar of the orthodox Church, whereby Christmas, *Shob,* is celebrated on January 6. Even in my part of America, the middle mountains, the old folks used to observe the same distinction between "New Christmas" and "Old Christmas." (See my poem "Presents. Presence.": *The day the "younguns" think to gift / Is on December twenty-fifth. / The oldsters feel that they should mix / The day of January six.*) Anyhow, when you responded to the knock on your door that Tuesday morning and found Kenny standing there with a big smile and bright eyes and a package done up in shiny red wrap and bow, you thought at first that he had simply "snitched" for you one more item, as he was always doing, except that never before had he bothered to gift wrap any of his snitchings.

"Come in," you invited. "What is this?"

"Merry Christmas!" he said. Taking the package, you thought that his greeting was simply, like Len Dalrymple's, in advance of the occasion, but you realized that, unless America had drastically different customs, one would present the gift on the day. "Go ahead, open it," he urged you. And you sat down to open it, almost dreading to find that perhaps thoughtful Kenny had bought you a wig of real brown hair. But the box was too heavy to contain only hair. Slowly, taking care not to rip the

paper, you undid the ribbon and Scotch tape and opened the package.
It was a small radio. Plastic and black-brown, two knobs and one switch,
capable of being switched from AM to FM. "Now you can, like, grab
some sounds," he said, and took it and plugged it in, and fiddled with
the dial until he found a station playing some heavy rock. "Or do you
want some longhair?" he said, and began twisting the tuner again. On
the job, I arranged for WQED to come in, playing Tchaikovsky, my little
Christmas gift for you. "How's that?" Kenny asked.

"Oh, wonderful!" you said. "Thanks so much, but I do not have
Christmas present for you yet."

"You didn't have to get me anything," he said. "I know you don't
have any money."

"But I must give you something, when Christmas comes."

"Huh? Today's Christmas," he declared.

"It is?"

"Sure. We've already unwrapped all our stuff downstairs, and Mom
and Dad are already bombed on eggnog and, like, out of it, and I'm
trying to fix a turkey in the oven. You know anything about cooking
turkeys?"

You were in confusion, not from his language. You had an idea what
bombed meant, and you could guess what *eggnog* was, and you'd seen
turkey recipes in that *Ladies Home Journal,* so you resisted your impulse to
fetch your paperback dictionary, which was falling apart by now anyway.
Nor were you confused by his question "Do you want some longhair?"
realizing it likely had nothing to do with a wig. You were perplexed to
find that Christmas had somehow arrived twelve days before you'd
expected it, and you were distressed that you were unprepared to return
the favor of Kenny's gift. Indeed, you had spent some time thinking
about possible presents for him—an astronomy book, perhaps, or a nice
shirt, or even a subscription to his favorite magazine, *Playboy*—but you
had concluded that the very finest present you could give him, knowing
him as you did, knowing what he might most appreciate, would be to
divest him of his bothersome virginity. Now, closing your eyes to the
magnificent sound of WQED's (or my) Tchaikovsky, you thought about
that: You didn't have time to plan it, to get up your courage, to learn

the right words to offer it, to make it happen. It was too soon, Christmas. Give you twelve more days and you could do it, but not now.

When you said nothing, he waited for a time, and then he tried again, "Can you do it?"

Lost in thought, you snapped back to this world, and asked, "Do which?"

"Help me cook the turkey."

"Oh, sure, I could try," you offered, and you rose to your feet and cast a wistful look at your unmade murphybed.

"First I've got to see if your neighbors want to help eat it. Mom says we should invite Dr. Koeppe and the Jerk. You know if they're in?"

You shook your head. You hadn't heard any movements in the adjacent apartments. During the more than two weeks you'd been here, you'd only seen Edith Koeppe on a couple of occasions, and you'd scarcely exchanged words with her: an overweight woman, early forties, perhaps, stringy short blonde hair; she seemed to spend very little time in her apartment, coming home late, leaving early. For a sociologist, she was very unsociable. As for Knox Ogden . . . You hadn't seen him since the last time he'd given you a lesson in English, when he had been in such poor condition he hadn't been able to rise from his sofa and had begged you to make a drink for him, which you had refused to do. Now you realized that you had intended to give him something for Christmas, too, and had been caught unprepared. You hoped he wouldn't have a gift for you.

"I'll knock and see," Kenny said, and left your apartment. You made up the murphybed and lifted it, folding it up into its compartment in the wall, listening to the sounds of knocking, first on one side of you, then the other. After a while Kenny returned, his demonstrative face furrowed into a frown. "Neither one of 'em's home." He made a variety of puzzled expressions. "Maybe they, like, went off somewhere together for Christmas." He screwed up his brow. "But they're not even on speaking terms with each other anymore." He spent some moments in thought. "Probably she went to visit her sister," he determined, "and I guess he's maybe just gone and finally croaked at last."

" 'Croaked'?" You didn't know that one.

"You know, kicked the bucket, bought the farm."

You didn't know those, either, but you had an uncomfortable approximation of a guess. "Talk straight, Kenny," you requested.

"Gone west," he tried, nervously, although he'd started out jokingly—unable, like all the inventors of all the hundred and one euphemisms and euphuisms for the condition, to come right out and say a word so final, so irrevocable, like the last word in the last sentence on the last page of a novel.

But his use of one of my favorite ways of putting it (because in truth that's precisely what I've, what we've all, done, turned our puny corporeal locomotions in the direction of the setting sun in order to accept the eternal weightless omnidirection that is our lot) roused me out of my half-listening state and made me take a quick, determined jaunt into the next room, where, sure enough, I found Knox Ogden's extract trying to learn how to exist without gravity.

"For crying out loud," Ogden declared in exasperation, striving to give some dignity and uprightness to his topsy-turvy levitation, "where are the handholds?"

"There are no handholds, Og," I told him. "Try not to hunt for them and you won't miss them."

He stared at me, and ceased his undulations. "Who are you?" he demanded. "Not the devil, I hope."

"No, Og, just a poor defunct transient like yourself," I said. "Dan Montross was my earthly name."

"Not Daniel Lyam Montross the poet?" he said.

I was moved, and more than touched, that he'd heard of me, possibly even knew my work. "At your service, forever," I said.

"But you're . . . you're . . ."

"Say it, Og!" I commanded, for it was very important that he acquire that ability, that honesty. "You must be able to say it."

"Gone to a better world?" Knox Ogden tried. "Out of your misery?"

"Come on, man!"

"Passed on? Called home?"

"*Og.*"

"Dead?" he tried.

"Very good!" I complimented him. "That wasn't so hard, was it?"

"But . . . " he said, "but . . . but . . ." He looked around at the dull walls, the many mirrors (in which he could no longer see himself), the bookcases, the things he'd never have to heft again. He saw, with detachment and what did not amount to pity so much as revulsion, the stiffening body sprawled out on the sofa, in one hand the sheet of yellow lined paper on which he had attempted unsuccessfully to scrawl his last poem, in heroic Drydenish couplets, "Ekaterina," but indecipherable to you and to any except the critic Lawrence Brace, who would not attempt its decoding for another few years; and in the other hand the almost empty glass of Jack Daniel's, tilted at a steep angle, its ice slowly melting.

"Ick," said Og. "An odious corpse, aren't I?"

"It will take you a while," I pointed out, "to become accustomed to the new sense of aesthetics that we have on this side, where every-thing's so beautiful that earthbound forms seem to be incomplete, if not inelegant."

"Funny," he observed, rubbing his plasmic hands along his gossamer arms, "I don't feel dead. How do I know I'm not just blind drunk and you're some joker pulling a trick on me?"

"There's someone who wants to meet you," I told him. "Someone who—if you'll forgive the expression—is just *dying* to meet you." I gestured dramatically with my hand, in presentation, and out of the ether the extract appeared in all its glory.

Og gasped. "Lawren!"

"Hello, old buddy," said Lawren Carnegie, and I left the two chums to chew the fat, settle old scores, explain a few things to each other, and my colleague to undertake the business I didn't want to handle: determining if Og desired to remain here and compete with him for the possession of this mansion or to accompany his remains to their burial in his home state, Utah, out west.

I returned to you and Kenny, who was fishing his keys out of his pocket and suggesting, "Maybe I oughta, like, open up and see?" And then, his voice quavering, he requested of you, "Would you go with me?"

"Sure," you said, and went with him, hoping to find that, as he sometimes did when he'd been drinking too much, Knox Ogden was simply sleeping late. Kenny unlocked the door, and the two of you stepped inside and at once saw the odious body sprawled out on the sofa. His murphybed had not been pulled down from the wall. You were more interested in studying Kenny than in studying the corpse. You did not know whether the boy had ever had any encounters with death or how he would take it, and you were apprehensive; Kenny's eyes were very large, and his mouth was open, and he could scarcely speak—just whisper to suggest that one of you, ideally you, not him, should shake the man. You went through the motions of shaking the man by his shoulder, just to buy time, just to give Kenny a few more moments to get used to the inevitable, because you already knew, from the moment you'd seen him, that Knox Ogden was dead. Your experience was great: In Svanetia, in Tbilisi, in Leningrad, and especially in Camp 39 at Ishimbay, you had seen dead people. You knew that the human body, once it is no longer inhabited by the *kvin,* is as harmless, as expired, as meaningless, as a fallen tree. Except that a fallen tree can be cut into firewood, or it can be left to nourish many generations of mushrooms, but a human body can do nothing, can do nothing, can do nothing at all, ever, anymore.

"Kenny," you said as gently as you could, "Professor Ogden is not any longer living."

"Oh, shit, *no!*" Kenny insisted. "How can you be sure? Did you feel his pulse?"

You lifted Ogden's wrist, the one holding the sheet of yellow lined paper, as if to offer it to Kenny to feel. "You want feel?" you asked. He declined, and when you released the wrist it dropped obviously like a deadweight, but not before you'd grasped the sheet of paper and, attempting to read it, made out what appeared to be, at the head of a column of verses, your name. You were very sad, then, thinking that the last thing he'd done was to try to write something to you, or for you. And you'd never even been able to tell him what you thought of his poems. And now it was too late. Soundlessly, because you were not yet ready to make the sounds, you wept; your cheeks were bathed, and you had to turn your head so that Kenny could not see.

"Jesus," Kenny said. "Oh, holy shit. I didn't hate the dude. I mean, sure, I said some bad stuff about him, sometimes, and yeah, I, like, probably made him feel bad, I guess, but I didn't hate him. He wasn't so bad. Why did he have to go and *die?*"

You wiped away your tears so that you could turn and face Kenny. "Is not your fault," you said. You saw that his own eyes were very wet, his mobile face very stricken, and he was clenching and unclenching his hands as if he wanted to make a fist and hit something.

But his lip began trembling, and then his whole jaw was trembling, and he stared at you beseechingly, as if there were something you could do to help. He said one thing more; it was like a question, not a statement: "He was probably a real good guy?" And then he sprang, lurched, fell into your arms. He wrapped his arms tightly around you and buried his face against your breasts. You tightened your arms around him. It was the first time you had been hugged since Dzhordzha had let go of you. It was the first time you had hugged someone with passion since you had last held Dzhordzha.

The two of you remained clenched there, thus, for a very long while, longer even than you actually needed just to comfort each other, while we three Magi, having seen the star in the east, turned our attention to the spectacle of the chemistry in your hormones, each of you, the rainbow-colored spectra, the atomic fusings and burblings, the microscopic kaleidoscopic splash and splurge.

"Hey," remarked Og. "Is that boy getting an erection?"

"'Pears so," observed Lawren.

"But isn't that rather unseemly," Og asked, "at a time like this?"

"Didn't you ever get a bone on," Lawren retorted, "when you got too close to a woman?"

"Can't she feel it, up against her?" Og wondered.

"Of course she can," I assured him.

OF COURSE YOU COULD, dear Kat, and it took your breath away, and took the fiber out of your knees, and it dampened you in your groin and grabbed you by your heart and twisted and wouldn't let go, and you knew that if Knox had left the murphybed down you would have tumbled into it despite the presence of his lifeless form, which couldn't decorously be dragged off the sofa so that you could use it, and you began to disapprove of yourself angrily for such thoughts, you began trying very earnestly to ignore that darling bulge in the *dzhinsy* down below and concentrate instead on the practical matter before you: Somebody had to be notified.

The rest of that day that had been a surprise Christmas to you, was not Christmasy at all. The fact of a death on the premises sobered up Dr. and Mrs. Elmore sufficiently to get them to handle things: A coroner's assistant had to come and supervise the removal of the corpse, and an autopsy had to be performed and a cause of death determined (advanced cirrhosis of the liver), and distant relatives had to be notified (distant only in the sense of the physical distance to Utah, from where a younger brother sent directions for transporting the body home). Kenny's turkey was forgotten, and, as near as you could remember, the dinner was a quartet of Swanson's frozen deep-dish turkey pies.

Knox Ogden's *kvin,* to my modest disappointment, decided to accompany his remains to Utah for the burial, to enjoy the final tributes of kin and Mormon clergy, and to remain forever among the bees in that state of hives, hanging out at old boyhood haunts below the Wasatch Range and along the river and in the town named after his ancestor the trapper Peter Skene Ogden. Lawren and I were sorry to see him go, but, as we agreed, two's company, three's a mob scene, and we took leave of him by accompanying him on his last expedition in that great city—an expedition made for the purpose of testing his new powers, to put the whammy on his department chairman, or rather chairwoman, who had caused him some grief over real and imagined derelictions of duty. He shamelessly haunted the poor old girl for forty-eight hours, until the train with his casket pulled out, leaving her with a permanent case of halitosis that could be helped only by constant gargling of Listerine. We refused his request to spend his last night here as your incubus. You, observing the old Svanetian custom of providing sustenance for the departed in the afterlife, left out a tumbler of County Fair bourbon, and Og raged at his inability to consume physical spirits. After three nights, only a small amount was gone, possibly through evaporation, and you drank the rest yourself, discovering that bourbon is not at all bad or undrinkable.

For the rest of the holidays, until the winter term of classes began, you and Kenny were inseparable . . . Not literally, for you did not dare, either of you, to hug that tightly again. You didn't have a good excuse. For his part, he kept trying to think of an appropriate pretext for hugging you, but it would have been premeditated, not spontaneous, and it wouldn't have worked. He spent a lot of time in your room, or you in his—although your room was more private, with Knox gone and Edith Koeppe still on holiday, and his room, as Loretta kept saying, was "a disaster area" (and she was embarrassed for you to see it): the piles of clothes everywhere; his "toys," some of them outgrown; his collections, some of them, too, outgrown; and, beneath his murphybed, a considerable pile of back issues of *Playboy*. Once, he let you borrow a few issues of his favorite reading matter, and you discovered that the magazine was much more daring than the one issue of *Playgirl* he'd given you, as if boys had different, or more profound, interests than girls. But both, true to their names, were play; and *lishdral* (or *ludus* in the Latin), play in all its forms—prelude, interlude, allusion, collusion, illusion, delusion, and ludicrous—was your heart's delight.

Most of the playing that you and Kenny did, apart from an occasional silent hand-language game of rock, scissors, paper, was confined to chess, in which he was steadily learning how to hold back, wait, think, and attempt to reach a mating.

But during that interlude of the holidays, most of what you and Kenny did was talk. He had many questions. What happens when a person dies? Is it just a matter of the heart no longer beating and the lungs quitting, or does some other stuff start beginning at the same time the old stuff is ending? Does the dead person know when the other stuff starts happening, does he understand what's going to come? If people didn't die, there would be just too many people on the earth, wouldn't there? Eating everything up? Everybody has to die, sooner or later, don't they? Is there any such thing as somebody never dying? Have you ever been afraid of dying? What have you wondered might happen to you when you die? Would you rather die in your sleep or when you're wide awake? If you had to choose, would you rather freeze to death or burn to death? What about dying in a car wreck? Or if the Bomb fell? Would you want to be shot? Or choked, or stabbed, or what? Do you think maybe when a person dies, everything just suddenly becomes blank or black, or just stops, like a movie or a book, and that's all, there's just not any more? Or do you think, like, you know, like you could always pick up another book or go watch another movie, there's another life afterward? Is there any sort of life after death? Do you think that what I'm doing now, I don't mean right this minute, but what I'm doing all the time nowadays, is going to determine what will happen to me after I die? You don't believe in hell, do you? But don't you think there might be some kind of heaven? I wonder, if a person goes to some kind of heaven, can they remember everything that happened to them when they were still alive? Or what do you think about the idea that maybe a person gets another chance here on the earth, only it's as a different person? I mean, what if I come back but find out that I'm just a dog, or a horse, or a girl, or something? Who would you like to be if you could come back as anybody else? If I died all of a sudden, would you miss me? Would you try to find another friend right away to take my place?

Now, Kat, I suppose I ought to tell you about the experience that Kenny had already had with what is so charmingly called the "little death," that brief exquisite pang that so many mortals, totally without any expertise at actual dying, have compared to it, as if there were any analogy at all. So far, alas, it had happened to you only a few times. The first time it happened to Kenny, for a terrible instant at least he wondered if he might actually be dying. And when the instant passed, he felt immortal, indestructible, everlasting, and couldn't wait to die all over again. Of course all his little deaths so far had been suicides. Many of them had been abetted by the fold-out pictures in *Playboy,* the magazine that, indeed, had verbally implanted the original suggestion in his just-turned-twelve mind with an article, "Doing It Without Chicks"—or rather, doing it with a surrogate cutely identified as "Mary Fist." Clumsy Mary had brought him, after several failures and dry runs, to his first little death, his first liquid death, a liquid that because of its composition and color had led him to suspect that if he wasn't dying he had something virulent and pustulant. By the time you came into his life, six months later, he had already learned, from his magazine and from his less ignorant schoolfellows, the basic facts of life and loving, and he knew he was normal and healthy, and doing it all the time wasn't going to cripple him or derange him or even leave telltale growths of fuzz on his palms . . . although he had been unable to resist the superstition that small amounts of the liquid applied to one's chest would cause one to become hairy chested, which accounted for the musky, woodsy fragrance that sometimes emanated from him and drove you wild.

But you did not know the source of the fragrance, just as you did not know that he had already died a little, several times. You continued to hope, as you pictured your first seduction of him, that his initial experience of the little death would come at your hands or—let me rephrase that—with your presence beside him to explain to him what was happening and to vicariously share the thrill of it, as you had done with both Islamber and Dzhordzha—because the supreme joy of the older woman with a pubertal boy lies not in what he can do to you or for you but in your vicarious pleasure in what he gets from you.

Never had you experienced the "little death" yourself with another person, neither Islamber nor Dzhordzha. The few times you'd reached an orgasm had come from listening to music, specifically Tchaikovsky, more specifically his First Piano Concerto.

You wondered, but never aloud, why Kenny didn't ask you any questions about sex—he was filled with questions about death and everything else, but not sex. Because, Kat, he already knew, or thought he did, all that was to be known about sex. But why didn't he ever, on any of the numerous private occasions when it might have been possible, express a desire to see you without clothing? Both Islamber and Dzhordzha, at his age and at about the same stage of familiarity, had been all too eager to have a look at you. You could still see Islamber's face at the instant he first beheld your breasts. And you recalled that first night you met Kenny, when he'd asked, so sweetly, "Could I stay and watch you take off that scarf?" If he could be so bold the first night, why had he not, more recently, asked, "Could I stay and watch you get ready for bed?"

The answer, and I'm sorry you've had to wait this long to learn the particulars from me, was simply that he did not need to ask. He had seen your head without the scarf. The hair on your scalp was growing back, and you would have been relieved to know that he did not find your bare head "gross," to use his word. He had seen your entire body without clothing. More than once. How? In the hall outside your door, there was a small closet, a so-called broom closet, for the convenience of the upstairs maid (a comely Scottish lass named Christal) in the days when the mansion was inhabited by Lawren's physical body. Kenny, familiar with every nook and cranny of this mansion, had discovered that it was possible to make a small hole through the wall of the broom closet that would, if he stood upon a box, provide him with an overlook of your murphybed. You never discovered the hole for two simple reasons:

it was hidden by the machinery that held the murphybed to the wall in its closed position, and he always plugged the hole when he wasn't using it.

By the time you wittingly gave him an erection, holding him close beside the body of Knox Ogden, you had already unwittingly given him a dozen or more erections, which he had served to Mary Fist, disguising her in his imagination as you, or part of you. It was a wonder, sometimes, that you hadn't heard, through the wall behind the murphybed, the panting and the gasping.

In the Hirshhorn Museum of Washington, D.C., is a painting titled *Eleven* A.M. by the supreme American realist of the twenties, Edward Hopper, which depicts a girl alone inside her room, naked except for her shoes, sitting in a stuffed armchair, staring out the sunlit window. Her long brown hair obscures her face, which might be identical to yours. Her body, naked, not nude—and the distinction is important— is not as desirable as yours, but the painting's mood, its theme, its gentle eroticism, and above all its loneliness will remind any viewer/reader of my Ekaterina, and it would certainly, years later when he saw it on a trip to Washington, bring back to Kenny the most haunting recollection of how he'd seen you in your room at the mansion, sitting in a chair like that, naked like that, enjoying your nakedness and the eleven A.M. sunlight warming it, staring out the window, thinking, remembering, planning.

Shocked at his recognition of the painting, Kenny would say to himself, "I wonder if what she's thinking at this moment is how she can get me into bed with her."

But what you were actually thinking at that specific moment was simply whether you ought, when you got your first paycheck, to buy a wig the exact color of your own hair, or to buy the auburn one and improve upon your already gorgeous looks. Then you heard sounds in the next room, Ogden's room, and you got up from the armchair and clothed your nakedness and peered through your blinds at the people through the window of the room opposite, which because of the building's staggered facade was at a visible angle to your own room.

Loretta Elmore was showing the room to a prospective tenant. Kenny had spent much of the holidays helping to clean the room after Ogden's belongings had been removed. (Ogden had left a will and had, despite his antipathy for his department, left all of his books and papers to the university's Hillman Library). Now Loretta was showing it to an Oriental assistant professor of physics, Dr. Chou Wen-Tseng, who was tall, handsome, and wore a constant smile of affability and contentment: a striking contrast to the previous tenant. Kenny later told you that his mother had been very eager to "land" Dr. Chou, a real good old joe, but that, unfortunately, the man had a Pekingese toy bitch from whom he was inseparable, and the Elmores had a strict no-pets policy (which would keep you from fulfilling one of your three wishes, to have a cat).

The next prospective tenant was a tautly muscled figure of swarthy cast, flat nose, and huge lips, named Roosevelt Smith, who had learned of the vacancy through his friend and former teacher, Edith Koeppe, now back from her sister's; Dr. Koeppe was as eager to have Smith here as he was to live here, on the same floor with his friend and former teacher . . . albeit with you separating them. But despite Dr. Koeppe making herself increasingly visible and vocal for a change, in order to lobby for her protégé ("He can drink me under the table," she declared in one of her rare attempts at humor, thinking it a qualification for the tenancy), the Elmores decided that Smith, because his dissertation (in criminology) was not completed and he was therefore, strictly speaking, despite teaching four sections of Intro Soc, still a graduate student, was not eligible to join the faculty on the mansion's second floor. He would be welcome to have one of the third-floor apartments, but there were no vacancies this coming term, and none anticipated. Rest assured the Elmores had no prejudice against blacks.

Two days before the winter term was scheduled to start, on the day that you would have celebrated, or that I would have preferred celebrating, in my young-manhood, as Christmas, you returned to the mansion from an hour of sitting in your office in the Biological Sciences Building, just sitting there, getting the feel of it and trying to rehearse your opening remarks to your students, and found this message from Loretta: *E. V., There's a man coming to look at the apt. this P.M., but I'm downtown on some business, and just in case I don't get back, and if Big Kenny is not back from Hillman or Little Kenny is not home from Schenley, could you show the apt. to him? Here's the key.*

Thus it was that Loretta, or Anangka, or, who knows, maybe even I, arranged for you to be the one to welcome into the mansion, and into your life, the *dzhentlmyen* who, in this tale, was, and was not at all, fated to become your agent, your *deus ex machina,* your "helper" (as your Vladimir Propp calls them): your conductor to your ultimate destination.

How about if I call him Professor Agathon N. O. Dirndl? Would you buy that? Nor would I, but here is certainly a situation where the real name will not do. I've played around—I did this before, as noted below—with such ludicrous rearrangements of the real name as your fellow Svanetians might carry: Thornan Dlogdani, Handon Ingaldort, or Dorn Glonthadani. But he wasn't Svan, though he looked it. Nor was he Norton Idhagland or Thogdon Inlandor. I like best of all Anthoni Gradlond, but that's a real name and we don't want to get ourselves into trouble.

Twenty years ago I published (posthumously, of course) a novella called *A Dream of a Small but Unlost Town,* wherein this same person served some critical functions akin to the demanding but entertaining job I now had laid out for him. That was ostensibly a work of fiction, and, according to the accepted tradition, I did my best to conceal his actual name, calling him, finally and consistently, by a mere initial. I'm tempted to do the same here. It's convenient and lends itself to collusion and allusion as well as delusion, to the sort of playing around that is so dear to you. But I can't reveal ("re-veil" is the meaning of that word: to replace one veil with another) the actual initial used therein, which was west of his real initial. So, to make a long veil short, I'll just shut my eyes and pick the initial to the east of his real one. I.

Let it stand, as it will, for Irresponsible, for Incognito, for Inept, for Indiscretion, for Inebriated, or for Idhagland, Inlandor, Ingledew, Ingraham. Just never, please, dear Kat, let it stand for *I,* meaning me, your phantom lover. You'll have to endeavor to keep us apart.

WAITING IN DREAD that the man might show up before Loretta or one of the other two Elmores returned, you began to convince yourself that this would indeed be the expected Bolshakov at last, although probably he'd known where you were all along and was just waiting for the right moment to move in next door to you, to inhabit (appropriately) a dead man's room and to haunt your days and nights from that proximity, to taunt your "pretense" of being sane, to flaunt his warped sense of "reality," to daunt your efforts to know what is true, to want your body finally and fully. You had never yet told Kenny about Bolshakov, though you had wanted to; you hadn't been sufficiently confident that your English was adequate to explain to Kenny just who Bolshakov was, not confident that Kenny was old enough to comprehend just what Bolshakov had done to you. But you realized now that part of your motive for desiring so urgently to tell Kenny was to inform him that you intended to kill Bolshakov if you ever saw him again, and precisely why, and to ask Kenny if he knew where he could "snitch" a gun.

Waiting, you told yourself it wasn't unreasonable to expect that cunning Bolshakov might have found you. All the time you'd known the man, he had boasted of his mobility, calling himself "the best-traveled psychiatrist in the Soviet Union." He was free to come and go as he pleased, and several times each year he attended conferences in England, Italy, Germany, even the United States.

You could not wait in your apartment listening for the downstairs doorbell to ring. You paced the mansion's foyer, pausing to look out the front door's sidelights at the driveway. The mansion's driveway, now covered with snow, cut in abruptly from the busy avenue, climbed slowly in front of the mansion, made a loop around the building, and gained the spacious parking lot behind the mansion, where at least half of the building's tenants kept their cars, along with the two belonging to the Elmores, in spaces that Kenny had to keep shoveled free of the snow. You expected to find Bolshakov arriving by rented car.

Thus, because a Hertz or Avis vehicle is usually clean and shiny and new, the vehicle coming up the driveway fooled you. It was a truck, or some kind of trucklike vehicle, with a white hard-plastic top or cover over a body of rust-cankered metallic blue. It was, in fact, although you had no familiarity with American vehicles, a seven-year-old Chevrolet Blazer, a four-wheel-drive car good for back roads or *bezdorozhye,* roadless areas, and snow and middle mountains. You watched it pass the front entrance; it seemed to be loaded down with stuff: boxes, clothing on hangers, rolled-up things. It had an out-of-state license, from one of the New England states, with what we in this country call "vanity" plates: personalized words or messages or names, this one six capital block letters: BODARK. It did not look at all like the kind of vehicle Bolshakov might have obtained, and thus you were taken aback when it stopped and he got out of it.

Yes, he was wearing a trench coat! You wanted to run out the mansion's rear exit and keep running. But no, this trench coat had a fur collar, and Bolshakov had never worn one of those. Walking up the front steps, the man appeared also to be much taller than Bolshakov, and he was not wearing a beard as disguise, simply a mustache that might have been his own. He rang the doorbell. You continued studying him, at close range, through the door's side window. He saw your face behind the glass. He watched you studying him. He studied your study. He attempted a smile, failing as miserably as Bolshakov would have failed.

You took a deep breath and opened the door. His mustache was real: the center of it was well seasoned with nicotine, and it was grizzled like his hair, which was too grizzled to reveal its original shade of berry brown. He wore glasses, one lens thicker than the other. Protruding from his ear appeared to be an immature mushroom, perhaps *Amanita phalloides*. You could not take your eyes off the mushroom.

"This is a *mansion*," he observed in a booming bass voice. "Are you sure you've got an apartment for rent?"

He did not sound at all like Bolshakov! And you decided, because of his great height, his deep voice, and the fur trim on his trench coat (which up close seemed to be very—what was Kenny's word?—very *grungy:* seedy, grimy, threadbare, manifesting a complete lack of neatness that Bolshakov could never have brought himself to permit, even for disguise), that he was no threat to you. Months would pass before you discovered that although he was not Bolshakov he had in common with your nemesis a total misunderstanding of "reality."

"Yes. Yes," you said. "Do come in."

You led him upstairs and unlocked Knox's—you'd have to stop thinking of it as his—unlocked the vacant apartment. He did not spend a long time looking around.

"Why all these mirrors?" he wanted to know.

"The better for see yourself," you observed, "and proof you exist."

"Pardon?" he said. He pointed at the mushroom in his ear. "I'm extremely hard of hearing."

"So is Dr. Elmore," you told him, thinking it a qualification for his liking it here, as a drunkard might like a house with other drunks in it.

"Are you Mrs. Elmore?"

"No, I am but living here. That is my room, next door down hall."

"I'm sorry," he said. "I can't hear a word, I'm afraid." You started to repeat yourself, louder, but he held up his hand. "No, it's a matter not of volume but of clarity. You have a luscious mouth, but I can't read your lips."

"I am not Mrs. Elmore," you tried, and whether or not he got it, you could not tell. You decided you'd better demonstrate the sleeping apparatus, and silently you opened the mirrored doors, pulled out and down the murphybed. "Behold," you said.

"Hey!" he said. "How about that!" He lay down on it, to try the length of it, which was too short for him. But if he slept slanticularly, it would do. He got up. "Well, I'll take it," he declared.

That was quick. But how did you explain to a deaf man that since you were not the landlady you didn't have the authority to rent it to him? The owners did have some standards to be met.

"Do you have pets?" you asked.

"What?" he asked. "Bats?"

"Pets," you said, and pantomimed the stroking of the ghost of the beautiful cat you could never have.

"Mats? Do you mean *mattress?* I'll need my own mattress, is that it? No, but I could get one."

"*Dog,*" you enunciated carefully. "Cat. *Goldfish.* Monkey. Parrot. *Budgerigar.*"

"Oh, *pets!*" he said. "No. No, I don't. Just me."

"Do you finish dissertation?"

He took a bunch of cards out of his shirt pocket, common three-by-five index cards, unlined, blank. He took out his ballpoint pen. You thought for a moment he intended to finish his dissertation on the spot. "I could understand you a lot easier if you'd just jot down a key word or two," he requested.

You took a card and the pen and wrote, *Dissertation?*

He read it and said, "Many years ago, at Harvard, my dissertation adviser read the first draft and told me I ought to be writing novels instead, so I gave it up."

"But you are faculty?" you asked, and wrote down the word *Faculty?* "Not simply graduate student?" And you wrote down, *Graduate student?*

"Oh, I'm a student all right, and graduated," he said, "and I'll always be a graduated student. But right now, starting day after tomorrow, for one term only, I'll be teaching."

"What do you teach?" It was not a test question; you were simply curious and wanted to get to know as much as possible about your next-door neighbor. You wrote the question down: *What do you teach?*

Maybe he should have written down his answer, because now it was your turn to misunderstand. "Riding," he said, or you thought he said;

his pronunciation was not of the best. If he'd said "Riding," then that explained his appearance and his grungy coat: He had just come from the stables.

You had only one more question, which was not a test so much as an effort to see how he would fit into the climate of the mansion. "Do you drink?"

You started to write it down, but he apparently had understood you. "Why, thank you!" he said. "Don't mind if I do. Would you happen to have any bourbon and branch?"

You decided against trying to make the effort to clarify your question. "On the rocks?" you asked, and once again he heard you, and he nodded, and you went next door and got the rest of the bottle of County Fair you'd kept for Knox Ogden, and you made a drink for this man, who was clearly not at all Bolshakov, and another drink of the same beverage, for conviviality's sake, for yourself.

BY THE TIME THE ELMORES came home, the new man had already moved in. Pausing after each trip to swill his drink, he had made a dozen trips out to his Blazer to carry in his stuff. You had offered to help in some way other than merely keeping his drink refilled, and he had let you carry in the lighter stuff, some of his wretched shirts, on hangers, odds and ends from the corners of the back end of the vehicle. He had carried in the heavy things: his big black electric typewriter, his boxes of books, his two suitcases, his grocery bag full of liquor bottles. By the time the Elmores came home, the carrying in was completed, and you had had several drinks together, and, although you had declined his offer of a handshake (because it had not yet been two hours), you had exchanged some basic information, your names and your places of origin; where you'd grown up. On a card, you had written your name for him in three languages. First in English:

EKATERINA VLADIMIROVNA DADESHKELIANI

and beneath that, in Russian:

Екатерина Владимировна Дадешкелиани

and beneath that, in Georgian:

ეკატერინე ვლადიმირის-ასული დადეშქელიანი

He had wanted to know how you would write it in Svanetian, and you had had to explain that Svanetian has no written language, no alphabet, that it is, like the American Indians' languages, entirely a spoken language . . . which did not mean, as Bolshakov had insisted, that you had only "imagined" it. It existed, as Svanetia did; a mountainous country, a mountainous language. Right then and there you and I. began to discover some things you had in common. On one of the trips down to the parking lot, he had explained his vanity plate: BODARK referred to that area of mountains in middle America from which he had originated. Later, over drinks, you wrote on one of his cards, *What do you miss most about the Bodark Mountains?* and he got glassy eyed—or maybe it was just from all the drinks he'd had or all the driving he'd done—and he answered that what he missed most was the smell of tomato plants, the particular acrid tang of their leaves. And you had written on a card for him: *That is exactly one thing I am missing most about Svanetia.* And he said, "You must tell me all about Svanetia." And you wrote: *You can be sure I shall.*

When the Elmores came home and you went to tell Loretta about him, she said, "What? Already? How does he spell that name? *E-I-G-H* or *A-Y-E* or *E-Y-E* or *A-I* or what?"

"Just I., I think," you said.

"What department is he in?"

"Equestrian Department," you said. "He is riding master."

"PA!" Loretta yelled into her husband's ear, "HAVE WE GOT ANY HORSE PEOPLE AT THE SCHOOL?" But she had more trouble getting across to him than you had had with I., and without the advantage of note cards to write upon. You realized one thing you liked about I.: The necessity of writing things down was good for you; you could communicate better in written words than spoken ones.

"No pets," you assured Loretta. "Also, he drinks like fish."

"Well, I guess I'd better run up and say hello," she declared, and took her glass of bourbon with her.

You remembered your own first night at the mansion, how the

Elmores had fed you, or rather Kenny had: the simple cheeseburger with fries. You assumed that I. would be in no condition to prepare his own supper, even if he had groceries. He had told you he'd been driving all day in the snow, sometimes in blizzards. You assumed he'd probably want to go out for supper to Burger Chef or some such; none of his clothes were good enough for a nice restaurant. It occurred to you to offer him something that Kenny had not wanted, or had not shown much interest in: a real Svanetian supper of *chikhirtma* soup, chicken *tabaka,* and eggplant salad, with hot *khatchapuri* bread. You got busy in your kitchenette. You hoped that I. would not think you were making a play for him, trying to lure him, trying to find your way to his heart through his stomach. You hoped he would understand you were only being neighborly and considerate of his first weary night here and that you did not intend to do it again. And you hoped that the coziness of having supper together would not make him want to use a familiar name for you prematurely.

But his first question upon sitting down at your table, as you began to serve the *chikhirtma,* was, "What can I call you?"

You wrote down on a card for him the information that in Georgia, as well as in Russia, unless you know somebody very, very well, or unless somebody is clearly your inferior (and how are you to know?) you could not use a nickname; you should use both the full first name and the patronymic. But Loretta, you told him, had taken to using just the initials of your first two names, which she had converted into the nickname Evie.

"That Loretta," he said, shaking his head. "Quite a bimbo."

You wrote, *Many words I am slow to learn, yet. What is "bimbo"?*

"Probably it comes from the Italian for *baby.*"

You smiled and wrote, *Because she is childish?*

"No, baby in the sense of a babe, a dame, a gal, that is—although it might be considered disparaging or offensive—a girl or woman, possibly an attractive one."

You wrote, *You remind me of Knox Ogden.* But then you realized that you were not going to tell him about Knox Ogden, not yet. You tore up the card.

"Hey!" he protested. "Don't *ever* destroy the written word." And thus you discovered that writing things down had both its advantages and its disadvantages: It was easy, more comfortable than speaking, and helped you to master the language, but it could not be taken back, it could not be forgotten, it was *too* permanent. "What did you write?" he wanted to know, and shoved a fresh card to you. But you simply wrote, *Let us eat, and then I will write to you about Loretta.* There was another disadvantage to note writing: You couldn't eat and write at the same time.

I. did not seem to have the appetite that you would have expected from a man his size, although he was properly appreciative of the food, especially the *khatchapuri* bread, which was hot (and in Svanetia must always be served hot). But he did not finish his soup, ate just a small bit of the chicken, and did not touch the eggplant salad. Months later, in a different part of the country, you would learn that his drinking sometimes killed his appetite.

When you were finished eating, you held out your hand and said aloud, "Give me four or five," and he did a strange thing: slapped his hand down on top of your open palm. You looked puzzled, even wounded, and wondered if he was already drunk.

"That's five," he said. "Although it was more a low-five than a high-five."

"Cards," you said. "Four or five cards."

"What?"

He could not hear you. It required a card to ask for a card: You took a used card, turned it over to its blank side and wrote, *Please give me 4 or 5 cards.* Which wasn't sufficient, as it turned out, for all you had to write: You told him about the Elmores: Once upon a time, and upon no time at all, Loretta, a local girl or bimbo, then twenty-four, had been working as a typist, not even a full secretary, in the university's Anthropology Department when the then-distinguished Professor Elmore, fifty-four at the time, had seduced her, starting a torrid affair that had resulted in Dr. Elmore's divorce from his first wife and his invitation to Loretta to accompany him on one of his periodic expeditions to Manaturu, in the Cook Islands of the South Pacific, where he was gathering material for what was intended to be an exhaustive document on the quaint sexual customs of the Manaturuans. It had been quite a culture shock for Loretta, whose father was a steelworker and whose grandparents had been West Virginia mountaineers, to find herself living among the Polynesian "savages" and eventually, on the second and third expeditions there, learning their language and serving as an interviewer of the women, who were too shy to tell their most private customs to her Kenneth Elmore. It was on the fourth and final expedition that Dr. Elmore and Loretta, then sixty-two and thirty-two, had themselves experimented with one of the customs and in the process had conceived Kenny, who was born upon their return to America and their marriage.

I. read your cards, occasionally attempting a smile. Then his only response to your narrative on its five cards was to ask: "Who's Kenny?"

You will meet him very soon, you wrote on a fresh card, and you paused, and reflected, and sipped your drink, and then continued, *He is 12, tall for his age but skinny, and he thinks he is the superintendent of this building. Perhaps he is. He is very*—again you paused and sipped your drink and did not know how to write this, but tried—*jealous and protective of me. He is probably downstairs at this very moment becoming angry because I am feeding you and talking to you.*

Inebriated, I. read this and chuckled and said, "Your boyfriend, huh? Well, bring him on, and let's see."

Almost as if in response to this request (and actually Kenny had been spying for some time through his peephole), there was a knock at your door, and you called out, "Come in, Kenny."

"How did you know it was me?" Kenny asked, coming into the room. He was not pouting at you or glaring like a panther at the professor.

"I knew it wasn't Professor Ogden," you told Kenny, and then you introduced them to each other. They shook hands; Kenny was tall, but he had to reach up to take I.'s hand.

"Have you got everything you need?" Kenny asked him, very politely. "In your apartment, I mean? Have you got all the lamps and stuff you need? Have you got all you need to cook with and eat with and stuff? I could snitch you anything you don't have."

"Thank you," I. said. "I think I'm all set." I. seemed to be following what Kenny was saying. Probably Kenny's voice, you realized, was clearer than yours, or, you decided, it was undergoing a voice change, as Islamber's and Dzhordzha's had done, and was lower in pitch than yours, therefore more intelligible to a deaf man.

"Have you got enough to drink?" Kenny asked him.

"If I don't," I. said, "she does."

"Well, good," Kenny said. "We want you to be happy here."

"Thank you," I. said. "I'm sure I will be."

You were amazed that Kenny was being so nice to him, and then it suddenly occurred to you that Kenny probably still felt guilty over Knox Ogden's death, or that at least he was overcompensating for his hostility toward Ogden. And you realized that you yourself were trying to atone for not having been as nice to Ogden as you could have. Also, it crossed your mind that Anangka intended this new man for some specific purpose, perhaps to divert you from your lust for Kenny. You could not conceive of yourself lusting for this new man, or even pretending a sexual attraction toward him, but possibly Anangka intended for you to receive his sexual attentions and thus be distracted from the temptation of seducing Kenny.

"Kenny," you suggested, "maybe I. will let you ride his horses."

"Yeah!" Kenny said, lighting up. "I've never been on a horse, but, yeah, I'd like to learn how to, like, get off and on one of them like you're supposed to."

I. was looking puzzled. He reached for his cards, but you already had one ready for him: *You might offer to let Kenny ride the horses. You don't have to teach him a lot.*

"What horses?" I. asked of both you and Kenny. And neither you nor Kenny knew exactly how to answer that question. You scribbled on a card, *Do you not say you teach riding?*

I. read it and laughed, or made a sound that was painfully like the way that Bolshakov on rare occasions had got something caught in his throat in an effort at expressing mirth or sadistic glee. "Oh, dear, no," I. said. "Not riding. *Writing.* What they choose to call 'creative writing,' as if there were any sort of writing that wasn't creative."

You and Kenny stared at each other, and then at I. Kenny said,

almost with a sneer, "You mean you're just, like, in the *English* Department?" I. nodded. Kenny observed, "Just like Knox Ogden!"

"Who?" I. asked, and you wrote the name on a card and showed
it to him, but he shook his head. "Who is Knox Ogden?" I was a little
disappointed myself, at the moment, to discover that I. hadn't heard of
Knox Ogden, whose poetry, after all, was not without some national
recognition and who had, after all, heard of *me*.

You whispered to Kenny, "Let's not be telling him yet." And then
you wrote on a card, *What are the courses that you will teach?*

He read it and showed you three fingers, and ticked them off one
by one: Intro Fick, Short Story, Narrative Techniques. *No poetry?* you
wrote. He shook his head. "Just fiction. Only fiction."

"*Ivasu khari,* Anangka," you said, realizing what the Lady of Fate had
in mind for you (actually I ought to get some of the credit). You wrote
on a card: *Have you publish fiction?*

"Some," he said, and on four fingers he ticked off the titles of novels
he had published. Then he observed, "I couldn't help but notice, Ekaterina
Vladimirovna, how bare your bookcases are. Would you like to decorate
them with some of my volumes?"

He ran next door to fetch you some of his books, and while he was
gone Kenny said, "You like him a lot, don't you?"

"Oh, not more than you," you said.

He blushed. "What did you tell him about me?"

"How do you know I tell him anything about you?"

"He asked you."

"How do you know he asked me?"

But before Kenny could answer that one, I. returned, with a stack
of four books in his hands, which he placed into your hands. They were
still in their dust jackets—nice designs on the jackets, and photos of
the author at different times of his life, usually with a beard, which
made him look older than he did now. "Just a loan, you understand,"
he said. You admired each book, one at a time, and passed them along
to Kenny, who did not read novels but was impressed with the author
photos and observed, in an aside the author could not hear, "He's

published almost as many books as Ogden, but his are, like, much thicker, so I guess he's published more words."

You wrote on a card, *Could I take one of your courses?* And you came perilously close to giving him the card, but you decided, for several reasons that we are to examine, that it wouldn't be a good idea. You tore up the card.

"That's *twice*," I. told you.

"Twice what?" Kenny asked.

"Twice she's torn up a card, although I told her not to," I. said, and then to both you and Kenny he said, "I'll tell you a little joke from the Bodark Mountains. There was this old boy, Dingletoon, reticent but tough, who married a strong-willed, domineering vixen named Sadie, and all the fellers in town laid bets to see which of them would get the upper hand. Well, Sadie had a little dog, and the first day after they were married the little dog up and bit Dingletoon. 'That's *once*,' says Dingletoon, and he pronounced it the way they do in the Bodarks, '*wunst*.' And about a week later, the dog bit Dingletoon again. All he says is, 'That's *twice*,' pronouncing it '*twice-st*.' Everything went just fine for another month, and then the dog bit Dingletoon again. 'That's *thrice-st!*' he says, and whipped out his six-shooter and let the dog have it right between the eyes. Sadie threw a fit at the sight of her dead dog, and she began cussing Dingletoon all over the place, and then she hauled off and slapped him as hard as she could. He just blinked a couple of times and said, 'That's *wunst*.' And from that day forward, Sadie and old Dingletoon got along fine and never had another squabble between 'em."

"That's funny," Kenny said, but he wasn't giggling or even smiling. Then he said, "Well, I guess I'd better go do my homework." You knew that of all the things on this earth that he hated most, he most hated homework. "Maybe I'll catch you later," he said to you, and then he said to I., "Just remember, if you ever need anything, I'm your man." He said one more thing, to both of you, pointing at his chessboard and pieces, which he'd left on one of your occasional tables, "If you want to use my chess set, that's okay with me."

BUT I. WAS NOT YET READY to play chess with you. In the coming few months, you and I. would play chess many times, and he would eventually succeed in mating you, but this first night he was simply too tired to think, and he declined your offer of a game, saying he'd have just "one more for the road" and then take off. *Road?* you asked. The "road" between your apartment and his apartment, he explained, which, as it would turn out, over the next months became a well-traveled road, in both directions.

But that night he had more than one more for his road. And so did you. Kenny came up more than once to creep into his broom closet and put his eye to the peephole, and to see that you and I. were still sitting there at the table, whose surface you could use for the cards you wrote. Finally Kenny's mother made him go to bed; he had school tomorrow and hadn't done his homework. But school for you and I. was not until the day after tomorrow, and you could stay up very late this night, exchanging your fears. You were both scared of facing your students. Without telling him anything of Ishimbay Camp 39, yet, or of Bolshakov, yet, you told him (or wrote on cards for him) that it had been four years since you'd last conducted a class in elementary botany, let alone mycology, and that while you had no doubt of your mastery of the material, you were petrified at the thought of talking to the students in a language that was still strange and new to you.

It was the other way around with I.: He had no fear of the students, plenty of experience with talking to (or at) students, but his classes for the last twenty years had all been in art history, which was his real field, and he had no experience teaching creative writing, which he was now going to do for this one term simply because he needed the job: The small liberal arts New England college where he'd been teaching art history had suddenly gone defunct through mismanagement and declined enrollment. His life was filled with deaths: His college was dead, his marriage was dead, his father was dead, his current novel was dead, his relationship with his publisher was dead, his ties with New England were dead.

"I'm an impostor," he said. "I can't teach writing. I've been telling anybody who would listen, for years now, that 'creative writing' cannot be taught. It can only be learned."

You wanted to write on a card, *Then would you help me learn it?* but you'd probably have torn up the card, and that would have been thrice.

You both became almost drunk, as Kenny observed in his last view through the peephole. Neither of you became dizzy or stinking or addled or sloppy or roaring, but both of you were a little loopy and pie-eyed and mellow and woozy and piffled. Old Lawren got rather supercharged at the sight and began to rattle the mirrors: No, he didn't actually rattle them audibly, but he caused them to vibrate, to shimmer. The shimmering mirrors were nothing new to you, but they caused I. to wonder aloud if there was a train going by, or a heavy truck. You wrote, *Just our resident spook.* "Maybe we should offer him one," I. suggested. You wrote, *I have.* You wanted to write words for him telling him about Knox Ogden, if not about Lawren Carnegie, but knew you'd probably have to tear up half the cards you wrote.

You wrote, and did not tear up, and he preserved (he kept all your cards, the hundreds upon hundreds you would write over the next few months), several cards about Svanetia, that mountainous wonderland that sometimes seemed like only an Arcadian dream to you and was the secret lost heart of the Caucasus just as I.'s Bodarks were the secret lost heart of America. You did not tell him, yet, nor did he guess, as Ogden had, that you were a princess. All you said in that regard was that the

Dadeshkelianis had owned large houses with towers in Etseri, Betcho, and your own native village of Lisedi, the three principal towns of the most beautiful valley of the Ingur, between massive Mount Layla (13,169 feet) and glacial Mount Ushba (14,882 feet), but that the houses had been collectivized by the Soviets, and now each contained many different families, which was ironic, in more ways than one, for originally the purpose of the towers, the four- to seven-story stone structures with battlemented caps, was defense: defense not against outlanders or invaders but against neighboring families, fellow Svanetians. Family rivalry, clan warfare, blood feuds, or simply mountain feuds, as I. told you they are called in the middle mountains of this country, were widespread and constant, a way of life in the old days, the seventeenth and eighteenth centuries, when the towers were built.

These towers seized I.'s attention, drunk though he was. He had spent a good deal of observation on architecture in one of his novels, and in his art history classes he had always been fascinated by the symbolic "human" qualities of buildings, the personalities of houses, and he wondered if the Svanetian defense towers, which dotted the whole valley of the Ingur River for fifty miles, had any possible phallic significance. The thought had occurred to you more than once. Your own interest in mushrooms, as you consciously knew, and as we shall see, but as I. was not to learn yet on that night, arose because of their suggestiveness and their insinuative reminder of the towers of Svanetia. Although Bolshakov had refused to believe in those towers, claiming that such a rustic and unsophisticated backwater as Svanetia couldn't possibly have built them, he had repeatedly tried to show that your "invention" of them was a possible clue to your worship of twelve-year-old penises. Your story of how you'd lost your virginity to Islamber in the top of one of the towers only confirmed Bolshakov's claim that you invented and mythologized your life.

But that night you were somewhat taken aback by the boldness with which I. discussed phallic matters, and you declined to make comment, or card, and he did not come to possess a single card of yours concerning penises. Attempting to change the subject, you wrote on cards that what you missed most about Svanetia was not the skyline of frequently upthrust towers in each village, the man-made erections, but the natural tumescences of the countryside: the fantastic flowers; the elephantine plants; the monkshoods taller than a man on horseback; the great *Heracleum,* with its yardlong leaves and ten thousand blossoms; the so-called enchanter's nightshade; not even to mention such mushrooms as the strange four-legged earthstar, *Geastrum fornicatum.* These were the things that Bolshakov had cited as proof that you were only "inventing," these were the splendors that he could not accept, and you were curious to see if I. would believe you, as Bolshakov had not.

But I. began singing. In a vibrant bass voice that you would have considered abominable had you realized how off-key it was but that you considered operatic because you didn't know the key and because you'd never heard a darkie crooning, he began singing this: "Way down upon de Svani ribber, Far, far away . . . Dere's whey my heart is turning eber, Dere's whey de old folks stay."

When he finished the song, you wrote, *There is no 'Svani River.' The rivers of Svanetia are the Ingur and the Nahkra and the Tskhenis Tskali.*

He explained that he'd just been making a kind of pun on a famous song by Stephen Collins Foster. Did you know Foster, America's greatest troubadour? No? Well, he was a native of this city and had lived most of his life here. I. intended to do a little research on Foster while he was in this city, for a possible future novel. Supposedly the university's campus contained a building, the Stephen Foster Memorial, that was the only museum and archive devoted to an American composer. Foster wrote wonderful, nostalgic, sometimes overly sentimental, but always folk-inspired songs, like "Beautiful Dreamer," "My Old Kentucky Home, Good Night," "Jeanie with the Light Brown Hair," and the aforesung "Swanee River," or "Old Folks at Home," as its proper title was. (There really is, I. told you, a Suwannee River in Florida, and a Sewanee College and *Review* in Tennessee.) "When he was only thirteen," I. said, and your ears perked up, "the age when most boys are just learning to play with their little flutes, he wrote his 'Tioga Waltz' for an ensemble of flutes!" But like so many creative geniuses, Foster drank too much, and he died of it at the age of thirty-seven.

"All de world am sad and dreary," he repeated.

You wrote a card, *We drink too much. We must go to murphybed.*

"Sure. Yours or mine?" I. asked, lighting up.

You wrote, *You for yours and I for mine.*

He read it and smiled and pointed to one of the pronouns, *I.* "This is me," he said.

You wrote, *You are very tired man, very sad man, and you must get sleep so you can be good teacher, and teach all your students, including me, how to learn to write.* You read this over and crossed out, blacked out, the *including me.* And you helped him up and to the door.

Again, in your sleep that night, you entered your old familiar dream of climbing and descending an endless sequence of steps, stone steps, concrete steps, iron steps, wooden steps, staircases that led up or down to significant places whose significance always eluded you.

The next day, bright and early, you counted up your remaining money. You had little left, just enough; the new term's first paychecks would be received on the fifteenth, just a few days off. You could afford to buy some things, and you took a bus downtown to buy the following: an inexpensive wig of long artificial hair, not in Chaucer's berye or even in a tasteful auburn, but in a rather garish and flaming red; a lipstick to match, that is, equally reddish orange; some rouge; and a pair of dark sunglasses. And at your request, Loretta was all too happy to let you help yourself to her vast collection of costume jewelry, boxes and boxes of it; it took you nearly an hour to pick out what you needed, the wildest items to match the wild hair, and then one of Loretta's somewhat outmoded but still brazen dresses, shorter than any you'd ever worn; and one of Loretta's old hats that she hadn't worn for years, a broad-brimmed thing like a parasol that would completely shade your face. "Evie, you're not gonna wear that stuff to *class?!*" Loretta said.

"No," you said, telling your first little lie. You were going to wear that stuff to class, but not to *your* classes. For your classes, you had made up your mind what to wear, and you would wear it: your *dzhinsy,* which so many women wore for all occasions in this city. You would wear your blue *dzhinsy* beneath the white laboratory coat that Marilyn the secretary had given you, with your name embroidered in script on the breast pocket: E. V. Dadeshkeliani. And on your head your bright Paisley scarf that had brought you good luck on the day you got the job.

Your first classes went, as we say in this country, without a hitch. No sweat. A piece of cake. Section Two of Intro Bot met a little too early in the morning for you, but you needed an excuse to have to get to murphybed earlier. Giving them their first assignments and a small pep talk on the joys of botany, you did not commit, as far as you knew, any major gaffes in the use of the English language. They seemed to understand what you were saying, and you apologized sweetly to them for your inability to speak more fluently. "I am just arrived in this country," you said, "and, like you, I have much to learn."

You stayed on the campus after class, ate a light supper at a grill nearby, returned to your office, and changed into your "costume," taking a full hour to put on your makeup, especially the cheeks and lips. You were as excited as you'd been the very first day of school when the bus had taken you to the collective school in Mestia. You were as excited as the day you'd started at the university in Tbilisi. You were far more excited than you'd been this very morning getting ready for your own classes. And as on those previous school-starting occasions, part of your pleasure had been in getting the equipment you needed: your clean, fresh spiral-bound notebook; a packet of fresh three-by-five index cards (pink); a yellow highlighter; and the required texts (which fortunately the bookstore had let you charge to your faculty account), three paperbacks and a hardbound: Wayne C. Booth, *The Rhetoric of Fiction;* William S. Strunk, Jr., and E. B. White, *The Elements of Style;* Wallace and Mary Stegner, eds., *Great American Short Stories;* and a thumb-indexed Crowell *Roget's International Thesaurus.*

You tucked your books and notebook in your arm and stood for a moment in front of the mirror in your departmental office. The mirror lied totally, for the young woman facing you was your first and finest fictional creation: your broad-brimmed floppy hat, your dark sunglasses (it was nighttime now, and only celebrities wore sunglasses at night . . . or people with eye problems), your makeup, atrociously overdone: a heavy application of a lipstick too brightly reddish orange and circles of rouge so unblended you looked like a clown, and all over you Loretta's loudest costume jewelry: cackling bracelets and jangling earrings and clacking necklace, and, best of all, your hair, a cascade of red flames that billowed out from under your hat and spilled down your shoulders.

If only Bolshakov could see you now. But, indeed, if he did see you now, he would not know you at all. Or, if he knew you, it would confirm the falsehood he'd spent three years trying to get you to believe: that your whole world is your own fabrication.

I SWEAR I HAD NOTHING to do with the coincidence that English 101/
801, Narrative Writing, met in the Scottish Room of the Cathedral of
Learning. I have "arranged" many things for your life in America, dear
Kat, but not that. And I doubt that Anangka concerned herself with it.
And I'm sure that I. himself had no choice in the matter; it's where he
was assigned to meet the class, and he probably wouldn't have chosen
it if given a choice: The room was too large, and too long, and too
formal, and he had to stand up there beneath that elaborate blackboard
covered by oak folding doors that he didn't know how to open and was
too drunk to cope with, doors carved with the names of great Scots:
Robert Louis Stevenson, author of The Strange Case of Dr. Jekyll and Mr.
Hyde, which Nabokov adored; James Boswell, Johnson's biographer; David
Livingstone, the African explorer whom Stanley presumed to find; and
Sir Henry Raeburn the portraitist, all of them surmounted by the canny
Scottish proverb GIF YE DID AS YE SOULD YE MIGHT HAIF AS YE WOULD,
which you could almost make out from your seat in the rear of the
room, although you could not then "translate" it, and you still can't.

I floated in the vicinity of the single window at the rear of the room,
over your shoulder, which was blazoned (the window, not your shoulder)
with the arms of the Montrose clan, a red rose on a silver field; and
from there I observed you and your professor both, and I thought how
appropriate it was that you were disguised from him in this room.

According to Scottish history, King James V of Scotland (1512–1542) loved to mingle with his people disguised as a peasant. You would have loved the man; he was "erected" king at the age of his first erection, twelve; and his last erection, at the age of only twenty-nine, produced his daughter, Mary, Queen of Scots. Once while he was riding around the countryside disguised as a peasant he was attacked by brigands, and an aide beat them off and washed his wounds; a lineal male descendant of that aide was Reginald Fairlie, the architect of this Scottish Room.

The professor, who was wearing not a jacket and tie but one of his grungy sport shirts, had clearly soused himself to prepare for facing this large group of night students, forty mostly older men and women who had worked at wages during the day and were now indulging a dream: to learn from somebody, even this drunk, deaf, unknown visiting novelist with a Bodark accent, how to put words on paper creatively. You shared that dream, and if your assessment of the instructor was more charitable than theirs, it was only because you knew some of his reasons for being drunk, disheveled, and defeated.

He began by pointing to the oil painting over the nonfunctional fireplace. "That's Bobby Burns, isn't it? Yup. Probably a copy of the original by Alexander Nasmyth. How do I know this stuff? This is my first time in this room. I'm as new here as you are. Newer, if you've ever had a class here before. I know that's a Nasmyth because I'm an art historian by profession. It's what I ought to be teaching instead of *this*. I write novels for a hobby, you might say. I've never made any money at it. I'm not going to teach you how to make money, writing." He paused, waiting to see if this would elicit any response. "Nobody wants to leave? You've resigned yourselves to the possibility that you'll never get rich from writing anything? Okay, then, let's begin."

You wished you had sat a little closer, to better hear what was to follow, but you couldn't risk being too close to him in the bright lights of the room. You took notes in your fresh new spiral-bound notebook. Writing, he said, is an art, not a science, and he wasn't going to mess around with "scientific" concepts like *plot, characterization, tension, conflict,* and especially that hideous thing called *POV* for "point of view," with such resulting diagnoses as *POV shift.* Breaking the act of writing down into such components would be like breaking the act of lovemaking down into *suggestion, maneuver, foreplay, penetration, optimal thrusts, climax,* and *post coital tristesse:* The lovemaker so conscious of what he is doing or trying to do is not going to be doing anything worthwhile, let alone pleasurable.

"Art has nothing to do with 'reality,' " he said, and paused, and then said, "I see several people not troubling to write that down. Write it down!" He went on to point out that Nabokov, one of the greatest of novelists, said that "reality" should always have quotation marks around it because there is no such thing, and with the first two fingers of each hand wiggling in the air, I. made the quote-marks that would often separate "reality" from art. You underlined your recording of this in your notebook twice. How Bolshakov would have hated that!

"If we avoid 'reality,' what have we got left?" he demanded. "If we were musical composers, we would have notes, tones, tunes with which to express our deepest feelings. If we were painters, we would have pigments, hues, lines, and shades. But we are writers, and all we have are *words.* Words are our salvation and our delight. Let me give you a gift of four words."

It was then that he had trouble with the reality of the blackboard, trying to open the oak doors covering it. It took him a while, and finally a student who must have been in this room before leapt up and assisted him, and they got the doors open, revealing the blackboard, upon which some previous teacher had left a hodgepodge of algebraic formulae. I. erased this, then replaced it with block letters:

EXTRAVAGANCE

OUTRAGE

EXAGGERATION

OFFENSE

He proceeded to take each word and explicate it: that *extravagance* means, literally, "wandering beyond," and that the art of fiction lies in wandering beyond the conventional into the original and the outrageous; that *outrage* is closely related to the French *outré,* "deviating from what is usual or proper," and that good fiction is always eccentric. How does one deviate into wandering beyond? By heaping, by piling word upon word: *exaggeration* means literally "piling up," but art often involves magnifying beyond the truth, distorting "reality" into a new truth, often at the risk of offending: *Offense* comes from the Latin for "to strike against." The good fictionist must always strike against something, if that something is only convention, putative "reality," bourgeois morality, philistine taste.

You covered pages of your notebook. "Now, are there any questions?" he asked. "If you have any questions, you'll have to write them down, because I can't hear you." He waited a long time, long enough for them to write, but only two questions were presented to him: *Do we have any tests?* and *WHAT are we supposed to write?*

No, he answered, there would be no tests, and as for what you were "supposed" to write, he said, "I'm afraid you'll never hear me say to you, 'I want you to—' or, 'I would like for you to—' with the idea that you will be doing 'assignments' to my specifications, prescriptions, or liking. The task of truly creative writing is always purely voluntary. Forcing your writing to conform to what you think is expected of you is foredooming it to mediocrity. Your greatest 'assignment' is to develop the ability to assign yourself." He paused and waited, and then asked, "Are there any other questions?"

One question was passed to him: *But what do you want us to DO?*

"Okay, I want you to read a few things. For next week, and I'm sure you know we meet only once a week, each Thursday night, please read the first story in the Stegner anthology, 'Rip Van Winkle,' by Washington Irving." There were some audible groans in the class, and I. said, "You were hoping, perhaps, for John Irving instead?" Several students nodded their heads. "Well, the Washington Irving story is sufficiently filled with extravagances, outrages, exaggerations, and offenses."

A question was passed to him: *But don't you want us to write anything?*

"Sure," said I., "write something."

But what? Can we write a poem or a story or a novel or what? Can we write science fiction? Detective stories? Can we write true confessions?

" 'True confession'? No, you don't ever want to write anything autobiographical. Fiction based on yourself is poison. Get it out of your system. I'll have more to say on this subject next week. Good night."

Nobody got up. Several students wrote on slips of paper and passed them down front to the teacher. "I can see you're disappointed that I've kept you for much less than the full three-hour period. And all of these questions ask the same thing in different ways: What do I want you to write? Okay, if you *must* have an assignment to get you started, let me suggest that you write your obituary. Write it as it might appear on the front page of the *New York Times* forty years from now . . . or on the back page of your hometown newspaper the day after tomorrow. This will be your last chance to write about yourself, so make it good, fill it with extravagances, outrages, exaggerations, and offenses, let it all hang out, and get it out of your system. Class dismissed."

BECAUSE YOU FOLDED UP the murphybed each morning upon arising, you couldn't hide your books beneath it, as Kenny hid his *Playboy*s. And you certainly couldn't leave them on the bookshelves, shoulder to shoulder with I.'s novels. You had thought of leaving them in your office, where you kept the wig and hat and other articles of the "costume," but then you wouldn't have been able to consult your books in the middle of the night if you needed to. So you hid the books in your closet, beneath your folded grungy coat, which you would keep forever for sentimental reasons (you now wore a nice new one). And this first night, as soon as you got rid of I. (he dropped by to ask, "Well, how did your first day go?" and to invite you to his apartment for drinks, but you said you had much, much work to do—which was true), you started on your homework: reading "Rip Van Winkle" very thoroughly and making copious marginal observations about its exaggerations and outrages, pausing to look up certain words in your dictionary: *posthumous, henpecked, termagant, virago,* etc., etc. You were fascinated with the Kaatskill Mountains and their being haunted by strange beings. You identified with Rip and reflected upon your incarceration in Russia as akin to his long sleep. And the strange figure with the keg of liquor who put Rip to sleep was unquestionably Bolshakov with his syringes. You wondered: If you were finally able to return to Svanetia, after even five years, let alone twenty, would you know the place? Your homesickness brought tears to your eyes and a profound depression came upon you, but you ignored it and went on with your work, reading and rereading until you knew almost by heart the seven points of Strunk's and White's Elementary Rules of Usage, and then Wayne Booth's first chapter, on Telling and Showing, wherein he debunks the myth that the good writer should always do the latter rather than the former. You made notes to obtain, on your next trip to Hillman, two of the books that Booth discusses, Boccaccio's *Decameron* and Flaubert's *Madame Bovary*.

You could scarcely wait to get to Hillman, and you went there the next morning, right after your mycology class, which had some good students in it. You surprised yourself during your first mycology lecture, speaking in English of the concepts you knew by heart in Russian as well as Georgian, although your mind kept wandering: You were thinking constantly of your obituary. You found yourself prematurely introducing into your mycology lecture your reflections upon the mortality of mush-rooms. It is of course an essential characteristic of their being that they endure upon this earth such a short span, just long enough to fulfill their intended destinies, but you had usually not taken your students deeply into the ephemerality of fungi until late in the semester, when they had been prepared for it by appreciating the sensational aspects of the brief but spectacular life span of the fungi.

At the Hillman, you ran into Dr. Elmore, on his way to his private carrel, and you attempted unsuccessfully to get him to hear your polite answer to his polite question "How's school?" then you began to load your arms with books: In addition to the Boccaccio and the Flaubert, you got several volumes on Scotland and Northern Ireland. When you had more books than you thought you could carry home, you realized you had more than you could safely hide at home, and you determined then to do much of your work in your office.

"My office," became your standard reply to the frequent question of Kenny, "Where have you been all day?" and the occasional question of I., "Where've you been keeping yourself?" A question that I. asked more often than that, "Have you had a chance to sneak a glance at my novels?" bothered you for its echo of Knox Ogden and made you wonder if your failure to have sneaked a glance at his novels would drive him to drink. But he was already driven to drink, so you couldn't be blamed for that. You would look at I. and smile and imagine writing down on a card, *The reason I have so little time for you is that I am spending all of my time on your "assignment."* But then you would try to be polite and friendly and as accommodating as you could, to both I. and Kenny, leaving them both to believe that the beginning of the term had simply overwhelmed you with responsibilities and that you hoped later, sometime conceivably later, to accept I.'s invitation to take you to a movie, and to do something about Kenny's marvelous, expanding libido, manifested in his more frequent telling of the latest risqué joke or story he'd heard or read. The chess set collected dust. "Let's play *something*," Kenny urged you one night. Soon, you promised. Soon, but for right now you had an enormous job to complete.

And finally, just in time, on Thursday, the day it was due, after an all-night session with the dictionary and your new thesaurus ("A good writer," Professor I. had told the class, "will wear out, entirely wear out, at least one thesaurus a year"), it was done and remained only to be made presentable. Marilyn the secretary, who was so kind and amenable, gladly agreed to type it for you, appropriately on her latest-model futuristic IBM Executive. "One of my favorite students," you explained to Marilyn, "is too poor to have a typewriter and needs this for another class."

April 24, 2021

Cathlin Ursula McWalter, the popular novelist known as "Scotch Mist" to her many readers, died yesterday in her hotel suite at Suwanee, North Carolina, at the age of sixty-nine. The editors of the New York Times *are pleased to publish herewith the first document produced by IBM's newly developed Telemedium, the machine capable of recording messages from the afterlife.*

EXCUSE MY DUST. It won't take me as long to get the hang of this thing as it did to discover that there are no guides over here, no officers, no bureaucrats, no delegates, no committees. Of course there aren't any restrooms or restaurants either, but I wasn't expecting those. I was hoping I'd be met, however, and it came as a surprise to discover that there's nothing social about death: It's the most solitary condition imaginable.

The first thing you'd like to know, if I'm reading your mind correctly from this distance, is: Who done it? I was in good health. Certainly I drank more than was good for me, but year after year my doctors said that wouldn't kill me. Every day, including yesterday, just before my death, I went for a twelve-mile hike into the mountains, collecting young specimens of the elusive Cathlin-weed (*Datura mcwaltera*) for inclusion in the book that looks like it's going to have to be posthumous, volume two of my avocational *Wicked Weeds of the Western World*.

There was nothing organically wrong with me. And I had scarcely one white hair among the thousands of scarlet strands that prompted so many of you to write me complimentary notes about my appearance, my fantastic jewelry and eccentric hats as well as my flaming hair. Thank you. It might pain you to learn that we don't have *any* appearance over here, not even phantasmagoric—not even smoke, not even, if you'll forgive me, Scotch mist.

Speaking of which, I'm bound to point out that all of the McWalters of that ilk were notoriously longevous, and I should've lived much longer than a mere sixty-nine years. My great-great-way-back, Parlane Mc-Waltir, he of Auchinvennell, in the shadow of Ben Lomond in Dumbarton, the first of our line to leave the ould sod and emigrate to North Ireland in 1609, lived to be almost a hundred, and many of his male descendants, including my grandfather Francie McWalter, of Londonderry, where I was born in 1953, managed to reach the age of at least ninety.

Of course, there were some who met untimely ends: Margaret McWaltir, a Covenanter, was tied to a tidal stake and left to drown in 1685, and Joanna McWalter, my aunt in Londonderry, leapt to her death in the Foyle River.

Could my untimely exit, you're asking, have been suicide? Not me. Oh, certainly the reception given by critics in the popular press to my last novel, my thirty-second and possibly best book, *Lady McBovair,* would have depressed any author to the point of self-murder as a substitute for not being able to murder the *Times* reviewer who called it "watered-down—or McWaltered-down—Flaubert." But what the hey? as they say; it was both a BOMC *and* a Literary Guild selection, and it made a mint, which I didn't need, despite what my first writing teacher said forty years ago—a forgotten novelist named I.: "You'll never get rich from writing anything."

Do you think I might have been done in by some person driven mad by envy of my riches? (Even Professor I. himself?) Then why didn't he or she murder me thirty-five years ago, when my first novel, *Geordie Lad,* catapulted me to fame? Or when my collection of retellings of Boccaccio,

The Ten Ludic Rooms, brought me serious literary recognition as well? The time to have murdered me out of envy or spite would have been right after the appearance of *The Long Sleep,* my epic psychobiography of Rip Van Winkle, which more than any other volume probably got me my Nobel in 2007.

I wasn't ready to die, and no one was more shocked by it than I was. But I've lived all my life by Murphy's Law (although he was Irish, not Scot) and to the extent that extinction of one's life is something gone wrong, it sure went wrong. And yet I had so many things going right for me: that lovely suite of rooms on the top floor of the Moonbeam Hotel, with Jacuzzi and Jenn-Aire, with my own futuristic kitchen where I could whip up one of those chicken dishes that grace the pages of *Cathlin's Quick Chick Cookbook;* a dozen absolutely beautiful cats of every color and breed who were contented beyond their wildest expectations by the attention lavished on them by their owner and by Miss McTavish, my maid; and my almost completed research on John Ross, the Cherokee Indian chief (half Scotch) who grew up in these mountains and came to lead his people into exile from them. At the moment of my death, I still had not determined whether Ross would be the subject of my next novel or of my fifth nonfiction book on American Indians. And now he will be neither . . . unless the IBM people aren't lying when they brag about their Telemedium.

And I was scheduled to start, this very afternoon, a best-of-seven match with American Grand Master Billy McFarland, who, even as I speak, is down in the lobby crying his little heart out. He would have beaten me, of course, and probably with several of his clever Sicilian Defenses, but just to mate him once would have made the day, the month, the season, for me.

Is he a suspect? Not Billy: He has already convinced the detectives that he was still on his bicycle, pedaling this way but ten miles off, at the moment the death occurred, and they, not even knowing he's a grand master but taking some account of his age, eleven, have let him go and are concentrating all their brutal "grilling" on poor Timmy McLachlan, my houseboy. That's stupid. Timmy is . . . Well, no, it's stupid to suspect Timmy. I have never denied that I hired him because he reminded me of Geordie McGraw, the model for the hero of *Geordie Lad.* But now, for heaven's sake, he's pushing fourteen and was planning to leave my employ next week.

So who are the suspects? I'm a writer, after all, and I can't give away endings, and this isn't the ending. You haven't heard the last of me. But my devoted readers who are familiar with my memoirs, *Louder, Engram!* will recall that I spent some years in my early twenties incarcerated in Armagh prison for my part in the Belfast riots of 1976, and that subsequently I was committed to the Ulster Psychiatric Hospital in Coleraine, where I came under the "care" of a Dr. ~~Fomin~~ Bolshakov, a Viennese-trained psychoanalyst whose job apparently was not to "treat" any real mental disorder I might have had but to punish me by giving me a mental disorder. For three years, this ~~Fomin~~ Bolshakov tried everything he could to drive me insane, and in the process he developed an overpowering sexual lust for my body. He was unsuccessful in both. For the rest of my life thereafter, following the daring escape that Geordie McGraw helped me make and that I have truthfully recorded in the otherwise fictional *Geordie Lad,* I was certain that ~~Fomin~~ Bolshakov was still, literally, out to get me: that he was bent upon finding me and obtaining revenge for my frustrating his efforts and his desires.

I'm not going to tell you, yet, who killed me. But I can say this much: ~~Fomin~~ Bolshakov is actually at large. He is out there, even in the vicinity of the Moonbeam Hotel on its hilltop in Suwanee, North Carolina. In my present condition I no longer need to wear the very dark glasses that I wore all my life because of photodysphoria, and I can see him clearly without them. I could bore you with a long analysis of ~~Fomin's~~ Bolshakov's own peculiar mental disorder, a delusion that all "reality" must conform to his own limited concept of what "reality" is, and I could warn you he is out there, waiting for all of you. But I won't. It would take away what little pleasure you find in your remaining physical inhabitance of that earth.

Please tell those guys to put away that Hammond organ and bring out instead a Steinway grand. For my funeral I want them to play, as you'll discover when you take the trouble to open my will, the Piano Concerto no. 1 in B-flat Minor by Peter Ilyich Tchaikovsky.

I WAS MIGHTY PROUD of you, Kat. It remained to be seen what I. would think of it, but I personally thought you did a splendid job, an inspired job—although I must disclaim any direct influence on your brilliant decision to write the piece as if you were a ghost, a true ghostwriter, ghosting that "Cathlin" on behalf of Ekaterina. Of course I immediately understood that your alias names were allusions to your own: *Cathlin* being the North Irish form of *Ekaterina, McWalter* a Scots form of *Vladimir,* and that middle name, *Ursula,* as close as you could get to *Dadeshkeliani,* both deriving from *bear.* Would I. catch these allusions? You were gambling that he would not. You were distracting him with the multiple allusions to Nabokov to keep him from catching the more subtle allusions to yourself. I was nervous about that "Suwanee, North Carolina." (There is no such place, although there is a Swannanoa, North Carolina.) Wouldn't he recall that he'd told you about Florida's Suwanee River and Tennessee's Sewanee and wonder about the "coincidence"? You were gambling that he would not.

I was especially pleased with your development of the Scottish angle: I suppose there's sufficient topographic similarity between the Highlands and Svanetia for you to feel "at home" there in your imagination. My ancestor Glendenning "Mountain Horse" Montross, who emigrated from Scotland to Connecticut and fought in the American Revolution, had been a feuding crony of some of those McWaltirs of Dumbarton. Your research was almost as meticulous as the research that "Cathlin" had been conducting into the life of the Cherokee John Ross (about which, as they say, more later).

And I think I understood why you took the risk of keeping Bolshakov's actual name, as an afterthought following an unsatisfactory attempt to disguise it as *Fomin* (which is also Russian, a form of *Thomas*). Bolshakov himself, with his insistence upon authentication and "reality," would have disapproved of becoming a fictional character. Would I. wonder how a Russian psychiatrist could come to be practicing in Northern Ireland? You were gambling that he would not.

The only minor correction I would have made to your otherwise flawless piece (your newfound grasp of English astonished even me) was "Cathlin's" assertion, in the beginning, that "it came as a surprise to discover that there's nothing social about death: It's the most solitary condition imaginable." This isn't, as I hope you'll find, strictly true. At the moment of arrival at "the other side," the lifeless are often overwhelmed to find that *every*one is there! I'm reminded of those surprise birthday parties, only with, if you can possibly imagine it, the entire departed population of earth in attendance. The lifeless are free to pick and choose which of those billions they may communicate with, but *all* of them are there, almost like a multitude of angels dancing on the head of a pin. So death, angel, is unimaginably not solitary but social.

Unlike your classmates, you didn't have to wait a whole week to find out what your instructor thought of your obituary. The very night after you'd handed it in, he arrived at your door with a drink in one hand and a stack of papers in the other, asking, "Want to have some fun?" and then explaining to you that he had assigned his Narrative class to write their own obituaries, and here were the results, and some of them were pretty darn good, if you'd care to read them. This one. And this one. Here, this guy writes it as if it appeared in a newspaper on Mars. And this lady writes a very short but funny piece from her hometown newspaper as if her wake had been held in a swimming pool. What do you think? Wait, here's a great one. Read this one. I want to know what you think of this one.

Reading it and pretending, like the very best writers ought to be able to do all the time, that what you'd written had been written by someone else, you couldn't suppress a giggle or two, particularly over *Lady McBovair* and *Cathlin's Quick Chick Cookbook*. And when you finished it, you felt that sure enough this Cathlin student of his was pretty darn good, certainly better than the others whose obits you'd just read.

"Well?" said I.

"Clever," you said.

"More than clever," said I. "Dynamite. Out of this world. The real George."

"George?" The name grabbed you, but it wasn't a name.

"State of the art. Something else. Cracking. This is some kind of superfuckingfantastic."

It was the highest accolade you'd ever had, and you came perilously close to saying, "Thank you." But all you said was—or, rather, you wrote it on a card—*You have some talented students in that class. You must be enjoying them.*

"Yeah, but the work load is driving me crazy. I've got forty papers to correct and grade for this class, and sixty short stories to read and correct for my other classes. I need to take a break. Want to go to a movie?"

You wrote, *Yes. I am not so busy, now. I have finished project. Let us see movie with three X's.*

He read it, and his eyebrows went up. He coughed. "I don't guess they have those in Russia. Or Georgia. But sure, let's go find one, if you want."

Yes, there are certain places in Leningrad (or Saint Petersburg, as it has regained its real name), and even in Tbilisi, where one may watch a *pornografeechyesky feelm,* but you had never seen one before. Driving you downtown in his Blazer, I. gave you the American synonym, *skin flick,* and said he hoped you would be ready for it. You strolled together down the street of cinemas, reading triple-*X*'ed marquees. "Take your pick," he suggested. "They're interchangeable. One is as good—or as bad— as the other." You discovered that *The World According to Gwyn* was no longer showing at the place where the lady in the booth had suggested you come back with your boyfriend. Now you had your "boyfriend," but the movie wasn't there. It was, however, showing at another theater just down the street. Interchangeable. "I don't like that title," I. protested. "It reminds me of a guy I would have liked to 'do in,' to quote that Cathlin's obituary, because I was driven mad by envy of his riches."

But you and I. went to see it. It bore not the slightest resemblance, I. told you afterward, to the novel about one Garp. The actress Gwyn Tiffany (not her real name; she was born Thelma Jean Mankowicz) was a sudden surprise when first you glimpsed her, because of her resemblance to Cathlin McWalter—except that Gwyn's flames were not the gaudy scarlet of Cathlin's; rather, a more tasteful shade of sienna ginger. But she wore much jangling jewelry, and dark eyeglasses! At least in the beginning, because it was California and the sun was hot and bright. Soon she took them off. Soon she took everything off. So did some male, the actor Scott Irish (real, but pseud.). You did not understand the role of the male in the plot; perhaps his function was to persuade her to undress. His nakedness was utter: even his dangling *qvem,* his generative organ, was exposed to full view. You said aloud, "*Ot!*" which is "Oh" in Svanetian. There was a great contrast of skins: hers light, undulant, soft, flowing, circular, flowerlike; his dark, knobby, hirsute, hard, lumpy, diagonal, animal-like. You were reminded then, and throughout the movie, of the things you do not like about grown men, mature men, developed men: their hairiness, their musculature, their swagger and aggression, even their smell, which you were almost certain you could detect here: the excrement of certain fungi and bacteria that infest only the full-grown man. "*Ot!*" you could not help saying again as the smelly man put his hand on Gwyn's head and forced her to her knees, where she was required to devote the next many minutes to the use of her *vishkv,* which in Svanetian means "face" or "mouth," or both together, especially her *nin,* tongue. The eye of the camera, which reminded me in a limited way of the telescopic and microscopic vision we have here in the happy hunting ground, kept zooming in to reveal the wet quiverings of the frenulum and the glans, making them gigantic and scary, like certain mythical toadstools you'd seen only in dreams. Was Gwyn allowed to stop when she had the thing ready for its proper use? She was not: She had to continue, many minutes, until, with the aid of her *jugvmard,* fist, as well as her *vishkv* and *nin,* she caused the toadstool to erupt and spew its spores, which resembled dollops of toothpaste, all over her pretty *vishkv.* *"Ot! Ot!"* you cried, not even aware you spoke.

I. must have heard you, however limited his powers. "Want to go?" he asked.

But you could not. You had to sit there the whole eighty minutes, thinking, *This is like a recording of dreams, like a peephole into fantasy, but I like my own fantasy and dreams much better.* Before it was all over, it had become repetitious, trite, unimaginative, almost boring, and the actresses and actors seemed to view their work as an assignment, a workout, a perfunctory fucky and an insouciant sucky. "Here comes the obligatory lesbian scene," I. warned you, and a full ten minutes were consumed by another actress, Candi Dare (pseud.), pretending that she had a lust for Gwyn, and employing her *nin* all over her, and later an artificial penis with rubber glandes at both ends of its yardlong length for mutual male becoming. *Ot.* The movie was full of props and devices: There were several bananas fondled, peeled, licked, and eaten; several phallicized instruments of different shapes that seemed to have on-off switches and that pulsated; and a string of small balls to be inserted rectally and jerked out. *Ot.* As the movie progressed, the motions and devices became more and more stilted, synthetic, and desperate, until you were no longer aware of individuals or any pretense at plot, but only of a variety of light and dark *lefva,* meats, in constant urgent motions that were some-times aimless, pointless, funless. You stopped saying *Ot.* Eventually you discovered that you could appreciate the film as a total abstraction, like a nonobjective painting by Kandinsky: thrusting diagonals and oscillating circles, overlapped, underlapped, lap upon lap.

Back at the mansion, you offered I. a nightcap and he offered you his cards and said, "Well, tell me what you thought of it."

You wrote, *There must be a better way to earn a living.*

He asked, "For the actors, you mean? But didn't the movie make you horny?"

" 'Horny'?" You reached for your dictionary.

"You won't find it in there," he said. "What I meant was, didn't it make you want to go to bed?"

Yes, put me to sleep, toward the end, you wrote.

I. did something he hadn't done yet: touched you. He put his hands, his palms, on the sides of your arms, as if to draw you to him. "The movie made me horny," he said.

You put two fingers up beside your head, horns, and then wrote, *Like cokewold?* You remembered only the way Chaucer spelled it. *Or like bull? Or like points of crescent moon? Or maybe you are impaled on a dilemma.*

He read it and made his strangled chuckle. "Not like cuckold," he said. "Maybe like bull." He waited to see what you would say next, and when you said nothing, he waited more, and then said, "To be blunt, I want to screw. How do you say 'screw' in Svanetian?"

"*Tchackrog,*" you said, and then you wrote it down: *čaxrag.* You pantomimed the insertion of a corkscrew.

He corrected your pantomime: not a spiral motion, but an in-and-out one, like the urgencies of the movie. Then he asked, "How do you say 'fuck' in Svanetian?"

You wrote: *It depends on who is doing to whom, bull to cow, man to woman, man to man, man to cow, man to himself. Different word each situation. Basic root is čoš-. I pronounce it for you.* "Chosh," you said, forming your beautiful lips carefully.

Again he put his hands on your arms. "Let's me and you chosh."

"In Svanetia, one never does 'chosh' without having known each other for at least two months." This was a fabrication of yours, Kat, an improvisation; it's not true at all. But how else to handle him?

"Really?" he said. "I'll remember that, then." He consulted his wristwatch, which had a calendar but badly needed cleaning. "On March eighteenth, I'm going to chosh you out of your eyeballs."

THAT REMAINED TO BE SEEN. When that March with its sweet showers had rolled around, as we shall see, I. had given up horning after you. He had fallen in love with someone else, we might say, and had left you alone . . . or left you to Kenny.

At the beginning of the third class in narrative techniques, the professor, who uncustomarily was wearing a necktie, returned the obituaries to their authors. Written in red on a sheet attached to yours (Cathlin's) was the letter grade A + and this note: *I am mightily impressed with this. It is the only obit in class written in the first rather than the third person, an achievement of singular inventiveness. It is also the only obit with a true narrative thread of suspense. It is one of the few obits with good humor and an attempt to observe my guidelines re exaggeration, extravagance, outrage and offense. To whatever extent it is "real," i.e., based upon your own life, you are a marvelous person and I am dying to get to know you better, even if you call me "a forgotten novelist." Ha ha! But you will get rich if you continue to develop the talent you show here. What would you like to write next? Do you really know about John Ross the Cherokee? I once thought of doing a novel on him myself. Let's get together for a chat after class, shall we? But meanwhile, do you mind if I read this obit to the class? If you don't mind, hold up your hand momentarily after you've read this note.*

And from his vantage at the head of the Scottish Room, he kept throwing glances toward the rear of the room, where you were slumped in embarrassment in your seat. You didn't want him to read your work to the class. Proud as you were of it (proud as I and *I.* were of it), you hadn't written it with *this* audience in mind, and you didn't want them hearing him read it aloud. So you did not hold up your hand, and after a while he gave up waiting for it, although he continued glancing at you, as if to assure himself that you actually existed. He read other obits, commenting upon their shortcomings and their good points. He analyzed in detail the work of the lady whose wake was held in her swimming pool. You sat half listening, wondering how you could get out of any after-class meeting he had in mind for you.

He began to discourse about, or against, autobiographical fiction, telling the class that now that they had their obituaries out of the way they could start to ignore themselves. Stories about oneself are doomed, he said, not because of lack of objectivity nor because of their egotism but because art must always transmute "reality," and the reality of one's own self is the hardest to transmute.

"Allow me," he said, "to read you a poem. Not mine. A colleague's, and you may have heard it or read it before. Don't stop me if you've heard it. The title is, 'My Penis.' " Without embarrassment I. proceeded to read the forty lines that describe, in infinite lyrical detail, the configurations, the associations, the sensibilities, the impressions, the history, and the uses of the poet's personal *qvem,* the organ whose Svanetian word, in one of those coincidental transpositions wherein *mama* means "father" and *deda* means "mother" in Georgian, is closer to the English female *quim.* It was a good poem. Too good. "Now, if that had been my own poem," I. said, "you'd think me a dreadful exhibitionist, a flasher. It's a marvelous example of the so-called confessional school of frankly self-obsessed poetry. Is it art?"

I. began to stroke his necktie, and you began to guess why he had worn it, that broad regimental-striped silk foulard that was, as far as you knew, the only necktie in his closet. "Now consider this," he said, fondling his necktie and presenting it. "See how long it is. See how it hangs down. Notice the swelling down here. Look at the brilliant stripes all over! See how the knot expands at the top and clinches it. If men are advertising their pricks with their neckties, the double-Windsor knot must be a big pair of balls, right?

"The question is: Which would you rather look at and *believe* in, this necktie or"—he suddenly unzipped his trousers and thrust his hand inside.

"*Ot!*" you cried out, but your Svanetian was drowned amid the gasps and exclamations of others.

But I. did not expose himself. He had made his point, and he zipped himself up and said, "I want you folks to write some gorgeous neckties and leave your pricks in your pants."

Thus it was that you spent the rest of the class period secretly practicing Cathlin's handwriting, to make it as unlike your own as possible, so that, after class when the professor caught up with you outside the Cathedral of Learning despite your hurried footsteps, you could stand there beneath the glare of the street lamp and hand him a card, not one of his blank three-by-five whites but one of your own lined pink ones, already inscribed: *I am only a necktie. You do not want to see my prick.* He was standing closer to you than you'd ever expected him to be, and while you knew that the combination of the floppy hat and the dark glasses was shielding you from his identification, you began to wonder if possibly you smelled like Ekaterina.

"I hope this doesn't mean you're a transvestite in drag," he said.

You did not know those words, but you had another card ready for him: *Thank you so much for the kind things you said about my obituary, but I think you and I should be teacher and devoted pupil, not pals.*

"But, pal, we have so many interests in common!" he said. "Did you know I'm part Scotch-Irish myself? And I'm crazy about that Tchaikovsky first piano concerto."

You did not have a card ready for that one, and you had to write it down, using your books as a desk, there beneath the street lamp. *Can you hear music?*

"Listen," he said, "you don't have to write down *every*thing. Sure, I can hear music, and I can probably hear your voice. Try me."

But of course you could not. *You could not hear me,* you wrote, *because in addition to my photodysphoria and hebephilia I also have speech defect.*

"Hebephilia?" he said. "What is that? Did you mention it in your obituary?"

I alluded to it, you wrote.

"Speaking of allusions," he said. "Talk about *allusions.* In your obituary, those allusions to Nabokov really killed me. Nabokov, I should tell you, is one of my very favorite writers, but so few of your classmates have read him."

You wrote, *I have not read him myself, but I know of him.*

"Who have you read?" he asked. You hesitated. Whom, indeed, had you read? You started to mention Gogol and Dostoyevski and Turgenev, but decided against it. Fortunately, he took your hesitation to mean that you were exasperated to be standing here under the street lamp on a cold winter night talking about literature, and he said, "Say, there's a nice little pub down the street there, called Tiffany's. Do you know it? Could we have one drink together as teacher and devoted pupil without becoming pals?"

So you stopped off, farther along the avenue, at the bar at Tiffany's, the only oasis between the campus and the mansion. It was rather posh, a quiet, dimly lighted lounge, and he was poorly dressed and you were overdressed, his trench coat threadbare and soiled, even if he was wearing a necktie, and your coat (borrowed from Loretta) a fluffy, shaggy thing that belonged to some flightier era. You wanted vodka but had to be careful not to give anything away, so you had Scotch instead and found it not at all undrinkable.

You discussed many things over more than one drink. Several drinks. I. chain-smoked his Pall Malls but you had decided, in order to distinguish Cathlin from Ekaterina, that Cathlin would not be a smoker. It took much willpower for her, for you, to do this.

I. started off by observing that the light in Tiffany's was awfully dim, so why couldn't you take off those dark shades? Because, you said (or wrote), your photodysphoria, extreme light sensitivity, was really terrible. In fact, it was the reason you had come to this city, to be treated for the condition at the university's medical center, whose chief of ophthalmology, Dr. Morris Heflin, was doing his best for you. For old Inquisitor's benefit, and in answer to his several questions, you began to assemble the details of Cathlin's current situation in life: You worked days as a typist in the payroll office of one of the steel manufacturers. In the eighth form of school, back home in Ulster, you had begun to manifest the symptoms of hebephilia, which, along with the speech and vision disorders, had led you to leave Ulster and come to America. You were also under the care of Dr. Horace Mifflin, specialist in personality disorders at the Western Psychiatric Institute. The depth and extent of poor Cathlin's afflictions brought empathetic tears to your eyes, and your sunglasses couldn't conceal them as they rolled down your cheeks, and you concluded a card, *I am a crazy mixed-up kid.*

I. laid one of his hands on top of yours and said, "But a potentially brilliant and successful writer." He skipped just a beat before his next question, which caught you by surprise: "Was there really a Bolshakov?"

Yes, there is really a Bolshakov.

"Then perhaps you ought to write, for me, for the course, about the story of your experience with Bolshakov."

But you insist we write neckties, not penises.

"Wasn't Bolshakov a prick?"

You laughed. It was the first time since coming to America and escaping from that prick that poor Cathlin had really experienced a good, resounding laugh. Oh, Ekaterina had shared a good laugh or two with Kenny, and with Dalrymple, her boss, and even with I., but Cathlin, who was destined to become, if her own predictions and Instructor's came true, one of America's wittiest writers, had not yet had a good laugh on these shores. It was almost like having her first orgasm, and laughter is, after all, a close cousin to climax.

And such was the relaxation and release of the laughter that your guard was down when the old Inveigler said, "Why don't we stroll over to my apartment and talk about chess and Cherokees and Tchaikovsky? Without becoming pals, of course."

You went, challenged by the task of pretending you'd never been there before, challenged by being that close to your own room and having to think of it as a place remote from you, and challenged by something else too, although you could not quite formulate the words or even the thought for it—but I can do that for you: Ekaterina was passionately enamored of faunlets and almost constitutionally incapable of feeling desire for a grown man, but might not Cathlin possess the "psychological distance" requisite to such desire? You were curious. And curiosity, as I. or I could have told you, is the supreme faculty of the creative artist. When curiosity flourishes, worlds can be changed.

On the way upstairs, Kenny spotted you but looked at you only long enough to convince himself that you were some bimbo that Professor I. was bringing home with him. You were glad that Loretta hadn't seen you; she might have recognized her clothes and jewelry. In I.'s room, you looked at his accommodations as if you were seeing them for the first time: the mirrors, the tall windows, even the murphybed, an interesting contraption. On his windowsill, in a Burpee Seed-N-Start container, he was sprouting twelve tomato seedlings, and, remembering that Cathlin was interested in weeds, you dutifully sniffed them. He tried to get you to take off your huge hat, but you couldn't, and you insisted that he leave the room's illumination as dark as possible: just one reading lamp on, nothing else.

"I'd like to show you my novels," he said, "but I've loaned all of them to my next-door neighbor." His face lit up with a thought. "You'd like Ekaterina. She's about your age and has some interests in common: ghosts, and chess, and Indians. She's a European too. Comes from Svanetia, in Soviet Georgia. Why don't I pop next door and ask her if she'd like to meet you? She's read your obituary."

You didn't like the thought of his having shown your obituary to his neighbor. And you didn't like the thought of some woman as his next-door neighbor. You wrote: *Is she single? Is she attractive?* And you lifted an eyebrow while he read it. "Yes, she's alone, and she's quite beautiful, but I'm not having a relationship with her or anything like that. I'll be right back." He was gone three minutes, knocking next door longer than he needed to, in order to bring the woman out of her shower or her bed or her trance or whatever she was in. She was not in. "I guess she's working late," he said. "She teaches botany at the university. Are you really interested in weeds?"

Not especially, you wrote. *But I needed to give myself in the obituary an avocation. Didn't Nabokov chase butterflies?*

"I can't believe you haven't read anything of his," I. said. He scanned his bookshelves and fetched a paperback for you. "As I say, Ekaterina has all my novels, but I can loan you this. You must read it." It was *Pale Fire,* and I. gave you a précis of it: a professor named Kinbote who thinks he is the exiled king of Zembla comes to extensively annotate a long poem, "Pale Fire," by his colleague John Shade, who was mistakenly murdered by an assassin out to get Kinbote, whose annotations of the poem become the story of himself. "The main reason I was hoping Ekaterina would be in was so I could borrow a cup of Cutty Sark from her. I've only got bourbon. Can you drink bourbon?"

You could, and he certainly could, and the two of you proceeded to get pickled. You told yourself to be careful; you wanted enough to relax your inhibitions, to make you amenable to things your sober self wouldn't want, but you didn't want enough to let you do something you'd be sorry for tomorrow or something that might give away your disguise.

I. apparently had no restraints, and he threw back a snootful. After a while, he got up and staggered next door again to pound on Ekaterina's door, and he staggered back to say, "Maybe she'sh gone out on a date." Then he sat down beside you on the sofa (where Knox had died) and said, "Y'know, I t'ink I like you a lot better'n her anyhow." When he was not sober, I. pronounced "I" as "Ah," so for the rest of this evening, and whenever he's drunk, I think that I shall call him that instead.

Ah began to sing. In the same vibrant bass voice that he had sung his "Svani Ribber" for Ekaterina, which she and you would have considered abominable had you realized how off-key it was, but which you considered operatic because you didn't know the key, he began singing this: "Oh, Danny Boy, the pipes, the pipes are calling. From glen to glen, and down the mountainside . . .

"The summer's gone, and all the roses fall-ll-ling.
It's you, it's you must go, and I must bide. . . ."

Even off-key, it was lovely, beautiful (even my own exquisite sense of pitch was not offended, since the words are addressed to one Danny, and I, after all, am Dan), and after the first stanza, he interjected, "Don'tcha know it? Ah wish you washn't mute and could sing it along wif me." And he resumed singing,

> "But come ye back, when summer's in the meadow,
> Or when the valley's hushed and white with snow.
> It's I'll be here . . ."

But he faltered then and asked, "What comes next? How does the resht of that line go?" and handed you your pen and one of his cards.

But you did not know what to write. Making Cathlin into a very good Scotch-Irish lass who would know not only the tune of "The Londonderry Air" but all the words to "Danny Boy" was going to take you a while. All you could write was: *I am too drunk to remember.*

"Really? Well." Ah moved closer to you on the sofa, draping one arm over the back of the sofa as if to embrace you. You got yourself ready for the touch of his arm on your shoulders. Preparing the nerve ends of your shoulders, you were caught by surprise when his touch came not there but on your bare knee. He put his other hand on your other knee and then began to slide it up your thigh.

"*Ot!*" you exclaimed.

"Say! You aren't mute," he observed. He removed his hand and looked at it. "Ish my hand hot? Did you say 'hot'?"

You nodded your head.

"Ah wish you could take off those glasshes, so's I could see your purty ahs. Couldja maybe closh your ahs tight and then take 'em off?"

You shook your head.

He lifted his glass, bourbon and branch on the rocks, and after draining it, he held the glass with its cubes in his hand for a while, then said, "Now my hand's not hot." And he slid the hand up your thigh again, almost to your *bud.*

"*Ot!*" you said.

"No, it's not," he protested. "It's cold. "Why're ya sayin 'hot'?"

You took card and pen and wrote: *Excuse. I am not uttering "hot." I am vocalizing "och," which is Scottish expression of surprise.*

Ah stared at you, long and lovingly, and then he declared, "You fashcinate me, y'know it? And y'know, you'd be a *ravishing* creature without all that makeup and that getup. That hat and hair and dressh and jewelry and sunglasshes." You drew back from him as if he'd insulted you. "I mean, really," he tried to elaborate, "didn't anybody ever tell you that you're sort of too much?"

Identifying so completely with the poor mixed-up kid that Cathlin was, you felt humiliated. Cathlin couldn't be blamed for her honest attempt to express her personality through her attire, and it certainly wasn't her fault that the photodysphoria required her to wear the sunglasses. You took a fresh card, and you spent a while with it, scribbling furiously on both sides, and then you stood up from the sofa and thrust the card at him. *No, nobody ever told me that. And you are very rude to do so. Do I tell you that you dress shabbily and haven't bathed recently and you don't even comb your oily hair? No, but it's true. And you smoke too much, and drink too much, and your breath reeks. I hope this isn't going to affect my grade in your course, but I wanted very much to talk to you about Bolshakov and a novel I want to write, and all you've got on your mind is your prick. You've hurt my feelings. Good night.*

Then you grabbed your coat and the paperback of *Pale Fire* he'd lent you, and you stormed out.

Ah made only a feeble, drunken effort to follow you, to stop you, to apologize, to get you back. Probably he was still sober enough to realize that you'd have to walk home alone in the dark, wherever you lived, and he ought to offer to accompany you. But you fled from the mansion and gained the street before it dawned on you that you did not know where Cathlin lived. And this time of night, you weren't about to walk all the way to your office to change out of your costume.

You waited in the dark street for a time, casting an occasional glance upward at the windows of Ah's room, hoping his lights would go out and he'd go to bed, but knowing that he wouldn't. Finally you let yourself back into the mansion very quietly and went up to your apartment and quietly entered and removed your costume and your makeup and went to murphybed.

FEBRUARY WAS YOUR BUSIEST month ever. In addition to giving and grading quizzes for each of your classes, attending departmental meetings, and finding yourself elected to the chairman's advisory committee, which would consume large chunks of your free time, you actually began, without quite knowing it yourself, the long story that would become Cathlin's first novel, *Geordie Lad*. What started as merely an attempt to fulfill one of Professor Ah's peculiar assignments—"Observe and describe a place, and through description of the place alone attempt to evoke the person(s) whose place it is"—became Chapter One of the novel because the place you chose to describe, from memory more than invention, was Dr. Bolshakov's office in the Serbsky Institute. Without any mention at all of the man himself, except to note and translate the diplomas on the wall, you began spinning a web of depiction all around him, so that the reader already knows him before first meeting him.

But it was a chore. You did most of the writing not in your office but in your apartment; the meager accoutrements and auras of your office would have spoiled your vision of the office of Bolshakov. Thus the questions of Kenny and I. were not Where have you been all day? and Where've you been keeping yourself? but rather When can you come out and play? and Are you doing anything in there that I could help you with? You were not able to find much time for them. You could pretend, to Ah, that you were indeed a bit miffed over his relationship with this red-headed student of his: he had clearly tried to make you jealous in his full "report" on the visit of Cathlin to his apartment, embellishing the truth of what had happened that night. He claimed that he and Cathlin had sung a duet of "Danny Boy," and that she trilled her R's thrillingly. He claimed that Cathlin had spent the night with him. "Well, since you can't 'chosh,' " he said, "it was either her or Edith Koeppe. I'm a horny man."

For Valentine's Day, I. gave Cathlin a copy of the hardback (not a first edition) of Nabokov's *Lolita*. But he also gave you, for Valentine's Day, the same thing. Thus you had two copies, and you managed eventually to read one of them, the only novel you finished while in this city.

Although you could avoid I. because he was "two-timing" you with Cathlin, you had no pretense or excuse to offer to Kenny other than "work." Kenny had been all too eager to let you know, in case you didn't, that Professor Ah had brought "some dishy broad" up to his room, and Kenny wondered how you liked that. You told Kenny that I. wasn't your boyfriend. "*You* are my boyfriend," you told him, and he blushed and screwed up his face, and said, Well, if you were his girlfriend then you ought to "make time with" him.

"Soon I will make time with you," you promised.

One of your greatest problems with the chapter was describing Bolshakov's dolls truthfully. He had a large collection of *matryoshka* dolls, the peculiarly Russian playthings made of hollow wooden shells, one doll inside another, like Chinese boxes, ever smaller. Some of his *matryoshki* were quite large and made of exotic woods; some of them were cheap lacquered lathe turnings. All of them had in common that the outer doll, the one containing all the others, was a man, shaped somewhat like a bowling pin; inside him was a woman wearing a babushka, round spots of rouge painted on her face (the source, you suddenly realized, of Cathlin's overdone makeup); inside the woman, yet another doll, a lad of not-yet-puberty; and inside of him was the smallest, most reducible of the dolls, a little girl.

Bolshakov had used the dolls didactically, to illustrate his theory that males have females inside themselves, and that females have males inside themselves, and that grown-ups have children inside themselves, and that you, Yekaterina Vladimirovna, have inside yourself both a little boy wanting to be seduced by an older woman and a little girl wanting to grow up and acquire a penis.

Contrarily, you had seen Bolshakov's dolls as a manifestation of his problems with "reality": For him, your external personality was only a disguise, an outer shell covering up an inner self that was not your own but a creature of his invention.

Your big problem, now, for Cathlin's chapter, was whether or not to prop the dolls hither and thither around Dr. Bolshakov's office. If you stressed the Russianness of Bolshakov's dolls and explained their historical significance, mightn't you make the reader (I.) suspicious that Cathlin might actually be Ekaterina? You tried to find out if there were a Scottish or Irish equivalent of the *matryoshka,* but a thorough search in Hillman Library failed to uncover any. It was too late to change Bolshakov's name, but you considered Anglicizing (or Scotticizing) his first name and patronymic, which were Vasili Timofeyevich, into something—William T., perhaps calling him Wullie, a Scottish diminutive of William. But finally, late one night with the help of a large quantity of vodka and some Tchaikovsky coming from WQED (and from me), you convinced yourself to leave Bolshakov's names as they were and to let him keep his dolls-within-dolls, although you did not call them *matryoshki,* and to have certificates on the walls licensing a man of Russian origin and Viennese training to practice psychiatry in Ulster. You finished a brilliant first chapter without any human characters, just objects in a room.

That was when you discovered that a good novelist, finishing a good day's work, often feels not only elated but horny.

There was a timid knock at your door. Not like Bolshakov's. Not like Ogden's. Not like Ah's.

"COME IN, KENNY," you called quietly, because on both sides of you there were professors grading papers or gone to murphybed. You turned down the volume on WQED.

"How did you know it was me?" he asked, coming into the room. He was in his plaid bathrobe, it covering his pajamas.

"I *wanted* it to be you," you said.

"Huh?" he said.

"In Svanetia, there is superstition, *tval,* that if you want something and call it by name before it appears, it will appear as you called it. Please sit."

He sat on your sofa. "Teach me how to talk Svanetian," he requested.

"This late at night?" you said. "I love to, but it would take many lessons." You were thinking of how Knox Ogden taught you English.

He sniffed the air, your breath. "Have you been drinking a lot?"

"Some," you admitted.

"How can you work and drink at the same time?"

"Drinking helps me think," you said. "You should try it sometime."

He made a face. "No, thanks," he said. "But I could sure use a cigarette." You gave him your pack, took one for yourself. He gallantly lit yours for you, after only two attempts at igniting a book match. "Mom and Dad are both fried. I could be gone all night and they wouldn't know it."

"Be gone all night," you echoed, suggested.

He studied you, to make sure your repetition wasn't a mockery. "Are you working hard again?"

You lifted the stack of pages, flourishingly handwritten in Georgian and yet to be translated into English, that would constitute Chapter One of *Geordie Lad.* "I am done," you announced.

"Well, that's good," he said. "We could play chess or something."

"Or something," you said.

"Or you could, like, teach me a few words of Svanetian."

"You point at something, I give you the word," you offered. He pointed at your dining table. "Table? *Tabog.* Say it." He tried to say it, then pointed at a chair. "Chair? *Skom.*" He pointed at himself. "Boy. *Nafvzhur.*" It took him two tries to pronounce it, then he pointed at you. "Girl or woman? *Dina* or *Zurail.*" He spoke the first, but moved his pointing finger closer, almost touching your breast. "This? My *lisv.*" You touched it and smiled and told him, "In Svani, the word for breast is very like the word for 'to dance,' *lisvbi,* perhaps because"—you stood and held out your arms as if to dance, and I arranged for WQED to be playing something slow and soft and shuffling, and he eagerly stood and put out his cigarette and came into your embrace—"because we dance breast to breast, see?" It was not exactly breast to breast: His breast mashed against your stomach, yours against his chin. Kenny did not know how to dance, and neither did you, but you took enough slow drifting dance steps around the room, tightly in each other's arms, to illustrate the relation of *lisv* and *lisvbi,* and to have all the excuse you needed, for the first time since Knox died, to hug, and this embrace, just as it did *that* time, began to straighten and stiffen his *qvem,* and if he could feel your breast mashing against his cheek you could feel his *qvem* mashing against your thigh.

He tried to whisper, and it made his cracking voice drop a register. "How do you say 'kiss'?"

You honestly did not yet know the word in English. "Point at one," you requested. "Or touch one." He touched your lips. "Face? Mouth? *Vishkv?*" He touched his own lips, then transferred the fingertips to your lips. "Oh, *patchy!*" you said, in a transliteration of the Svanetian child-language word *pači.* "Kiss-kiss."

"Let's *patchy,*" his cracked voice croaked. You puckered and gave him a little peck on his mouth. Quick and light as it was, it was enough to turn your knees to jelly, and you had to let go of him and fall on the sofa. He stood over you, his face warped into an expression of disappointment. "That's the way they kiss in Svanetia?" he demanded. He dropped down to sit beside you.

"They who?" you said. "Babies *patchy.* Little boys and girls *patchy.* Men and women *lickwhál.*"

"Then let's *lickwhál,*" he hoarsely whispered.

You showed him how they do it in Svanetia, men and women, or nineteen-year-old girls with boys of eleven in the top of the abandoned towers, which was your only Svanetian experience with it. You and Islamber had stood beside the embrasure looking out over the valley of the Ingur. You and Kenny sat side by side on the sofa with your arms awkwardly shifting for a comfortable embrace. You and Islamber had eventually wound up on the stone floor. You and Kenny would wind up in your murphybed, where anything that can go wrong will go wrong. But nothing would, except in the sense that it may be very wrong for a twenty-seven-year-old woman to sleep with a twelve-year-old boy.

A *patchy* is quick and light; *lickwhál* goes on and on, and involves all parts of the *vishkv,* inside and out, especially the *nin.* Kenny had kissed girls before but never touched tongues with them, let alone entwined tongues, wrestled tongues. Boys this age can do this sort of thing for only a short time before becoming uncomfortable. It was he who broke the *lickwhál* with an exaggerated panting as if he'd run a *verst.* In his lap some fruiting body had pitched its tent, which peaked beneath his robe. "I know one," he said, thinking to tell you something that would lighten the heaviness of the *lickwhál,* like coffee after a liqueur. "It goes, What's dry and hard when I put it in, but soft and sticky when I pull it out?"

You stared at him for a while before asking, "Is this another riddle?" He nodded, and smirked, and waited. You thought. After a suitable time, you announced, "I give up."

"Chewing gum!" he cried, and roared with laughter.

"*Chvotirk!*" you hushed him. "Shh! You'll wake Dr. Koeppe."

"Aw, she never sleeps," he declared.

"How do you know? Have you been in her murphybed?" You nudged him with your elbow.

"What if I have?" he said.

"So you are not . . . a virgin?" you said, teasing, not believing that he had ever slept with anyone, and certainly not wanting to believe it.

"Nope," he said, proudly.

You hoped he was kidding. You would not be able to bear it if he was not kidding. "Truth?" you said. "Did you put it in dry and hard and bring it out soft and sticky?" And you laughed, nervously, though not loud enough to be heard beyond the confines of the sofa.

His face grew thoughtful, and he decided to stop kidding. "No," he admitted. "I can't even, like, imagine, like, what it's like. Did you?"

"I have nothing dry and hard," you said.

"Aw, shoot, you know what I mean. Did you ever 'chosh'?"

You stared at him, and your mouth fell open. "Kenny! I did not teach you that word! Where did you learn it?" He hung his reddening head and wouldn't let you see his eyes. You wondered if he had been talking to I. Or maybe he'd just been listening outside your door, which is what you asked him, giving him a way out: "Have you been putting your ear to my door?"

"Yeah," he gladly confessed. "That's it. I was just, like, getting ready to knock one time when you were talking to Professor I."

"Bad boy!" you said, feigning a severe reprimand. "Snoop! You said you would never snoop. I ought to spank you."

"So spank me," he requested.

Laughing, you grabbed him and turned him face down over your lap. You pulled up his robe and tugged down the bottoms of his pajamas, exposing his *samt'rock,* buttocks, the sight of which made you abruptly all moist in your groin. You began to give his buttocks mild slaps with your hand, not hurting him at all. His *qvem* was extending down between your knees, and by closing your thighs you could squeeze it as you spanked him. He was making murmurs and groans and occasionally speaking the name of Jesus. You stopped and said, "Okay. Enough. You can sit up," and you hoped that when he sat up he would not reclothe himself.

"Don't stop," he said. "That feels way rad."

But you could not strike your hand against his buttocks again. You could only rub your hand over them, slowly, with much love, all over, allowing your fingertips to wander to the wonderful place beneath his scrotum and even to touch the small, hairless, crinkly balls.

Abruptly he sat up, but he did not pull up his pajamas. He sat there studying his *qvem,* which was exposed to your full view for the first time. It was longer than Islamber's, but not as thick or erect as Dzhordzha's. It was a tower of Svanetia, a mushroom of the forest, but it was made of human flesh. And it was very hard, but not quite dry: A dewdrop glistened on its tip. Kenny stopped studying it and began to study your face, which must have been in some kind of trance. "Do you want to hold it?" he asked you in his hoarse whisper.

"How long have I known you?" you asked him.

He thought. "Over two months," he said, breathing hard. "Why?"

"Is enough," you said, and reached a hand over and wrapped your fingers around his *qvem.* His whole body shuddered. His pelvis jerked upward, and he gripped the sofa cushions tightly in both fists and clenched shut his eyes, and a great gasp came out of him just an instant before his *dwis* exploded out of him, shooting onto the floor, the sofa, his legs, your hand.

When the last gush had subsided, he sighed, "Nobody ever held me before. Except me, I mean. I guess it was, like, just too much."

Dzhordzha, the first time, had lasted only a little longer and had, you recalled fondly, been ready again within minutes. "Do not worry," you said. "It will now be soft and sticky." You laughed. "But soon will be hard again. And"—you drew your *nin* over your lips—"and I will lick it dry."

"Oh, Jesus," Kenny said again.

KENNY STAYED ALL NIGHT. Of course there was penetration, eventually, and more than once, but that was not your goal, just as your goal was not the orgasm that you failed to have. What mattered most was not consummation but recreation: a good time of exploration and discovery, of experiment and play, greatly enhanced by the multitude of reflections in the mirrors on the walls. For you the very best phase of it all, as you had tried unsuccessfully to explain to unbelieving Bolshakov, was not the actual sequence of coital wrenchings and plungings, which any animal can do, but rather the explorative quests of eyes, fingers, hands, tongues, an abandonment to the wonder of discovery, a marvelous sexual hide-and-seek in which the seeking is always more fun than the finding. You became Kenny. As you would learn to become your readers, as you had already become your readers in the opening of *Geordie Lad,* you wanted the slow, playful reconnaissance of the room to be more important than the inhabitance of the room. "You cannot believe in *real* fucking," boorish Bolshakov had said to you in Russian. "You can only contrive infinite fanciful foreplays." You had attempted a retort: that one never gets pregnant from such; and you had to explain to Kenny, this night, answering his fears, that it was unlikely you would bear his baby because the moon's stage of ripening was not yet. "Do not worry about it," you whispered to him. "I can take *all* of your *dwvis* inside me, in my *vishkv* as well as through my *bud,* and it will not tonight make me *liffnavy.* But we must get you some balloons to wear on your *qvem* for the next time, so that I do not become *liffnavy.*"

And sure enough, Kenny snitched some balloons the next time he came to spend the night. Where had he snitched them from? you asked. From his father? No, somewhere else, he said; his father couldn't even "get it up" anymore. How did Kenny know? Did Kenny snoop on his father and mother? No, his mother had told him. Did he and his mother talk a lot about such things? Sometimes. He wasn't going to tell his mother about this? Of course not. Never. What did you take him for? Did you think he didn't know from nothing? "Do you think I'm a mushroom?" he demanded.

"Yes," you said.

"I mean, like, no, that's not what I mean. A mushroom is a nerd, a goofus, who doesn't know jack shit. I may not be a rocket scientist but I've got sense enough not to rat to my mom and dad."

The balloons, a brand named after an Egyptian pharaoh, didn't fit Kenny; they were too large for his *qvem,* and they easily slipped off afterward; so you had to be careful, especially when the moon's stages were very ripe, not to let any of the *dwvis* spill before he could withdraw.

When he came to you one night, one of the many nights that he was certain his parents were bombed into such deep slumber they would never notice him missing, he had a package of a whole dozen of the pharaonic balloons, and you demanded to know where he had been snitching them. "From a drugstore, of course," he said, and you told him that stealing was bad and he ought to let you give him some money to pay for them.

But Kenny continued to steal from the drugstore, not only the balloons but candy and, eventually, items he did not need, women's things, useless medicines, greeting cards for occasions he would never have for greeting.

One night when Kenny was with you, a graduate student on the third floor was holding a party that was becoming increasingly noisy and drunken, with loud music from open doors and drunks wandering down to the second floor, and Kenny got up and dressed and said, "I guess I got to go do something about it." That was only the first of many occasions when Kenny would have to leave your murphybed to handle his duties as "super."

Another time, you and Kenny were just drifting off to exhausted slumber together when you smelled something burning. It smelled like —the only resemblance you could recall was from an incident at Ishimbay—like human hair burning. Kenny went to investigate, and he returned to ask you to go with him, as he had when he went to find dead Ogden, and you followed him down the hall to Edith Koeppe's door, which he opened with one of his keys. She was sprawled out in a drunken stupor up against the wall's built-in gas heater, her hair and one side of her face badly burned, but she was alive, although unconscious. Kenny phoned for an ambulance, and Dr. Koeppe spent several days in the hospital.

"This is a terrible town," I. said to you once, over drinks in his room, and waved a stack of student stories. "These kids write endlessly about this city's murders, divorces, muggings, rapes, child deaths, wife beatings, suicides, infidelities, betrayals, and endless dope addictions. The only student who doesn't write about this city is Cathlin, and she writes about killings in North Ireland and a psychopathic psychoanalyst."

Kenny couldn't stand having you talk to I., but he always seemed to know when I. was in your room, and he would interrupt rudely. As if his stealing and increased truancy from school weren't sufficient man-ifestations of his becoming what Knox Ogden had called a "punk," Kenny began to act increasingly tough, coarse mouthed, and mean, and his manner toward I. became as hostile as it had been toward Knox Ogden. You experienced an uncomfortable déjà vu: Here was your next-door neighbor drinking too much, coughing too much, almost on the verge of whatever terminal debility had required Knox to cancel his remaining classes the previous term (I. insisted he didn't have cirrhosis but admitted to "some problems with pancreatitis"), and here was Kenny openly hostile toward him. You did not see I. all that much—not as Ekaterina; you saw him more often as Cathlin—but you had to be very careful when you saw him that Kenny not discover you, because Kenny would become furiously jealous if he did. "I wish the old fart would hurry up and die off, like Ogden did," Kenny blurted.

"*Kenny!*" you replied.

One day Kenny brought home a stack of pamphlets from somewhere, and giving you the first one and telling you to be sure and read it, he went from door to door throughout the mansion, slipping one of the pamphlets under every door. It was entitled 20 *Questions for Alcoholism,* and it began, *If you can answer 'yes' to half of the following questions, you should seriously consider joining Alcoholics Anonymous.* The questions each had *drink* as their verb, and out of curiosity you decided to score yourself on them: *Do you ever crave to drink at a definite time daily?* (No.) *Do you feel under tension much of the time while not drinking?* (No.) *Do you need to drink the next morning?* (No.) Of the twenty questions, the only ones which you answered positively were *Do you drink to escape from worries or troubles?* and *Are you at times possessed with unreasonable fears?*

At the end of each pamphlet was scrawled in pencil, *If you scored more than 10 yes's, please see me for free book,* Twelve Steps and Twelve Traditions. *Kenneth Elmore, Jr., Superintendent.* Half-jokingly, the next time you saw Ah, you asked him if he'd taken the test and what his score was. Seventeen, he said; you? Two, you said. Good girl, he said. After a week, Kenny admitted that only one person in the building had asked for a copy of the book, and "it sure wasn't that asshole who lives in the next room." But he gave you a copy of the book and asked you to make sure the asshole read it.

Late one night, when Kenny was "staying over," you had a bad scare when you answered a knock at your door and there was Loretta, who was supposed to be bombed. She was somewhat drunk, and half-asleep, but lucid enough to ask if you had seen Kenny, who had crawled under your murphybed. You feigned drunkenness and sleepiness and said you hadn't seen him since "before murphybedtime." Loretta apologized for waking you and declared, "Well, that brat's probably taken up running around with street gangs."

Kenny did not take up running around with street gangs, but his tendency to juvenile delinquency escalated from his shoplifting the drugstore and supermarket to the cultivation of a new hobby: amassing a considerable collection of automobile hubcaps. His room was filled with the ones he couldn't sell, and his complaining mother was told that he'd found them in the street, which was partly true.

If, sweet Kat, you were inclined to blame yourself for his descent into delinquency, truancy, and punkdom (and there is a small but substantial body of recorded cases of such effects of older women's seductions of youths), you did not consider that his premature assumption of a full sexual life was what corrupted him. You thought, rather, that he had been corrupted because you were not able to accept, and had thus declined, his proposal of marriage.

Kenny had made a mistake in falling in love with you and proposing marriage. He never used the word *love,* but he began to exhibit all the symptoms. Falling in love wasn't so bad—both Islamber and Dzhordzha had professed the same condition, *liltuneh* for Islamber, *vlyubeetsya* for Dzhordzha—but Kenny had become obsessed with making you into Mrs. Elmore, Jr. You had laughed when he first brought the subject up, and you thought he didn't mean right away but eventually, when he grew up, but he was serious and wanted to "run away" with you as soon as you consented to it. You couldn't consent. You tried to explain to him that you had a job that you would have to keep, even if you married him, and that meant not running away. "Aw, you said your job would be over in April," he insisted. Yes, but then you had to find another job somewhere, and you couldn't take him with you.

"Why not?"

"It is against the law, I think," you said.

"So? Lots of things are against the law, but people still do 'em."

"I cannot marry you, Kenny," you said. "You are very sweet to ask, but when you are truly old enough to be married, according to the law, I will be . . . Let me think . . . I will be in my midthirties, much too old for you." And you told him about Svanetia, how the women there, although they often live past 100 (you had a great-aunt who was still living, the last you'd heard from home, at the age of 123), often become "old" by the time they reach their midthirties.

"I don't care," he said. "I'm still going to marry you."

YOU BEGAN TO UNDERSTAND, as you reached the chapters of *Geordie Lad* in which Dzhordzha (or Geordie) first appears, that poor Kenny Elmore, for all his simple attraction and likability, was nothing at all like Dzhordzha. Would Kenny have devised a plan to get himself into the prison camp and extricate you from it? Would Kenny have been able to stand up to the bogeyman Bolshakov and humiliate a man four times his age? Would Kenny know how to drive a truck over a tract of *bezdorozhye* to get you from Ishimbay (Armagh) to the road to Tbilisi (Londonderry)? Could Kenny, for all his toughness and his devotion to you, kill the three guards who tried to stop you and the five who followed you?

Be careful here, Professor Ah scribbled in the margin of your (Cathlin's) manuscript. *You are "telescoping." Or is it "telegraphing"? Whatever, you are telling the reader too much information too early about this boy, Geordie. You want to make him into a superhero, but too much extravagance and exaggeration too early can only lead to disbelief.*

For all of his increased drinking, Ah still somehow managed to read his students' submissions dutifully, slowly, and critically, and he continued to give Cathlin's ever-expanding *Geordie Lad* an honest appraisal and sufficient suggestions and encouragement to keep her going, and to keep her coming back to class each week with another twenty or thirty pages of new material. Ah's assignments to the class had taken an erratic turn, an eccentric sequence of directions on experimenting with flashbacks, "collages," "lucky accidents," and shifts of tense and person that confused many of them and that he privately told Cathlin to ignore or follow, as she wished.

Ah no longer made any pretense of assigning stories from the Stegner anthology or other outside readings. He told Cathlin, again in private, that he simply didn't have time to keep up with the readings himself, because he spent all his hours reading student stories. The last reading he was able to assign, Edgar Allan Poe's "Fall of the House of Usher," fascinated you, Kat, (although you had already known a bad Russian translation of it) and enthralled you, Cathlin; and you both hoped, for different reasons (Kat for its supernatural elements, Cathlin for its fear and trembling), that Ah would discuss it in class, but he never did. A student in class handed in a question, *What are we supposed to be reading?* and Ah ungraciously lost his temper and lectured them on the use of *supposed to*—as if creative people are *supposed* to do anything. Eventually he announced, "Y'all just read whatever y'all want to. It hardly matters. I never did like for anybody to *tell* me what to read."

One night in late March when Kenny was out somewhere stealing hubcaps, Ah knocked at your door and you let him in and did not need to offer him a drink because he brought his own. In his other hand he held a sheet of paper, a piece of stationery, a letter that he showed you. "This was forwarded to me from my most recent residence," he said.

The stationery bore the letterhead of something called BOW: Bodark Organization of Writers; and Ah himself was not certain whether it should be spoken as something you do from the waist or a weapon you hold. The letter, from a woman named Agnes Roundtree Mazzarelli, secretary of BOW, said some flattering things about his "famous" novels set in the Bodark Mountains and then invited him to be the main speaker at BOW's eleventh annual conference, to be held in the Halfmoon Hotel at Arcata Springs on April 27. BOW would pay his transportation, provide lodging for the three days and two nights of the conference, and offer him an honorarium of one thousand dollars.

"Frankly," Ah said to you, "I long ago made up my mind that I would never attend a writers' conference, for any reason. But until this letter came in the mail today, I had, really, nothing much to live for.

So I'm ready to swallow my scruples . . . provided, that is, that you will go with me."

Me? you scribbled hurriedly. *Why should you want me to go with you?*

"Because you are so homesick for Svanetia," he said. "Of course, you'll find that the Bodark Mountains are nothing at all like your homeland. They are mere pimples on the arse of the midcontinent, the highest of them less than three thousand feet, not to be compared with your eighteen-thousand-foot Mount Elbrus. But some of the valleys of the remotest parts of the Bodarks may remind you of your Ingur Valley. There are no towers, of course, but this Halfmoon Hotel, if I remember it correctly, has stone towers that may resemble your Svanetian strongholds."

You were greatly attracted, or at least intrigued, by his invitation, but you wrote, *I should think you'd rather take your girlfriend, Cathlin.*

"I considered that," he admitted. "Although to call her my 'girlfriend' may not be accurate. We've never gone out on a date. I've never been to her place. She's under constant medical supervision for some problems, photo—phototropism, or some kind of eye disorder, and a severe personality problem called hebephrenia or something like that. Maybe her doctors wouldn't let her take a trip with me. But the main reason I can't take her is that she'd look terribly out of place there. Do you know, she's never changed her hat or her dress since I've known her? She looks *weird.*"

You controlled yourself, did not wince, and made a mental note to take Cathlin shopping for a new outfit. You wrote, *But perhaps it would crush her if she knew that you were asking me. I think you should invite her.*

"Okay. But if she won't go, or can't go, will you?"

You wrote, *I would have to give that some careful thought.*

At the next meeting of the Narrative class, the instructor was visibly surprised to discover that his star pupil was wearing a new dress and a new hat and had left off some of those cackling bracelets, and that her earrings were pendulous but not noisy, and that she did not have quite so much rouge on her cheeks, and that although her lipstick quite obviously attempted to redraw the entire shape of her mouth it was not a gaudy orange but a relatively modest pink. She may still have seemed too weird to be in the company of the ladies of BOW, but she was no longer a caricature.

And whatever her appearance, she had been knocking herself out doing the work for the course, not only writing, diligently, a new chapter each week (with the help of much Hillman research into the history, folkways, and features of North Ireland), but also assigning herself the readings that the instructor had been neglecting: many chapters of the Booth, many stories of the Stegner. As but one example of her conscientious devotion, she had made an honest effort to locate, and learn, the words to "Danny Boy," so that if the instructor ever sang it to her again, drunk or sober, and wanted to know any of the words, she would be able to tell him.

But try as she might, Cathlin had not been able to find the words to that song. Even with the help of three reference librarians at Hillman, one of whom said, "Sure, everybody knows that song," but had been able to sing only six lines and hum the remainder, Cathlin could not find any book in Hillman that contained the lyrics.

I am yours, precious Kat, and I did not feel obliged to perform any favors for this alter ego you had fabricated to permit the mycologist to study writing undetected. But Cathlin's beating her brains out trying to find the words to that song finally got to me, and I decided I'd better give her a hand. So I arranged for her to stop off, on apparent impulse, at a back-street secondhand bookshop, where I arranged for a dusty volume to fall off a shelf into her hands, and for her to flip through it and chance upon, on page eighty-nine, "Danny Boy." The book was *Songs that Changed the World,* edited by Wanda Willson Whitman, Crown, 1969. Cathlin bought it for two dollars. It would also furnish her, if she needed them, with the words and music to "Old Folks at Home," "Loch Lomond," and "The Blue Bells of Scotland."

But after all that trouble, Cathlin did not get an opportunity to demonstrate her knowledge of "Danny Boy" when she accompanied her instructor back to his apartment after class. For the first hour or so, I. remained I. and did not become Ah, and sang no songs, because there was something important he wanted to discuss. "Your latest chapter," he said. "Chapter seven. As I attempted to point out in my note, you are getting lost in your flashbacks. This may be a result of what I've warned you about: the mistake of making your heroine, Cathlin, yourself. Cathlin is too obviously nostalgic for her County Derry, and she is carried away with all these lyrical descriptions of her native countryside and the people and their way of life and all."

I. went on, making his perhaps valid point that the narrative pace of the story was considerably slowed and hampered by Cathlin's abandoning herself to romantic longings for the somewhat idealized highlands of the Foyle Valley. As you listened, divorcing yourself for minutes from your *Doppelgänger,* you realized that everything he was saying about Cathlin's being lost in her highlands applied painfully to your own feelings about Svanetia, and you were overcome with such a terrible homesickness that your tears could not be concealed as they rolled down from beneath your opaque spectacles. I. laid a hand on your arm and said, "I know how you feel, believe me. Sometimes I'm so eager to see the Bodarks again that I'd sell my soul to the devil for just a glimpse of them. But I have to struggle not to let that yearning contaminate my writing. Here, let me freshen our drinks."

It was almost welcome to watch I. becoming Ah, and Cathlin began to hope he'd sing "Danny Boy" so she could tell him the missing words to the other stanzas, wherein Danny's sweetheart, left behind to die, tells him what it's going to be like for him when he returns and finds her dead. But Ah, despite tossing back several that he no longer diluted with branch, remained sober enough to say, "I've got a theory. Many of the people who first settled the Bodarks in the first half of the nineteenth century were descendants of those Scotch-Irish you write about. I've never seen the Ulster highlands myself—the closest I got was a visit to Yeats's Sligo—but from your description of them I think there must have been something in the genetic memory of the Bodark settlers that made them seek out a countryside that looked exactly like your County Derry."

Cathlin waited, and she wrote nothing in response. She had not got out her pink cards once so far this night. She had thought a lot, with your help, about his upcoming invitation, and she knew, more or less, what she would have to write when it came.

"Is it true," he asked, "that if you went back home you'd be arrested?"
And without lying at all, you were able to nod Cathlin's head.

"So you'll never be able to see your home country again? That's terrible. Here, let me freshen our drinks." Although he never touched the stuff himself, Ah had acquired a bottle of Glenlivet unblended Scotch for Cathlin's benefit. "I have an idea," he said, pouring her fourth drink, and he proceeded to explain to her what BOW was, an organization of amateur free-lance poetesses and poetasteresses and a few fair writers who actually sold something to the Sunday supplements, and then he told Cathlin that he had been invited to address their annual convention in April, and he "wondered" if "there was any chance" that Cathlin's doctors might not have apoplexy if she were to accompany him for a few days to that "enchanted land of glens and dells and gentle peaks."

Ah got so carried away in his description of it that she wanted to caution him against "too obvious nostalgia," but she only wrote, *These Bodarks. Are they in North Carolina?*

He read it, puzzled momentarily, but then he seemed to remember her "obituary" and said, "No. That's the Appalachian Mountains, south of here. The Bodarks are a sort of range of Appalachians misplaced westward"—he gestured—"out in the heart of the country."

You thought he said—or maybe it was his tipsy mispronunciation —"apparitions." You wrote, *I would like to see the Apparition Mountains.*

"Would your doctors let you go for a few days?"

You wrote, *They cannot cure me. They have given up.* And in sympathy for poor Cathlin's hopeless condition, you shed a few more honest tears.

He did not have any Kleenex. He got you a paper towel. He said, "I'm sorry. But are you okay to travel?"

You dried your eyes (careful not to dislodge the sunglasses) and wrote, *I could not share a room with you.*

Ah wanted clarification. "You mean a room, period, or a bed?"

You and Cathlin had given this much thought and discussion between yourselves, and had considered the possibilities. Did he intend to drive his Blazer to the Bodarks? How far was it? Would you not have to stop at motels overnight en route? And this Halfmoon Hotel, would they frown upon your presence? Also—and this was the biggest hitch—

making the trip would mean that he would see Cathlin, often, in broad daylight. Thus far, he had only seen her at night, in dim illumination. Wouldn't he perhaps recognize you in the strong glare of sunlight? And one of the reasons (there were several) why you could not share a room with him was that you couldn't sleep in your red wig with your sunglasses on. For bed, you'd have to remove all your disguise.

You took the last card you'd written and wrote additionally upon it, *Room, period. Bed, whatever. We could not be pals.*

"But aren't we already pals? How could we spend all that time together without becoming better pals?"

Not sleeping pals, you wrote.

"Well, thanks anyway," Ah said, and dropped the subject. He did not take it up again. You and Cathlin both began to wonder if he had simply abandoned the invitation. He proceeded, as usual, to become very drunk, but when he began singing, it wasn't "Danny Boy." It was something truly operatic but waltzlike that went:

> *"Ah! sweet mystery of life, at last Ah've found thee!*
> *Ah! Ah know at last the secret of it all!*
> *All the longing, seeking, striving, waiting, yearning:*
> *The burning hopes, the joy and idle tears that fall!"*

You thought, for a while, that the "Ah" he was addressing was himself, and you thought it a conceited song, though it had its tender sentiments. Cathlin hoped it wasn't a North Irish song that would require more library research. It was, in fact, Irish of sorts, or rather the composer was Irish in origin, one Victor Herbert, who, Ah explained, had been an American master of light opera, or operetta, and had, coincidentally, spent much of his life in this city, as director of the burgh's symphony orchestra.

"He wash a drunk, too," Ah said. "Like Stephen Foster, only worsh. Do you know, as soon as Ah knew Ah was coming to this town, Ah started thinking of Foster and Herbert, and that melody started helplessly playing itshelf over and over again in my head: *Ah, sweet mystery of life, at last Ah've found thee!* Does that ever happen to you? I mean, do you ever get some tune stuck in your head and can't get it out? Stop looking so spooked. I *don't* know the secret of it all. I haven't found any sweet mysteries of life. I never shall."

THAT APRIL WAS NOT the cruelest month you'd ever known, but it ran a close second or third. The mansion began to go to hell. You couldn't help thinking of the Poe story: This was "Fall of the House of Elmore." Poor Kenny couldn't cope with the heavier responsibilities of superintending the place: He could fix plumbing, but trying to fix the electrical problems that were developing was too much for him. He almost electrocuted himself, and you fussed at his mother and demanded to know why she didn't hire a professional electrician. "Why are *you* out to take up for the brat?" she retorted with a supercilious glance that was your first indication she had an inkling of where Kenny was spending his nights.

On one of the rare nights when Kenny stayed in his own room because his parents weren't sufficiently bombed for him to sneak out and up to yours, you were lonely, and Lawren visited you. He actually, confound him, materialized, and you knew you'd had too much vodka but not *that* much. He actually spoke to you, as a Svanetian *lanchal* would have done (he even spoke Svanetian, your first experience of another talent we ghosts have). He told you you'd better think about getting out of here. He told you the house's days were numbered. He said, "If you don't believe me, watch this." And he caused one of the tall mirrors to detach itself from the wall and crash to the floor.

Elsewhere in the mansion, including next door in the rooms of

Professors Ah and Koeppe, mirrors crashed to the floor. The spring's first thunderstorm began, with much dramatic lightning, although it was only like fireflies compared with a real Svanetian *lirkunal*. It woke everybody and petrified them, and gave them an explanation for all the falling mirrors, but you knew that the mirrors had fallen *before* the thunder crashed.

Sometimes your little radio came on by itself, without your having consciously turned it on. It was always WQED, but that station had invariably played good "longhair," as Kenny called it, and this hair was rather short and curly: Stephen Collins Foster's "Beautiful Dreamer," "Old Folks at Home," and "Swanee River." Victor Herbert's "Ah, Sweet Mystery of Life," as performed by both Nelson Eddy and Jeanette MacDonald. And, over and over again, night after night, "Danny Boy," as sung by Colleen MacNamara. The question of Ah's you'd never answered, "Do you ever get some tune stuck in your head and can't get it out?" (of course you did; everybody does), began to take on new meaning, only this wasn't stuck in your head, it was stuck in your radio, and if you turned your radio off, it would turn itself back on. You thought of complaining to Kenny, but he'd get himself electrocuted taking your radio apart.

Ah never brought up the subject of the trip to the Bodarks again, so after a while you went to him and asked him (writing it on a card) if Cathlin had agreed to go with him. He was already so drunk that he held your card upside down and stared at it for a long time before righting it and responding to it. Then, half-incoherently, he delivered himself of a tirade against Cathlin. She was a "maybe talented" writer, he said, but she was a goofball, a clown, a "daffy damshel."

But why won't she go with you?

"She'sh just too dumb to 'chosh'."

But you told me she's been sleeping with you here.

"I lied."

Toward the end of the term, you began to cut several of your morning classes, preferring to stay in murphybed. You examined your motives and decided that since you were only a "temporary" and would be out of work in another week or so, and since the students appeared free to cut classes whenever they wished (and they often wished), you might as well. Len Dalrymple called you in for what was to be your last visit with him, and not a pleasant one. He had been watching you, he said. Did you know they had considered extending your appointment? Bill Turner would be taking over mycology again, but they had thought of finding "some use" for you. Now, however . . . You seemed to be indifferent to your work, and you weren't doing any research at all, were you? So it would be difficult to recommend you for continuance. What were your plans for the future?

WQED was playing in your head, and you were strongly tempted to sing to Dalrymple, "Oh, Lenny Boy, the pipes, the pipes are calling . . . ," but you said, "I'm doing a research project in the Bodark Mountains." How interesting, he remarked. *Phallales? Geastra?* Everything, you said, and Len Dalrymple said, Well, he hoped you'd show up for your final examinations. And you cleaned out your office, everything except your "costume."

Ah came to your room that night, not yet drunk or, rather, still sober enough to declare, "I never wanted to ask Cathlin to go with me, anyway. I just did it because you suggested it. You said that if she wouldn't, or couldn't, you would consider it. Have you?"

You had, but you wanted his sober answer to a question, *Why do you prefer me?*

"Because . . ." He had to give it some thought. "Because you're much smarter, and nicer, and more attractive. You've got everything she hasn't. The only thing she's got is a perfect nose, but it's not a bit better than your nose."

You smiled and resisted the impulse to feel your nose. You did, however, feel your hair, which was now long enough that you did not need to cover it with the scarf when you were at home. *She has such beautiful red hair,* you wrote.

"How would you know? Have you seen her?"

Yes, once when you were bringing her here, I saw her.

"Every time I've brought her here, I've pounded on your door so I could introduce the two of you. You've *never* been here." You were slow to think of something to write in response to that, and he, looking around the room to emphasize "here," let his eye fall upon something you'd forgotten to hide. He spotted it on the small table beside your murphybed, and grabbed it, and waved it at you. "Where did you get this?"

It was the paperback of *Pale Fire* that he had loaned to Cathlin. Was the jig, as they say, up? Had the time come to confess, to reveal the masquerade? If so, then all was lost, because it was Cathlin who really needed him, not you. It was Cathlin who wanted his help for the writing of *Geordie Lad*, Cathlin who would love to visit the Bodarks and perhaps even meet some of her McWalter kinfolk, Cathlin who could, if given time, possibly persuade herself to share his bed. There was no way on earth that the Bodarks could be found to resemble Svanetia, but they probably did look much like County Derry.

All right, I., I will tell you, you wrote, stalling for time to think something up. *Cathlin was here. After you invited her but changed your mind because she told you she couldn't share your murphybed, she came to see me, to tell me that she thought it was I who should go with you. We argued much about it. I insisted I could not go with you. She felt I should. She showed me that book. She said I must read it, to see how much I am like Kinbote: he was the exiled king of Zembla, I am an exiled princess of Svanetia.*

You handed him that card to read while you grabbed a fresh card and continued, *So I read it, and yes, perhaps I am like Kinbote, his story is mine, and there is even a Gradus on my trail, but I insisted to Cathlin, because I had read her "obituary," that it is she who must go with you to the Bodarks, not alone because of the fantasies of the Halfmoon or Moonbeam and of the Indians and all that, but because she needs your help in order to become a published writer. You must help her.*

You gave him that card also and took yet another one, a third one. *And it is she who can help you more than I, if you will but give her the opportunity, and if you are patient with her. She explained to me about her photodysphoria and her hebephilia. The former can never be cured, and she must always wear those dark glasses, and you will never see her eyes. But the latter, someday, she hopes, you will help her heal.*

He read each of the three cards, more than once. Then his only response was a question, "Are you really a princess of Svanetia?" You nodded your head. He stared at you, got up, and helped himself to your bourbon, County Fair, which Knox Ogden used to drink when he came to your room. And, like Knox, he began to address you formally: "So Your Highness cannot go with me?" You shook your head. "Because Your Highness is royal, or because there's something else wrong with you?"

In Svanetia, you wrote, *they are saving me for the wedding night. If I slept with you, the men of Svanetia, all the warriors of Lisedi—and they are fierce and terrible—would track you to the ends of the earth and destroy you.*

Later that same night, Ah enticed Loretta Elmore into his room, without any difficulty, and got her as drunk as he was, without any difficulty, and took her to bed, with some but not much difficulty, which is where Kenny, with his key, leaving your bed to investigate the strange noises coming from the next room, found them. Kenny took one look and retreated without being seen, and told you, "The old fart is fucking my mom!" He didn't like it one bit, but you persuaded him, with some difficulty, to return to your bed, for what would be, as it turned out, the last time you ever slept with him . . . or tried to sleep; the radio blared Colleen's "Danny Boy," and then there was another horrendous thunderstorm that actually approximated a Svanetian *lirkunal* and could be blamed for all of the other mirrors of the mansion crashing down.

The next day, the next evening, the police arrested Kenny in the act of removing the wheel coverings from a Lincoln parked on Forbes Avenue, and they obtained a search warrant for his room, where they found a considerable collection of similar stolen articles.

After his parents posted his bond and removed him from jail, he, in retaliation against his mother's scolding ("You're not going to sneak out of the house any more nights, buddy boy"), told them that he had not been sneaking out of the house, but up to your room, where you had taught him how to fuck.

Loretta came to you and said, "I want you out of this house tonight, Evie. And don't forget to give me back my jewelry and clothes and stuff, especially that coat."

IN SVANETIA, APRIL 23 is always observed as Saint George's Day, and Svanetians worship the dragon slayer almost on an equal footing with Christ. Indeed, Saint George takes third place in the holy Trinity of the Svanetian church. Since the day before, April 22, was observed throughout the Soviet Union as Lenin's birthday, Svanetians had a two-day feast that left them stuffed and still and silly. But did you know that both Shakespeare and Cervantes died on April 23, and that our friendly ghost Nabokov was born on that day? And is it entirely a coincidence that Cathlin was scheduled, according to her obituary, to die on that day?

It would have been further serendipity if April 23 marked your leaving this burgh, but it was simply the day you left the mansion; another day would pass before you could get out of town.

Late that afternoon, you stuffed everything you owned into the one pasteboard suitcase that you had arrived with: your few books, the manuscript of *Geordie Lad* (all except for the chapter that the professor had not returned), your little radio, and your few books, including the songbook, the Russian–English dictionary, and the two Nabokov novels. You cleaned out your room as you had cleaned out your office, and you folded the murphybed up into the wall. All that remained were the four volumes of I.'s novels, not one of which you had ever had time to read. You stacked these outside his door, with a note folded into the top one.

Dear I.:

Suddenly I received an unexpected opportunity to teach at another university, and I regret that I have to leave without saying good-bye to you. Here are your novels, and you must forgive me that I am apparently not the novel-reading type. Let me, as a final word to you, in addition to thanking you for the pleasure of your company during so many dull times in this mansion, urge you from the bottom of my heart to reconsider your feelings about Cathlin.

With fondest regards and best wishes,
E. V. D.

Then there remained only one more note to write. You sat at your desk for the last time and stared for a while at your last sheet of paper. You gazed out the window and noticed one more of April's thunderstorms brewing, the first drops already falling. You touched your pen to the paper and wrote, *Dear Kenny,* but that was as far as you got. You realized, with embarrassment and regret, that you really had nothing to say to him. It was a question not simply of how to say something, but of what to say. You stared at the salutation a long time and tried to think of polite expressions of sorrow, words of grace, courteous good-byes.

You were spared the task by his breathless arrival in your room. He saw your suitcase ready to go beside the door and said, "You can't go!"

By way of answer you simply declared, "You told your mother."

"I was real pissed at her," he said. "It was, like, the only way I could fix her wagon."

"But you fixed my wagon, too, and now my wagon is heading west."

"Huh? Where are you going?"

"I'm not sure. But I must go. Good-bye, Kenny. I wish for you much happiness. I wish for you that you will stay out of trouble, work hard in school, be a good boy."

He stared at you, his mobile face warped into an expression of disappointment. "Is that, like, all you've got to say to me?"

Yes, it was. But then WQED, which was driving you nuts (your little radio was stuffed into your suitcase and wasn't plugged in, but you

could hear it clearly, all the same), compelled you to begin singing. Even
I, who thought I knew you so well, was surprised at the lovely soprano
of your voice:

> *"Oh, Kenny boy, the pipes, the pipes are calling,*
> *From glen to glen, and down the mountainside.*
> *The winter's gone, and all the mirrors falling,*
> *It's I, it's I must go, and you must bide.*

> *"But I'll come back, when summer's in the meadow,*
> *Or when the valley's hushed and white with snow.*
> *It's you'll be here, in sunshine or in shadow,*
> *Oh, Kenny boy, oh, Kenny boy, I love you so!"*

"I guess I sort of, like, love you so, too," he said when you finished.
"But will you really come back?"

You lifted your suitcase, kissed him on the forehead, and got yourself
as quickly as possible out of there, out of the mansion, into the pouring
rain, down to the street, the avenue, where you caught the first westbound
city bus, which took you down into the heart of town, where you checked
in, wet and weary, for your last night in the burgh, at the Young Women's
Christian Association hostelry.

But most of that stormy final night you spent not in your YWCA
room but in your office at the Biological Sciences Building, where you
graded final examinations and filled out grade reports.

And while you were engaged in this activity, an Avis rented car
pulled up in front of the mansion, where I was still hanging around,
keeping an eye on I. and making sure that he was staying sober enough
to get his stuff ready to go. He had been so saddened to find your
farewell note that he had immediately gone to his bottle and was tying
one on. The driver of the Avis was a man in a trench coat who waited
for the downpour to cease and, when it didn't, jumped out of the car
anyway and rang the doorbell, and then spoke to Loretta in thick English
with a Slavic accent, asking for you. Loretta informed him that you had
just moved out. He demanded to know where you had gone. She said

she had no idea, but she was quite certain that she would never see you again. "I'd just better not," she said. The man asked to speak with Dr. Elmore. Loretta informed him that her husband "can't hear worth a damn; all this thunder doesn't mean a thing to him."

The man returned to his car but did not drive away. He was still there the next morning when Dr. Elmore came out, tested to see if he would need his umbrella, found that he would, and started off for Hillman Library. The man in the trench coat followed him.

And that night, when Ah met his last Narrative class in the Scottish Room, the man in the trench coat followed him to the Cathedral of Learning, where he parked and waited patiently for the class to end. The man waited with more patience after the class while Ah stood outside the Cathedral talking to one of his students, a girl with very long red hair and dark sunglasses. The man was not close enough to hear what they were saying.

"As I told the class, I've already submitted my final grades," Ah was saying to her, "but I was sorry to discover that your name was not even on the computerized class list and grade report. You made an A, of course, but how can I report it so it will be on your transcript?"

The man in the trench coat observed that the red-haired girl was writing something on a pink card, which she then gave the professor to read; and after reading it the professor spoke to her again, and again she wrote something on a pink card. And so it went. The man in the trench coat surmised, correctly, that this professor, like Dr. Elmore, could not even hear the thunder, and this was the student's way of communicating with him. But what was it that required so much communication? The man in the trench coat was a very patient man. People who mistrust "reality" must cultivate an exceptionally high level of patience in order to survive.

"Yes, I'm sober enough to drive, but I wasn't planning to leave tonight. I suppose I could, though. Where are you staying?" The red-haired girl apparently had only one more card for the professor to read. He read it and spoke to her: "The YWCA? I'll pick you up there in an hour," and they said their good-byes, and the professor started out walking to the mansion.

The man in the trench coat, before following, wrote something on a card of his own. It was his business card, without much room on the blank reverse side, but it had enough to write his question. The man was waiting in his Avis rented car at the mansion when the professor arrived, and he presented his question to the professor. The professor read it, answered it briefly, stuck the card in his shirt pocket with his other cards, excused himself, and entered the mansion.

The storm was still abroad in all its wrath. The man waited and watched as the professor carried his clothing on hangers out of the mansion and to a trucklike vehicle. The man wrote down the license plate's inscription, BODARK, and the state, a New England state noted for its maple syrup and red covered bridges. The professor made several trips from the mansion to his vehicle, carrying several boxes and a large typewriter, and, finally, made six trips to carry gingerly, two at a time, twelve small potted plants. They appeared to be marijuana. Then the professor stood at the door and said a long good-bye to Loretta Elmore. They kissed briefly.

The man in the trench coat followed the BODARK-plated vehicle as it drove through the dark, mostly deserted streets (it was almost 10:00 P.M.) downtown to the building of the Young Women's Christian Association. The red-haired girl came out bearing a cheap suitcase and got into the professor's vehicle. The man in the trench coat recognized the pasteboard suitcase! The red hair was obviously a disguise to fool the man in the trench coat, and he cursed himself for not having recognized her figure, her way of walking, her lovely nose, her confounded *aura!* His heart leapt up, and eagerly he followed the BODARK plate and would not let it out of his sight as it gained the throughway, crossed the bridge over the Monongahela, and entered the Fort Pitt tunnel. Emerging from the tunnel on Interstate 279 just a few car lengths behind his quarry, the man was startled to discover that the radio of his rented Avis, although he had not turned it on, was playing some local station, some abominable operetta, some atrocious baritone screaming in English something about the sweet mystery of life. The man tried to turn it off. The blasted radio would not turn off. He pounded at it with his fist, but this only had the effect of increasing its volume, the wailing of all the longing, seeking, striving, waiting, yearning—the man in the trench coat thought he would go mad, and he cursed these American capitalist machines that always went wrong with burning hopes and joy and idle tears that fall!

He was so distracted by the malfunctioning apparatus that he did not notice the professor's vehicle taking a veer from Interstate 279 to Interstate 79 South. The vehicle he found himself trailing had taken Interstate 79 North, and by the time he caught up with it he found that its plate did not say BODARK.

BY THE FIRST LIGHT of dawn, somewhere in western Ohio, he showed her the card. On one side printed in Cyrillic letters were the name, title, and Moscow address. Cathlin didn't know the Cyrillic alphabet, nor did I., and all you needed to know was the one word **Большаков**, which somewhat resembled its English form so that you were surprised I. hadn't recognized the name of Cathlin's psychiatrist. Cathlin turned the card over and read the English on the other side: *Prof. I.: It is imperative that I find Ekaterina Vladimirovna, and I have reason to believe you know her where-abouts. Can you help me? I will make it worth your while.*

"I simply told the guy," I. told Cathlin, "that I was sorry but I had no idea, that I'd just received a note from her saying good-bye, she was taking a job somewhere else, but she didn't say where. You know, she was a very strange woman. Lovely but mysterious. This guy was obviously Russian, maybe a secret agent or something, but he was just a day too late. She used to tell me about an imaginary companion of hers called Anangka, sort of a pooka, you know—aren't they Irish?—this pooka of hers was always looking out for her and taking care of her, and maybe the pooka warned her that this guy was coming soon."

Cathlin tried to stay awake enough to remain Cathlin and to write a pink card in response to this, resisting the impulse to look over her shoulder to see if they were being followed. She had found herself nodding off in the middle of the night and becoming you, and she had had to share I.'s coffee. He miraculously kept on driving, never seeming to tire, but needing to stop periodically along the vast, straight Interstate 70 in order to buy more coffee or to relieve himself. Two things appeared to keep him going—or three, if you counted his dream of the Bodarks: The interior of the Blazer was filled with the tangy fragrance of the small tomato plants that were lined up across the dashboard and on the floor behind the seat, and just the inhaling of this fragrance was enough to turn Cathlin into Ekaterina if you weren't careful; and occasionally, whenever the interstate approached a bridge, I. would suddenly pull over to the shoulder, stop, and take a lusty swig from his quart of bourbon. The first time he did this, he explained to Cathlin, "I have gephydrophia. That's not as good as your photodysphoria and hebedysphoria or whatever it is, but it's a big problem anyway. It means 'fear of bridges over water,' and somehow it doesn't bother me if the bridge is a viaduct or the creek is dry, but just let me get out over water and I panic." His occasional swigs from the bottle had given him courage to cross the bridges without apparently affecting his driving ability. You and Cathlin, even bringing in Anangka for a third consultation, had huddled nervously to discuss this problem of committing yourselves into the hands of a drunk driver, but as it turned out I.'s driving never once showed any sign of being affected by his drinking. Maybe it was the coffee, but I. was never Ah with his hands on the wheel.

Don't you want to stop soon? Cathlin's card asked, and, *Yes, Kati told me some Russian KGB agents were on her trail, because, you know, she was a* ~~dissident~~ *dissenter.*

"Soon," I. said, and then he said, " 'Kati'? Did she let you call her Kati? I knew her for a whole term and she didn't want me to call her anything except Ekaterina Vladimirovna, no more, no less."

He had mispronounced the nickname but Cathlin decided not to attempt to correct him. *We became very good friends in the short time I knew her,* she wrote.

"I don't think she even let little Kenny Elmore call her Kati," I. said, and cast Cathlin a glance before going on, "and the funniest thing about Princess Dadeshkeliani was that she and Kenny, age thirteen at most, were lovers. Did you know that?"

No! Cathlin wrote. *How do you know? Did she tell you? Did Kenny tell you?*

"Loretta Elmore, Kenny's mother, told me. Apparently she had known about it, or at least guessed, for months. The Elmores were even stranger, I think, than our 'Kati.' He was a retired professor of anthropology, and what the Elmores had done in the South Pacific was investigate the sexual customs of some primitive peoples, Manaturuans, who often permitted, or even encouraged, their pubertal boys to lose their virginity to experienced mature females. Yeah. It had been Loretta's job to ingratiate herself among the Manaturuan womenfolk and try to learn the real facts of the matter, but the Elmores had never been able to discover if the experienced mature females, who were usually married women and mothers, had actually enjoyed their duties in teaching the boys how to screw, or if the young boys were in any way adversely affected by their 'initiation,' and both of the Elmores had a kind of scientific curiosity as to what was going to happen to their son Kenny in the company of this Russian—or Georgian—woman who had the hots for him. They had made a bet, I don't know for how much money, over Loretta's contention that Kenny would turn into a juvenile delinquent if he lost his virginity prematurely. And Loretta apparently won her bet, at the same time that she was required to tell Ekaterina to leave."

Could you stop soon? Cathlin wrote. *Aren't you exhausted?* The sun was coming up now, behind them. Cathlin cast a glance at it and in the process noted with relief that there were no cars to their rear.

"Can you drive?" I. asked. "Do you want to take over?"

I am sorry, Cathlin wrote truthfully, *I never learned to drive. I should have warned you of that beforehand.*

"Like warning me beforehand that we can't share a room? Do we have to stop at a motel where we can take separate rooms?"

In Nabokov's book you gave me—not Pale Fire *but* Lolita*—there is much discussion of the American motel. I have never been in a motel. I think I would* *not like that aspect of America. If you can find a hotel, however, I shall share a room with you. Not a bed, but a room.*

He read it and laughed. "But they have only motels near the interstate," he said. "To find a hotel, we'd have to leave this throughway and go into some city."

The sun was fully up now. The light was behind you, but it was sufficient to show him, perhaps, that you were there with Cathlin. Her profile was yours. *Then let's do it. Aren't you exhausted?*

The small city of Richmond, Indiana, is only a couple of miles off Interstate 70, a short detour, and I gave I. a little help in finding the street that would lead him to the Eagle Hotel, erected in 1887 and scarcely changed since its heyday, except by the addition of a multilevel parking garage for the convenience of the very rare motorist who prefers hotels to motels. The level where the Blazer parked was even with the third floor, on which your room was located, a room that bore no resemblance whatsoever to the typical motel room, furnished as it was with Victoriana and flocked wallpaper, with chromolithographs instead of offset lithos in the picture frames. There were twin beds. I. had a nightcap (or rather a morning cap) of the remainder of his bottle and went to sleep immediately, fully clothed. The thick draperies blotted out most of the sunlight coming into the room. Cathlin woke about noon to discover that her red wig had got twisted around and was covering her face. She hoped that wouldn't happen again. She woke again, finally, at about four in the afternoon. I. would sleep another hour before she woke him. Waiting for him to wake, she read the various literature in the room, including a menu for room service. She counted her money, the remainder of your April paycheck, all she and you had in this world in the way of cash, and decided against calling room service. When I. woke up and they got in the Blazer again, he treated her to breakfast at a stop on the interstate.

He made other stops, on the highway shoulder, before crossing the Wabash River and, later, the Kaskaskia River, in Illinois, in order to fortify himself with bourbon against his gephydrophobia. But neither of these bridges nor any of those encountered thus far on the trip had prepared him for the bridge over the Mississippi at St. Louis. It is a large river. It is much wider and deeper than the Kura at Tbilisi or the Neva at Leningrad, or, as far as Cathlin was concerned, the Foyle at London-derry or the Lagan at Belfast. The preparatory dose of bourbon was not enough; I. panicked before reaching the midpoint of the high, long span. Luckily, that late at night there was little traffic coming behind. Still, there I. was, his hands gripping the steering wheel so tightly he had no control, asking desperately once more, "Can't you drive? Can't you drive?" You could only shake your head, which he, with his eyes glued to the roadway of the bridge, could not see. You couldn't write him a note. He couldn't read it in the dark.

"*Ot! Ot!*" you began to lament. But something had to be done. He was clearly incapacitated.

Only poltergeists make things move. I, your garden variety ghost, had never before so much as rattled a mirror. Sure, I'd messed around with a couple of radios, but that was a matter of invisible waves or sparks, not physical objects like steering wheels and gas pedals. I was nearly as panicked as I. But somebody had to do something to get you off that bridge and across the great river. Visible even in the darkness, because floodlighted, was the great parabolic arch, gleaming aluminum, Saarinen-designed, officially the Jefferson Memorial Arch but called the Gateway. Here you were, dear Kat, at the Gate. I. couldn't get you through it. You'd have to do something yourself.

But I think I held your hands as you grabbed the wheel and I think I held your feet as you thrust one of them toward the gas pedal and with the other one attempted to lift his heavy foot off the brake. His foot was frozen. "FOOT OFF BRAKE!" you screamed at him.

"What?" he said. He hadn't heard you, but just the sound of mute Cathlin speaking something other than "Och" had loosened his foot on the brake, and you got it off, and the Blazer began to creep forward again. It seemed to take forever, but you steered it over the water, then far enough beyond the water that he regained his awareness, his com-posure, his driving skill.

Miles beyond St. Louis, switched to Interstate 44 now, he was still breathing hard, and he asked Cathlin in wonderment, "How did you do that, if you can't drive?"

But there was no way in the dark of the car, without turning on the dome light, that he could read any answer she cared to write. So she was spared trying to explain that she hadn't done it, that somebody, maybe Anangka, had "taken over."

Rolla, Missouri, was the last real town you passed through; the rest of them from here on in will have to be pseudonymous. I. told Cathlin he had several friends in Rolla, and he even deliberated with himself, aloud, the possibility of stopping there, but it was the wee hours before dawn, no one was awake yet, and he decided to drive on. But Rolla, he explained to Cathlin, was the portal to the Bodarks; these hills all around, although you couldn't see them, were the first foothills of the Bodark Mountains. By the time the sun came up and you had reached the city of "Summerfield," you were on the mostly flatlands of the dull "Summerfield Plateau," and I. could not yet point out any mountains to Cathlin to remind her of Londonderry.

Summerfield also has an Eagle Hotel, as well as many other nonmotels, but I. would not leave the interstate, even though Cathlin was flashing the same cards from the morning before: *Could you stop soon? Aren't you exhausted?* I. shook his head and concentrated with demonic intensity upon the road ahead of him, until at last he could point out a mountain of sorts, not very high, but a mountain all the same, the first since leaving the burgh where you'd spent the winter. It was full springtime now, and full daylight now. Even from the dull, tedious interstate you could see flowers, and the omnipresent pink-blooming *Cercis canadensis* and the white-blooming *Cornus florida*. I. was so intent upon the road you lost your sense of discomfort over the possibility of his seeing you clearly in the daylight, and what little you had of this discomfort soon was forgotten as you studied the changing scenery and even began to imagine, out there in those woods, that special boletic reek that makes your nostrils dilate: the dark, dank, satisfying blend of damp moss, rich earth, and rotting leaves.

Suddenly I. pulled over to the shoulder and stopped, although there were no bridges in sight ahead. He jumped out of the Blazer and ran to the roadside and fell to his knees. You thought perhaps he was going to upheave his consumption of bourbon and the "fast food" that had nourished the two of you at many stops along the route. He knelt forward and brought his face right down to the earth.

He returned to you with crumbs of dirt still clinging to his lips, and he declared, "That's the state line. We're here!"

And you realized that he had gone to kiss his native soil.

THE HALFMOON HOTEL was built of native limestone in 1886, originally as a mountain retreat for wealthy railroad executives and their families (Lawren Carnegie once slept there, when he was still alive). It is five stories of one hundred rooms, high on a hilltop overlooking the quaint Victorian spa of Arcata Springs, an alpine village of steep, narrow, winding streets lined here with shops, there with massive limestone walls and huge shade trees. After its heyday as a rich man's lodge, the Halfmoon had a second incarnation for twenty-four years as a junior college for girls, Halfmoon College; and later, during the depression, it suffered a third incarnation as the hospital of a quack doctor who claimed to cure cancer, and among the several ghosts who have taken up permanent inhabitance of the place are a couple of nurses who endlessly wheel gurneys with terminal lymphoma and carcinoma patients and are some-times spotted by the modern guests, who are motel-shunning tourists enchanted by the views, the elegance, and the promotional slogan, "A Castle in the Air High Atop the Bodarks."

It is indeed a castle, its peaked roofs and towers looming over the town, and your first sight of it, sweet Kat, would be a delicious jolt of recognition—not of anything from your past, because in all honesty not even its rugged stonemasonry reminded you of the towers of Svanetia, but of a kind of answer to that half-formulated search that we all carry around with us all our lives, most of us never finding anything.

The first part of the *Ot!* you began to sigh was so long, a vowel so continuous, that by the time you got to the end of the exclamation you had the presence of mind to change the terminal consonant to *k* instead of *t* and make a Scottish "Och." Then you wrote on a card for I., *It is fabulous!*

"Anything like that in Londonderry?" he asked. You shook your head and went on shaking it. You would be even more fascinated when you discovered, as you would soon, that the original settlers of the town had not been the railroad executives or even the earliest health-seeking white Americans, but Indians. Long before the water-faddist bathers, dippers, and drinkers of the 1880s mushroomed the village into a city, the Osage Indians had discovered the curative properties of the springs and had a small village of their own on the mountain where the Halfmoon would come to be. Indeed, they named the principal spring of water flowing out of the mountain's east slope (water good for curing erysipelas, scrofula, photodysphoria, and dyspepsia, but not cancer or hebephilia) *Mionba Athigezhe Nithní,* Osage speech for Magic-Water-Beneath-the-Two-Horned-Moon, and this halfmoon spring gave its name to the hotel.

Checking in at the magnificent curving walnut-and-marble registration desk, I. discovered that the room reserved for him by BOW, in expectation that he would be alone, contained only one bed, albeit a double. "Have you ever heard of our colonial American custom of 'bundling'?" he asked Cathlin, and when she shook her head, he said to the clerk, "My wife and I would really prefer twin beds."

The clerk, a girl named Sharon, gave Cathlin a glance, then said, with a slight lisp, "We have no twin beds together. There are some rooms with a double and a twin, a queen and a twin, or a king and a queen, and some with two doubles, but . . ."

I. was having trouble hearing all of this. "Anything," he said, "so long as they're separate."

". . . but they are all taken," clerk Sharon went on. "The BOW meeting has reserved everything." You learned then that the name of the organization is pronounced as something done from the waist, rhyming with *how,* the Indian greeting.

But I. missed the pronunciation and said, "I'm the main speaker at the BOW meeting," pronouncing it to rhyme with *go,* an injunction of leave-taking. The clerk glanced again at Cathlin and studied I. Neither of you were very presentable; neither of you had bathed since leaving the burgh, and Cathlin's dress was wrinkled from the long car ride; I. was dressed in his customary grungy shirt and trousers, and he hadn't shaved for two days.

"There are many motels along the highway," the clerk said.

A cat leapt up onto the registration desk and settled there as if he owned the place. He was a yellow-striped tabby with a white-ringed tail, fat, and you could not resist stroking him—the first time you'd had your hand on a real cat in years. Worse, you could not resist asking Sharon her cat's name. She answered, "Morris," the terminal *s* lisped as *th.* You hoped that I. had not overheard the exchange.

Cathlin began to write on a card and gave it to I. *Go ahead and take the one reserved. We can work out something.*

I. smiled hugely at the clerk and waved the card at her and said, "My wife, who is here in hopes the water can cure her aphasia, says that it's okay if we take the one we've got."

Sharon said, "But I should warn you, that room has a history of being haunted." She lightly lisped her *s*'s again.

Was she trying to get them to go? You wrote quickly, *Tell her I love ghosts.*

"My wife hopes your ghosts are friendly," I. said. "Now do I have to hire a bellhop or can I carry my own stuff?"

Finding Room 218 without a bellhop was slightly difficult: The brass numerals had been removed from the door, and only a *pentimento* of the numerals was still faintly visible. Detecting the room number, 218, you nearly blurted that it was the same number as the room you'd recently vacated at the Elmores' mansion. But you soon discovered some major differences: It was considerably smaller than your room in the mansion had been, yet the view beyond the walnut jalousies was far grander (spoiled only at one edge by an enormous cement statue of a robed male with extended arms, possibly meant to be Jesus), the furniture was much swanker (at least the bed was not a murphybed but an ornately head-boarded Victorian), the yellow floral wallpaper matched the window draperies, and, strange to relate or to discover, there wasn't a single mirror in the room. Not even in the bathroom, which had gleaming tiles and porcelains and chromiums but no silverbacks. How could you, after showering (which you immediately did), look at Cathlin afterward to restore her disguise? At your request, I. went down to complain to Sharon and returned with a hand mirror, which was better than nothing.

Then there was the problem of the smallish bed. You were so tired that you were ready to tumble into it even if half of it was occupied by a grown man, a very large man. But even if you could risk waking up to find yourself in his arms, you couldn't risk waking up to find that your wig and sunglasses had come off. I. solved the problem by graciously offering to let you take a nap while he reconnoitered the Halfmoon Pub. You fished in your purse for a much-used card: *Aren't you exhausted?* and showed it to him once more. He shook his head and said he was too excited to sleep. So you thanked him, but you requested that he leave the key with you and knock when he returned. You didn't want him letting himself into the room if you were sleeping.

I. was Ah when he came back, hours later. He was thoroughly Ah. You came out of a very deep sleep, during which you'd alternated between dreams about the Osage Indians (although you knew nothing about them) and your old familiar dream of climbing and descending an endless sequence of stone steps, concrete steps, wooden steps, staircases that led up or down to significant places whose significance always eluded you. You answered Ah's knock, using the hand mirror to make sure it was Cathlin who let him in. She managed to understand, from his slurred speech, that in the Halfmoon Pub he'd encountered a gaggle of the ladies of BOW, who had bought his many drinks and attempted to engage him in conversation and used up every last one of his cards. He was out of cards. He had resorted to paper bar napkins and had a fistful of those, which you read after he had fallen into the bed for a long sleep, embracing the pillow you'd vacated. Many of these women had covered the napkins with their names, home addresses, their current room numbers, and the red bow-shaped imprints of their lipstick. Many of them had, apparently, read all of I.'s novels with, apparently, much appreciation and relish. You regretted that you'd never had a chance to read anything of his. You resolved to do so as soon as you got "settled."

While I. slept, you also read the hotel's list of services, which was vast: in addition to the Halfmoon Pub, there was the main dining room, called the Crystal Room, a movie theater, and an observation deck on the top floor, a game room in the basement, outdoor games of tennis and shuffleboard near the swimming pool, and a hiking trail. There was also a bus that took an audience to the Passion Play, and a carriagelike vehicle called *Tally-Ho* that took guests down to the town's shops and later to something called the Cook-Out. At 5:00 P.M., you put on your *dzhinsy* and your only fresh blouse and decided to leave off the extravagant hat and sunglasses, as long as I. was sleeping. But you wore your red wig, and you rode off on the *Tally-Ho* to the Cook-Out, for a real American eat-and-sing, with hot dogs, baked beans, potato salad, dill pickles, rolls, and pop. One of the songs everybody sang was "Loch Lomond," which you had previously learned from the book. Some of the picnickers, apparently all BOW members, had their children with them, and there were a couple of adorable boys, age eleven or thirteen, that you would have loved to become acquainted with, if you'd had the courage. One of their fathers flirted with you and tried to persuade you to go off on the hiking trail with him "and hunt for mushrooms or something," but you told him your husband was sleeping and might wake up anytime. "Are you a Russkie or something?" he said. "Where'd you get that accent?"

You learned, from your conversation with him, that the membership of BOW was not exclusively female, nor was it limited to amateur wordsmiths. There were artists and photographers also aspiring to publication, and several males, young and old, published and unpublished. The president was a man, even if all the other officers were women. A monthly newsletter, *Take A BOW*, kept members informed of workshops, contests, events, and hot tips on free-lancing, and the March and April issues had given prominent mention to this annual convention, at which the main speakers would be the two most celebrated Bodark writers, I.

himself and a woman named Halfmoon Berryfairy. "Yes," you said, in your Russkie accent. "I am Mrs. I."

"No shit?" the man said. "Well, hey, tell me something. If it's not too personal. Does the guy do all the stuff in bed that he writes about?"

You gave the man a coy sidelong glance and said, "He does things in bed he *never* writes about."

WHEN I. WOKE UP, sometime in the middle of the night, and was ready to give the bed back to you, he found you reading one of his novels, which you'd fetched from a box in the back of the Blazer. The novel had a bookmark: Kenny's pamphlet, *20 Questions for Alcoholism*. When I. woke up, you inserted this back where it had been and you closed the book. The main effect of his fiction on you was to make you want to write, and you were burning to get back to *Geordie Lad*.

Before giving the bed back to you, I. told you of an old Bodark custom called "ride-and-tie": when two travelers on a long trip had only one horse between them, one of them would ride so many miles ahead of the other, dismount, tie the horse, and continue on foot. When the other traveler, on foot, arrived at the horse, he would untie it and ride on so many miles beyond the first traveler before dismounting and tying the horse. And so on, taking turns. "That's what we're doing with this bed," I. said. "Riding and tying. I wish we could ride together."

The horse won't hold us, you wrote.

"Do you sleep with those sunglasses on?" he asked as you got into bed.

If there is any light, you wrote.

"I was going to sit here, while you slept, and work on my speech," he said. "But I guess I could put out the light and go down to the lobby." He looked at his watch. "Nobody's up at this hour. The Halfmoon

Pub is closed. I don't have any notion what I'm going to talk about tomorrow . . . or, rather, today, because I'm supposed to speak right after lunch. I've never given a speech to a writers' group before. Have you got any ideas?"

Sleepy though you were, you tried to think. You could not imagine, then or ever (and you've turned down many an invitation since), telling people how to write, or speaking to a hotel full of free lances, broken lances, daggers, and toothpicks. You got the bookmark, Kenny's pamphlet on alcoholism, out of his book and gave it to him, and you wrote on a card, *Maybe this will inspire you.*

He stared at it, and then at you, as if you weren't any help at all. But he took the pamphlet and turned out the light and went down to the lobby.

The next day, or rather, later that same day, in the Crystal Room, to the assemblage of a hundred members of BOW, who had during their consumption of luncheon cast an occasional appraising glance at Cathlin sitting beside him at the head table, I., or rather, Ah, who had fortified himself in advance with the all-morning help of a bottle of bourbon, rose after the flattering introduction by Agnes Roundtree Mazzarelli and said, "Somebody recently gave me a pamphlet published by A.A., called *20 Questions for Alcoholism,* and just this morning it occurred to me that you can take that list, go through it, substitute the word *write* for the word *drink,* and come up with a perfect list of questions to determine whether or not you are a genuine, dedicated, incurable writer. As follows:

"*1. Do you ever crave to write at a definite time daily?*

2. Do you feel under tension much of the time while not writing?

3. Do you need to write the next morning?

4. Do you lose time from work due to writing?

5. Have you ever had a 'blackout' (complete loss of memory) as a result of writing?

6. Do you write to build up your self-confidence?

7. Do you write to escape from worries or troubles?

8. Do you have feelings of guilt or inferiority?

9.   *Are you at times possessed with unreasonable fears?*

10. *Do you write because you are shy with other people?*

11. *Have you become noticeably short-tempered, irritable, opinionated?*

12. *Is writing making your home life unhappy?*

13. *Does your writing make you careless of your family's welfare?*

14. *Is writing jeopardizing your job or business?*

15. *Have you ever gotten into financial difficulties because of writing?*

16. *Is writing affecting your reputation?*

17. *Do you lie about your writing?*

18. *Have you become extremely self-centered and selfish?*

19. *Do you hold bitter resentment toward certain people—wife, hus-band, employer, associate, or friend—and do you continue to harbor these resentments?*

20. *Have you lost your self-respect?"*

The ladies of BOW, and the gentlemen too, loved his speech, and Cathlin was proud to watch their faces during it, almost as if it really were her husband who was giving it to them. Afterward, before adjourning for the sessions on how to sell to religious periodicals and how to cope with rejection slips, the members were as eager to shake Cathlin's hand as they were to shake his, almost as if they knew she'd put him up to it.

The speech had a lasting effect on the convention: Everybody made a beeline for the Halfmoon Pub, where they lost their tensions, built up their self-confidence, escaped their worries and troubles, and shed their guilts, inferiorities, and fears. Among these people, you were startled to notice, was bold Bolshakov. If not Bolshakov, his twin. No trench coat, and no widow's peak in his hairline, but wouldn't he disguise himself as a . . . perhaps a Bodarks dentist? He appeared, however, to be with some women who were clearly BOW ladies. Could even Bolshakov have ingratiated himself so quickly with the natives?

"You'll have to excuse me," I. said. He truly was exhausted. Driving for hours nonstop had not drained him as much as preparing and giving that speech. "I'd better go ride and tie."

Don't leave me just yet, you wrote. *Do you see that man over there, sitting with those women? If I am not mistaken, that is Bolshakov, the North Ireland psychiatrist, the prick.*

I. squinted his eyes and studied the man, and you waited in dread to hear him say, "Yes, that's the guy who gave me his card when I was leaving the mansion." But he didn't. All he said was, "Are you sure?"

Does he look familiar to you? you wrote.

"From your description of him in *Geordie Lad*, yes. Looks just like the creep. But come on, Cathlin, what would he be doing here in Arcata Springs?"

You wrote, *You have not yet read the chapters of* Geordie Lad *that will make it very clear why he would be following me, trying to kill me.*

"Well, gosh, Cathlin, do you want me to go ask him if he's a shrink? He looks more like a dentist to me. Or an insurance salesman from Cabool, Missouri."

You sighed. The man had not thrown a single glance in your direction. Finally you wrote, *I am being silly. Forgive me. You go on and get some sleep.*

I. got up. For appearance's sake, he gave you a kiss. Or maybe it wasn't only for appearance's sake. Shortly after he left, the man you'd mistaken for Bolshakov also got up, with one of the ladies, and left, without having thrown you a glance. You removed your hat and your sunglasses and joined the fun. Morris the cat, as if waiting for I.'s departure, leapt into your lap and began purring.

Several people wanted to talk with you, to ask you what it was like living with the "celebrated" author. One of the ladies slapped you on the wrist and said, "You're not really married to him, now, are you? You're not wearing any ring." And you had to confess that you were living in sin.

"Are you a Russkie or something?" another lady asked. "Where'd you get that accent?"

You passed up an opportunity to attend sessions or workshops on Environmental Writing and Selling Your First Novel (although you might have learned some helpful hints in the latter meeting). After tiring of the ladies in the pub, you visited the game room, where people were playing cards, checkers, and chess. Morris followed you down there. You got yourself into a couple of chess games and demolished your opponents so handily that one of them asked, "Are you a Russkie or something? Where'd you learn to play like that?"

Later, declining an invitation to accompany a group taking the bus to the Passion Play, you and Morris rode the elevator up to the observation deck on the fourth floor, and you got your first complete view of the lovely surrounding countryside, although a distant hill was grotesquely marred by that colossal cement hunk called *Christ of the Bodarks:* a quasi-primitive statue of a stiff, legless man with his arms outspread. I. had not told Cathlin that this town, for all its charm, was smack in the middle of the Bible Belt, and you, dear Kat, an unbeliever not because of Soviet atheism so much as Svanetian paganism, were going to find yourself sometimes exhilarated by the religious *poshlost* of these people.

Morris and I stood beside you, he visible, I not, and I was almost tempted to take inhabitance of his body, but it was much too early in our relationship for that. You did not know it then, but you were standing on the observation deck (near one of those huge, robotlike coin-operated binoculars-on-swivels, which for a dime would have given you a close look at Christ's stern face) almost within touching distance of the slate-roofed slopes of the penthouse peak wherein, just a few years later, you would have your own lavishly appointed triplex suite of rooms with its futuristic kitchen where you could whip up one of those chicken dishes that grace the pages of *Kat's Quick Chick Cookbook,* and, if not your "dozen absolutely beautiful cats of every color and breed," at least this selfsame Morris, who would attach himself to you and in whose physical entity I would attempt to manifest what remained of my spiritual entity. I was so glad to have you there, at last, that I was desperate to give you a foreglimpse of your future, to point out to you the penthouse's highest picture window, where your bedroom would be, to show you even the window ledge on which Morris (or my incarnation), by then permanently attached to you, would bask away his old age, approaching nineteen. But I could not yet speak to you of these things so that you could hear me. Nor could I contrive to have Morris communicate with you in any manner.

I did the next best thing. I "arranged," if we must persist in using that verb, for you to be approached by my kinsman, or rather kinswoman, kinschild really, a charming girl just a couple of years older than yourself, whom you'd already briefly met, and to whom you assumed, wrongly, that Morris belonged. Sharon was a golden blonde with blue eyes that seemed to have depths of experience (in such contrast to your innocent eyes), and her eyes came to gaze into yours almost with recognition, as if she knew the history of your soul.

Beneath the deck railing's gas lamps, she leaned her arms on the iron balustrade in a meditative pose identical to your own, right beside you. "Is you Cathlin or Kati?" she asked.

You stared into those deep blue eyes. What was this? You didn't mind being mistaken for a Russkie but you didn't want to be somebody you were trying not to be. "I beg your pardon?" you said frostily.

"I said, 'Is your castle in Arcaty?.'" She tried to correct her lisp.

" 'Arcaty'?"

"Here," she said. "Arcata Springs. We just call it Arcaty."

" 'Castle'?"

"Don't you know, they call this place the Halfmoon Castle? 'A Castle in the Air High Atop the Bodarks.' I was just wondering if you'd found your long-sought castle, that you dreamt of all those nights in Lisedi."

"In *where*, pardon me?"

" 'Endlessly,' I said. Do you have trouble with English, or is it me?"

"Not as much as I used to," you said.

She offered you a cigarette, a filtered Tarreyton, and took one herself, and lit yours for you. Then she exhaled her smoke with the words "Where the devil did you find I.?" So you told her that you'd been a student of his, the past term, in the municipal university of that burgh, far away. "That's just like him, seducing a student," she said.

"Do you know him?" you asked. He hadn't seemed to recognize her during registration.

"I know his stuff," she said, and you understood that all-purpose "stuff" to mean his writing. "And I know his country. My name's Sharon." She told you her last name too, but you didn't hear it or understand it. It started with *I* but wasn't I.'s. She wasn't related.

Morris had continued to rub himself up against your leg and was completely ignoring her. Of course, many cats are often more friendly to strangers than to their own masters. "You have a nice cat," you remarked. "He's beautiful."

"Morris isn't mine," she told you. "He doesn't belong to anybody. He just sort of comes with the hotel, and some people call him the General Manager. He just wandered in, as a kitten, seven years ago, and took over the place."

"Have you worked here long?"

"Here in Arcaty, or here in the hotel? The hotel job I just started. I've been in Arcaty for a few years. But I grew up in Sticker Hound." She waited for your response, and when there was none, she asked, "Haven't you read any of his stuff?"

"I just started reading some last night," you declared.

"Hasn't he told you about Sticker Hound?" she asked. You shook your head. She explained. "That's the name—one of the names—of the town that he writes all his stuff about, 'way off in the deepest, lostest part of the Bodarks. Do me a favor, will you? Do us all a favor. Ask him when was the last time he came back to visit Sticker Hound. And then ask him when he ever plans to come again."

" 'STICKER HOUND'?" HE SAID, reading your card. "Where did you meet this girl?" You wrote another card while he was getting dressed and combing his hair. It was late at night, you were ready for bed, for your share of ride-and-tie, but he was just getting up. And he was still half-asleep. "Sticker Hound?" he said again. Then slowly recognition spread over his face. "Oh," he said. "I think you might have misunderstood her. Sharon, huh? Yes. If I'm not mistaken, she's Vernon Ingledew's older sister, one of Hank's four daughters. Or was it five? Anyway, what she must have been saying to you was the name of that village—only it isn't an inhabited village anymore—it was named Stick Around."

She wanted me to ask you when was the last time you were there?

"Why didn't she ask me herself, when we were checking in?" he said.

She also wanted me to ask when you plan to visit Stick Around again.

"Maybe she's on night duty at the desk," he said. "I'll go see. Have a nice beddie-bye and ride-and-tie."

You slept a full eight hours, more than your share of the ride-and-tie, but he was not waiting for the bed when you woke. You showered and dressed and went downstairs. The desk clerk was not Sharon but Cathy. You asked her if she'd seen him. She said he was in the Crystal Room, and there you found him having coffee with the man you'd mistaken the day before for Bolshakov. Both men got to their feet as you entered, and I. motioned for you to join them. You hadn't had breakfast yet, although it was lunchtime, and your head wasn't clear enough to discount the possibility that this *could* be Bolshakov.

"Speak of the devil," I. said to you. "We were just talking about you." He gave you a wry grin, and there was something in his eyes that made you suspect, for a terrible moment, that Bolshakov had been telling I. all of the untruths he had fabricated about you. I. spoke to him: "Dr. MacLean, this is Cathlin McWalter herself." Then he said to Cathlin, "Sweetheart, you were right. He's not an insurance salesman from Cabool or a dentist. He's a sure-enough psychiatrist!" Your knees buckled, and I. grabbed your elbow. "Not from North Ireland, though! He practices in West Plains, Missouri."

"Hiya," said Dr. MacLean. "Pleased to meet you." He didn't sound anything at all like Bolshakov. I. was motioning for the three of you to sit, but the doctor said, "I've really got to run. The wife is over there waiting for lunch. Nice to've met you, Cath. You take care of this guy, hear?" The doctor departed.

"Nice guy," I. remarked after you'd ordered some brunch. "He's not a BOW member himself; just keeping his wife company. She writes children's books."

What were you telling him about me? you wrote.

"Oh, I was just mentioning that you'd been getting treatment for your eye trouble, and I wondered if he knew anything about photodysphoria. According to him, it is pretty psychosomatic. He told me a little story about Dr. Alvah Jackson, the man who first discovered the halfmoon spring, after the Osage Indians had left it, back around 1832. Jackson's twelve-year-old son, Timothy, had a sort of photodysphoria that almost blinded him, but after treating the boy with water from the halfmoon spring, his son was apparently cured. For years after that, the doctor bottled and sold the water as 'Dr. Jackson's Eye-Water.' Too bad they don't make it or sell it anymore. Dr. MacLean says that all the springs of Arcata Springs are now polluted, and you can't even use them to bathe in."

Did you find Sharon? your next note asked.

"Yeah," he said. He said nothing else. It was almost as if you'd introduced an unpleasant subject or something he wanted to avoid. His attention shifted to the Crystal Room's head table, which was filling up with the officers of BOW and the day's guest speakers. Following lunch, a very pretty girl with dark hair, introduced by Mrs. Mazzarelli as "our most distinguished writer, and a resident of right here in Arcaty, the one and only Halfmoon Berryfairy," gave a speech on the subject How I Use the Bodarks, which was so encouraging that it made you too, Cathlin McWalter, believe that you could write about the Bodarks. But she was followed by a lengthy succession of ladies who read their poems, mostly saccharine odes and funereal dithyrambs.

You slipped a card to your companion: *Maybe the club should be called not BOW but SCRAPE: Sisters Composing Romances And Pretty Elegies.*

He laughed. Several members cast him looks, because the poem currently being declaimed was somber, even pathetic. But then it was all over, except for the afternoon workshops, which I. was not required to attend.

He rose from his table. You rose with him. He looked at you for a while, smiling . . . or perhaps smirking. Then he asked, "Are you ready to go to Stick Around? Or Sticker Hound, as the case might be?"

You nodded.

"Wear your jeans," he said.

As you were leaving the hotel, standing out front waiting while I. returned to get the suitcases, there was Morris, to say good-bye to you.

"You be a good kitty, Morris," you said to him. "And I'll be back, don't you worry."

I. was at your elbow, with the suitcases. "How come you can talk to the damned cat," he asked, "but not to me?"

BUT IT WAS I. who did not talk, all the way to Stick Around. He seemed to be lost in thought, perhaps dwelling upon the world of his fiction that he had created out of Stick Around, that he had not successfully re-created for going on five years now. Perhaps he was a little scared, or apprehensive, not wanting to find that the actual Stick Around was nothing at all like his idealized conception of it. He had no illusions that it would be anything other than a ghost town. He knew that no one was living in the village itself, that the few remaining citizens were all on the outskirts of the village, and that the abandoned buildings of the village would be either in ruins or in bad repair. But he didn't really know what to expect, seeing again with his own eyes what he had only seen in his imagination for years.

If that was what he was thinking, you thought, then you could easily identify and sympathize with him, because you knew that if you were ever permitted to see Svanetia again, it might be nothing at all like the gorgeous place you'd seen only inside your head (and heart) all these years. Indeed, the closer you got to this Stick Around, leaving behind the big highway and climbing up into the remote fastnesses of "Isaac County," passing across the Buffalo River (a real name; he didn't need booze to cross) through the mountain-locked village that was the small county seat, "Jessup," and then taking an unpaved back road that meandered toward the dying-but-still-post-officed village of "Acropolis," you began to be constantly reminded of Svanetia. There were no enormous glacier-clad peaks like Ushba or Layla as backdrops, but the small mountains uprose ever more precipitously and were covered with the great oaks, beeches, and junipers that reminded you of Svanetia's woodlands, and the flowery meadows . . . Ah, the meadows were thick with ripening hay that took you right back to the fields of Lisedi. You rolled down your window to inhale the air.

Here you were, Kat, almost home. I was beside myself with—I nearly said *impatience,* but if there's one commodity we ghosts have in endless abundance, it's patience. No, I was beside myself with triumph: This was the culmination of all the tricks, large and small, that I had pulled in order to get you here. My biggest trick was your driver, and unfortunately his services were about to end. I still had not made up my mind just how to get rid of him. Soon I would want him to "get lost," and I decided I would practice by having him literally get lost.

As the steep dirt road climbed south of Acropolis, I gave I. a fork in it, and he took the wrong one. The prong he took became increasingly rough, weedy, and circuitous. He had, for the first time, to stop and shift the Blazer's gears from two-wheel to four-wheel, to use the gear called "low lock." He also had to take the tomato plants off the dashboard, to keep them from falling off. He arranged them on the floor behind the seat. After a steep mile on this route, the trail petered out.

"I thought I knew this country, but I guess I don't." It was the first time he had spoken since leaving Arcaty, seventy miles before.

You wanted to write on a card, *Are we lost?,* but the Blazer was bouncing so much you couldn't hold your ballpoint steady. Once, the car hit a bump so severe that your wig shifted its position, and you had to right it as inconspicuously as possible.

One of I.'s several flaws was that he was never able to admit defeat, nor to backtrack from a stubborn destination. He could not turn around. If he had gone back to the place where he'd taken the wrong turn, all would have been well. But he insisted on going back only as far as the next westward divergent trail, which was scarcely better than the one you were on. This trail, which obviously hadn't been used for years, meandered up hill and down vale all over the countryside, like the sledge paths of your Mount Layla. The only advantage of it, because it clearly wasn't getting you anywhere, was that it afforded you a view, in passing, of some interesting mushrooms. You couldn't ask I. to stop so you could get a closer look at them.

It was late afternoon. The sun would be down in another hour. Would you have to spend the night in the woods? The prospect almost elated you. More than once, you had spent the night in the woods above Lisedi, among the bear and roe deer and gazelles of Svanetia.

But I decided I'd given you and poor I. enough exposure to the rough forest, and I arranged for the logging trail you were on to drop down from the mountain and emerge, abruptly, beside a small white church and cemetery. In shape and size, if not in whiteness, the church reminded you strongly of little Saint George's in Lisedi. "Hey!" I. exclaimed in recognition and exultation. "That's the Stick Around churchhouse!" The sweat was running down his face, almost as if he'd been carrying you through the forest and down the mountainside. "I'd like to show you the cemetery, but we're running late," he said.

And then you were on a dirt road smooth enough, level enough, for you to write, *Late for what?*

"We've got a lot to do before dark," he said.

Then you were in a valley filled with green pastures and broad meadows and surrounded by thousand-foot deep-forested mountains whose tops were nearly lost in scarves of mist that could have been transplanted directly from Lisedi. Dear Kat, you almost felt what I wanted you to feel. "Yonder's Leapin Rock," I. pointed. "But you've never read my novels, have you?"

Another mile down this valley, you reached the village proper, or what was left of it: a few buildings standing but abandoned, several buildings fallen or remaining only in traces. I. gave you a quick tour without getting out of the Blazer, driving in a circle over the terrain, through a couple of creekbeds—"Banty Creek, there," he said, "and this is Swains Creek" (both real). Here's where the gristmill was. And here's the tomato-canning factory, what's left of it.

The only building in good repair was a two-story house that had a verandah, ornately inset with carved balusters, running the length of its porch and making the place look for all the world like one of the Svanetian houses of the Dadeshkelianis. If it had only had a tower beside it, it would have been perfect. "That used to be the hotel," I. said. "But before it became a hotel, for many years a strange woman used to live there by herself. You'll hear stories about her. She was once the mistress of a governor of the state—who, incidentally, built this house—and was one of the town's settlers." This hotel/house, you'd be surprised to discover years hence, would come into your possession, even if it never came into your occupation.

"Now, *this,*" he said, pointing to another building, at a fork in the road, "used to be my favorite. It was the last post office of Stick Around, and also the house of a woman"—his voice caught, snagged on some memory, and he could not finish the sentence. He slowed just enough for you to get a good look at its long porch, which again reminded you of the verandahs of Lisedi. "Our friend Sharon is going to move into this house a couple of years from now," he declared. "Of course, she'll have to fix it up and get rid of the cockroaches."

How do you know? you wrote. *Did she tell you that?*

He read the card, then brought the car to a full stop and turned to you and said, "Listen, Cathlin, we're in Stick Around now. I can *hear* you, and you *can* speak. You don't have to keep on writing these goddamn cards."

But you were not able to speak. He drove on, up the eastward prong from the abandoned post office. He drove past the first apparently occupied dwelling, a two-pen log cabin with an open breezeway between the pens. There were flowers planted, and the yard seemed to be kept, and there were chickens roaming free. Even the arrangement of the logs reminded you of Svanetian log cabins. "I'm *not* going to stop," I. said, as if talking to himself, persuading himself not to stop. "That's where the woman—the last postmistress of Stick Around—she lives there. She is, by the way, Sharon's grandmother, and she can tell you enough stories to keep you writing for years."

Still, you could not speak, or write, in response to that. He drove on. In less than another mile, he came to a clearing with gardens, tilled fields, and a charming old house painted yellow, the only painted building

in the environs, its eaves and porch trimmed with fancy jigsaw work in
the fashion of Svanetia's *quelvoni lisoque,* "crazy carpenters." The house
was obviously occupied: there was a thriving vegetable garden beside it,
a pig pen, a goat pen, and free-ranging chickens everywhere. "I *will* stop
here," I. declared. "But I'll just be a minute. I need to borrow a shovel."

You watched as he got out and approached the porch, calling out,
"Hello, the house!" Two dogs ran to meet him but did not bark. He
patted their heads. Soon the door opened and a boy came out. Still your
leaping heart, Kat; he wasn't old enough for you. He wasn't yet eleven,
and even when he got to be twelve, he was not going to be your boyfriend.
So you could put that out of your mind.

The boy was followed by his mother, a woman you thought could
have been Sharon's sister: the same blonde hair, only longer, the same
blue eyes. But she was not Sharon's sister. Soon enough you would find
out who she was, but she was not related to Sharon. Interrupted in the
act of preparing supper, she was wiping her hands on her apron. But at
the sight of I. she suddenly screamed his name and practically leapt off
the porch and into his arms. They did not kiss, but they hugged tightly
a long time, the boy standing close and touching his mother's back as
she did so.

You watched as they talked. Wasn't I. going to bring her over to
the Blazer and introduce her to you? Apparently not. Or not yet. Soon
the yellow house's door opened again and a man came out, the woman's
husband, the boy's father. You guessed the couple were in their early
thirties. The man shook I.'s hand vigorously and slapped him on the
back, and I. chatted with him, and the couple both looked out at the
Blazer, in your direction, at your eyes hidden by the dark glasses. Wasn't
I. going to introduce them? Apparently not. After a while, the man went
out to a shed beside the house and returned with a shovel, which he
handed to I., and I. talked for just a minute longer before returning to
the Blazer. He threw the shovel into the back and got in.

You wanted to write, *What's the shovel for?* but he had asked you not
to write, and you remembered, "That's once. That's twice."

"The man who built that house," I. told you, "was a fabulous old
character who came originally from Connecticut, and he lived here as a

hermit. He wrote some far-out poetry. I met him once when I was very young, and again . . . after he died."

The fabulous old character's spirit arranged for I. to easily find the logging trail that led straight up the mountainside to a grove of *Juniperus virginiana,* a glade on the bench of the mountain, where there was a cemetery-of-one, a single gravestone in the clearing. I. stopped the car, turned off the motor, and said, "Well, we're here."

Although the motor was off, and although the decrepit radio in the Blazer had not been functional for years, I managed to get it to pick up, from some far-distant college town, a station called KUAF, which began playing the Piano Concerto no. 1 in B-flat Minor by Peter Ilyich Tchaikovsky.

You recognized it from the first urgent calls of the keys. You were then thoroughly torn between an elation of love for the music, an overwhelming expectancy of what the music was going to do to you, and an enormous fear: this was the music, you'd written in Cathlin's obituary, for her funeral.

"Get out," I. said. He took the shovel out of the rear and walked with it to a spot in the clearing, not very close to the lone tombstone, where he began digging. Listening to the Tchaikovsky, you reluctantly got out of the Blazer and moved slowly in his direction. The music's volume increased so that you could still hear it away from the car. You arrived at a place where you could make out the inscription on the tombstone:

DANIEL LYAM MONTROSS
June 17, 1880–May 26, 1953
The last Montross of Dudleytown
The only Montross of Stick Around
"We dream our lives, and live our sleep's extremes."

You had not even brought your ballpoint and cards with you. "Who was he?" you asked. The Tchaikovsky had reached the passage where the piano, finding itself lost in the wonderland of strange emotions, is guided by the strings onto the right path and discovers the first glimpse of heaven.

I. continued digging. "He was the man I just mentioned, who built that house down yonder. I wrote a novel about him once, which you never got around to reading. That girl, the blonde, is his granddaughter. Her name is Diana Stoving. But she's also his daughter, too. And their son is named after him. They call him Danny Boy."

Is it possible to carry two tunes in your head at once? At least it was, for you, this time, because there beside the Tchaikovsky but not in tune to it was this, from County Derry:

> But when ye come, and all the flowers are dying,
> And I am dead, as all the flowers must die,
> Ye'll come and find the place where I am lying.
> And kneel and say an Ave where I lie.
>
> And I shall hear, though soft you tread above me,
> And in the dark my soul will wake and see.
> For you'll bend down and tell me that you love me,
> And we shall sleep in peace for all eternity.

"What are you doing?" you asked. "Please tell me."

"I was just thinking of maybe transplanting my tomatoes here," he declared. "But I guess it's not the best spot for it. And my hole's too deep, isn't it? It's nearly deep enough to bury somebody in."

The look he gave you with these words sent shivers up your spine, but you weren't sure the shivers had not proceeded from the music: the Tchaikovsky had reached the passage where the soft strings alone, while the piano is silent, attempt to tell the piano how heaven really appears, before the piano can complete the job of describing a mortal response to it.

You knew what was coming soon. The music was building up to it. You swayed. You closed your eyes and lost yourself in the music's losing itself in paradise; you hugged yourself and stroked your arms and took deep breaths; the tingling of your spine was almost visible to me and the goose pimples on your skin actually were visible, and your expression revealed your longing and exultation and tender aches: The full orchestra and piano were having at it for all they were worth, and then the melodic line began to buck and jerk and thrum and heave in an ecstasy that seized your whole body, and you knew that if you did not grab I. for support you would fall on the ground and have your climax there.

You grabbed his arm. It was not simply for support during your spasms. It was almost a gesture of pleading: Don't do to me what I think you may think you are doing.

You reached that unfamiliar summit standing up. During the last throes of it, as you and the music subsided, he gently lifted the extravagant hat off your head and threw it into his hole. Then he removed your wig and threw it in. And then your sunglasses.

He addressed the hole. "Rest in peace, Cathlin." Then he turned to you and stroked your own hair, brown as the forest floor that nurtured the mushrooms that were your singular overriding interest in this life. And I, powerful and mighty there beside my grave, arranged for the forest floor all around you to sprout with the most marvelous mushrooms you'd ever seen.

He stopped stroking your short hair and lifted your chin. "Damned if I'm going to keep on calling you Ekaterina Vladimirovna, though," he said. "So what can I call you?"

"I have been called all kinds of things," you said, and he heard you. Katerinka. Katerinochka. Trina. Katrusya. Katsyaryna. Kotya. Kitti. Ka-trusenko. Keesa. "In camp at Ishimbay, they called me Keesa, which is a cat's name. In Leningrad, they called me Katrina. But in Svanetia, they called me Eka, or Kati. Kati is a good nickname in Georgia, in Hungary, in Yugoslavia, in Czechoslovakia, in Finland, everywhere. But I think"—you paused and thought, and cast a fond glance at my grave—"I think that in this country I would like for those I love most to call me Kat."

"Kat," he said, and liked it. "Those who love you most will call you Kat."

And thus both of you circumvented the awkward direct professing of love.

How had he seen through your disguise? Oh, long before, he had guessed, had become suspicious of the similarities between Cathlin's obituary and Kat's life, had realized that Bolshakov "belonged" not to Cathlin but to Kat. Despite the extravagance, exaggeration, and outrage of Cathlin's face and costume, she could do nothing with Kat's nose or Kat's neck. They were clearly Kat's perfect nose and Kat's long, graceful neck. And then there was that exclamation, *Ot!* I. wasn't as deaf as you thought, and here in Stick Around he wasn't deaf at all.

"But the clincher," he said, "was when I asked Dr. MacLean this morning what hebephilia is. He told me: an abnormally passionate interest in pubescent people. In your case, boys of twelve. And now that I've told you how I saw through your disguise, it's your turn to tell me: Why did you do it? Why did you have to go to such lengths to cover Kat?"

"I only wanted to be your student, to study to be a writer, without your knowing it was me," you told him, which was the truth. But only part of the truth. You tried to tell him also the rest of it: that you wanted to create Cathlin, that you needed to see if you could make a woman different from yourself who could write *Geordie Lad* as a necktie, not a penis. And you had also wanted to see if knowing him as Cathlin might have helped you overcome your hebephilia.

"It didn't work, did it?" he said. "Tonight, in the bedroom that was Dan Montross's, we're going to have to ride and tie again, but for the last time. After you've gone to bed, I'm going to stay up very late talking to Diana and to Day Whittacker, her husband. Then, after you give me the bed and I get a few hours' sleep, I'm going to take off. I'm thinking of going back up to Rolla, Missouri, and visiting some friends, and then maybe hunting for a job teaching art history somewhere."

"What about me?" you said.

"You're going to stick around here for as long as you like," he told you, and when you looked surprised, he added, as if to persuade you, "Bolshakov could never find you here. Day and Diana will be happy to have you for as long as you want to stay . . . and so long as you don't molest Danny. You could finish *Geordie Lad* here, although my advice, my final advice to you, is to forget Cathlin and write *Dzhordzha Boy*. Or,

if you do it in English, call it *Georgia Boy*. No, wait, Erskine Caldwell
wrote a novel of that title. But hell, there's no copyright on titles. What's
so funny? Why are you laughing?"

"Forgive. I was just thinking, or remembering: Bolshakov was always
accusing me of 'embellishment.' He had an obsession with 'real life.' Do
you think he would ever believe what you, and Anangka, and . . . the
spirit of Dan Montross have done with me?"

I. said, "But now you're going to do for yourself. I'm not going to
write about you, or about *this*." His hand swept the glade of the cedars,
the tombstone, the magic place on the mountainside. "Let me correct
myself. I said a moment ago that tonight's the last time we'll ride and
tie. Yes, I may never see you again, but I hope . . . and I think possibly
Dan Montross would also hope . . . that you'll like Stick Around enough
to maybe write some books someday about it, about him, or maybe even
about the Indians who once lived here. I can't anymore. These people
won't let me write about them. I've already used them in stories, and
once I do that they demand the right to be left alone. But you . . . you
could ride and tie my country with me, picking up where I left off and
creating your own characters, as you created Cathlin. It's your turn now.
Stick around. Ride and tie."

Dusk was fallen. The long day was over. My bag of tricks was empty,
but I had you here . . . almost. You needed time to think about it, but
both I. and I were confident you'd stay, because, you see, you had
absolutely nowhere else to go.

Riding down to the yellow house in I.'s Blazer, going off to meet
his friends, who would become your friends too, you informed him, "I
love the little serendipities of life, but this coincidence I like best: in
Svanetian, *Lisedi,* the name of the town I came from, means 'to remain,
to stay more, to stick around.'"

PART TWO

LOUDER, engram!

(from the Memoir, chapters 17–25 only)

BEFORE DEATH TAKES ME TO HER BREAST, I'll show you the Indian shelters and their little burial mounds in this glen of the waterfall. People lived here once. I was an Indian once, and so were you; our people lived here. We might live here again.

—Daniel Lyam Montross,
A Dream of a Small but Unlost Town

17

I

BUT HE ACTUALLY DID LEAVE, early the next afternoon, and I would not see him again for two years. His friends in Stick Around were disappointed that he'd blow in like that, deposit me like excess baggage or castoff ballast, and take off again, without even, I was soon to learn, troubling himself to say hello to some of those who had loved and missed him most. Ingraham, as I think I've shown conclusively in the previous chapter, was a man with many problems, some of them beyond hope. I did not wish to become another of his problems, and thus I might almost be forgiven for allowing myself to believe, eventually, that his function in the story of my life had been simply that of a temporary assistant to beloved Anangka, who'd had her gentle hands full supervising my destiny . . . although, as we shall see, it was not Anangka but a male arranger to whom Ingraham was in thrall.

The next several months that I spent in Stick Around were among the most idyllic of my life, despite, or because of, the total contrast to Pittsburgh, where I had at least been gainfully employed and faced with the unremitting difficulties of learning the language and coming to grips with my deracination and festering homesickness, not to mention vastly diverted by that ardent sport with young Kenneth Elmore, the memory of which was going to have to suffice me for a while, because I had given Ingraham my solemn oath to refrain from seducing Daniel I. Stoving-Whittacker, the son of my host and hostess. Danny Boy, as they

called him, had just reached his tenth birthday, and while he was precocious in ways that would surprise me (my solemn oath did not prevent
me from spying upon him in various stages of nudity and observing his
semierections), he would not be ready for his first sexual encounter until
such time as I had quitted for good the room where I slept and wrote
Georgie Boy, the room that had been the bedroom of Danny's grandfather
(I hesitate to complicate matters by revealing that he was *also* Danny's
great-grandfather as well as his father), the late poet Daniel Lyam Montross, the same complex, inscrutable figure—half hillbilly, half mystic—
whose tangled life and small body of work would soon attract to Stick
Around in search of answers the critic Lawrence Brace, who incidentally
was the lover of my good friend Sharon Ingledew . . . But I am plunging
ahead of my story, as I have already done frequently and inexcusably—
or with the excuse that there are so many warps for my woof to cross
that my shuttle jumps ahead of me.

Too many people in a story diminish the reader's trust in any one
of them, as Ingraham tried to teach us in that class in Pittsburgh. Thus,
I must give Diana Stoving and Day Whittacker a slighting scrutiny less
than equal to their actual substance to me. But knowing them, as I came
to do, I think they would like it this way; they were very private people,
utterly devoted to each other and to their son, keeping to themselves
and to the world of nature that surrounded them and loved them,
cultivating their own little gardens in the best Voltairean sense, knowing
home and staying at it. I will offer no details of their sex life, although,
sleeping as I did in the next room for many months, I was privy to it
in all its variety, frequency, and music. I will not even essay to describe
them, beyond pointing out that both were beautiful and she was perhaps
three or four years older than he. I am not even going to describe their
son, beyond saying he was (and is) the loveliest male I've ever seen.

Surely Day and Diana were not totally comfortable suddenly having
a stranger as their interminable houseguest; surely their rich, cultivated
sense of privacy was taxed, if not abused; surely they had some discussions
between themselves about the best way to get rid of me. But they never
once expressed any displeasure toward me, nor committed any lapse of

complete hospitality. What could I offer them in return? Money was a subject never discussed; I had none and would soon have to think of some way to meet my minimal obligations. But the third day I was there, Anangka (or Whoever) came up with a way I could make a token gesture of repaying their hospitality with what little talent I possessed.

The murmuring engrams of that afternoon remain audible in my mind even from this distance of eleven years. Day and Diana happened to remark, over lunch, upon the dearth of morels encountered that season. Themselves good amateur mycologists who could easily tell an edible bolete from a deadly amanita, they lamented that their favorite annual spot for picking the *Morchella esculenta,* a once-burned-over stand of woods up the hill, had apparently not produced any of the succulent fungi this springtime and that now it was too late for them. Yes, I said, throwing in my tiny two pennies' worth of expertise, the season for morels lasts scarcely two or three weeks. They looked at me. "Do they have morels in Svanetia?" Diana asked. Apparently their friend Ingraham had entirely neglected to tell them that I was, by training and profession, a mushroomologist of no small merit, and I was not about to boast of my credentials. But I offered to find them some morels. It was relatively easy. Day and Diana had been correct in assuming that the most favorable habitat for morels is a burned-over substratum of woodland (because the fire tends to kill competing myceliae), but I knew that there were other conditions of the substrata (type and density of leaf rot, moisture, pitch of slope, etc., etc.) conducive to footholds for *Morchellae,* and I conducted Day and Diana, with inquisitive, sponge-brained woods-creature Danny in tow (even then he already matched Kenny's eagerness to learn Svanetian, at least for *tqubul,* "the mushroom"), on a tour of their upper acres, where, in what was once an apple orchard, long abandoned and overgrown and carpeted with a dense leaf fall from third-growth timber, we began a search that was soon fruitful, despite the pessimism in their not having brought any containers to hold the almost full peck of the spongy delicacies I found.

"But how did you *find* them?" Day wanted to know. "I just searched this spot yesterday, carefully."

"Both ways?" I asked, trying not to sound at all smug. "The best way to find something, morels or other, is to re-search the same spot from an entirely different direction."

And thus they had from me, not simply enough morels to grace our table for the next week or so, but also a handy tip that will do for life's quests as well as for mushroom hunting. I could not resist further pointing out, to my rapt audience, that morels are of the class Ascomycete, not the Basidiomycete class, to which most other mushrooms belong, and that I subscribe to that theory of mycology which holds that Basidiomycetes evolved from the Ascomycetes; thus our porous morel was a primitive creature who had not learned how to cap or striate its spore sacs, or to manufacture protective poison, or to diminish its delectable taste. In other words, like certain people it was still innocent, naïve, vulnerable, and exquisite.

On the way home, and often in answer to Danny's eager discoveries-and-questions, we paused to talk about many other mushrooms, and thus by the time we reached the house I had to confess, in response to Day's "How do you *know* all this stuff?" that I was not simply an *amateur* mycologist. "But Ingraham told us you were just another novelist," Day said, and the way he put it was not without some disparagement, as if the world were full of novelists . . . with their feet sticking out the windows, to use a charming Bodarks expression of overcrowding.

They understood, my hosts, why I preferred to spend so much time alone in my room: I was indeed attempting to write a novel. My dormer window faced the dirt road (on which there was scarcely any traffic) and a splendid vista of Ingledew Mountain that couldn't rival but could impersonate to the desperately homelorn the bulk of Mount Layla (2,300 feet versus 13,000 feet). The walls of the room, all four white plaster walls, plus the extra surfaces within the dormered gable, had been covered thirty years before with the penciled script of the poet, as a kind of open journal, a mural of erect tablets, containing his soliloquies (for I understood from his daughter, Diana, that except for a space of a week when she at the age of three lived there with him, he was entirely alone, virtually a hermit): MONTROSS, HIS BECOMINGS; MONTROSS, HIS LEAVINGS; MONTROSS, HIS NAMINGS; MONTROSS, HIS HUMMINGS; MONTROSS, HIS

BLESSINGS; MONTROSS, HIS DAMNINGS; etc. Only two of these latter formed
engrams in my mind. If I hadn't been so preoccupied with the novel, I
would have transcribed many of Montross's words into my own journal,
but I didn't, and all I could recall were Damnings Numbers Two and
Six: *Wretched are they who work for wages; for the one is never equal to the
other;* and *Wretched are they who think themselves only male or only female, for
the one is not equal to the other.* I had cause to remember the first because
it would be a while before I could find any wages to earn, and the second
because it helped open up one of Bolshakov's *matryoshka* dolls that had
been resisting my probes, and it prepared me for that gender switch, or
gender disguise, that eventually made me famous to millions.

It was almost as if Montross's ghost were in that room with me.
Not literally: If his ghost did indeed exist, and did indeed "haunt" his
former house, he was careful never to let himself be manifest to its
inhabitants, even though, on occasion, I challenged him, talking to those
walls, flirting with them, even teasing them. I have had experience, as
I showed in Chapter Five, with summoning a *lanchal* back from its limbo
and getting it (he or she) to prove its existence by some slight sign:
action, utterance, or appearance. But nothing I tried on Dan would raise
so much as a chirp or vapor out of him. I knew he was there but was
keeping himself silent and invisible . . . Or, no, he was waiting patiently
for me to understand, as I finally did, the important truth that his essential
spiritual manifestation was in the *Word:* Words themselves are all the
ghosts we need. And there were plenty of these in that room . . .
including those that, day by day, I amassed for *Georgie Boy.*

II

ONE OF THE QUESTIONS most commonly asked of me by reporters,
especially those interviewing me for the more literate and literary media,
is, "What books did you read those years at Stick Around?" Usually I
reply, after first correcting the tenure (it wasn't years but months), that
one of the several books I read was *One Hundred Years of Solitude.* Diana
owned a copy, along with a number of American novels by Updike,

Barth, Cheever, Toni Morrison, Lee Smith, and of course, Ingraham. I was never without something to read, and Diana also had, in addition to *Lolita* and *Pale Fire,* the other fourteen novels by that Russo-American master whose life, or life style, I have been accused of emulating, and in all candor I did read most of these in Stick Around; but the one novel that remains most strongly encoded in my engrams is the masterpiece not of Nabokov but of García Márquez. *Newsweek*'s interviewer asked me, bluntly, "Did Stick Around remind you of Macondo?" and I told her I've never been to Macondo. But I was being coy. Yes, I suppose one could enumerate countless similarities between the Colombian ghost town and its American counterpart, and one should be careful to mention the essential difference: that Macondo disappeared into "a fearful whirlwind of dust and rubble," while Stick Around yet manages to survive, and always shall, as if heeding the pathetic injunction of its own name. The total population, when I was there, was not more than two dozen, and this was all outside the "town limits," whatever those limits were. The village itself was not populated, although my friend Sharon would eventually move into the old post office/general store/house that had once belonged to her grandmother, and shortly thereafter her erstwhile lover, Lawrence Brace, would come to occupy (and nearly destroy) the old hotel for less than a year. I was told that early in this century there were over five hundred people in Stick Around.

The only truly permanent resident (and I trust I'm using *permanent* advisedly) was Sharon's grandmother, an extraordinary woman, then approaching eighty years of age, although ageless surely, whom I shall have to call, out of deference to Ingraham, "Lara Burns." If Stick Around has the equivalent of Macondo's Pilar Ternera, it is she, but again with essential differences: Lara was never a prostitute, despite rumors to that effect, and Lara will probably outlive Pilar, who outlived the most longevous old ladies of my Caucasus, where it is not uncommon to find a Svanetian dowager of 120 years. Lara was still youthful when I knew her, or at least I, fifty-odd years her junior, couldn't keep up with her in mental or physical activity.

Ingraham had pointed out to me her house (actually a two-pen log cabin), but I did not even trouble myself to wonder, then, why he would not stop to say howdy to her. I first became really aware of her when I told Danny one of my very favorite Svan tales of *lanchali* and he commented, "Gran Dahl already told me that one." I thought he said "Grand Doll," and my confusion was to continue through his several repetitions of it: "Grand Doll loves to fish," "You should see some of Grand Doll's cats," and "No, but I bet Grand Doll can."

Finally I asked Diana who was this Grand Doll, and she explained: the widow of "Everett Dahl" (as Ingraham has shaded him), Lara Burns Dahl, the town's last postmistress and, now, the town's oldest native-born resident. And then Diana repeated Ingraham's words almost exactly: "She can tell you enough stories to keep you writing for years." How could I meet her? Diana gave me a look as if it had been a silly question, then said, "Just go up and bang on her door, if she's not already outside, as she usually is."

In *Original Flavor,* my most recent novel, I did indeed incorporate several of the stories I first heard from Lara Burns, and I used a number of others in my one venture into so-called "nonfiction," *Dawn of the Osage,* which sold well for such a work, although it was not translated into very many foreign languages. During my months in Stick Around, I probably spent more time in her company than with anyone else, not excluding Diana and Day and Danny. She was the only person I've ever given permission to address me familiarly from the beginning: When she asked me to call her simply Lara, I said she could call me simply Kat, and she said, "Sure thing, but I've got a plenty of those already," and indicated her yard, where a variety of felines were lolling and sporting, and declared with a wink, "A cat arena." Whenever I sat with her, one of her cats would jump into my lap, and at first she'd try to shoo it away, but I protested that I was very fond of cats, and she said, "They know it, too."

Of all the many things that Lara and I had in common, this is the most noteworthy: She, too, in her early twenties, spent three years in a psychiatric hospital, specifically the state asylum for the insane. Unlike me, she was not confined for political motives, and I will not pretend that our incarcerations were identical, beyond the fact that neither of us was certifiably mad: She was diagnosed as having "aphasic catalepsy" (whereas in truth she was simply so angry at those who were trying to steal her baby that she would not speak to anyone), and I was diagnosed by Bolshakov, as we have seen, as having "creeping schizophrenia," the Serbsky's convenient catch-all category for nonconformists. But both Lara and I had spent three years exposed to genuinely sick minds, among the doctors as well as the patients, and we could spend many an hour swapping memories of the dazzling flights of the truly possessed. More, even, than our repertoire of ghost stories, wherein we were constantly delighted to discover the kinship of the Bodarkian spook and the Svanetian *lanchal,* these tales of bughouse behavior cemented a bond between us. There are, come to think of it, many affinities between the *lanchal* and the lunatic: both have left this sorry world behind. Neither Lara nor I entertained Danny with tales of loonies, but we practically competed with each other in telling him ghost stories. It is a wonder we didn't give him bad dreams, but if we did, he kept them to himself. The highest accolade I ever earned as a storyteller, more meaningful to me really than all the praise the reviewers have heaped upon my work this past decade, was when Danny told me that I could tell better stories than Grand Doll could . . . and he meant not that the content of the stories was any better (or even any different, considering the enormous resemblances between Bodarkadia and Svanetia) but that my way of telling was perhaps more deft than hers.

We swapped, Lara and I, not only our full and frightening repertoire of specter yarns, but also the similarities (and the essential differences) between Svanetian and Bodarkadian customs and superstitions, e.g., there is a Svanetian equivalent of the Bodarkadian *shivaree* for newlyweds, in which much noise is made and the bridegroom has to "ransom" himself by furnishing the revelers with much food and drink. There are also in Svanetia many little habits designed to help someone who has lost something find it, such as Lara's superstition of bending down the stalk of a mullein plant. I recall the evening, after a very warm day in late May, when Lara and I were sitting in her breezeway (*dogtrot* was the local name for such, but only cats trotted—or minced—in hers), and we saw the season's first firefly hovering over A Cat Arena, the first firefly I had seen since summers agone in my homeland. Soon there were so many of them that I was transported back to the verandahs of Lisedi and lost, for a long moment, in the legendary Svanetia of my girlhood.

"I'm sorry," Lara interrupted my reverie. "For a while there you got to talking in your own language, and I couldn't follow you. Is that how they say 'lightning bug' where you come from?"

Yes, and there was something else, how in Svanetia we worship trees (as I've made a motif in *Lamshged; or, The Shady Side of the Mountain*): Trees, no less than people, are thought to possess souls and to survive after death. Trees feel and suffer and communicate with one another. Lara herself could understand all this, not because the Bodarkadians had ever worshiped trees or even respected them, but because she herself knew that trees have souls if not minds and are capable, in their own way, of speaking, even singing. One night, when the breeze died down and everything was still, except the slow drift and twinkle of the fireflies, she said, "Listen. Can you hear that?" And I strained my ears, which, long-removed from the cacophonies of Pittsburgh, had regained their discrimination, and indeed I thought I heard a sound, almost as of a distant wordless hymn or chant. Trees, Lara said.

"Or maybe," I offered, "the spirits of old trees long gone." And then I asked her a question that strikes me in retrospect as pretty stupid. "Did you ever know Daniel Lyam Montross?"

"Of course," she said, but she said nothing more, then, by way of elaboration.

III

ETYMOLOGICALLY, *BODARK* derives from the French *bois d'arc*, "archer's wood" or "wood for bows," the name given to that common tree, *Maclura pomifera*, used so exclusively by my Osage Indians for their bows that it became known as Osage Orange (the fruit resembles an oversized orange, but greenish). Other bynames for the tree are mock orange, ironwood, yellowwood, hedge, and bowwood, and other place-name derivatives around this vicinity are the lake, creek, and wildlife refuge named Bois d'Arc; the village Bozark, or Bozarth; the town Bodark; and this whole range of mountains. Lovers of fated links, or "happenchances," as Stickarounders call them, happy serendipities, will appreciate this connection between the basic root, *arc* or *ark,* as "a place of shelter or refuge," and my *Svan,* which means, yes, "a place of shelter or refuge." The latter was deliberate, given anciently to that inaccessible region where people could cut themselves off from the rest of the world (but not, alas, from each other), while the former is just accidental, a true happenchance. Since I thought I could never go home again, it was good for me to discover that I was in a place of refuge in America.

Falling into a steady routine of work on *Georgie Boy,* leaping out of bed at the first proud crow of the *qwich* (who I was charmed to learn was called *rooster*), walking a couple of miles in the morning-fragrant, sunrise-fresh woods while waiting to help Diana make the breakfast of coffee, biscuits, bacon, eggs, and that quaint corn-derivative called grits, then returning after it was eaten to my (or Dan's) room, where I'd sit at my (his) little desk and first warm up the brain traces by browsing through one of the three volumes that had constituted Dan's entire library: a Webster's unabridged, an anthology of Elizabethan poetry, and a King James version of the Bible—Diana told me that Dan had "read" the dictionary as one would watch a movie, following a dramatic plot, and I sometimes attempted to do that myself, with limited success. Then I would pause, before letting myself be carried off to Moscow or Ishimbay, and reflect upon the security and peacefulness of my mountain hideaway, in such contrast both to Pittsburgh and to the settings of my novel.

One reason I think I was able to depict and characterize V. T. Bolshakov as "the most nefarious villain to appear in fiction since Faulkner's Popeye," as the *Atlantic's* reviewer called him, was that I felt so safe from him. Much as I gave him credit for mobility, cleverness, subterfuge, and strategy, I did not believe there was any way he could find me in Stick Around. Bolshakov in the Bodarks? Inconceivable. Thus I felt absolutely free to malign him with a loaded brush, to slap the pigments of his delineation onto the canvas with vengeance and honest scorn, as if belatedly completing the insults that had freed me from him. The miserable son of a bitch.

Nights, I lay awake for only moments in Dan's bed, listening to the serenade of night-courting insects and reptiles, before falling into a deep, snug, safe sleep, during which my unremembered dreams sorted out, classified, rearranged, and coded all the intricacies of the next day's verbal art, and even my familiar dreams of climbing and descending an endless sequence of stone steps, concrete steps, iron steps, and wooden steps seemed to have a new symbolic significance to the work I was doing.

As I said in my interview for *Paris Review,* I consider myself not a novelist but an idyllist, even though the one work that first brought me to the world's attention was not an idyll so much as a buskin, stamped with the thick-soled cothurnus imprints of the Soviet regime. If I'm granted half the chance, I'll write an idyll about Stick Around, not in competition with Ingraham, whose territory it is, but in tribute to the pastoral life I was allowed there. But the difficulty is, it would have no plot, no story, no conflict, no tension. Nothing happened to me in Stick Around . . . except that I finished a novel.

One thing I'd explore in my idyll, which I can only mention here, is the lone stint of labor I performed to earn a modicum of wages, as if Anangka had taken over my accounts and knew when I was penniless and would need some money just to buy the essential necessities: writing paper, cigarettes, toiletries, vodka. In early June the hay harvest started and was threatened by rains (as it turned out, the last rains for months) and every available "hand" up and down the valley of the Little Buffalo River was recruited to help, and I abandoned my novel for five days of hard work that left me sunburned, scratched, blistered, sore, and exhausted, but remunerated sufficiently by the farmers who owned the fields to buy my needs for the rest of the summer. In Lisedi (where of course there were no landowners but only managers of the *kolkhoz,* or collective) I had always been a spectator at the annual haying and knew the difference between *chem* and *neni,* the kinds of hay, and *meri,* the second mowing of hay. (There was to be no *meri,* or merry, in Stick Around because of the awful drought that year.) This was the first time I had actually helped at a haying, and it was sufficient to implant my engrams permanently with the smell of the new-mown hay, the feel of the lashings and stabbings of the stalks and strands, the straining of never-used muscles in my back, and the intensification of pleasure that the hard work gave to a simple pause for a glass of iced tea, or, at the end of the day, a "skinny-dip" in the creek.

Mention of this engrammatizes the picture of some of my coworkers and my first awareness that outside of Stick Around, in the hills and hollers that had once belonged to Anglo-Saxon and Scotch-Irish peasants, and before them to the Osage Indians, there now existed no small number of dropouts from society, people who, ten or fifteen years earlier, had been called flower children or hippies, and now were as outmoded as those labels but still carried flowers, or wore them, along with headbands, Indian-print fabrics, quilted things, and lots of beads. Day and Diana knew most of these people but had had their own brief fling, eleven years before, with the so-called counterculture in some other place, and now were resolved to share nothing in common with them except their devotion to back-to-the-land subsistence agriculture. Ironically, the only people I'd known in Georgia like these latter-day hippies were the bands of brightly dressed Gypsies, who had no interest in the land at all.

When, at the end of the first day's haying, after sundown, everybody headed down to the creek and eagerly divested themselves of clothing, and the girls too, wearing no brassieres, stepped out of their beaded moccasins as well as their bedspread dresses or embroidered jeans and plunged naked into the cool stream, I was obliged to join them. All of these girls—I should call them women because most of them had passed the age beyond which they had been advised never to trust anyone—had long hair, and I felt more self-conscious about my short hair (although it was long enough now that no one would know it had last been cut by a prison razor) than I did about my nakedness. On the riverbank there was also much lighting up and passing around of "joints," and if one passed up one's turn to pinch and pucker the smoldering roach, one was considered uncool, unhip, or at least unsociable. There were a few men, three or four, who made nuisances of themselves to me, attempting to "start something."

The cultivation of marijuana was indirectly responsible for the one serious disharmony in the idyll of Stick Around: At least once a week, a helicopter would patrol the valley, officers of the law searching for illegal plots where the narcotic weed was grown, and the sight of this airship, not to mention the awful noise of it, ruined the day for me. My hosts grew none of the stuff themselves, nor used it, but for some reason the lawmen in the air seemed to think their property was an ideal location for shady raising, and they swept our airspace redundantly.

The helicopters disturbed the peace of the livestock more than that of the people, who at least understood the intentions of the disturbers. Day and Diana owned a number of goats, several pigs, a milk cow, and countless free-ranging chickens (in the course of my stay I taught Diana my best recipes for preparing chicken in the Svanetian manner), and a few minutes' surveillance by the helicopter would leave these animals neurotic for several days.

Lara Burns, if she and her animals, including those in A Cat Arena, were exposed to the flight of the raucous whirlybird, would stand and defiantly raise a fist, at the top of which stood her middle finger. If I was with her, I'd join her in this gesture, and I did so on several occasions before she finally explained to me its origin and significance. That recent photograph of me in *Time,* lifting my hand and finger to make this sign, was inadvertent; the photographer was one of those paparrazzi who had virtually camped out at the Halfmoon in order to shoot me.

"I learned that signal, by the way," Lara Burns told me, "from Dan Montross."

IV

FROM JUNE 8 UNTIL September 23 of that year, according to my journal, it did not rain a single drop in Stick Around. This, even more than the craggy heights of its snowcapped peaks, set Svanetia apart from Bodar-kadia, because I had never in my life there known a drought; indeed, the annual rainfall in Svanetia is not only dependable and predictable but awesome. The event called by old-timers in Stick Around "a toad-strangling downpour" was a common summer day's occurrence in Lisedi. That summer, I had not yet read any of Ingraham's books, and I did not realize that severe droughts recur every dozen years or so. Along about the middle of July, when Ingraham's tomatoes, which I had transplanted and staked into a corner of Diana's garden and had been weeding and watering whenever I volunteered this effort for the rest of the vegetables, began to wither and droop, I was told by my hosts to cease using the fresh water that came from the well and begin using, if any water at all, "scrap" water from our baths and clothes washings (we had been required to give up showers and take only tub baths in a few gallons of water). Ingraham's tomato plants managed to bear a few misshapen fruit not living up to their varietal name, Big Girl, and I abandoned the notion I'd been tinkering with, to find his address in Rolla, Missouri, and mail him a few of the mature "love apples." We ate them. Diana's own tomatoes were not plentiful enough for her usual canning and freezing, and then in August the tomato vines languished and wizened beyond hope. For three months we had been eating marvelously, we three cooks (Day was himself no mean chef) vying with each other in succession, and using an abundant supply of homegrown vegetables, fruit, and meat, but from August onward there was a noticeable falling off in the fare. I had just had time to discover that treat, corn on the cob, when the corn gave out, much to the distress of our local distiller-by-the-light-of-the-moon, a young man I shall have to call "Jack Chisholm" because his operation, which I understand is still flourishing in nondrought years, is just as illegal as the cultivation of marijuana. I considered his product at least superior to the County Fair I once kept to serve to Knox Ogden, and it would do in a pinch when my vodka ran out and no one was going to the nearest liquor store, which was many miles away in the next county.

I could write an idyll about Jack Chisholm, who was, for his youth, one of the very last of the real Bodarkadians and lived "'way back around up in there" in some remote aerie. But I have taxed my reader's patience with these notes about Stick Around when it is another town, Arcata Springs, that serves as a far more important setting in my life. Let us head that way, with a backward glance that regrets all that has been omitted from this chapter. I see I have made no mention whatsoever of that grandson of Lara's, my friend Sharon's "kid" brother, who is currently attracting much attention because of his campaign for governor.

Over the years, I have made three promises to Ingraham: one, to keep my hands off Danny, I've already affirmed; another was that I'd leave Vernon as Ingraham's "property" for some future novel.

But I don't like giving the impression that I didn't even know Vernon those months in Stick Around; we played many a game of chess together, and he beat me on occasion. He told me several stories about his ancestor Jacob Ingledew, who foreshadowed him as governor. And it was Vernon whose knowledge of the Osage Indians' long tenure of that valley not only helped me to identify some of the projectile points I found while searching (both ways) for mushrooms but also prepared me for that one great sally into truthful prose, *Dawn of the Osage.* I don't think it will hurt his candidacy for governor if I confess, in this memoir, that of all the grown men I have known I found Vernon Ingledew the most attractive.

His wife, or mistress (does it matter?), Jelena, I did not come to know as well as I would have liked, although, in this world where everybody had an announced "best friend," she called her best friend my hostess, Diana Stoving, who reciprocated by announcing that Jelena was her best friend. But another woman living in a geodesic dome near Stick Around also claimed Jelena as best friend, although it was not reciprocated at all, and this other woman, whom I shall have to camouflage as "Lillian Sparrow" because a lawsuit is still pending, was one of those full-fledged (with many feathered garments), outworn hippies, whose very talk was still sprinkled with archaic cant—*groovy, dig,* and *outasight*—and who had waist-length hair and a hat that made our Cathlin McWalter's seem a pillbox, and who supposedly held ice cubes to her nipples to make them protrude beneath the gauzy cotton of her ankle-length dress. She happened to have a son, sired in a one-night group grope thirteen years before by one of those rock-stoned smackhead electrical guitarists, a boy who had been afflicted with a name of stunning synthetic cuteness that I regret I must transform here into "Ashram Tarot Atman." I saw Ash, briefly, from a distance, not more than twice—once when his mother came to visit Diana and brought the boy to play with Danny, who to his credit did not like the kid but felt sorry for him. Watching them from my upstairs window as they attempted some tagging game in the yard, I studied the kid only long enough to determine that he held no attraction whatsoever for me.

Ash is now twenty-three years old and is sitting on death row in the state penitentiary for having shot a convenience-store clerk. Lillian, his mother, has told anyone who will listen (and many tabloids and even respectable newspapers have listened) that on that afternoon while she visited Diana I took her son on a mushroom hunt (but the woods were parched and the only things growing were chiggers, ticks, and copperhead snakes) and instead of uncovering mushrooms I uncovered his penis, which I subjected to such a variety of tactile, lingual, and venereal manipulations that the boy became almost instantly corrupt, spoiled, and delinquent.

That kind of falsehood, which would have confirmed Bolshakov in his convictions that we none of us can tell the truth, was going to be just part of the price I'd have to pay for becoming famous.

18

I

IF PEOPLE ARE PERMITTED in this world to have a "best friend," then Sharon Ingledew Brace is mine. As I've shown, my girlhood in Svanetia was singularly without playmates of the same sex; in college at Tbilisi there was that roommate I despised, and later, at Leningrad, those other roommates I tolerated but did not like; and the inmate at Ishimbay whom I have called Evgeniya was a wonderful companion who probably helped me preserve my sanity after those terrible episodes of SHIZO, *shtrafnoy izolyator,* solitary confinement. But Evgeniya was a sister, perhaps, or even a partner, not a "best friend."

To be your best friend, the other woman must not only observe the golden rule but live it without being aware of it: doing, acting, thinking, and speaking toward you as if you were herself, keeping nothing from you, wanting you to keep nothing from her . . . and being totally comfortable, natural, and unforced in this ingenuousness.

Sharon was the fifth daughter of John Henry Ingledew and Sonora Dahl, Lara's only child. Sharon's father, like so many fathers, had wanted a son desperately and had kept trying, and when Sharon was born he was not only ready to give up trying but also ready to make Sharon's childhood miserable for her having failed him. She was known as Little Sis, which everyone called her in preference to Sharon. She felt not only estranged from her father but unwelcome to her four older sisters, who also considered her unnecessary or superfluous.

The major difference between my girlhood and Sharon's was that I had no playmates of the same sex; Sharon was surrounded by them but they would not play with her. Which of us, therefore, was the more deprived?

She understandably had some bad experiences with men, trying to find one who would give her the love her father never gave. At the age of sixteen she eloped with a Stick Around man, Junior Stapleton, twelve years her senior, who was one of those chronic losers so intimidated by the rest of the world that they have to take out their frustrations on their wives, and who regularly slapped, punched, and mauled Sharon. She related to me, with a wry smile, that the only time her father ever showed her any attention was the one occasion when he accosted Junior, after her husband had broken one of her arms and left her jaw needing to be wired, and "beat the living shit" out of him, leaving Junior in the hospital, from which he never returned to Stick Around.

Sardonically, Sharon Ingledew Stapleton kept her married name and monogram, SIS, for several years after the marriage had been dissolved and she had left Stick Around and gone to Chicago to see if a big city might have a few good men in it. She worked as a waitress to put herself through the nursing school of Northwestern University, and she took a degree in nursing and worked for a few years in a hospital. She met a great variety of men among the restaurant customers, medical students, doctors, and patients, and she went to bed with anyone who asked her, including a few of her patients, which cost her the job in the hospital; she did not reapply at another hospital.

But one of those patients whose bed she entered was a young professor from the University of Chicago, Lawrence Brace, recuperating from a simple operation on one of his knees, which had been damaged in a game of touch football. He was not able to move his leg or the lower part of his body, and he told Sharon after she made love to him that nobody had ever made love to him like that before, in that superior position, and some weeks later, after he had abandoned his crutches and was mobile again, he returned to the hospital to find her and ask her for a date but discovered she had been fired. He spent months searching Chicago for her, and of course Chicago is a big place. Perhaps she had her own Anangka, or he his, because he happened one day to take his stereo turntable to be repaired at a shop where she was working in sales. He invited her to move in with him.

Sharon and Larry lived together almost two years. He was an assistant professor in English at the university, and, like some English professors I have known, he drank too much. He excused his immoderate consumption on the grounds that some of the greatest poets (he was a specialist in modern poetry) had been boozers. But when he drank too much, he did not listen very carefully to anything Sharon had to say, and in time she discovered that she was talking to herself. She cultivated the ability to have conversations, aloud, with herself. She became such a stimulating and witty self-conversationalist that Larry, sober enough on one occasion to eavesdrop, became jealous. He listened long enough, and carefully enough, to determine that she found herself a more entertaining talker as well as listener than he, and he wrote to her a long and sarcastic poem (this was in the days when he had not yet abandoned the creation of poetry for the criticism of it and was publishing a few poems himself) in which he so much as accused her of being in love with herself. It was a difficult poem, and she was never certain she understood its allusions, but she got its message. Writing him a short, angry note in response, she stole his car, intending to drive it home to Stick Around. En route, her Anangka arranged for the car, a decrepit Ford Fairlane, to break down in Arcata Springs, where a day later her Anangka arranged a pileup of two trucks, three cars, and a passenger bus on a treacherous curve of scenic U.S. 62 to overtax the employees of the Arcata Springs hospital, who gave Sharon a temporary job that became more permanent, at least until she found herself once again unable to resist the invitations of male patients to climb into their beds.

When I first met her, Sharon had been living in Arcaty (as she and they, and now I, call it) for four years, working at a number of different jobs after being fired from the hospital, most recently as the desk clerk at the Halfmoon Hotel. As often as she could, she "went up home" to Stick Around, ostensibly to visit her grandmother, her brother, and the one sister who still lived there, but actually to talk to herself about her childhood in relation to certain scenes of memory in the village, certain buildings that had special significance for her, or certain trees and turnings of the creek and secret glades. She had long since returned the Ford Fairlane to Larry in Chicago, parted amiably and civilly from him, and obtained for herself a used Chevrolet Camaro for the trips "up home," although the rugged roads south of Acropolis were terrible for that sporty vehicle.

She called the Camaro Camilla and personified it, and she talked to it almost as she did to herself. Cam was her best friend until Kat came along. Often, when she unexpectedly pulled into her grandmother's A Cat Arena, she would find Lara and me sitting together in the breezeway, and she would join us, occasionally in time to hear our most recently remembered ghost story. Once, a Saturday morning in October on one of those hikes of hers to a favorite glade on a hillside, she encountered me searching for mushrooms in the aftermath of the rain that had broken the drought. We exchanged greetings, made comments on the end of the drought, and then Sharon said, "How's the book coming?" Day and Diana, for the most part, had never betrayed any great curiosity over the novel I was writing, but on a couple of occasions Diana had asked, politely, "How's the book going?" Now, before answering Sharon, I meditated on the difference between *coming* and *going*. (In Russian, *idyot* can sometimes mean either, or both.) I am sure that Sharon did not intend any connotation different from that of Diana, but I have been struck with the way English uses *come* for the orgasm as well as for the male by-product of same, and Lara Burns had explained to me how *come* is what happens to milk in a churn when it turns into butter (Lara makes her own butter come). Pondering Sharon's question, I saw my months of labor on *Georgie Boy* as like the hard manual plunging of the churn dasher in cream, about to make it come but not yet turning the cream into butter. So I answered Sharon, "I'm poking the churn stick as fast as I can, but she aint come yet." I think I may even have captured some of Lara's intonations. Then I waited to see if Sharon would get it.

Sharon smiled. "Don't ye know," she said, doing a good imitation of her grandmother too, "that it aint the hurry that does it?" She made a fist of her hand and began jerking it up and down; it might almost have been wrapped around an imaginary male member. "It aint the hurry but the regularity."

That was when I decided, for the first time, to ask Sharon's advice. I had never asked anyone, not even Ingraham, for suggestions on how to create the "realities" of my story. Now I needed suggestions, from a fellow female, on how best to construct the climax of the story, wherein the bogeyman, Bolshakov, is demolished. The basic question I put to Sharon—What would she do if she really wanted to humiliate a man?—intrigued her so much that she could not answer it right then, but promised me she'd think a lot about it and tell me the next time she came to Stick Around. "Better yet," she said, "why don't you come to Arcaty and visit? You like the place, don't you?"

Oh, I liked it! And I had been feeling shut off from the world, all those months in Stick Around. Day and Diana did not own a television set (they claimed the reception was too poor, but Lara's son-in-law, Sharon's father, John Henry Ingledew, supposedly was capable of erecting antennae good enough for clear pictures), and the infrequent occasions we made a shopping trip to the county seat, "Jessup," or to the larger and better markets at "Harriman," the only real city in that part of the Bodarks, were not sufficient to provide me with a sense of the comforts of civilization such as I had known in Tbilisi, Leningrad, and Pittsburgh. I know it will come as a shock to those readers who have pictured me as a rural, nature-loving ascetic (the *Washington Post*'s critic recently called me, after my true sex was at last revealed, "Russia's answer to Annie Dillard" . . . and of course I am not from Russia) if I reveal that I prefer towns to the countryside, that I am suffocated by a constant exposure to nature, that the woods sometimes (even without their chiggers, ticks, and copperhead snakes) frighten me or at least make me uncomfortable. Given the choice, as Anangka (and the book-buying public) has given me, I'd prefer to dwell neither in a city like Pittsburgh nor in a village like Stick Around but in a town of modest size, of about three or four thousand people, with all of the amenities of restaurants, shops, interesting architecture, a weekly newspaper, a hospital, a drugstore, a movie theater, a courthouse, a bath house, many steep sidewalks for hiking, a colorful history (and a record of it in a historical museum), and of course a first-rate hotel. In short, Arcata Springs. By early November, I had the stunning conclusion to *Georgie Boy* and a place to live for the winter, both courtesy of my friend Sharon.

II

IT DOES NOT TROUBLE ME to confess that Sharon gets the credit for the ultimate comeuppance to Bolshakov in *Georgie Boy*. The beauty of it is that her solution for an ideal retaliation against the man for all those years he'd abused me mentally was not very far removed from what had actually happened. But it was far enough removed to provide that little transmutation that turns life into art, "reality" into fiction, or, as Ingraham taught us, penises into neckties, and it keeps *Georgie Boy,* as the better critics were quick to notice, from being merely a glorified roman à clef.

Sharon had a spacious, sunny, well-furnished apartment in one of those Arcaty houses—a carpenter-Gothic Victorian with multibalustered porches reminiscent of homes in my Georgia—that, like so many Arcaty houses, have their entries on street level but need two or three basements to let their back doors adjust to the slope of the mountain. The spare bedroom Sharon gave me for my own, much larger than my room in Pittsburgh had been, was actually level with the street, although its eastward windows were three stories above the backyard.

My first objective was to find a job. My second was to begin the translation of *Georgie Boy* from the Georgian in which I'd written it into English. The first objective was hampered by the off-season of the Arcaty tourist trade; that resort's major volume of traffic occurs in the summer months and the early autumn; in winter, it almost shuts down, except for a spurt of shoppers around Christmastime. I had sent my résumé to the state's major university, in a city only two hours distant, but their mycologist appeared to be entrenched. The community colleges, as well as the three so-called "universities" within commuting distance (assuming I could learn to drive and bought a cheap car), did not teach mycology at all and had no vacancies for botanists. Anangka preserved me from throwing myself upon the charity of Sharon (although Sharon had insisted, "I'll be glad to tide you over until your book finds a publisher") by finding me a position as a housekeeper for one of the wealthier widows of the town. It appeared that much of Arcaty's permanent year-round population consisted of retired people, older people, widows and widowers, and a "Mrs. Clements," who had another of those charming hillslope Victorians within easy walking (or climbing) distance of Sharon's house, hired me to come in five days a week (Wednesdays and Saturdays off) to clean her house and cook for her, and the wage helped me pay half of Sharon's rent, pay for half of the groceries, and, the next spring, pay for a typist to make a clean copy of the manuscript of *Georgie Boy*.

On Wednesdays and Saturdays, and most nights until bedtime, I sat at my desk with Daniel Lyam Montross's old unabridged dictionary (a *Webster's Second International*), a "going-away" gift from his daughter, Diana, and the *Roget's Thesaurus* I'd bought originally (and annotated) as Cathlin McWalter. There was not, or if there was I couldn't find one, any such thing as a Georgian–English dictionary, or even an English–Georgian dictionary. But at least Georgian is written, whereas Svanetian is only oral, and while Georgian lacks Russian's nuances and infinite shadings it is more liquid, more flowing, and more comfortable. So I had composed the "rough draft" of my first novel in that language, and now I had to "recompose" the draft in an English that, although it was going to require much work from a sympathetic, hardworking editor as well as a whole team of copy editors, was readable.

That unabridged dictionary was a magical book, almost as if its words were still haunted by the spirit of Dan Montross, who, I kept remembering, supposedly had been able to "read" it as if it had a plot. Often, using it, I had a strong sense of his being in the room with me, trying his best to help me find the right word. There were even situations in which I would be stumped for finding the English equivalent of some Georgian word, perhaps a word like *mdgómaréoba,* "situation," and I would eerily feel that Dan was making my fingers turn to the exact page of the dictionary where I would find it. But how could he possibly have known Georgian? Once, after I'd finished a long, hard session of constant thumbing of the dictionary's pages, Sharon happened to come into my room and, looking around, asked, "Did you have a man in here?"

Beneath my name on the title page I was almost tempted to write, *Translated from the Georgian by Daniel Lyam Montross.* This intense "collaboration" with Dan on the translation offered me a convenient excuse for declining Sharon's invitations, frequent at first, to join her for an evening at one of Arcaty's "night spots" (I loved that term as soon as I was able to determine that it did not mean a blemish on the evening, but I had little liking for the actual places). At least three nights a week, she would go out to the "Frog's Nest," the "Mole's Eye," or, her favorite place, up on the mountain, that same Halfmoon Pub where I, or Cathlin, had spent some fun hours during the BOW convention, and, invariably, she would either be gone until morning, spending the balance of the night in some man's room or apartment, or she would bring a man home with her. Once she brought two men home with her, "Michael" for herself and "Ted" for me. My only "blind date" was a very handsome, witty, well-spoken gentleman who, had I been at all romantically interested in a twenty-nine-year-old man, would have been a prize. But long after Sharon and Michael had retired to her bedroom, Ted and I were still talking, he genuinely fascinated with Svanetia and Russia and even Pittsburgh, and I pretending great interest in his boyhood and youth in a dull downstate place called Eldorado. Along about five A.M. he looked at his watch and said, "Don't you think it's time we got in bed?" He seemed to accept without question, as I showed him to the door, Svanetia's ageworn tradition that a woman can never "chosh" with a man without having known him for at least two months. Ted sent me things, flowers and books, and called me up on the telephone, and rang the doorbell, and even wrote me a long letter in which he called me the most beautiful and alluring woman he'd ever met even in dreams, but by the time the two months elapsed he had given up trying, or, like so many of Arcaty's transients, had gone on to some other place.

"Don't you like men?" Sharon asked me one day. And I realized the excuse of the work was wearing thin, although it was a genuine excuse. I also realized that Sharon and I had become very close, very open, and that we had no secrets from each other . . . no secrets except that one, which I then decided to reveal to her.

"Not after they've started to shave," I answered her. To Sharon's everlasting credit, she did not think I was making a joke, nor did she even say, "Really?" or "Come on!" or even ask for a clarification: At what age did men begin to shave? Knowing Sharon as I did, I might have expected her to laugh and say, "I can't stand whiskers either." But she didn't do that. What she said was: "Well, we'll have to find you one who thinks razors are for making model airplanes."

Which is precisely what she did. It turned out that Sharon's "heaviest" date, Michael, had a son, "Jason," who was constructing from kits, with much glue and many razors, quite an assortment of toy airplanes. Michael had been leaving Jason and his airplanes with an overnight baby-sitter, although Jason had been complaining that he was much too old, at eleven and three-quarters, to require the services of a baby-sitter.

In February, for Jason's birthday, Sharon suggested to Michael that the three of us bring the boy to the house for a birthday dinner, give him a little party with some presents, and then later the two of them, Sharon and Michael, might go out for the evening at the Halfmoon Pub, leaving Jason, if he needed any babysitting at all, with "Aunt Kat," who would be glad to keep him entertained with ghost stories or teach him how to play chess, or something.

Jason's birthday coincided with my last day of work on the translation of *Georgie Boy,* during which my effort at rendering into English the tragic death of beloved Dzhordzha not only filled me with a third attack of sadness over the event but also gave me that sense of postaccomplishment horniness that I have already described in my narrative of the first sexual encounter with Kenny Elmore, which had occurred, come to think of it, exactly one year earlier. Can a quota of one seduction per year be called profligate or promiscuous?

"You're just another baby-sitter," Jason accused me, when his father had departed with Sharon. "Only you're a take-out instead of a come-in baby-sitter."

"But I'm different," I declared, "from any baby-sitter you've ever known."

"How?" he demanded. "Except for being the prettiest ever?"

"Is there anything you ever wanted a baby-sitter to do for you but couldn't ask?"

He thought for a minute. "Yeah," he said. "Give me a bath."

"I will be happy to give you a bath."

"Aw, I'm too old for that, now."

"Or maybe you're not even old enough," I said, and winked at him. The wink got to him. "I bet I am," he said. "Let's prove it."

So I gave Jason a thorough bath, in Sharon's big white claw-footed tub. With much soap and lather and bubbles. With much fondness and attention. He was modest getting out of his clothes, not from the act of undressing so much as because he already had an erection, but after I praised it suitably he lost his self-consciousness about it and was especially appreciative of the way I soaped it.

Hours later, tucking him in just before his father and Sharon returned to spend the night, I heard him sigh and say, "You sure are some kind of different baby-sitter."

For the rest of that winter, and through the springtime too, Jason insisted that he would accept no other baby-sitter, and his father even teased him about it, telling him he was too old now for baby-sitters and asking him once in my presence, "What does she do for you?" and poor Jason blushed so furiously without being able to answer that I knew his father must have suspected something.

"It's all right," Sharon eventually assured me. "I'm not sure that Mike knows, but if he does know, he thinks it's an okay thing for the kid. Believe me."

Arcata Springs had a reputation, I discovered, for free-thinking libertarianism. A few years earlier, it had been tolerant of the largest concentration of hippies in the state, and the signs of its indulgence were still in the air. In addition to rampant heterosexual free love, there were communities of homosexuals, male and female, and assorted paraphilias: a community of transsexuals; a community of sadomasochists; and communities of sodomists, urolagnists, and coprophiliacs. To my knowledge, there was not a community of hebephiliacs. I was, and am, the only one.

III

THE VERY FIRST of the several million American readers of *Georgie Boy* was an Arcata Springs woman named Joni Lynn Miller, the receptionist, clerk, and secretary for a law firm, and thus an expert typist, whose years of typing wills, deeds, briefs, and contracts prepared her for the more exciting job of making a presentation copy of the manuscript of my first novel. She was a casual acquaintance of Sharon's, and Sharon told me that Joni Lynn could use the money, which, as I recall, was some ridiculously low sum like fifty cents a page. Doing the job only in her spare time, nights and weekends, she finished it in less than two weeks, and I was amazed. The manuscript was not simply "clean" in the sense of what publishers call "a clean copy"; it was immaculate: not a smudge on it, and its corrections, if any had been made, were invisible. With my permission, Joni Lynn had even corrected several misspellings and a few errors in grammar.

Best of all, Joni Lynn was still crying when she gave me the finished typescript. "I don't suppose you'd want to know what I think of it, would you?" she asked timidly and deferentially. I assured her I would be thrilled to have her opinion. She was, I told her, the very first person to see it. "Did any of that stuff really happen to you?" she wanted to know, foreshadowing dozens of reviewers who would put the same question in fancier language. And when I told Joni Lynn that most of it was genuinely a work, and a working, of fiction, although it had liberally utilized and converted some of my own experiences, she hugged me. She wordlessly wrapped her arms around me and held me for a long moment in an embrace of sisterhood, comfort, sympathy, and perhaps, I like to think, simply the wish to touch the author. Then she declared, "I haven't read a whole lot of novels, but I'd rather read a good novel than watch TV, I can tell you. I've read everything by Stephen King, which I guess isn't anything to brag about. And I've read everything by Agatha Christie and Dorothy Sayers. But I've read some 'real' novelists too, like Iris Murdoch and Muriel Spark and Joyce Carol Oates. And I just want to say, *Georgie Boy* is the best novel I have ever read in my whole life. I'll never forget it." Hearing that, I began crying myself, and we had a good cry together.

Sharon was the second person to read the manuscript. She apologized for being a slow reader, which she was, apparently not able to read it as fast as Joni Lynn had typed it. And she was not as well read as Joni Lynn, having confined her novel reading to Jesse Stuart, James Still, and of course Ingraham. I had mentioned to Sharon that my next step, in finding a publisher, was perhaps to locate Ingraham and send the manuscript to him and ask him if he could recommend it to his publisher. But when Sharon finally finished reading it, the first thing she said to me was, "You'd better not give this to Ingraham. It's so much better than anything he ever wrote that it would leave him crazy with envy."

Good advice, perhaps, but unnecessary, because I couldn't locate Ingraham, anyway. He had left Rolla, Missouri, the previous summer and taken a teaching job in art history at the only place he could find, some college in South Dakota, of all places. But he had left no forwarding address.

Sharon hadn't cried at the end of the book, she said. Why not? I asked her. "I realized that what is sad about it was my own invention," she said. It was indeed, I allowed.

But Sharon had a rather naïve conception of how authors get their first novels published, although her conception, I admit, was not all that much more innocent than mine. She thought *Georgie Boy* was so good that all I would have to do would be to mail it off to a publisher, and anyone who read it would accept it. Because of some of the "marketing tips" that Ingraham had given that class at Pittsburgh, I was skeptical of this notion, but partly to humor Sharon, partly to see for myself, I mailed the manuscript off to Random House. Knowing what I do now, I realize it was probably seen only by a young clerk whose job was to affix a standard polite rejection slip to it and return it. Sharon thought I ought to frame the rejection slip because it would be the only one I'd ever get. She told me I should send the returned manuscript to Ingraham's publisher with a covering letter saying that I was "a former student and very good friend" of Ingraham's. But when I mailed this letter with the manuscript to Little, Brown and Company of Boston, I received the standard rejection slip, upon which someone had written in pencil the information that they no longer considered themselves to be Ingraham's publisher.

Sharon had been asking around, among her more artistic friends in Arcaty, about the best way to get published, and she told me, "You have to have an agent." But I attempted to explain to her what Ingraham had explained to his class: the so-called "Catch 22" of publishing: You can't get published without an agent, but you can't get an agent unless you've been published. "Okay, so what can you do?" Sharon asked.

I told her of Ingraham's "Solution 23": It helps to know somebody who knows somebody who has an agent. "Do you know anybody in Arcaty who would have an agent?" I asked.

"I don't know her, but I know of her," Sharon said, and told me all she knew about Halfmoon Berryfairy. She was originally from New York City, with a Jewish name, and like so many among the influx of hippies in the early seventies she had chosen an alternative name of memorable countercultureness, taken in part from the town's major hotel. When she began to write she decided to keep her hippie name as a pen name, and had published several books, children's books, poetry, murder mysteries, and now a cookbook under that name. "But again," Sharon said, "if you showed *Georgie Boy* to her, she would just die of envy."

As it turned out, Halfmoon Berryfairy was too busy, at that particular time, proofreading the galleys of her latest book to have any time for reading my manuscript, and, furthermore, she had promised her agent that she would not "unload" any aspiring Arcaty writers on her. But Halfmoon (who has become a good acquaintance if not a close friend of mine in recent years) knew of another agent, not her own, who might be willing to take a look at an unsolicited manuscript from an unknown and unpublished ex-Soviet. This woman told Halfmoon that if I would write a covering letter describing my background and stating in twenty-five words or less why the book was publishable, she would "see" if she could find time to read my book.

So I carefully wrote and rewrote a brief autobiographical sketch, omitting any mention that the Dadeshkelianis had been royalty but attempting to depict Svanetia in a nutshell (or in a Fabergé Easter egg) and summarizing my troubles with the KGB, the special psychiatric hospitals, and the camp at Ishimbay. Then I wrote, *This novel is based freely and loosely on the author's own nightmarish experiences as a victim of the Soviet Union's campaign to quell dissidence with psychiatric "treatment."* Twenty-seven words, two over the limit, so I cut *and loosely,* and Halfmoon was kind enough to send my manuscript to the woman who might consent to become my agent. Solution 23 was put into effect.

Then I waited. And waited. Spring passed into summer. Sharon had a violent breakup with Michael, and she stopped going out to her night spots, spending her evenings in her room talking to herself and listening to music. Jason, Michael's son, managed to sneak away from home a few times to visit me before his father put a stop to it—not because he had any objections to the relationship as such but because he didn't want Jason visiting Sharon's house. So Sharon and I were alone, together often, but more often entirely alone, she in her room talking to herself, trying to cheer herself up or trying, as she put it, "to give a purpose to my dumb life," and I in my room talking not to myself but to Anangka. My fate goddess had done a great job so far, but now she seemed to have abandoned me.

"Still waiting to hear from a publisher?" Diana asked me on a Saturday in July when Sharon and I decided to escape from our apartment and return again "up home" to Stick Around for a visit. At least it wasn't a drought summer this year; there were plenty of toad-strangling downpours and plenty of mushrooms in the woods. I wanted to put some flowers on Dan Montross's grave, and Sharon wanted to inspect the old building that had once been her grandmother's house, store, and post office. She was giving serious thought to restoring it and moving into it.

"Still waiting to hear from an agent," I answered Diana, and added, gratuitously, "only an agent."

And then I took my flowers up the hillside to place on Dan's grave. There I soon discovered that I could talk to him more freely than I ever talked to Anangka. Not only that, but I began to believe that he had more power to help me than she did. I didn't want to eliminate Anangka;

she had been so good to me for years. But it was almost as if I had moved beyond her territory of expertise.

IV

WHETHER OR NOT DAN had anything to do with it, on a day in mid-August two significant things happened: I received a letter of rejection from the agent along with the returned manuscript, and we had a visit from Sharon's old boyfriend Larry Brace. The agent was even chattily informal: *You wouldn't believe all the problems I've been having lately,* she wrote, and she described a few of her more interesting problems, including a broken foot. The upshot was that her main problem was simply too much to read. *I've found scarcely a moment to give your novel the attention it deserves. I gather that it could be made into a much-wanted book. I don't feel that I have the time or enthusiasm to give your work the necessary care to secure a publisher for it, but I want you to know that I sincerely hope you will find a person who can bring to the task the qualities that I lack.*

Sharon read this, swore, jumped into her Cam, and returned shortly with a half gallon of vodka. "Let's get loaded," she said. We sat on the porch of the house and proceeded to do precisely that. I hadn't become so tipsy since some of those days in Pittsburgh, and Sharon, who had a great talent for nursing one drink at a night spot through the whole evening, didn't hold herself back. Soon she was yelling at passersby. There weren't a lot of them, summer tourists choosing to tour the town's picturesque neighborhoods on foot instead of in their cars. "YOU WOULDN'T BELIEVE ALL THE PROBLEMS I'VE BEEN HAVING LATELY!" Sharon would yell at anybody who came along, and, if they stopped to listen (most of them didn't, but hurried on), Sharon would add something like, "I WANT YOU TO KNOW THAT I SINCERELY HOPE YOU WILL FIND A PERSON WHO CAN BRING TO THE TASK THE QUALITIES THAT I LACK!"

Soon I got into the spirit of it myself and joined her in the yelling. "SCARCELY A MOMENT!" I would yell.

"THE ATTENTION IT DESERVES!" Sharon would add.

"I DON'T FEEL I HAVE THE TIME!"

"OR THE ENTHUSIASM!"

"TO GIVE YOUR WORK!"

Perhaps our noise was frightening off the pedestrians, for eventually we were reduced to yelling only at passing vehicles. Some of these vehicles would slow down and pause long enough to attempt to hear what we were yelling, then speed up and go on.

"I GATHER THAT IT COULD BE MADE!"

"INTO A MUCH-WANTED BOOK!"

One of the cars, a Ford Fairlane, came to a complete stop and parked at our curb, and its lone occupant sat listening to us run through the whole sequence of phrases yet again. My first inkling that this was not a tourist came when Sharon slightly modified what she was yelling:

"BUT I WANT YOU TO KNOW, LARRY, THAT I SINCERELY HOPE YOU WILL FIND A PERSON WHO WILL BRING TO THE TASK THE QUALITIES THAT I LACK!"

He yelled back at her, "GODDAMMIT, SHARON, THERE AREN'T ANY QUALITIES THAT YOU LACK!"

"WELL, GET YOUR ASS OUT OF THAT OIL BURNER AND COME HAVE A SNORT WITH US!" Then, as he accepted her invitation, she said to me in her normal voice, "Here is ole Larry, my onetime best fellow."

It did not take Larry very long to catch up with us, in consuming the vodka, and when that ran out he had his own half gallon in the Ford. He was a good-looking man, although his beard and mustache were so heavy it was difficult to imagine what he'd look like cleanshaven. My first impression of him was that he was what the late Knox Ogden must have looked like thirty years before. Sharon showed him the letter from my agent—or rather, would-be but never-was agent—and Larry declared, without any inkling of what manuscript of mine had accompanied it, "What fatuous bullshit!"

And he added his loud bass voice to our streetward yellings for a little while, until Sharon decided she'd rather just talk. "So what brings you to the Bodarks?" she asked.

"You, of course," he declared. "But I want to see your Stick Around before you disappear thither. I've been thinking. As soon as I finish the Ogden study, I'd like to do some research on this Daniel Lyam Montross."

I did a genuine double take. Two different names he'd dropped, both of intimate familiarity. Or was I just very drunk? "Pardon," I said. "Did you say Ogden?" He smiled, and nodded. "Knox Ogden?" I said.

Again he nodded, and he smiled even bigger. "Do you know his work?" By way of answer, I jumped up, stumbled, staggered into the house and into my room, and got the book and brought it back to show it to him, *The Final Meadow,* with the inscription on the flyleaf. He peered closely at that inscription, and then his mouth fell open. He stared at me. "This is you?" he asked. "Are you Ekaterina Vladimirovna Dadiankeliani?"

As I had once done for Knox himself, I corrected him. "Dadeshkeliani," I said.

"I told you," Sharon said to him. "I wrote and told you I had a roommate named Ekaterina."

"But I had no idea . . . ," Larry said, and then he drew himself up and declaimed:

> *"Ekaterina, hear my final song:*
> *The dying bird drops down from breaking bough*
> *To perch on earth, and not continue long*
> *The notes and cries that deafened broods allow.*

"I think that's what it says. That's all of it I've been able to decipher at this point," Larry said. "I was just inspecting it the other morning, among his papers at the Hillman Library in Pittsburgh."

"Larry makes a specialty," Sharon said, "of writing books about poets that nobody's ever heard of. So who is this Knox Ogden?"

I told Sharon, "I lived next to him the last few weeks of his life. And Larry has just been quoting from the very last thing he wrote."

"Isn't it a small world?" Sharon said.

Larry stayed a week. It was, he revealed, the last week of summer before the fall semester began, and he'd meant it as a kind of vacation, a final fling after a stint of hard work at the Hillman, but now it looked like it was going to turn into a "working vacation" for him, especially because he needed to preserve, on his tape recorder, everything that I could remember about Knox Ogden, and also because Sharon wanted him to use his nights, instead of trying to sleep with her, reading the manuscript of *Georgie Boy*. She promised him that if he would read it and give us his honest professional English teacher's opinion of it, she would take him to see Stick Around, and, possibly, she might even consent to sleep with him.

Sharon and I gave him a good tour of Arcata Springs, dining out evenings (at his expense) at the Plaza, the best restaurant in town, and having great lunches at Bubba's Barbecue, and we even went swimming, one splendid afternoon, at Lake Lucerne, a tiny fraction of the size of its namesake in the real Switzerland and obviously so named because it was the only substantial body of water in close proximity to "America's Little Switzerland," as the Arcata Springs Chamber of Commerce called the town.

The fifth morning of his visit, Larry announced, over breakfast at the Paragon Café, that he had been awake until approximately 2:30 A.M., finishing *Georgie Boy*. He took a dramatic pause to stuff his mouth with a doughnut, which required several long moments of munching before he could answer Sharon's "Well—?" and my "So—?"

"What did Knox think of it?" he asked me.

"He didn't read it," I answered, "for the simple reason that I hadn't started writing it before he died."

"Have you shown it to anybody?" he asked.

"Sharon, of course," I said, "and the girl who typed it, and that agent, who didn't, I think, take even a peek at it."

"Knox would have loved it," he said. "In some ways it confirms his final view of the world."

Sharon put in, "But did Larry love it? Does it confirm any of your views of the world?"

He nodded. "Can you ladies give me a couple of days to think about it? Just to think about it, before I let you have my thoughts?"

"Let's go to Stick Around," Sharon suggested.

We took Larry for the full tour of Stick Around, such as remained of it. Sharon introduced him, first, to her grandmother, Lara Burns. "I didn't know anybody lived in log cabins anymore," he remarked, then was surprised to discover that in Lara's modest library were volumes by two of the poets, John Clare and Christopher Smart, on whom Larry had written monographs, copies of which he promised to send to her as soon as he got back to Chicago. Sharon and I conducted him on a tour of what was left of the village, including the building, its post-office boxes still intact but dusty, that Sharon was thinking of turning into her next home. She showed him also the house that had once been a hotel, now vacant and deteriorating rapidly, in the attic of which he found, among the detritus of yesteryears, a letter once written by Daniel Lyam Montross to the woman who had been the last occupant of the hotel. Larry asked for permission to borrow this and photocopy it, but Sharon had to explain that the house and any contents of it legally belonged to her brother, Vernon. We took Larry to meet Vernon and his Jelena in their extravagant nonconformist house (yurt? dome? bubble?) on the mountain, and Larry got permission to borrow the letter. Larry asked of Vernon, "Would you consider renting that old hotel sometime?" For what? Vernon asked. "For a scholar's retreat," Larry said.

We also introduced Larry to Day and Diana and showed him the upstairs room where I'd written *Georgie Boy* . . . although I didn't boast of this; the reason we showed it to him was so he could see all of the thousands of words on the walls, in the handwriting of Daniel Lyam Montross. "God! I've got to come back!" Larry declared. "I've got to come and photograph all of this!"

Our last stop was Dan's grave. The flowers I had put on it a month before were still miraculously fresh . . . Or else somebody, maybe Diana, had replaced them with fresh flowers of exactly the same kind, daisies, Queen Anne's lace, black-eyed Susans, and buttercups. Larry stared, properly reverential, at the gravestone for a long time, and then he demonstrated his ability to quote the rest of the poem that provided the gravestone's inscription, a pretty villanelle called "The Dreaming," whose message is that the purpose of sleep is the manufacture of one's future.

"He's living his sleep's extremes," Larry observed. "Knox Ogden and he would have really appreciated each other."

"Maybe they did," I said, and then corrected my tense: "Maybe they do."

That night, back in Arcaty, Sharon let Larry sleep with her. I listened, almost envious, until they hushed and went to sleep. And in my own dreams, later, I joined them.

The next morning, before getting into his car to drive back to Chicago, Larry said to me, "Let me keep your manuscript. I know a novelist in Chicago who would love to read it. He's not famous, but he's important. And he's got a wonderful agent. Your book must be published, Ekaterina."

19

I

LIZ BLAUSTEIN THOUGHT SO, TOO. And she did not keep me waiting forever for her answer. In late September, just a month or so after Larry had taken the book to his novelist friend (a brilliant but little-known writer whose entire output of thirteen books I have since read, and who, in his enthusiastic report on the novel, promised to "fix me up" with his agent, Liz Blaustein, on condition that I never tell anyone that he had done it . . . so he must remain anonymous here), I received a letter from her that began, *You did not give me a telephone number, or I would have called you sooner with this good news: You and I were meant for each other.* Georgie Boy *is everything that _____ _____ told me it was, and more! It literally and figuratively cannot be put down. I have already sent it to a publisher who has a special interest in this kind of book.*

As I tried to explain to Sharon while we were finishing off a bottle of champagne in celebration, I wasn't entirely comfortable with those words *this kind of book,* which implied that *Georgie Boy* wasn't completely original, in a class by itself. At that point in my career, I had no idea if any other novels had been published in America by Soviet dissidents, and during the weeks I waited for Publisher W's reaction I visited the Arcata Springs Public Library, in a quaint limestone building donated to the town by that philanthropic cousin of our old haunter Lawren, and tried to find out what "kind of book" Publisher W published. But the only similar thing they'd done was not a novel: *A Question of Madness,* by the twins Zhores and Roy Medvedev, published a decade earlier. The book had been widely circulated in *samizdat* in Russia, and I had read it years before: the compelling story of how Zhores was railroaded into a mental hospital because of one of his books and because of his campaign to open up the Soviet scientific establishment to dialogue with the outside world. Alternate chapters of counterpoint—Zhores inside the "special psychiatric hospital" and his brother Roy outside it—chronicle the desperate battle to gain Zhores his freedom. It is paced like a novel, nervous like a novel, but it is not a novel.

And perhaps Publisher W would have preferred that *Georgie Boy* be nonfiction too. After six weeks during which I spent a lot of time walking the steep streets of Arcaty, up to the Halfmoon and around it and back, Liz Blaustein sent me a copy of Publisher W's letter of rejection. Several editors had read the book, and they'd even had a fact-checker attempt to verify the "truth" of it. Their only criticism, if that's what it was, was that "this Bolshakov character is such a beast that he stretches credulity." But that wasn't their reason for rejecting the novel. "The young boy-narrator's voice," the letter said, "is somewhat arch, glib, even disagreeable."

"I disagree!" Sharon yelled as we sat on the porch swigging vodka in the early November chill, watching the leaves fall. In this off-season, there were no tourists, pedestrian or vehicular, to yell drunken remarks to. Sometimes, during the off-season, Sharon would let me come up to the Halfmoon and spend the night in one of the rooms there, pretending I could afford it. Given a choice, I would pick Room 218 and hope to meet its ghost, but I never did. I did meet Morris the cat, who was always thrilled to see me. The first time I saw him I said, "I told you I'd be back, didn't I?" and he purred loudly and rubbed against me as if he'd been waiting patiently for me ever since.

Liz Blaustein next sent the book to Publisher X, who had published Vladimir Bukovsky's magnificent (but nonfictional) *To Build a Castle: My Life as a Dissenter*. Now, there was a voice that was arch, glib, and sometimes disagreeable, but I had loved it, and so had all of us in Russia who had worshiped Bukovsky as a brave, obsessed, articulate victim of the system of psychoprisons and the horrors of their "treatment." Like myself he had suffered the double punishment of stretches in a "strict regime" prison with much time in solitary confinement, as well as time in a mental hospital subjected to the same "regime" of drugs and little tortures like the "roll-up" in a wet canvas sheet that wracks the victim excruciatingly as it dries. Also like myself (and like, I might add, Solzhenitsyn), he was educated as a scientist, a biologist, and became a "literary" person almost by default because of his experiences in the prisons and hospitals. Yes, I felt good about having his publisher, Publisher X, look at my novel. I seemed to detect some of the footprints of Anangka in that contingency. But if they were hers, they were pointed the wrong way, for Publisher X, too, turned me down.

At least Publisher X, when they rejected *Georgie Boy* in the week before Christmas, made some flattering comparisons to Bukovsky, calling my experience "comparable" to his, "reminiscent" of his, and acknowledging that "the narrator's voice is often as unrelentingly cocky and self-obsessed as Bukovsky's." Their main reason for the rejection appeared to be the editors' personal distaste for the concept of sexual relations between a twelve-year-old boy and a woman nearly twice his age. "Liz, we don't need our noses rubbed in this."

For consolation, during the dark days of the holiday season following that rejection, I reread Nabokov's charming essay "On a Book Entitled *Lolita*" at the end of that volume that Ingraham had given me. For further consolation, I was tempted to visit Ingraham, who, I had learned, had returned yet again to his native state; but, eschewing Stick Around for whatever reasons he had, he was living in a shack on a lake, or a reservoir, named for the dam-building rodent. Not two hours away by car, if I could drive, or if I could get Sharon to take me. But I suspected, rightly as it turned out, that he might be plunged into some depression or soul searching himself and would not be able to respond to my bad luck.

For bad luck it certainly was, as the Nabokov essay reminded me in narrating his own unhappy experiences trying to find an American publisher for *Lolita*. The reactions of his Publisher X, who thought the book too long, Publisher Y, who thought it had no good people in it, and Publisher Z, who thought he'd go to jail if he printed it, somewhat surpassed the feeble rejections I'd had so far. I had still to hear from

Publisher Y, the third place Liz Blaustein sent the book. Publisher Y had brought out, just the year before, Victor Nekipelov's *Institute of Fools: Notes from Serbsky.* I had known Victor Alexandrovich, had been a fellow victim of incarceration in the Serbsky Institute, had enjoyed several opportunities of talking with him, but had not yet read his book, which of course had the same principal setting as mine (although I disguised the Serbsky Institute as "the Laboratory"), and many of the same cast of characters, including the *nyanki,* a word like *baby-sitter* that he applied to the ward orderlies. Now, while waiting to hear from Publisher Y, I ordered for myself for a Christmas present—through the Gazebo, Arcaty's lone bookstore—a copy of Nikepelov's book, and I spent January reading and rereading it, partly out of envy, because there it was, in cold print between hard covers, the same place, the same people, some of the same doctors, including a thinly disguised Bolshakov, in a nonfictional memoir that was distinctly Chekhovian, and, despite being deliberately oversimplified or nonarch in style, was greatly readable. I consoled myself that if my book never did find a publisher and thus could not bring any pressure to bear to stop the psychiatric abuses of the Serbsky, Nekipelov's book could do the job, for all of us—a damning document of evidence against those doctors.

Publisher Y liked my book very much . . . which is why they kept it so terribly long before rejecting it. It reminded them very strongly, they said, of the Nekipelov, but it had the "virtue" of being a novel, and thus of "enjoying the benefits of the author's rich imagination." In the final analysis, however, the editorial board's vote, very close, was to decline, because there appeared to be two irreconcilable separate stories involved here: that of Kathy with Bolshakov, and that of Kathy with Georgie.

"Bull manure!" Sharon said, hauling out a fresh half gallon of vodka. We could sit on the porch again: Springtime had returned; the daffodils and tulips were blooming, the trees leafing. " 'Irreconcilable,' my hind foot! The jerks don't even realize that you meant to play off the relationships one against the other, the badness of Bolshakov, the goodness of Georgie."

"I love you, Sharon," I said, holding back my tears. The next day, with a hangover, I sat myself down and composed a little letter to Liz Blaustein. *Could you please,* I requested, *try the book on some publisher who has not published any books by Soviet dissidents?*

And thus, ever after, I had myself to thank for the book's finally going to Publisher Z, who took it.

II

THEN, AS NOW, IT REQUIRED roughly an entire year to take a manuscript from the author's hands and put the finished book on the shelves of bookstores. That span of twelve months, it seems to me in retrospect, is a kind of "missing year" of my life: There aren't any engrams for it upstairs in my head. Oh, if I took the trouble to consult my journal, I'd find plenty of little jogs to my memory of that year, March to the following year's April, when *Georgie Boy* finally appeared: During that twelvemonth Sharon moved out of our apartment and took up residence in the heart of what had been Stick Around, where, within that same year, her Larry followed, not to move in with her (which she would not permit) but to take up lone occupancy of the old hotel; my employer, Mrs. Clements, became very ill and was required to move into a nursing home because I had to decline her request to move in with her and work for her seven days a week around the clock. Unemployed, I once again attempted to find a teaching post, and luckily (or with intervention by Anangka) the mycologist at the state university took an on-campus sabbatical and turned his fall semester classes over to me, one semester only: no general botany courses, mycology alone, at junior, senior, and graduate levels, with many idyllic field trips into the autumnal woods outside that city which is called "Athens of the Bodarks" because it is an intellectual oasis in a state without intellectuals.

To my surprise, Ingraham was also living there, as I discovered by accident when I bumped into him one Saturday afternoon at the supermarket. We embraced, then blocked an aisle with our carts for nearly an hour. He expressed surprise and delight at how "gorgeous" I looked with my hair grown long again. I observed that he looked healthier than

I had ever seen him. He was able to report that he was on the wagon, for good as it turned out, and had acquired a girlfriend who, in October of that year, was scheduled to become his second wife. (He would invite me to the wedding, a Bodarkian "costume" affair, but a previous commitment to take my mushroom-hunting students on a field trip would keep me from it.) Ingraham was not employed at the university but was doing some research there in preparation for a nonfiction book he and his wife-to-be were collaborating on, concerned with, naturally, ghost towns. For some reason that I was never able to determine afterward, I could not tell him that my novel had been accepted and was "in production." I thought, possibly, that to do so might leave him envious and discouraged. Later during that one semester I lived in that cultural oasis (which Ingraham told me could be spelled either as celebrative *Fêteville* or as momentous *Fateville,* so I shall opt for the latter) I met and liked his wife, Kay, a charming blonde who was about my age yet had a beautiful son named Andrew who was just turning twelve. "Unt-uh," Ingraham grunted at me, wagging his finger back and forth negatively in my face when he introduced me to Andrew.

But Fateville was filled with many other twelve-year-old boys, although few of them found their way into the pages of my journal that fall. Most of my available free time off campus was spent in writing letters and making phone calls to my editor at Publisher Z. Since, as I'm about to show, that editor was responsible for tampering with my gender, making me sexless, or more implicitly male than otherwise, I think I shall return the "favor" (or the sex-change operation) by never revealing that editor's sex, if he or she actually had one.

So I shall call the editor, him or her, "H. (for Heinrich or Henriette) Wölfflin," which happens to be the name, Ingraham pointed out to me, of a famous Swiss art historian. Heinrich Wölfflin (1864–1945) is dead, and my dear editor nearly, not so long ago, became dead because of me, as I'll ultimately have to reveal.

The many long letters I received from Wölfflin while *Georgie Boy* was in production concerned such matters as choice of words (my editor's forte was the exact word, the perfect word, the, to use Wöfflin's own oft-employed French, *mot juste*), narrative (excising the more clinical, less lyrical descriptions of lovemaking between Kathy and Georgie), grammar (I confess I am still not certain about the distinction between *that* and *which*), and even such mundane matters as choice of "dingbats" (not, as I first thought, silly eccentric persons but the ornamental pieces of type for separations, chapter headings, etc.). But in one of the letters there appeared suddenly one day this sentence leaping out and shaking me: *Do you know, dear Kat, that your full name is entirely too long to appear on the title page, let alone the spine?*

My first reaction to this was that I had never given any thought to the spine. My second reaction was to run to the university library and check the title page of *Princess in Uniform,* the autobiography of my great-aunt and namesake, Ekaterina Alexándrovna Dadeshkeliani, one of the few Svanetians ever to publish a book. Naturally the library did not have the book, but a young woman named Debby Cochran who was running the interlibrary loan department was able to obtain it for me within a few days. And, alas, there on the title page, instead of Auntie's full name with patronymic, was simply, *By Princess Kati Dadeshkeliani.* (And also, *Translated from the French by Arthur J. Ashton, London, G. Bell & Sons Ltd., 1934.*)

"All right," I conceded to Wölfflin by return mail. "So what do you propose?"

I have been giving this some serious thought, Wölfflin replied in the next letter. *Your narrator is, of course, not only male, but a twelve-year-old male. This is a tour de force, I assure you, that puts such child-narrator novels as* To Kill a Mockingbird *and* True Grit *entirely to shame. But I think many of your readers (and particularly your reviewers) might be thrown by the discovery that you are female. Don't answer this precipitously or impulsively. Please give it some long and hard thought. But let me suggest that you consider using only initials that would not reveal your sex.*

I gave it some long and hard thought, perhaps a month's worth. Until I had to return it to Interlibrary Loan, I kept and reread my great-aunt's book, *Princess in Uniform,* in which she tells the exciting story, a true story, of her life: how after a conventional childhood in Svanetia not very different from my own and a study of medicine until the age of twenty (and an early marriage to an aristocrat who turned out to be a homosexual), she found herself by a fluke of destiny in the First World War given an opportunity to masquerade as a Russian soldier on the Austrian front. Her disguise would have shamed Cathlin McWalter. (And I refer the curious, especially those with access to interlibrary loan departments, and especially those who are badgering me for a photograph of myself, to the frontispiece of her volume, with its stunning photograph, full-length in uniform, of "Prince Djamal," as my great-aunt was known during her imposture. If you look carefully at the "prince's" face, you will see a very close resemblance to my own. It was this photograph of my aunt in her soldier's cap that inspired me to have the jacket photo and the publicity photos for *Georgie Boy* show me wearing my short hair inside an American "farmer's bill cap," like a baseball cap, and wearing a denim jacket that does not reveal the bulge of my breasts, and thus to appear more masculine than feminine.)

As far as anyone in my family was able to determine, or as far as I could determine by a careful rereading of the autobiography, there was nothing bisexual, let alone androgynous, about Aunt Kati. She was simply a strong willed and beautiful woman who found it expedient for the duration of the war to serve as a man. As she pointed out, Svanes take an enormous pride in having fine guns, and she enjoyed carrying and using guns. She genuinely adored the czar, Nicholas II, and considered the revolution that occurred shortly thereafter "the greatest and bloodiest tragedy that the world has ever known." But for the space of a few years she transcended her womanhood and got herself into an adventure, with some narrow escapes, that would keep her for the rest of her life. In Paris, where she remained forever in exile after the revolution, and during my brief trip there as a student from Leningrad, I talked with her in her old age—she reminded me, come to think of it, of Lara Burns—and she was the most remarkable woman I've ever known.

Would she, I asked myself, have approved of my decision to become male, or sexlessly initialed, in my *nom de plume?* And the conclusion I reached was *yes.*

I thought also of beloved T'hamar, or Tamara, queen of all Georgia during its golden age, A.D. 1184 to 1213, who was clearly a female and yet was thought of as a king. She was our Alexander the Great, and the chroniclers of our history call her the greatest of our *kings*. This gender confusion, if that is what it was, was part of my heritage. Would the Georgians approve of my decision to become male, or sexlessly initialed, in my *nom de plume?* Yes.

Yes, I wrote to Wölfflin. *So let's just make it V. Dadeshkeliani.* Using both initials troubled me for their association with the nickname Evie, what Loretta Elmore had called me.

Some time after that, Wölfflin thanked me for my decision but added, *Here in the office we are pretty much agreed that nobody can pronounce your last name, let alone remember it. Can you think of any way to shorten or Anglicize it?*

Keliani? I reluctantly wrote back.

How about simply Kelly? Wölfflin replied by return mail.

Would you shorten your name to Wolf? I replied. *No, I think Kelly makes me sound Irish. I wouldn't mind being Scottish, or even Scotch-Irish, but not Irish.*

We haggled. We experimented. We eliminated such choice cuts from my last name as Dade and Skelly and Deskel and even Liann.

We ended up with the compromise that is, of course, dear reader, the name that you and millions have come to know, and that adorns the spine of this book also.

III

THE *NEW YORK TIMES BOOK REVIEW,* in its catch-all "In Short" columns on page 47 ("That far back in the back just kills us," Wölfflin sadly commented) of that early April issue, said, *V. Kelian is apparently young; that appears to be all that is known about him. His publisher offers virtually no clues as to whether this stunning novel is autobiographical or not. We would like to know. At the risk of sounding like the despised Bolshakov, we wonder why he simply didn't tell the truth. Why couldn't he have simply given us the unvarnished Kathy, or whoever she was, without straining to turn her into a fictional victim? Kelian is going to have to decide whether he wants to be a novelist or a historian.*

The review did manage to give a capsule synopsis of the story that, like all plot synopses, was absurdly unreadable and demeaning. But the review itself, coming as it did and where it did on the heels of rhapsodic notices from *Kirkus, Library Journal,* and *Publishers Weekly,* was inexplicable, damaging, and so unfair it turned me into a lifetime enemy of the *New York Times Book Review,* not even changed by their favorable, indeed fawning reviews of my later novels. (Wölfflin tried to console me by pointing out that we were able to salvage that one adjective, *stunning,* for use in advertising.)

The April issues of two influential monthlies, the *Atlantic* and *Harper's,* both contained reviews that could be classified as "raves," albeit both of them succumbed to gender confusion. *V. Kelian is a new star in our literary galaxy,* the *Atlantic* said, but added, *His choice of a name for himself in the novel, and for the novel itself,* Georgie Boy, *brings to mind both Erskine Caldwell's 1943 best-seller,* Georgia Boy *(also narrated by a twelve-year-old boy, although not one who becomes involved in sexual intrigues with an older woman), and the 1966 film with Lynn Redgrave and James Mason,* Georgy Girl. *Of course there is no evidence that V. Kelian was familiar with either of these, or, if he was, that he wanted, for example, to convert his girl into a boy.*

The *Harper's* review, written by a woman, gave the first good and accurate plot synopsis, then digressed into a little essay on gender. *V. Kelian understands the sufferings of the female heart so admirably that I cannot help but wonder if he might not be a woman. The choice of George as a name reverberates with associations: Both George Eliot (Mary Ann Evans) and George Sand (Amandine Dupin) were women writers hiding behind that husbandman's name, and then of course we are today witnessing the pop phenomenon and androgyne known as Boy George, whose very name is almost an inversion of this great novel's title.* This blather was redeemed by a concluding paragraph: *No one who reads this totally original novel will ever be able to forget it. No one who reads it will remain unchanged by the experience. No novel in recent memory succeeds on every level as brilliantly as* Georgie Boy.

Congratulations on those splendid notices in Atlantic *and* Harper's, Wölfflin wrote, *but we are still waiting for a "biggie," in* Time *or* Newsweek.

But the biggie, when it came, was from a totally unexpected source: the *New York Review of Books.* Wölfflin phoned the joyous news, quoting at length from the lengthy review and promising to send me the issue by express mail. This periodical, Wölfflin explained, was not to be confused with the *New York Times Book Review;* it had been founded originally to counteract that powerful review medium. It was considered the "chief theoretical organ of Radical Chic," and if it had a flaw, it was that it was inclined to print long-winded discussions of obscure books that were in no danger of becoming popular. It rarely reviewed fiction, and *Georgie Boy* was the first *first* novel it had reviewed in a long time.

When I received my copy of the issue, I was amused to see that the review was accompanied by one of those striking pen-and-ink cross-hatched caricatures, by "D. Levine," based obviously upon the publicity photos of me that did not reveal my sex. The creature in the caricature manages to be very handsome despite what Levine does to him/her. I was told that Mr. Levine always did his caricatures of famous people or recognizable people, and that I was the first "unknown" he had ever attempted.

I would like to reprint the entire review, all 4,200 words of it.

IV

Evil Shrinks

Georgie Boy
by V. Kelian
Harcourt Brace Jovanovich, 348 pp., $15.95

Clive Henry

Ten years ago I. F. Stone observed in these pages, in his article "Betrayal by Psychiatry," that "socialism without freedom, whatever its declared intentions, turns into a suffocating nightmare." The literature of that nightmare has burgeoned apace; within the past few years these pages have carried reviews of important new indictments of the Soviet order by Eugenia Ginzburg (*Within the Whirlwind*), Vladimir Bukovsky (*To Build a Castle*), Lev Kopelev (*To Be Preserved Forever*), Zhores and Roy Medvedev (*A Question of Madness*), and Andrei Sakharov (*Alarm and Hope*), to mention only those that I have read myself.

But all of these, and the several others that I have not read, have in common that they are nonfiction, first-person eyewitness accounts of the merciless punishment that the Communist regime metes out to those citizens who dare to question its ideology. Without wishing to denigrate the very real worth of any of these accounts, I have the unmistakable impression that the voices of these victims become merged into a single, pathetic lament that seems to lose some of its strength or effectiveness because it is first-person and because it is eyewitness and because, after a while, it loses whatever novelty it possesses.

Now comes a voice that is unforgettably remarkable for at least three reasons: First, it is that not of the victim but of a child, literally, of the victim's oppressors; second, although it is clearly based upon, as I shall show, actual experiences in a Soviet psychiatric hospital and a Soviet politicals' prison, it never once identifies its locales, thus rendering them universal; and third, perhaps most important in terms of literature, although it must have come out of a profound personal experience, it is clearly a work of fiction.

That alone, its novelistic complexion, sets it apart from the entire body of Soviet protest writing, with the exceptions of Solzhenitsyn and Voinovich, with both of whom the mysteriously named newcomer, V. Kelian, must now be compared. The novels in English of both Solzhenitsyn and Voinovich have been translated from the Russian; *Georgie Boy* was apparently written in English by a Russian emigré (Keliansky? Kelianko? Kelianovich? One guesses, at least, that the V is for Vladimir).

Georgie Boy is not a political novel. It is not even, despite its surface, a novel about the political abuse of psychiatry. Nor can it, by any extension, be called a psychological novel, as such. Certainly it concerns corruption in the practice of psychology, but it has no "mission" in that direction. If by some miracle it reaches an audience in the general book-buying public, it may even come to be denounced as a pornographic novel about the intense affair between the victim, a beautiful woman in her twenties, and the narrator, her savior and lover, a boy of only twelve named George.

Inevitably, because of this "twist" of the story, comparisons may be made with the most celebrated novel by another Russian, Nabokov, but really the only similarity between the two books is the precocious sexuality, in the one, of a girl, and in the other, of a boy, vis-à-vis a "mature" lover. There is hardly a single point of resemblance between Monsieur Humbert and "Princess" Kathy, other than their awareness that their fondness for pubescent lovers is considered wrong by society. If the sometimes graphic scenes of lovemaking, as seen and told through the fresh eyes of the boy himself, serve to attract readers who otherwise would overlook this wonderful novel, then they will have accomplished one of their two purposes—the other being to examine the whole question of what is real, if the same "reality" is experienced by a woman of twenty-four, a boy of twelve, and an unscrupulous psychiatrist whose grasp of reality is entirely egocentric.

All of us have endured those mildly inquisitive moments, sometimes stretching into hours, waiting in a doctor's or dentist's (or psychotherapist's) office with nothing to do but examine the room, the tiles on the floor, the pictures and diplomas on the wall, the familiar and unfamiliar instruments, the furniture of boredom. *Georgie Boy* introduces us to the subject, and to our friendly narrator in the title role, with a brilliant opening chapter in which there are no people at all, and yet the major personae of the novel are not only presented but depicted clearly, as seen innocently by George (there are no last names in this novel, except that of the villain, Bolshakov), an eager, intelligent, kindhearted (for annealing reasons of his own) boy of twelve, the son not of the doctor whose room this is but of one of the doctor's professional colleagues, a woman psychiatrist in the same hospital—for this is clearly, as Georgie lets us know, an office not in a professional building or clinic but in a psychiatric hospital—and these documents and pictures and dolls that the boy describes and imaginatively analyzes in the room are clearly those of a senior staff psychiatrist in an institution whose purpose is ostensibly the treatment of mental illness but in "reality" is the punishment, through Pavlovian conditioning, of nonconformists, dissenters, the heterodox misfits in the social or political order.

Here, and throughout the book, Georgie refers to the hospital only as "the Laboratory," which is no part of its name but only the name his doctor mother calls an unused part of the hospital in which she "parks" her son, leaving him to play or somehow amuse himself while she works. Thus by imaginative synecdoche he applies to the whole institution the two "purposes" of a small part of it: the consumption and management of his idle hours, and radical experimentation with the mechanisms of the human psyche.

It may be argued—and the reader is certainly wary of this throughout the first chapters of the book—that young George is simply too perceptive for his age, in what he observes and illustrates around him in the Laboratory, and this wariness is encouraged by his lovely use of language. But the truth is that, as the reader abruptly realizes along about the end of the second chapter, George is not "interpreting" anything; he makes no value judgments, no appreciations or denunciations, of the world around him. He simply describes his world with the candor and innocence of his youth, the awkward age, and permits the reader to do all of the thinking. This is, of course, the highest condition of literature as opposed to the "entertainment" arts.

The closest George ever comes to voicing an opinion is when he betrays his real feelings for his (and our) heroine, whom he has chosen to call "Princess," thereby endowing his narrative with some of the charm of a fairy tale. We learn eventually that her first name may be Kathy, but we learn also that it could conceivably just as well be Kofryna or Catalina or Aikaterine or Caron or Katerina or Karena, "the pure" in any language. She might very well be from a royal family and thus actually a princess, or that may simply be a title George has bestowed upon her. She is not Russian—or, if she is, she is also Portuguese and Swedish and Scottish and American. In some unnamed city that could be any large city anywhere, she has been arrested, during a demonstration, for civil disobedience or for passive resistance or for her political or religious beliefs. An agency of the government (it is never identified as the KGB or the CIA, but it behaves suspiciously like an amalgam of both) arranges to have her incarcerated without a trial, which would attract unfavorable publicity, by sending her for psychiatric "evaluation" to the Laboratory.

Those of us who know Moscow's infamous Serbsky Institute, by reading Bukovsky or the Medvedevs or the more recent Victor Nekipelov in his brilliant *Institute of Fools,* will recognize at once that the Laboratory closely resembles the Serbsky. But, lest we think we are actually there, the Laboratory also closely resembles Saint Elizabeth's in Washington, D.C., and indeed one of the permanent inmates (there are several) of the Laboratory is an aged poet who writes deliberately obscure verses remarkably similar to Ezra Pound's. The fact that Pound was released from the psychiatric hospital in 1958 should not deter us from making the assumption that this poet is Pound and the hospital is Saint Elizabeth's. It may actually be not Pound in person but his ghost, of whom there are several in the spectral imaginations of Princess as well as George.

Out of curiosity, I referred to my copy of *Russia's Political Hospitals: The Abuses of Psychiatry in the Soviet Union* (published in America in 1977 as *Psychiatric Terror: How Soviet Psychiatry Is Used to Suppress Dissent*), in which authors Sidney Bloch and Peter Reddaway identify some of the personnel working at the Serbsky. Several of the actual doctors are recognizable here, as George sees them or depicts them from his "neutral" stance as the son of their colleague: Daniil Romanovich Lunts,

the chief of Section Four (Political) of the Serbsky, is clearly identifiable, as are Dr. Yakov Lazarevich Landau, his deputy, and Dr. Margarita Felixovna Taltse, another senior psychiatrist. Most remarkable is that George's mother in the novel, whom he refers to simply as Doctor Mom, is distinguishable as the actual Dr. Svetlana Iosifovna Rudenko, a blonde beauty who actually had, and doted upon, a young son, Dzhordzhi, or Georgy (named fawningly after the Serbsky's longtime powerful director, Georgy Morozov). Are we to assume that "V. Kelian" is possibly Dzhordzhi Rudenko, grown now into his twenties? Or did Dzhordzhi actually rescue a woman like his Princess and get himself killed in the act? . . . But I hesitate to give away the tragic ending of this novel.

If these various disguises and pseudonyms were necessary to protect or conceal, however thinly, actual persons, why then did V. Kelian (or George, or Dzhordzhi) choose to identify Dr. Vasily Timofeyevich Bolshakov by his actual name?

For a number of years Dr. Bolshakov has been in the forefront of the elite Serbsky psychiatrists who, by their Party loyalty and their willingness to abuse their profession for political ends, have enjoyed special privileges, inflated salaries, and the right to travel, including to the United States, where Bolshakov has been several times.

V. T. Bolshakov is the most disagreeable person I have ever encountered between the covers of a book, fiction or nonfiction. In a word, he stinks. But again, George never passes judgment upon him . . . until the very end, and then the judgment is final, severe, and eternally damning. If George even resents Dr. Bolshakov because the man once seduced and debauched George's own mother with George as a covert witness, he does not reveal his repugnance. Throughout the book, he is content, if that is the word, merely to chronicle Bolshakov's long, demonic, crafty campaign to deprive Princess of her sanity.

It is Bolshakov, of course, who "evaluates" Princess for the government agency and writes a report, which George finds in the doctor's files at the conclusion of the opening chapter discussed above, discovering that Bolshakov has classified her as schizophrenic. (The Serbsky, following the diagnostic system of the notorious Dr. Andrei V. Snezhnevsky, actually does classify all political prisoners as having "sluggish" or "creeping" schizophrenia.) Bolshakov's own pet diagnosis of his "patients," especially Princess, is a form of paranoid or delusional schizophrenia in which the patient is incapable of distinguishing truth from fiction.

How many of Bolshakov's sessions with Princess her Georgie actually eavesdropped upon, or how many he reconstructed from spying in Bolshakov's files or by simply being told about them by Princess herself, may only be surmised; we do not question his modus operandi, so fascinated are we by his modus vivendi. He captures the intonations and inflections of Bolshakov's speech, as the doctor talks to Princess, without making Bolshakov sound Russian or American. "How am I to believe you tell the truth?" becomes almost a litany in Bolshakov's questioning of his victim, Princess. There are endless variations: "Did you actually do that?" and "How can you be sure that it happened the way you think it did?" and "Aren't you simply trying to get me to see something that never existed?" and, always, the falling back on that one word: "Is this really *true?*"

For a man obsessed with truth, or pretending to be, Bolshakov has almost no awareness of the hideousness of the truth of his own existence. He has abjured his own mother, caused the death of his own sister, and dishonored some of his best professors during graduate school. He is a compulsive chronic masturbator, even after "normal" satisfaction from the great variety of women he seduces or coerces with threats, punishments, drugs. To Princess and his other patients, he freely administers sulfazine and atropine, two drugs whose effectiveness in psychiatry has long been disproved, but two drugs that cause considerable chemical discomfort and even derangement. (Sulfazine in particular, a form of sulphur suspended in peach oil, does nothing for the "patient" other than create disorientation and severe headaches.) When Princess's spirit continues to hold up under the regimen of abusive drug treatment, Bolshakov permits her to be subjected to tortures that are not chemical but physical, wracking her with stretchings and bruisings and even a form of Chinese water torture. And then of course there is his most diabolical torture: under pretext of "talk therapy" that he persuades her is for the benefit of "helping" whatever imperfections in her psyche have resulted in her predilection for youths, he submits her to what is essentially a "conveyor belt" of nonstop interrogation, an insidious campaign of questioning designed to invalidate her trust in "reality."

In his observation and description of the grotesque punishments that Princess must endure, George himself breaks, becoming, in his choice of words and images, a surrealist.

Surrealism as a mode of representation—or misrepresentation—in literature as well as in the visual arts has as its fundamental limitation its being private, personal, even hermetic. One man's dream is another man's nightmare. Or, to put it differently, one man's worst nightmare becomes a ludicrous farce to another man. Jung to the contrary, there is no collective unconscious that can interpret or even appreciate the illogical, anachronistic, asyntactical phenomena that well up from the depths of the soul and are consciously rearranged to form a "truth" or "reality" that can be communicated to another person.

V. Kelian knows this and has wisely chosen not to become cutely Kafkaesque when there are so many easy temptations for doing so, in a work of this nature, this setting, this cast of characters, and this exploration of themes. Young George's slow and subtle descent—or ascent—into a kind of madness of his own is not, we realize with a shock of recognition, a flight into inaccessibility but rather a voyage into the familiar if puzzling terrors and suspicions we all of us have known at the passage from childhood into adulthood. George's "loss of innocence" (concurrent with his loss of virginity) takes the form of his realization that the scenes of horror he is witnessing in the Laboratory are for him a symbolic albeit brutal indoctrination into puberty. The "rites" are of observation, not participation, and the only way he can communicate that observation to the reader is with language verging on the irrational, even poetic, with images that are magnificent in their strangeness and extravagance. One almost regrets the coming of the inevitable time when George, through the love of Princess, regains his prosaic rationality.

An instructive contrast has to be made between George's narration and the most famous first-person boy's voice in fiction, his that begins, "You don't know about me, without you have read a book . . ." Georgie and Huck might like each other, or at least understand and appreciate each other. Georgie would consider Huck self-consciously and deliberately rustic, uncouth, and unlettered. Huck would think that Georgie is prematurely wise, somewhat cocky, and maybe a little too spoiled by his mother's devotion. Probably the two boys would pick a fight and bloody each other's noses . . . but neither would be victor. Each would greatly envy the other's situation in life, the one's chance to explore the Mississippi, the other's chance to explore the way that people treat and mistreat each other in an institution. Perhaps, if only Huck could accompany Georgie when he runs away from home, from the Laboratory, and sets out on an epic journey across—again, is it Russia? or is it America?—if only Huck could be with George when George journeys a far distance to find the prison camp to which his beloved Princess has been removed, and to attempt to rescue her therefrom, then perhaps . . . But again I hesitate to give away the ending, even by suggesting ways that Mark Twain could have handled it better.

At least, when Princess is shipped out to the prison camp, she is escaping, for a while, from her tormentor, Bolshakov. (My first reading of these chapters led me to suspect that her prison camp may have been either the "strict regime" women's zones at Bereznyaki or Orel, but then I deduced from certain clues—descriptions of the bleak Bashkir landscape, primarily—that it may have been the notorious Ishimbay, the most terrible of all Russia's camps for women. Still, as far as the reader might be concerned, it could be simply Fort Worth or Frontera or any of the women's "correctional institutions" in America.) Bolshakov, having failed to seduce her, having failed with all his arsenal of physical, chemical, and mental weapons to drive her out of her mind, having failed (worst of all for him, as far as his obligations to the System are concerned) to convert her dissent and extract any recantation or apology from her, can only send her off to a prison camp where she will be subjected to a variety of abuses of which not even he is capable.

There are parallels, if I may draw them without maligning my own profession, between the psychiatrist and the book reviewer. Both are supposed to be intelligent if not intellectual persons of uncommon perspicacity and sufficient understanding of the foibles of mankind to be able to detect a warped psyche or a plot bent out of shape. Both are expected to be dispassionate, tolerant, and open-minded. Both are also expected to be honest, fair, and selfless. The virtues of kindness, sympathy, and fellow-feeling are not requisite,

although they are helpful. Both professions place their practitioners in positions of enormous trust, the one from his patient and his patient's family, the other from his audience of potential readers, not to mention the author himself.

The chief comparison is that both the psychiatrist and the book reviewer wield great power, the power to create as well as the power to destroy. The reputation of a book is as fragile, as malleable, as the spirit of a patient. These powers can be corrupted and abused. At its most recent meeting or congress, in Honolulu, the World Psychiatric Association, with a jaundiced eye upon the abuses of the profession in the Soviet Union, adopted the so-called "Declaration of Hawaii," amounting to a Hippocratic oath for psychiatrists. (The actual Dr. Bolshakov, incidentally, was in the Soviet delegation to this congress, and even had the audacity to deliver a paper, "Methods of Inducing Reality Acceptance into Mythomania.") Article Number Seven of the Declaration reads, "The psychiatrist must never use the possibilities of the profession for maltreatment of individuals or groups and should be concerned never to let inappropriate personal desires, feelings, or prejudices interfere with the treatment."

Those words could so easily be paraphrased, "The book reviewer must never use the possibilities of the profession for maltreatment of authors and should be concerned never to let inappropriate personal desires, feelings, or prejudices interfere with the review."

In *Georgie Boy*, Bolshakov as psychiatrist, in the end, is like a book reviewer who, having done everything he could to destroy the book's chances, must even visit the marketplace to ensure that the book is not displayed in bookstores, or, if it is, that its jacket is torn, its boards broken, its pages crumpled.

Let me make a bold hint to America's filmmakers, who seem to be running out of good ideas these days: the last fifty pages of *Georgie Boy,* if translated to the screen, could make a cinematic adventure of the highest order . . . even without Huck. Georgie travels alone, without money (because his mother neither gives him an allowance nor permits him to earn anything), across a thousand miles of country (it could be Russia, but the filmmakers will show us chunks of Kentucky, Illinois, Iowa, Kansas) to reach an impregnable, formidable fortress of a prison where his girlfriend sits, her head shaved, in a cell of solitary confinement, having abandoned all hope.

Hot on his heels, as the filmmakers say (and show), comes the team of two crazy shrinks, the evil Dr. Bolshakov and the flighty "Doctor Mom," who suspected Georgie's destination when he disappeared from the Laboratory. Georgie has a considerable head start on them but is on foot when he isn't successful hitchhiking. The two shrinks drive a car. There is considerable suspense: Will they catch up with him before he reaches the prison?

I will spoil neither the book reader's nor the moviegoer's pleasure by revealing how Georgie gets inside the prison. I will not even reveal what the filmmakers may choose to ignore: that

Georgie is no longer merely a lad of twelve; two years have passed and he is pushing fifteen now. The tense, harrowing climax of the book loses no credibility through our doubts that a young boy can pull off such a stunt. He is not so young anymore . . . and he does not pull it entirely off.

For me, the book's moment of truth, if not its actual climax, is the ultimate confrontation between the just-arrived pair Bolshakov/Doctor Mom and Georgie, in which the youth totally humiliates the both of them. It is the most satisfying "just deserts" I have ever encountered in literature, and I do not intend to give away one moment of its pleasure by quoting from any of it.

Throughout the book's final chapter, Georgie's articulate narrative voice, never boasting or vainglorious, the same voice that earlier "lapses" into surrealistic wordplay and apparent babble, becomes increasingly musical. There is a distinct tone and timbre to it that, if I am not mistaken in my own "listening" to it, derives straight from the popular First Piano Concerto of Tchaikovsky, or at least strongly reminds this listener of the elegiac, haunting moods of it, which seem to blaze a trail through an uncharted pastoral woodland.

The reader caught up in the very emotional music of the book's words may be puzzled, if not disappointed, to discover that the book does not end. The music stops, the last page is blank, the last sentence has no period on the end of it—but the book does not end.

Having already digressed, in this essay, into the nature of surrealism and the parallels between psychiatry and book reviewing, may I be permitted at the end a digression on endings? Any ending is sad (unless we are impatient to have done with a bad book) because, while we have spent the entire course of the book enjoying our privilege of actively participating in the creation of scenes and characters and even establishing the pace or time frame, we now find ourselves totally helpless to make the story continue. Given even the best imagination and inventiveness, we cannot visualize anything beyond "The End." It may be argued that even in the hypothetical happy ending, wherein the hero and heroine "live happily ever after," the hero and heroine are suddenly and certainly dead, as far as our access to them is concerned. Why then should they not literally die at the end of every story?

But when any time-factored work of art (including those works of visual art that require a certain amount of looking time properly to see them) comes to its inevitable conclusion, should we think of it, or of ourselves in relation to it, as dead? We can repeat our experience of it, we can bring it "alive" again and again, but we can never prevent, deter, or alter its ultimate demise. That demise is final.

Consider, as V. Kelian surely must have done, that none of the stories we experience in our nightly dreams ever has an "ending." We may wake up, or we may switch to another story, but we never end a story in a dream. "Every exit is an entry somewhere else," as a character declares in Tom Stoppard's *Rosencrantz and Guildenstern Are Dead.*

V. Kelian miraculously does not end *Georgie Boy.* Certainly, he, or his character in the title role, is killed. (We do not even wonder how this narrative could have come to have been written if he were dead.) Certainly his voice stops, or permanently falters. But he is not dead. Just how this is achieved I leave to be joyfully discovered by the reader impatient to put down my review and rush out to buy a copy of this remarkable, incredibly beautiful first novel.

20

I

THERE WERE TWO IMMEDIATE results of that lovely review. The first, coming within days, was that an influential director of the Book-of-the-Month Club, which had already passed up an opportunity to select *Georgie Boy* when it was still in manuscript, happened to read the review and was so taken by it that he brought strong pressure upon his organization to reconsider and to rush the novel into immediate adoption as an alternate selection for the month of June. This required a special printing of the volume (an edition somewhat more cheaply mass produced than Publisher Z's)—a printing that, as it turned out, had to be doubled, tripled, and infinitely multiplied after the membership read their copies of the *Book-of-the-Month Club News,* with a review of my novel quoting all of the other good reviews up to that point and making it look like the sensation of the season.

I was visiting Sharon in her newly restored residence in Stick Around, the house that had been her grandmother's general store and post office, by coincidence on the day the local telephone company was installing her phone; Sharon and I were staring at the instrument, one of the "old-fashioned" ordinary black plastic telephones with a dial rather than buttons, and Sharon remarked, "I wonder who will be the first to call," and the phone rang at that instant, the first call not for her but for me: I had given to Liz Blaustein Sharon's name and address, where I could be reached "in an emergency," although I wasn't expecting anything.

"Are you sitting down?" Liz asked. I wasn't, but that didn't deter her, and she told me about the BOMC selection, and also the second bit of good news generated by Clive Henry's wonderful words: a major British publisher, who like the BOMC had already once rejected the novel, had been influenced to change his mind and was paying an advance for British rights that was small but, more importantly, might lead other European publishers to consider or reconsider the novel.

Then, in rather quick succession, the "biggies" that Wölfflin had wanted began to appear. *Time, Newsweek,* and even *U.S. News and World Report,* the latter reviewing not so much the novel itself as its possible repercussions in foreign affairs: "Soviet Psychiatric Housecleaning Is in Order" was the title of their piece. *Psychology Today* had an essay-review under the title "What Motivates the Sadist?"

A belated but lengthy and clever review in the *New Yorker,* by John Updike, seemed to be more interested in my pen name than in the novel itself and went to great lengths to speculate about similarities between V. Kelian and V. Sirin (as the early Nabokov disguised himself) as well as B. Traven (as the mysterious Hal Croves or Traven Torsvan called himself, he who wrote *The Treasure of the Sierra Madre.*) But Updike took it for granted that Kelian, like Sirin and Traven, was male.

Book Digest ran a review of the *NYRB* review: a story about Clive Henry, the "thoughtful, wry, attentive" professor at Columbia University who had written the "brilliant" review for the *New York Review of Books* and had "dared" to compare the profession of book reviewing to that of psychiatry, both subject to abuses and corruption. Sharon pointed out to me that the photograph of Clive Henry accompanying the article made him look exactly like her old lover Larry Brace, and I agreed that the resemblance was indeed striking. I was tempted to write Clive Henry a fan letter but decided that authors ought not praise their own critics.

Liz Blaustein called again. "How do you feel about television?" she asked. Both "Good Morning, America," and the "Today" show had made firm offers for appearances, ten-minute minimum, and they were ready to fly me to New York or L.A., whichever I preferred.

"I'll have to get back to you on that," I replied, having picked up a few phrases of the polite jargon of the trade, and I called my editor, Wölfflin, and asked, "How do I feel about television?"

"You're beautiful," Wölfflin said, "but I'll have to get back to you on that." And Wölfflin called a day later to inform me that "our people have talked to their people," and our people had concluded that while television appearances would certainly boost sales, it would be better if I preserved the "mystery" of my identity. The public should not know that V. Kelian was a woman.

This meant that I had to decline not only all of the requests, and they began to multiply, to appear on television, but the urgent appeals from *People* magazine and *US* magazine for photo interviews. The more I (or rather Liz) refused the invitations, the more intense and aggressive they became. The so-called Sunday supplements, *Parade* and *U.S.A. Week-end,* ran articles with titles like "Who Is V. Kelian?" and "Mysterious Young Best-selling Writer Guards His Identity," but their discussions of the book itself denounced it for its pornography . . . which of course greatly helped sales.

The unpleasant *New York Times Book Review* had the duty of reporting *Georgie Boy*'s steady climb, week by week, up the exalted ladder of its Best-Seller List. Within two months of Clive Henry's review, my novel was firmly lodged in the top position on the list, where it would remain for over a year.

I moved into a suite of rooms in the Halfmoon Hotel, where I could have three meals a day in the Crystal Room when I didn't feel like walking to one of Arcaty's fine little eateries. Morris the cat immediately decided that he wanted to move in with me, or at least spend more of his time with me than elsewhere in the hotel, and one of the first of the many fine things I began to collect for my rooms was a wicker cat-cushion-cave for Morris to sleep in. I also began to pick up other things, folk furniture and folk crafts from the Bodarks and other southern highlands: an extensive assortment of baskets woven from white oak splits; a variety of quilts, some of them family heirlooms; and the beginnings of my collection of ladder-back, woven-hickory-seated furniture from Mount Judea, not far from Stick Around. And for my walls, in addition to the hangings of folk "finger weavings" and "wood pretties," I collected the time-warp and space-warp prints of M. C. Escher before they became fashionable everywhere. Soon my suite was overcrowded with my collections, and I began to think about more spacious quarters, especially after *Georgie Boy* rights were sold to Bantam for a cool million.

Commentators who have made much of certain similarities between Nabokov's later lifestyle and V. Kelian's have overlooked a crucial difference: Nabokov owned few possessions and boasted of being able to move easily from one lodging to another without anything in tow; I have collected so many things during my years at the Halfmoon that it is going to require several haulings with a four-wheel-drive truck to move my belongings from this hotel to my next destination . . . or else I am fated to remain here for the rest of my life.

How did Ingraham know I was living at the Halfmoon? Perhaps he guessed. At any rate, that was where he addressed his letter to me. The letter was ostensibly congratulatory. He was only assuming, he said, that *Georgie Boy* was the same novel that he had known and encouraged as *Geordie Lad* back in Pittsburgh and that he had "provided" me a place to finish. If I wanted to keep my identity a secret, he assured me, he would not brag to any of his Fateville friends that he had known me "back when" or that he had actually helped in the production of that runaway best-seller. He himself, he reminded me, had "pursued the bitch goddess, Success," for all of his long writing career, but "never got within sniffing distance of her body odor, even." So he was glad, and vicariously thrilled, that she had smiled upon me.

The real reason for his letter, it turned out, was that he, with the help of his wife, Kay, had finished six chapters of a nonfiction book about ghost towns. The book was quasi-autobiographical; in it he compared six episodes of his own life to the beginning, rise, and decline of the towns. He had not yet reached the Pittsburgh episode and rushed to assure me that he did not intend to capitalize upon his friendship with me or to reveal my identity. He might not even mention me at all. Anyway, what he really wanted to ask me was, would I consider using my "considerable influence" with Publisher Z in order to find an editor interested in his work?

Grateful as I was to Ingraham for all he'd done for me, I thought that was rather presumptuous of him, and I replied, *You have confused me with the notorious V. Kelian, the male author of the best-seller* Georgie Boy. *Have you read the book?* I knew that Ingraham, given his reading habits, or rather nonreading habits, had probably not purchased the book, let alone read it.

A month or so after that, I received a picture postcard of the quaint square in downtown Fateville, on the back of which he had written, *I am reading* Georgie Boy. *Have you read anything of* mine? Touché, old Ingraham.

It was a poor season for business at the Halfmoon; the motels on the highway were siphoning off the tourist trade, and there were occasions when I had the Crystal Room to myself at breakfast or lunch. The management was even considering closing down the building for the winter. I would be without a place to live, and, much as I appreciated an offer from Sharon to move in with her in Stick Around, I really preferred the advantages, such as they were, of my town life in Arcaty.

Then Trevor Kola, the illustrious Hollywood filmmaker, bought the movie rights to *Georgie Boy* for, as it was reported, "a very high six figures," making it possible for me to lease the entire north wing of the top floor of the Halfmoon, along with the penthouse that rose two flights above it, and I had a delightful winter, supervising the conversion of that floor and penthouse into one spacious triplex apartment, complete with a vast futuristic kitchen wherein I could use the latest microchip appliances and fixtures to prepare one of my Svanetian chicken dishes, *khenagi* or *tsitsila shkimerulat,* and two rooms devoted entirely to a huge walk-in closet wherein I could hang my burgeoning wardrobe, flanking a bathroom with pool-size sunken tub and Jacuzzi (requiring the lowering of the ceiling in the servant's bedroom directly below it), and a sauna-cum-shower that would easily accommodate a party. What fun I had equipping my music room! The speakers alone, Hartley Concertmasters, cost me over five thousand dollars, and I spent at least that much on a record collection.

There was also (why am I using the past tense? There *is.* I see it from where I pen—or pencil—these words) a chess nook, a special room without the windows that distract one with the gorgeous view of the hills surrounding Arcaty, devoted to a special chess table with a Bombay inlaid mother-of-pearl chessboard, upon which I placed an eighteenth-century Dieppe bone-carved chess set, found for me my dealer-friend Lennie Lewin of the Esoterica Gallery on Spring Street.

It was in that chess nook that I first played, and played with, young Travis Coe, at a time in his life when he was, if my reader can believe this, almost totally unknown.

II

IN THOSE DAYS before he ever had a lesson in diction, he pronounced his name "Tray-viss," as in B. Traven, and I, knowing no better, came to pronounce it that way too. The facts of his origins are all too familiar to readers of movie magazines and Sunday supplements: He was a found-ling, of sorts, born in the mountain fastnesses west of Stick Around, in a still-primitive area of the rural Bodarks where, as he put it, "the Coes is so thick their dogs caint tell 'em apart," his mother a Coe girl of thirteen who was first cousin to her inseminator, a Coe not much older than she—the two of them keeping him only long enough to name him, and then leaving him on the cabin doorstep of a spinster aunt, Fannie Coe, who grudgingly but dutifully raised him from infancy, teaching him the language and the ways of the deepest backwoods, to the age of twelve, when he ran away from home to see the sights of the nearest "city," actually just the large town I have called "Harriman." Trying to find his way home after discovering that Harriman had hardly been worth the trouble, he got confused on the highway and took the westerly instead of the southerly direction, which led him in due course to Arcata Springs, where he began living hand-to-mouth, artfully dodging the truant officers and welfare officers who couldn't get him to stand still long enough to be fingerprinted, let alone placed in a foster home and returned to school.

His formal education had ended with the fourth grade of the con-solidated school to which he'd ridden a yellow school bus for four years from Aunt Fannie's cabin. Of the American "three *r*'s," he was terrible in 'rithmetic, could scarcely 'rite his own name, but was, somehow, excellent in reading. And that was how I met him.

One chill morning in February I'd walked down the hill to the Arcata Springs Public Library, that small limestone edifice (with a pair of Doric columns and a frieze) donated to the town by the philanthropic cousin of my old spook acquaintance Lawren. I was searching for a book, John Joseph Matthews's *Wah'kon-tah,* which was crucial to the research on the Osage Indians that I was contemplating for my as-yet-uncommenced second novel. I knew I could not rest on my laurels much longer, or allow V. Kelian to rest on his, but I had vacillated for some time between trying to write a novel with a Svanetian setting, which might not be very popular in English-speaking countries, or indulging my longtime fascination with the American Indian to write something about my adopted country.

The librarian informed me that *Wah'kon-tah* had been checked out. When I protested, she, casting a glance toward the front door, told me that the library had a policy of never revealing the identity of one borrower to another, but that she could tell me that the book would probably be back "very shortly" because the borrower, who had just taken it that morning, was a "very fast" reader. For the price of a postcard, I could leave my name and address, and they would notify me as soon as the book was returned. When I gave my address as the Halfmoon, the librarian said, "Oh, you are just passing through?"

"No," I said, "I live at the Halfmoon," and I resisted the impulse to call her attention to the copy of *Georgie Boy* that was propped up on the counter under a sign that said, THIS WEEK'S NO. 1 BEST-SELLER.

Disappointed at leaving without *Wah'kon-tah,* I was astonished to discover, sitting on the front parapet at the top of the library's steep stairsteps, precariously high above Spring Street, busily absorbed in reading that very book, the boy who was destined to enter my life and heart. In the best tradition of contemporary confessional literature by and about the famous in American culture, I can now reveal that it was Travis Coe to whom I was referring in that recent *Paris Review* interview (see below, page 355: the audacious question was, "Just as Monsieur Humbert was genuinely in love with his Lolita, or Dolores, haven't you ever found yourself similarly in love with one of your boys?" and I replied, "Only one").

He moved his lips as he read, and his lips were a blur. They were full but not broad. His yellow hair was not combed; perhaps it had not been combed recently, nor trimmed in quite some time. The morning sun was warming up the day, and the burgeoning freckles on his cheeks were like little sunbeams, but it was still cold February, and his jacket was inches too short for his freckled arms and couldn't be zipped up the front, so that his dirty, frayed plaid flannel shirt was exposed. His shoes, or sneakers, were woeful, and there was a gaping hole in the knee of one his trousers . . . This was a year or so before the national fad for wearing blue jeans full of deliberate holes. But his freckled face, although it was still bowed over the book, was washed and clean and surpassingly lovely, and I had a great urge to get a better look at it, to say something that would make him look up at me.

"Would you rather believe in Wah'kon-tah than in God?" I asked. To the Osages, the name means something like "Mysterious Great Spirit."

For a long moment he did not look up, and when he did, he glanced first at me, quickly, then to the left and to the right of him to see if there was anybody else I might be addressing. At length he said, scratching his head with one hand and laying a finger of the other hand on his chest, "Me?" and when I nodded, he said, "I didn't hear ye." I repeated my question, and instead of answering it he asked me, "Air ye a hooky cop?"

I thought perhaps it was an Osage Indian word. "Hoog'kee-kop? What's that?"

"Air ye aimin to git me back to the schoolhouse?"

I think I understood, then, that he was truant and was mistaking me for a truant officer. "Why, no, I was just planning to read *Wah'kon-tah* myself, but you beat me to it." He scratched his head again, then closed the book and held it out to me. I would not take it. "No, no," I said. "You go ahead and read it, and I'll just check it out when you return it to the library." He reopened the book and made a pretense of resuming his reading of it, but he was clearly uncomfortable and continued scratching his head, waiting for me to go away. I still could scarcely believe that a boy just on the edge of puberty would be reading a thick, heavy volume on the Osage Indians, even if Matthews was something of a popularizer. It was almost as if this kid and myself were the only two persons in the world with any interest in the Osages, and here we were together in the same town where once those Indians had roamed and bathed and made love. I couldn't let him go out of my sight. "Could I buy you something to drink?" I offered. "A Coke or something?"

He looked up at me again, and his eyes narrowed. He retarded the hand that was scratching his head. "The last lady tried to buy me a Coke," he declared, "she also tried to get me to go back to the schoolhouse."

"I swear to you that I'm not a hooky cop or whatever. I'd just like to buy you something to drink . . . and perhaps talk about Wah'kon-tah."

He studied me. The hand on his head dropped to his lap. "Would you also give me a dollar?"

I studied him, pondering his question for a moment until I realized that he was—what's the expression?—he was panhandling. "Sure," I said, and I opened my purse and took out not a dollar but a ten, and offered it to him. His narrowed eyes opened greatly at the sight of it, and he took it quickly, as if afraid I might have second thoughts or expect him to make change. He stood up, closing the book and holding it at his side.

We walked together—and he was almost as tall as I—down Spring Street to one of the cafés near the New Orleans Hotel, which took its name from all the cast iron on its front. He ordered not a Coke but a cup of coffee and then asked me, "Could I also get me a doughnut?"

"Have a dozen doughnuts, if you want," I said. He ordered and ate four doughnuts and had three cups of coffee, to my one. Afterward, when I lit my cigarette, he looked at me so expectantly that I offered him one too, and he took it eagerly. We were the only people in the room except for the waitress, and if she frowned upon my giving a cigarette to a kid, that was her problem, as they say. "What's your name?" I asked him.

"Tray-vis," he said. "What's your'n?"

"You may call me Kat," I told him.

He resumed scratching his head. "Like in *kitty-kat?*" he asked.

I nodded and asked, "Do you live in Arcaty?" He nodded. "Where?" I asked. "Near here?"

He gave his head an encompassing toss in a noncommittal direction. "Oh, jist hither and yon," he said. "Whereabouts do you live at?"

"Do you know the Halfmoon?" I asked.

"Why, shore," he said, and tossed his head in a definite direction. "Up yonder on the mountain. I figgered ye was a tourister. You don't sound like ye come from this part of the country."

"I live at the Halfmoon," I told him. "Permanently."

He gave me a quizzical look and once more scratched his head. "Is that a fack, now? Do you own the place?"

"No, I just have a bunch of rooms there, on the top floor and penthouse."

"A whole bunch, huh? What do ye do for yore money? Or didje just inherit it or some'pn?"

I laughed. "How do you know I've got so much?"

"You jist gave me a big chunk of it, didn't ye?" he grinned. "And you jist have the look of a lady who's loaded."

"Thank you," I said. "I'm a writer, and I wrote a book that made a lot of money."

"You don't mean to tell me," he said, with genuine awe, and his fingers burrowed into his scalp once more. "What's the name of it? Could be I've done read it myself."

I debated whether to tell him. I was warming to him by the minute and fantasizing the "project" I could make of him, and I knew that eventually, if not this very night, he would find out the title of my book. So why not tell him now? Because I was still committed to preserving the secrecy that surrounded my *nom de plume*. But curiosity got the better of me: could it possibly be that this uncouth but not unlettered child of the backwoods had actually at least heard of my novel? "Do you read fiction?" I asked him.

"You mean whopper tales?" he asked. "Yeah, that's my favorite kind of book. Made-up stories. *Novels.*"

"Did you ever hear of a novel called *Georgie Boy?*"

"Sure, I heared of it," he declared. "Matter a fact, I even seen it a-settin there on the counter in the lie-berry. Matter a fact, I even tried to check it out, but the lie-berrian said it wasn't fitten for children, though she orter know I aint exactly no child no more."

"Well, I wrote it," I said.

He shook his head. "Unt-uh. That book was wrote by a feller name of V. Kelian. I don't know what the *V* is fer. Maybe Virgil."

"Vladimirovna," I pronounced. "It's my middle name."

"What-all kind of middle name is *that?*" he wanted to know.

"Russian," I said. "It means 'daughter of Walter.'"

"You're a Com'nist?" he wondered.

I shook my head. "I'm neither Communist nor Russian. I came from a beautiful country called Georgia, which the Russians conquered."

"I never been east of the Mississippi," he said, "but I heared tell of Georgia."

"Not *that* Georgia. Mine was a European country in the Caucasus Mountains."

"That's the one I mean," he said. "Where that Com'nist boss name of Joe Stalin come from. I read all about it."

"You read an awful lot," I observed.

"Ain't much else to do," he declared sadly. "Won't nobody give me a job of work, on account of I'm too young."

"What work could you do?" I asked.

"Jist anything, near 'bouts," he said proudly. "I don't reckon I'm old enough to write books, like you do, not yet anyhow. But I could do near 'bouts anything else."

"All right," I said, smiling, "I could offer you a job as my houseboy."

His eyes made that squint again, in disbelief, and I began to wonder if he kept scratching his head out of genuine befuddlement or if perhaps he had some skin itch. "Air ye a-funnin me?" he asked. I thought about his verb and decided it meant something like "making fun of." I shook my head, sincerely. "What-all does a houseboy have to do?" he asked.

I counted off some random things on my ten fingers. "Could you feed my cat? Bring up the newspaper and the mail? Dust the furniture? Run the bath? Help in the kitchen?" To each of these he nodded. "Could you polish my shoes? Carry packages home from shopping trips? Return books to the library for me? Check a few out?" He nodded. I had just one finger left. "Could you rub my back?"

"Why, shore," he said. Then he grinned and narrowed those eyes once more. "You want me to sleep with you, too? Or have you already got somebody that does that?"

My turn to narrow my eyes and grin. "Are you experienced in such work?"

"I never been nobody's houseboy before," he declared. "But if you got the money, I could do anything you pay me for."

"Would you like to see my rooms?"

"Why not?" he said. "Let's go." He stood up.

"What about your parents? Do you want to let them know where you're going?"

"Parents?" He snorted a kind of sardonic laugh. "My momma wasn't much older than me when I was born, and I aint seen her since. I saw my daddy, once, from a distance, when somebody pointed him out to me, and one look was all I could stand."

"So who do you live with?" I asked.

"You," he said.

III

VICARIOUSLY I WAS ABLE to inspect my new twelve-room triplex apartment, through the awestruck eyes of Travis Coe. He revealed to me that the classmates he'd once had in the fourth grade had called him Coelumbus (shortened eventually to just Lum), and it seemed to me that he was looking at my rooms with the wonder and astonishment and, yes, fulfillment with which Christopher Columbus must have first laid eyes on the New World. Because when he'd left home, left his Aunt Fannie's cabin and the nineteenth-century world of the Bodarks behind him, and set out on the journey that would take him eventually to stardom, he was setting out, as Columbus had, to discover a passage to a fabled world of riches that he had only read and heard about and that he scarcely believed he would ever find.

He was so absorbed with my rooms he forgot to scratch his head. He would point at a door and ask, "Who lives in there?" and when I would explain that that was simply one more of my rooms, he would shake his head, and then he would point at a stairway and ask, "Who lives up there?" and when I took him up to the second level and he found another stairway leading to the top level and he asked again, "So who lives up *there?*" and I said my own bedroom was up there he asked, "You mean you got all *three* of these floors all to yourself?"

"And you," I said.

Even though my library (on the first level) was not yet stocked with books, it seemed to be the room that most fascinated my new companion ("I never even heared tell of nobody havin a whole lie-berry room all to theirself"), and I was charmed when he decided to contribute to the stocking of the room by placing his copy of *Wah'kon-tah* in the middle of an empty stretch of walnut shelf and declaring, "There! Now we both can use it."

It was in the library that Travis met Morris. Whether Travis had an indifference to the concept of pets in general (not realizing that he himself was about to become one), or whether Morris simply had an instinctive dislike for young boys, the kid and the cat never would hit it off together.

After the library, he was most captivated by my personal rooms in the penthouse's top level. He simply could not believe the sunken bathtub. "Why, there's swimmin holes up on Thomas Creek aint near as big as *that!*" he exclaimed. And although I was tempted to offer on the spot to let him take a skinny-dip in it and try out its gushing Jacuzzi whirlpools, I was constrained to point out that his own room below, in the servant's quarters, had its own bathtub-with-shower, amply sizable for a thorough dip if not a swim. He found the fact of having his own quarters (on the main level with a splendid northward view) incredible. When he stood on the threshold of his bedroom, unable to move, unable to say anything, unable even to scratch his head, I suggested I might leave him alone while I looked at the morning's mail, and he was able, at last, to sigh and say, "I do believe I done died and come up here to Heaven." And he grinned at me and asked, "And wasn't I too young to die, anyhow?"

Later, when room service brought up our lunch, I attempted to give him his first instructions in how to be a waiter. He had had enough experience with Arcaty's cafés to know what waitresses do, and a waiter was simply a waitress in pants. He did an admirable job of keeping a fresh linen napkin draped over his crooked arm. He had some difficulty on his first attempt at using a corkscrew, but he got the hang of it and managed, by holding the bottle between his legs, to get the cork out, and he was very quick to understand my explanation of why he should proffer me the cork to sniff and then pour my wineglass only a taste pending my approval.

All that was lacking was suitable attire for my waiter/houseboy. Arcaty didn't have a real department store, or even a men's shop, as such, but there were some specialty shops on Spring Street that carried some clothing and shoes he could wear, and before the afternoon was over we had assembled a fairly decent wardrobe for him, although nothing really fit him well because of his skinniness and his height.

On the way home I asked if he didn't have any belongings, anywhere, that he would want to bring with him to the Halfmoon. "It'll take me just a secont," he said, and disappeared up some alley off Spring Street and was gone for more than a second, more like five minutes, while I stood and waited for him, having dreadful thoughts that he had changed his mind and had disappeared for good.

But eventually he returned to me, bringing a little red bandanna ("snotrag," he inelegantly called it) into which he had wrapped all his former earthly possessions, having kept the bundle stashed away in the crevice of a rock wall off Spring Street.

Back at our lodgings, he revealed the contents of the bandanna: a frayed toothbrush, a tube of toothpaste, an extra pair of socks, a broken black comb with teeth missing, some kind of shiny rock, a creased black-and-white photo of a homely young girl presumed to be his mother, a fishing lure, two nickels, three lumps of hard candy, four bottle caps from Dr. Pepper and Grapette, an arrowhead, a much-chewed pencil, a feather, a blue hair ribbon, a school report card with bad grades except in reading, some rubber bands and lengths of string, and an eight-times folded page from *Holiday* magazine depicting a pastoral valley of the Bodarks.

I suggested that before serving our dinner he might want to run up for a shower and change clothes.

"How come my privy's a two-holer?" he wanted to know, after his shower.

I didn't understand him. "I'm sorry?" I said.

"There's two toilets side by side in my bathroom," he pointed out. "Only somebody took the seat off'n one of 'em."

"That one," I said, "isn't a toilet. It's a bidet. It's for washing, not elimination."

"Washing what?" he wanted to know.

"Your bottom," I said.

He blushed. "I never heared tell of no sech a thang in all my life," he said. And it seemed I could hear the distant echo of the accents of his Aunt Fannie in his words.

At dinner he was neatly dressed. When he'd finished serving me, once again, as I'd done at lunch, I invited him to sit across from me and eat his own dinner (and sample the wine, too, if he desired, and he did), although I explained that, as a houseboy, he wouldn't always be invited to join me at meals. He giggled and remarked, "Back up home, in the old days, the womenfolks used to have to wait till the men was all done eatin before they could set at the table theirselfs. You're turnin it around, aint ye?"

"Right," I said. "In Svanetia, where I came from, the same custom prevailed, in olden times. The women never ate until the men had finished, but stood behind the men's chairs, waiting and starving."

"Tell me everthing about Svanetia," he requested, and I was pleased and flattered that he'd ask, but I didn't know where to begin. He prompted, "Does everbody got them bee-days in their house?"

"No, I never saw a bidet in Svanetia. I never saw one until I got to Paris. In Svanetia, they have privies that are just wooden shacks built around deep holes in the ground, out away from the houses, quite similar to the outhouses in Stick Around."

His face lit up, and his mouth dropped open. "Do you know Stick Around?"

"I lived there while I wrote most of my novel, *Georgie Boy.*"

He resumed scratching his head.

IV

WHY DID IT TAKE ME so long to investigate the real reason that Travis kept scratching his head? Quite possibly I knew from the beginning but was not willing to confirm my suspicion. Later that first night I reached the point—or rather, the two of us reached the point—of easiness, familiarity, and closeness where I felt I had to confirm my suspicion, even if it cost me repugnance toward this ideal youth.

But getting him to let me have a close examination of his scalp was almost as difficult as persuading a shy boy to take off his pants. I had to use subterfuge: It was easy enough to entice him into sitting at the grand checkerboard table in the chess nook and playing with the large ivory and ebony pieces (I let him have white for his maiden try). He was genuinely eager to learn the rudiments of the game. He had never even seen a chess set before, but he had read about the game in several books, including a biography of Bobby Fischer that had enthralled him. He "misdoubted," he said, that he would be able to make a match for me "for a good long spell," but that first night he tried his best to learn the basic rules and concepts, although the unusual license given to the movements of knights was very difficult for him to grasp, and under pretext of needing to guide his placement of his knight, I came around to his side of the table and bent over him. From long experience, I was able to "read" the board from his side as easily as from mine, and we continued the game that way, with me behind him, sometimes resting one hand on his shoulder while reaching out with the other hand to show him where and how to move his knight, or to move one of my own pieces in response.

The hand I laid on his shoulder became restless and curious: I let it slip down inside his shirt, over his chest, which I stroked. When my fingertip touched his nipple, he shuddered, shivered, lightly gasped. I ran my fingertip circularly around that nipple, then shifted to the other nipple, which was already swollen. I spoke quietly into his ear, "Does this bother you?"

His voice dropped a register to reply hoarsely, "Naw, that feels right good, but I aint gonna be able to concentrate on the next place my horsey wants to go."

I misunderstood, for a while, that what he meant by "horsey" was simply his knight. I unbuttoned his shirt so that I could slip my hand farther down the front of him. While doing so, however, my face rested against the top of his head, and my eyes were startled to discover in his hair a number of the nits of lice.

Excusing myself to go to the bathroom, I privately phoned a still-open local pharmacy, inquired about the best medications for lice, and had an assortment of solutions and soaps and salves sent up to the Halfmoon's desk, from where Bob the porter would bring them up to my floor. When I resumed playing chess with Travis, I returned to my own side of the board, and I concluded in a few moves our second game, checkmating him more savagely than I'd intended.

"Wooo, you creamed me!" he said, and I needed a moment to determine which of the slang meanings of that verb he intended: that I'd simply beaten him badly. Then he studied me quizzically and said, "It's okay if you wanter feel me. Why did you stop?"

I was spared replying by the porter's knock at the door, which I answered, taking the package from the pharmacy and tipping Bob a dollar.

"Who was that?" he asked, as I returned from answering the porter's knock.

"Do you like chess so far?" I asked. "Tomorrow we will play several games. But now, dear, I would like to ask you to take this special soap and wash your hair very thoroughly with it, and then I will put some of this stuff on it."

He blushed scarlet and hung his head. "Just don't call me 'dear,' okay?" was all he could say. But he reached out and took the package of soap and headed for his quarters.

I called after him, "You can just wear your new bathrobe."

And when he returned to me later, his wet hair plastered to his head and his whole young body smelling of the medicated soap, he was wearing only the bathrobe, a fancy velour of emerald green that complemented and complimented his red freckles, and on his cute feet a new pair of what he called "flip-flops," made of rubber.

But alluring as he was, whatever powerful attraction I had for him that night was canceled by the thought of his lice. I arranged him sitting on the floor with his back to me, his body between my legs, while I applied the solution and then spent several minutes combing it into his hair, each stroke of the comb bringing out a dozen or so of the nits. Having him between my legs like that aroused me greatly, but whatever lust I was feeling for him was spoiled by the unpleasant task of grooming him.

It was just as well I didn't feel inclined to seduce him that night. Looking back, I think I came eventually to appreciate how *gradual* our relationship was, how my seduction of him, if that was what it was, did not occur rashly and hastily. That first night, when I'd finished applying the medicine to his head and combing his hair, after he'd dutifully asked if there was anything he could get for me or do for me, and I'd declined his offer to brush my hair (for fear I'd catch a few of the nits off his hands), he went off to bed and put out his light, but with the door to his quarters ajar, at my request, in case there was anything I needed to have my houseboy do in the middle of the night.

Much later, after I'd had my vodka nightcap and was doing some reading in Sam Clemens, I heard him crying. It seemed so uncharacteristic of him that I had to listen for a good while before I convinced myself that indeed the sounds were of a twelve-year-old boy crying.

I got up and went in unto him, and I sat beside him and rested my hand on top of his head as if my touch itself could cure him. "What's the matter, Tray-vis?" I asked softly.

"I guess I been lousy all my life," he said. And then, intelligent enough to catch the double meaning of the adjective, he made a kind of chuckling laugh and said, "I mean, infested with louses."

"Lice," I gently corrected him. "But we're going to get rid of them. Wait and see if we don't."

He sniffled. "Still and all, you won't never want me to sleep with you."

"Do *you* want to sleep with me?"

"I need for you to like me," he said. "I wanter do whatever you want me to, just so's you'll always like me."

"I like you very much, Tray-vis," I assured him. "Your lice don't bother me. And I don't ever want you to feel you *have* to sleep with me."

"But I *want* to," he declared.

And oh! the way he said that, sincerely and with feeling, gave me a powerful urge to take him into my bed despite his lice. I knew that if I did, I'd have to wash and rewash the sheets, but that wasn't really the problem. There was something about the intensity of his wish that made me ask, paraphrasing my earlier question to him, "Have you ever slept with a girl?"

It is too bad that my verbal modesty prevented me from coming right out and asking him if he'd ever had sex with a female before. When he said, "No, I aint," he was truthfully declaring that he had never drifted off to sleep in the company of a female.

21

I

SO HE DID NOT SLEEP WITH ME that night. Nor the next. According to my journal, Travis Coe, whose bed hopping in Hollywood has become legendary, did not enter my bed until his tenth night under my roof. It took nearly that long for him to banish the lice from his hair.

We developed some daily routines. Each morning, the alarm clock in his room would rouse him at 7:00; he would shower, apply his dose of hair medicine, dress, open a can of 9-Lives for Morris (of whom he was grudgingly accepting, although the cat did not return the feeling), run down to the desk to get the morning's copy of the *Gazette,* the one decent daily published in the entire state, and a bouquet of fresh flowers left by the local florist, then chat (and possibly flirt) with Lurline, the cute desk clerk who had replaced Sharon and who, despite being a staunch Jehovah's Witness, "tolerated" my employment of Travis because she was under orders from the management to "do whatever that lady wants." He was back in my kitchen by 7:45.

Travis had volunteered to prepare breakfast, and it took him only a few mornings to learn how many seconds to leave the egg cooker running, and how many seconds the toaster required, and the exact amount of mocha java to scoop into the Mr. Coffee machine.

At 8:00 on the dot, he would turn on the Harman Kardon system, flooding all three floors of the apartment with something by Beethoven, a quartet or a sonata, the *Appassionata,* perhaps, then bring up to my bedroom, and present me with, a bed tray upon which were the breakfast, the flowers, and the newspaper. He would return at 8:30 to collect the dishes and ask if I needed anything further, then he would run my bath; it took a good half hour for the enormous sunken tub to fill with water and bubbles.

Once I was in my "soak," as he called it, he would be free to do what he liked, usually curling up on his own sofa with a book—*Wah'kon-tah,* which took him only two mornings to finish, and then, with my permission, *Georgie Boy,* which took him three or four. After my bath (and I must confess that I had discovered quickly how easily the vigorous jets of water coming out of the Jacuzzi were capable of arousing me, so that I had to restrain myself from summoning my houseboy to get into the water with me), I went to work: In lieu of any genuinely creative employment (for a good second-book idea still eluded me), I was busily attempting to read and correct the proofs of the French edition of my novel, *Le Garçon Georges.* I'd had a few years of French in college and had used it much during my visit to my aunt and namesake in Paris, and I thought I was capable, with the help of a *Cassell's French Dictionary* purchased at the Gazebo and some real or imagined promptings from the spirit of Daniel Lyam Montross, of spotting a number of misrenderings and *malentendus* in Claude Voleur's generally excellent translation, which in a few more months would become the number-one best-seller in France.

After lunch (I refused Travis's request to let him prepare it himself, not because I mistrusted his abilities but because in this off-season the Halfmoon's kitchen needed some excuse for staying open), we would digest our meals together in the chess nook, where I would introduce him to openings, the Ruy Lopez and the Benko Gambit particularly, and I would resist the temptation further to hover behind his back and feel up his chest.

Then we would go for a walk. The early March weather was often sunny, almost balmy, and while nothing was blooming other than tulips and daffodils I was able to predict, in our rambles along the woodland paths on the slopes of Halfmoon Mountain, the places where the first mushrooms would appear in April. "Just wait and see," I would say to him. "Right there will spring up a cluster of *Secotium agaricoides* next month. It looks like what you call 'puffball,' but it has a fleshy central stem like other mushrooms, just concealed." He said he would come back here next month and see if I was wrong.

But mostly our hikes took us not off into forest footpaths but down among the man-built erections of Arcaty: There are fifty-four miles of limestone retaining walls, built without mortar, lining the sidewalks of the streets, as well as the back streets and alleys, which spill and twist all over the knolls and ravines of that precipitous village (such is the meandering of the town's steep streets that none of them ever intersect). Walking between the looming blocks of limestone (Travis and I were the only pedestrians) gave us a snug, protected feeling, almost as if our walkways were ramparted. Behind the retaining walls, usually, are the quaint Victorian gingerbread cottages and mansions that are the town's major tourist attraction, since the springs themselves are no longer potable or even functional—but we would visit them too: Grotto Spring and Cave Spring, with their picturesque limestone formations; and the springs of Spring Street, beginning with the dramatic Halfmoon Spring itself, dry but enshrouded in a pergola-pagoda-gazebo within the crescent-shaped limestone ledge that gave the name of its shape to the spring and thus to the hotel; followed just down the street by Harington Spring, with its benches for resting; and Sweet (or Sweetheart) Spring, sur-rounded and surmounted by the steep climbing stairs.

The "shortcut" to get from one street to another in Arcaty is often not the conventional sidewalk but a steep flight of steps, of native limestone, or of old poured cement, or of iron or even of wood: stairs plunging and turning up and down the embankments of limestone, often flanked by steep cement gutters for storm drainage, and often, or always, flanked by iron or steel handrails. Soon after my arrival in Arcaty, I recognized these labyrinths of staircases as the earthly embodiment of those seen continually in my old familiar dreams of climbing and de-scending an endless sequence of stone steps, concrete steps, iron steps, and wooden steps, staircases that led up or down to significant places whose significance had always eluded me, and, once I'd seen the mazes of inclines in reality, I stopped dreaming about them. Now Travis and

I spent a lot of time going up and down the great variety of stairways that link the pathways of the town. Although I had lived in Arcaty for over two years and had done much steep walking there, Travis seemed more familiar than I with the routes or destinations, if any, of these steps. One of these stairways, almost hidden beside a shop where Main Street meets Spring Street, led us up to the grotto or cavern wherein were the remains of an old rock house purportedly built by the Osage Indians but actually erected by the white man who displaced them: Dr. Alvah Jackson, the discoverer of Halfmoon Spring and its magic properties. The rock house is open to the elements, uninhabited, secluded; and I was somehow reminded, climbing up to it, of going with Kenny Elmore up to his rooftop astronomical observatory. I would have enjoyed using the rock house as a symbolic site for taking Travis's virginity . . . except that on the March afternoon we visited it the sunless grotto was chilly and even damp, and Travis, having finished *Wah'kon-tah,* wanted to talk about the "spirit" of the Osages that he sensed in the grotto. We talked a lot and never touched.

Back at our penthouse after these long hikes, we would take turns using the sauna. Travis had enough difficulty accepting the sight of the sweat pouring from his own body without being required, or permitted, to watch it pouring from mine. Only after we'd showered and changed into fresh clothes would we see each other again.

And then was the "empty" part of the late afternoon, before supper. "Would you like to have a television set for your room?" I asked him. "If you want to watch TV, just say so, and I'll get you a big color screen."

He thought for a long moment before answering, "Naw, I reckon I've got along purty good without one this long, I don't want to pick up a hankerin' fer it."

So I would read and correct another chapter of *Le Garçon Georges* while he flipped through one of the several glossy magazines that arrived regularly in the mail. Sometimes Morris would saunter up to be stroked by Travis or myself, and for a time Morris liked to sit in Travis's lap; but after the novelty of Travis wore off, Morris resumed his usual feline superciliousness.

Then a young man from the Halfmoon's kitchen would bring up supper; Travis would drape his arm with a fresh linen napkin, uncork the wine, serve the meal, and, as often as not, be invited to join me in the eating and drinking.

II

THIS ROUTINE WAS BROKEN on the afternoon that Travis, instead of going with me on my daily hike, heeded my request to get himself a haircut. With my help and the drugstore's chemicals, the last louse and nit had disappeared from his hair, which, I suggested, needed trimming; I was uncertain of my ability to do the job myself, so I sent him off to the barbershop. After my hike, I used the post-sauna empty time to start a special supper I'd planned to replace the hotel's fare: *mtsvadi,* skewered lamb, the tastiest of all Georgian meats. Traditionally, the roasting of the meat over coals was always done by men, who were also responsible for preparing the fire and getting the coals just right, and throughout my exile from Svanetia I had been tortured by the memory of how much the very aroma of their activities had caused my mouth to water. My kitchen was equipped with a top-of-the-line Jenn-Aire, which had an elaborate grill with grill-rocks element, a suitable substitute for the requisite coals of hardwood and grapevine branches, and easily regulated to the correct temperature, but I had not yet had a good chance, or a good recipe, to try on it.

When Travis came home from his haircut (and a shopping errand for me, to find some cherry tomatoes to skewer beside the lamb chunks), he found me hastily trying to impale the lamb chunks on a couple of *shampuri,* authentic but wicked daggers imported from Georgia by my friend Lennie Lewin of the Esoterica Gallery. Travis, first asking me what I was doing and being told, offered to do it for me. And while he was doing it, alternating skewering the cherry tomatoes he'd found, it occurred to me to see if I could teach him to do the Svanetian men's work of actually supervising the grill and cooking the meat. Since he was so eager to learn the work of my kitchen, he took to the task with alacrity.

But he sniffed and asked, "What-all kind of meat is this-a-here, anyhow?" and when I told him it was lamb he asked, "You mean a baby *sheep?*" Many people in the rural Bodarks, where pork or chicken are the common meats, have never sampled lamb, and this was Travis's first encounter with it. But after his first wary bite of a chunk of it straight from the *shampuri,* he mmmed and declared, "Anybody who ain't never et this stuff don't have no idee what they're missing."

Our *mtsvadi* was served with sliced cucumbers, a Svanetian *shoti's puri* bread I'd baked and frozen some weeks earlier and now served thawed and hot, and a bottle of the best Gevrey-Chambertin that the local liquor store carried. Before the evening was over, my houseboy would be required to uncork a second bottle of it.

Nor had he ever eaten by candlelight before. He had eaten by the light of kerosene lamps ("coal oil," he called it) but tall, thin tapers were a new sight for him, and eight of them, in two silver candelabra, were sufficient light for us.

Midway through the elegant, luscious meal Travis, having finished his reading of *Georgie Boy,* abruptly asked me if this food was the kind that Dzhordzha and his Princess used to talk wistfully about the possibility of having (*Georgie Boy,* pp. 187–191 *et seq.*), a possibility that never ever became a reality, and, thinking of it, I began to weep, more for joy at having finally realized the meal than for sadness over the fact that it was Travis, not Dzhordzha, who was sharing it with me.

"Hey!" Travis said, solicitously. "What's the matter? Did I say the wrong thing? Am I using the wrong fork? Did you spot another nit still in my hair?"

I brushed away my tears. "No," I said. "I was just remembering a time when I was young."

"You're still young," he observed, refilling the wineglasses for both of us. "I could blink my eyes and play like you wasn't a bit older'n me."

"Blink your eyes," I requested.

And that was how we began the motif of the evening and night, which was not that I magically became twelve again but that both of us were without age, or, more accurately, that neither of us was bound to any actual years of life: neither was he older nor I younger, but each of us freed from time and from all the constraints of life except sex: He was clearly very male and I female and the two of us very attracted to each other, very curious about each other, very eager to seek the other's hidden self. But neither of us knew anything about sex. Both of us wanted to find out, slowly and wonderingly and gently.

I think it was then, that night, that I first realized the truth that would lead me to the answer I gave to the *Paris Review* interviewer (see below, page 356), who asked me bluntly, "Do you know why you are fixated upon twelve-year-old boys?"

Oh, of course Travis and I were intoxicated, but I like to think it was not just the wine or the music that was playing (I asked him if he had any favorites. "I reckon my favorite number must be Hank Williams's 'I'm So Lonesome I Could Cry,' " he said, "but if you don't have it, I guess Conway Twitty's 'How Far Can We Go' orter suit me." But I didn't have either piece, so instead my Harman Kardon system played some soft things by Gershwin and Rodgers-Hart). When we stood up eventually to leave the table, to move from the formality of the dining room to the comfort of the multicushioned conversation pit, which Travis had quickly christened "the visit hole" although I'd had no visitors yet, it seemed to me that we were the same height, that he had grown, or I shrunk, or both of us, just as we had done with our ages, had transcended whatever measurement of size bound us to the earth. Admiring his neat, masculine haircut and running my fingers through it, I was aware of how long my own hair had grown—to below my shoulders, or, as we would discover very shortly, long enough if hanging in front to frame and caress my bare breasts. And he returned my gesture, running his fingers through my hair—the beginning of a nightlong game of follow-the-leader: *any*thing I'd do to him, he'd do to me; whatever he chose or invented to do to me, I'd do to him.

Before we lowered ourselves to the cushions of the pit, I put Morris out to roam the hotel, although Morris complained at this so much that I wondered if he knew what we were about to do and wanted to stay to watch. Then I flicked a wall switch that began the simultaneous dimming of all the "house lights" and the opening of the curtain on the great skylight that hovered above the pit, so that we were eventually illuminated only by starlight and some moonlight, scarcely enough to reveal us fully one to the other or to deprive us of our imaginations and our fancies: he could have been Islamber in that Svanetian tower, or Dzhordzha in the cell of the Serbsky, or Kenny in the Murphy bed, or all three of them interchangeable with Travis Coe, the backwoods faunlet, who had been dropped here by Anangka, or by angels, or, as I was to learn eventually, by Daniel Lyam Montross himself.

I do not remember, at all, either of us undressing. I do not know what happened to our clothes. It was almost as if, having transcended age and height so easily, we transcended clothing with equal ease, finding ourselves bare beneath the stars in the cushiony pit, our flesh oblivious to whatever chill of February was outside the place, our skins warm and soft and soon touching, his fingers reaching out to find how full my nipples had grown, my fingers discovering that already his groin's heart had swollen to its fullest size, not man sized but as large as either he or I would ever want.

Did we make any conversation in the conversation pit? *Any* talk in the visit hole? Possibly, but I don't recall. It seems he expressed solicitude, or wonder, or a wish, or that he acknowledged a liking, or a request, or reverence, or that I spoke endearments and appreciations, but I think if we used many words at all we used the simple language of discovery, of searching and finding and knowing. Thus I became Travis, and he me.

I blew softly and warmly into his ear, and he shivered with both the tickling and the delight of it, and he couldn't wait until he had blown into my ear too.

We used our hands, our eyes, our mouths and tongues more than our bodies, at least in the beginning and for a long time through the night. We even used our toes, which was an especially youthful and playful thing to do, my piggies (as he called them) burrowing into the nooks of his nates and neck and armpits, his piggies venturing as scouts into the places he'd later want to poke his little pole. When his biggest piggie brushed against my cheek I seized it between my lips and rolled my tongue around it, and he laughed with surprise and pleasure.

We discovered, for the first time, both of us, a new and delicious sort of touching: of just the tips of our nipples, lightly and teasingly against each other's, having a playful struggle to position our breasts to make the nipples touch, and then to rotate each nipple around the other. It was wonderful, but my nipples were so much larger than his that we realized this was the only disparity between ourselves, and we turned our attention instead to massaging each other's chests with our hands and fingers and tongues.

We played so long, without any actual contact of our sexual parts, that eventually he lost his erection. All this time I had been aching to take it into my mouth, but I had hesitated for fear he'd think it perverse or even evil of me.

But while I was licking his stomach wetly, he observed, "You're shore gittin me all wet, ye may as well tongue me all over." And he requested, "Come on, lick me all over!" So I did, saving for last his wilted, drooping, shy penis, which I greatly slobbered upon, until it was not only drenched but resurrected. It was fully raised again, taut and proud, tougher than it had ever been and constantly quivering. I knew that it was near to exploding, and the noises he made told me that he knew it was. I assumed that he, like Kenny, had had some previous experience with self-induced orgasm, so it wouldn't take him completely by surprise. I didn't want to frighten him. I was tempted to bring him to fulfillment with my hand alone, but both my hands were busy elsewhere, one of them playing with his nipple, the other seeking to find the one entry to his lower body, and then finding it, and rubbing it with a forefinger that slowly but firmly entered it. He sucked in his breath noisily, and then, letting out his breath, let out also his semen, which splashed against my tonsils, as his body bucked and twisted and trembled. I kept my mouth upon his penis until both it and he were still and soft again.

What is it about a boy that leaves him uninterested in sex as soon as he's had his coming? Since all night long he had been duplicating my acts, my movements, my ventures, I hoped that he'd dare to return the deed I'd done for him. I waited a long while to see if he would do anything more, and when he didn't, I said, "Now you ought to slobber all over me too."

He rolled over and nuzzled my neck with his mouth and gave my shoulder one or two licks, but then declared, "Boy, am I guv out! I could jist go right to sleep."

"Go right ahead," I said, disappointed. And the way he snuggled into me, holding me, I thought he wanted to get himself comfortable for his snooze, and I resigned myself to simply holding him and perhaps trying to sleep myself.

But sometime not much later in the night he began to wiggle and stir, and said, "You know what I'd keer to do? I'd care for us to go up and jump in that big swimmin hole in yore bathroom and take us a dip." I told him to put lots of bubbles in it. While we waited the half hour for the tub to fill, we sat naked on the edge of the pool, having another glass of wine.

Then we jumped into the deep tub and became a pair of dolphins and played a long time, and he was surprised to see how he could lift my body in the buoyancy of the water and hold me above him. He adjusted and changed the Jacuzzi whirlpools and he discovered that by standing waist deep in the pool and maneuvering his groin near the nozzle, he could give himself another erection with the jets of warm water. "Wow! I bet I could shoot off again like this!" he observed.

And as I've said, I had discovered myself, some weeks earlier, that the Jacuzzi had the power to do something to me that no person could do. The beginning of the water orgasm had been so surprising and intense that I'd been leery of finishing it, but now, watching the Jacuzzi massage my Travis to the point of coming, I couldn't resist moving to an adjacent nozzle and letting it gush between my legs.

Travis became so absorbed in watching what the water was doing to me that he lost his concentration upon his own arousal. "You're fixin to turn inside out," he observed, and I, having never heard that expression before and wondering where he'd picked it up, was charmed by the accuracy of it, for indeed the water jet was manipulating me to the point of unbearable loss of control of my body.

When I felt that I could contain myself no longer, that indeed I might turn inside out, I was moved to see if I could bring about something that had never happened to me before, an orgasm with a boy's penis inside me. Quickly I turned him away from his water jet, as I turned from mine, and using the water to buoy my body I rose up and straddled my legs around his waist and impaled myself upon him.

"Now this is more like it," he said, as he hugged me to him, and I took it to mean that this was his first experience with intercourse, the real loss of his virginity.

Oh, I was so close to the edge! My mind brought back to me all the hours I'd had with Islamber, Dzhordzha, Kenny, and Jason, hours of futile and senseless thrusting on their parts, on their *parts,* which had inevitably ejaculated but left me unreleased and consumed with fears of being frigid. Now dear Travis was not interested so much in thrusting as in bouncing the two of us up and down in the water, and around. We danced. We were both thrilled at how easily he supported my weight in the lightness of the water, with my legs tightly around his waist and his feet alone touching bottom, enough to make us move, to make us skip and spring and drift. The whirlpools seemed to sense our mounting ecstasy and increased their pressure, until the water all around us was boiling and roiling, and we were covered in bubbles. His two hands tightly gripped my buttocks as he bounced, and my two hands clasped his as if to hold on, but then he recalled a turnabout-is-fair-play that he had left unreturned, and he slipped one of his fingers into my rectum, and I slipped one of mine into his, and almost as if those were the two buttons waiting to be pushed, we came off together, simultaneously, neither of us hearing the other's cries because we were too busy screaming ourselves.

In the profoundest sexual passages of *Georgie Boy* there is nothing, nothing at all, comparable to the ecstasy of that moment.

And yet, even in the throes of its excruciating intensity, something in my mind kept saying to me, "You'd better enjoy this, because you'll never have it again."

There is a poignant line in our collateral text, *Lolita,* wherein Humbert, in one of his frequent asides or direct addresses to his imagined jurors, declares, "Sensitive gentlewomen of the jury, I was not even her first lover."

And then he begins the next chapter, "She told me the way she had been debauched."

III

HE TOLD ME THE WAY he had been debauched. Not that night (when we were all finished with the Jacuzzi and climbed out of the tub, neither of us had energy enough to do more than stumble into my bedroom, pull back the down-filled satin comforter, and fall together into my queen-sized bed, where we were soon asleep in each other's arms) but the next morning, when he reverted to his routine of preparing and serving my breakfast, after his trip down to get the flowers and paper and to flirt with Lurline (or to be flirted with by her), and then complied with my request to turn down the Beethoven quartet that would make conversation difficult, and to sit down beside my bed.

Morris also sat, on the windowsill, pretending to keep an eye on the birds while actually observing Travis carefully.

When I had finished my breakfast, I gave Travis a fond but shy glance and said, "So. How did you like all of that?" My curiosity matched that of a novelist awaiting his first review.

"All of which?" he wanted to know.

"Well, everything last night, but especially what we did in the Jacuzzi."

He nonchalantly remarked, "That sure beats a bed of straw all to smithereens."

"Oh?" I said, taken aback. "Which bed of straw? Have you done it on a bed of straw?"

"Yeah, and it aint near as much fun," he said.

"With whom?" I asked. "You told me you'd never slept with a girl."

"Naw, I never slept with her. But we done it."

"Who was she?" I kept on. "Tell me."

Travis Coe asked for and received permission to get himself a cup of coffee, and while he was in the kitchen I prepared myself nervously for his confession, wondering at myself and asking myself if I would be able to tolerate the confession. My apprehension at my own intolerance grew steadily as he, during the drinking of his coffee, told me the story. The previous summer, his aunt had taken him on one of their frequent

Sunday afternoon visits to a kinsman's house, where, as was the custom of those country people (not unlike a Svanetian custom that was observed, however, on Saturday rather than Sunday afternoons), the grown-ups spent the whole afternoon, following a large feast of fried chicken and many desserts, socializing at leisure, the womenfolk gossiping busily in one part of the house while the men congregated on the porch or in the yard, and the children, of all ages, were left to their own devices . . . which devices were inventive enough to come up with some variation on the universally popular game of seeking.

Travis welcomed the chance to get away from the reading that usually filled his Sunday afternoons, and he was an "old hand" at the full repertoire of hiding games. His playmates here included a number of his cousins and neighbors, all of them of the same social class, rural poor, without any mixture of the children of the outsiders (ex-hippies and other subculture arty types). Some of the players were as young as eight or nine; those younger than that were really not clever enough to play the particular game they chose, but there were players as old as fifteen or even sixteen who had grown up playing it.

"Didje ever play I-draw-a-snake-upon-yore-back?" Travis asked me, and when I asked him how it was played and he told me the basics of it, I remarked that it was like a variation on the basic hide-and-seek and struck me as remarkably similar to games that I had known in my childhood in Svanetia, usually variations on *ligweb-upgosh,* as the universal game was known there (it translates roughly as "finding-the-secreted").

The essence of the variation is that it increases the "foreplay" (if I may be forgiven) of the basic hide-and-seek: whoever is "It" must turn his back on the others and bury his face in his arm against a tree while the leader slithers his finger down It's back, intoning, "I draw a snake upon your back. Who's gonna put in the eye?" and then a volunteer steps forward and pokes It in the back, "putting in the eye." It must then turn around and attempt to guess who among the other players has poked him.

He is not told, yet, if his guess is correct. He must first set a task for the other to perform, ideally a difficult, time-consuming task. Once the task is suggested (such as climbing a tree to its top and back down, or running around the house twelve times, or running down to the creek and bringing back a live crawdad), the identity of the poker, the eye-putter, is revealed. If It has guessed him or her correctly, then that person must perform the task, while all the others run and hide (and from that point on, the game reverts to conventional hide-and-seek).

But if It has missed the guess, then It must perform the task himself or herself while the others run and hide.

After the counting-out rhyme-chant of "Eeny, meeny, miny, mo," etc., a fourteen-year-old girl named Denise McWalter (!) was designated as It. After the snake had been drawn and "dotted" on her back, she guessed the poker to be her best friend, one Amy Murrison, and then she teasingly assigned as the task to be performed the deflowering of Travis Coe. "Take him to the bushes" was the expression. There was much giggling and joking about the task, and some of the older boys protested that they hadn't been selected instead. "I'm three years older than Lum and I aint never done it yet myself," one lad complained.

As it turned out, Denise's guess of Amy was wrong, and thus she herself had to carry out the task, which, Travis surmised eventually, was what she had been hoping for all along.

"It won't take but a minute," Denise kept saying to him as she led him not into the bushes but out behind the barn and then through one of its rear doors, into a stall floored with straw.

In the conventional playing of the game, the task assigned should take only long enough for all the others to run and find a good place to conceal themselves. But long after everyone else had hidden and someone kept crying, "All hid, all hid," Denise and Travis did not return. It took much more than a minute. The others eventually gave up on them and selected a new It and resumed playing without them.

Three things in Travis's memory of that episode remained strongest in his mind, all three of them part of his education about females: One was his first sight of Denise's pubic hair. He had just begun to grow the first peach-fuzz of hair around his own genitals and wasn't sure it was normal for himself, and he had no inkling that *girls* had hirsute groins. Denise, who didn't at all mind removing her jeans and her panties, surprised him not just with the swelling of her hips and the thinness of her naked waist but with her dense, thick, dark pubic hair, which did not frighten him so much as arouse his compassion, because he assumed, but dared not inquire, that something in that growth was abnormal and atavistic. For months afterward he puzzled about it to the point of obsession, until he discovered that I too had the same luxuriant mass of hair down there.

A second thing that would not leave his memory of the experience was his discovery that girls are capable of an intensity of feeling analogous to that which happens to the boy when he ejaculates. Girls don't exactly ejaculate but they do, to use Denise's expression, "start falling apart."

"There now," Denise had said to him, once she had guided him into her. "Now you aint a virgin no more. How's it feel?" (And what most inflamed me with jealousy was her privilege of being able to ask that question.)

He was uncomfortably aware of the texture of her pubic hair pressing against his groin, but that awareness was almost overwhelmed by the sensation of his penis adrift within the moist chamber. "Okay, I guess," he managed to allow. "How's it feel to you?" He solicitously wondered if the hairy growth was painful.

"Super," she said, and cooed, then groaned and began moving, tossing her hips. This was his third surprise, for, although like any country kid he'd had plenty of opportunity to watch the mating of animals, from barnyard fowl to enormously hung horses, he had never seen the female of any species devote any energy of her own to the ritual. Absolute passivity was the norm, and here again he suspected that Denise must have something wrong with her, that she was bucking and heaving as if she thought she was supposed to do all the work. He urgently tried to subdue her movements by the velocity and intensity of his own, but this only served to increase her ardor, until she was gasping and crying, "I'm gonna turn inside out!" Her warning slowed him only for a moment of wonder, because he felt as if he were turning inside out himself and wanted to complete the process, and tried hard, and did.

"Ohhhhh!" Denise sighed loudly as she let go, falling apart and turning inside out, and I involuntarily found myself sighing *Otttt!* in my Svanetian throat as I listened to Travis finish the story.

IV

FOR THE LONGEST TIME after he finished and I sighed my sigh, I was unable to say anything more, consumed as I was with jealousy. I had never felt this emotion before, not with Islamber or Dzhordzha or Kenny or any of the several others, all of whom had lost their virginity with me. My depression and anger over the thought of Denise as my rival, nay, as my predecessor in the indoctrination of Travis into the mysteries, made me ask myself the question that the *Paris Review*'s Barbara Phillips would ask (see page 356), "Do you honestly know why it is so important to you that your boy be a virgin?"

To which I answered, simply, "If he is not, it is as if the novelist discovers that someone else has already told his story. And perhaps done it better."

I think I must have gone into a kind of sulk or funk that lasted for most of the rest of the morning. I did not do any work on *Le Garçon Georges* that day.

"Did I mess up, or something?" Travis asked at lunch. "Have I done went and made some fool mistake?" I shook my head, but morosely, and he went on, "How come you're so standoffish, all a suddent?"

"Last night," I said, "throughout it, I was under the impression that you and I were doing all those things for the very first time."

"Huh?" he said. "You mean you never did it when you were a kid?"

"Not with you," I sighed, and I could not stifle a sob.

"Huh?" he said again. "When you was a kid I wasn't even born." This struck me almost as a repudiation of the sweetness of his earlier "I could blink my eyes and play like you wasn't a bit older'n me."

"But last night," I complained, "last night I was trying very hard to pretend that we were doing it for the very first time, together."

"Shoot, most of that stuff we did last night I never even thought of doing with Denise. *She* never thought of it. Golly Moses fishhooks, I never even knew there was such things to do! Not with no splishin and splashin and sploshin and all!"

I managed to smile lamely and brush away a tear. "Still, you had intercourse with her. Did you do it again?"

"Well, yeah," he faltered, as if reluctant to get himself in any deeper. "There was a good few other Sunday afternoons, but then she had this boyfriend, see, and Bobby Joe found out about it, and he's maybe five years older and bigger'n me, and he said he'd break ever bone in my body. That was jist one of the reasons I left home."

"How many times altogether did you do it with Denise?" It was like I was a novelist masochistically checking the library to see how many other novels told the same story I'd thought was my original invention.

He tried to remember and came up with a guess. "Oh, if you don't count a couple of times we had to stop because we heard somebody a-comin, maybe eleven or twelve, all told."

He was breaking my heart. I narrowed my eyes at him, matching his crafty squint, and said, "That day we first met, when I was about to hire you as my houseboy, I asked you if you'd had any sexual experience, and you said you hadn't."

"You ast me if I'd ever *slept* with a gal, dammit, and I said no I aint, and that's the gospel truth."

"But you fucked her!" I cried, speaking the English verb for the first time in my life. "You fucked her, and you were only *twelve* years old!"

"Heck, I'm *still* only twelve," he pointed out, "and you fucked me, and vice uh versey."

I could say nothing more, retreating once again into my sulking silence. I realized that he was hopelessly, to borrow another expression of his people, "used goods": he was pawed over, secondhand. I could never feel the joy of having ushered him into the first experience of sex, as the novelist wants the joy of introducing his reader to a unique story. The novelist cannot say, "Pretend you've never heard this before." The novelist cannot even say, "Stop me if you've heard this one."

All that the novelist can say is, "Okay. That's it. Good-bye, Travis. I wish for you much happiness. I wish for you that you will stay out of trouble, perhaps go back to school, be a good boy." It was not until after I heard myself speaking the words that I realized I'd said the same thing to Kenny Elmore.

"Huh?" he said.

"Leave," I said. "I'm sorry, but I can't use you anymore." I stood up and fetched my purse and took out my wallet and gave him five twenties: a hundred dollars. "Here," I said. "And you may take all of your new clothes and shoes with you."

He narrowed his eyes at me for one last time. Then he left a dependent clause dangling: "If that's the way you feel about it." He gathered up his things. He had a final request: "Could you see your way to letting me keep a copy of *Georgie Boy?*"

"I thought you'd finished it," I said.

"I need to read it again," he declared. So I gave him a copy of my book. I even wrote something on the flyleaf, nothing special, *Very Best Wishes to Travis, Kat,* something like that.

And he left me. All he left behind, I discovered later, was his copy of *Wah'kon-tah.* But it wasn't his. After I read it and discovered how much I didn't know about the Osages, I'd have to return it for him to the library.

22

I

FOR AT LEAST A WHOLE DAY after he was gone I cried. Not even the
arrival in the day's mail of the proofs of *Schorschi, ein Knabe,* the German
edition of my novel, could console me or distract me from my grief.
That grief, I was quick to realize, was whimpered not over his leaving
but over his prior loss of virginity, over my missed chance for the privilege
of being first in his history.

Not as an act of retaliation against my rival but as a rite of exorcism,
I began to create Denise McWalter, as I once had created her namesake
Cathlin McWalter, as I kept on creating Ekaterina; I gave Denise an
appearance and a personality and even a history: a drunken father divorced from an abusive, foul-mouthed, unfeminine mother, an infancy
and childhood in a squalid mobile home, a keen mind squandered upon
television soap operas and movie magazines, an ennui more acute and
restless than that of her few girlfriends, a precocious sexuality that had
her chronically playing with herself from the age of seven until she was
deflowered by Bobby Joe at the age of ten, a totally unsatisfactory five-
year romance with Bobby Joe punctuated and relieved by one summer's
search for and finding of an "ideal" boyfriend two years her junior in
the form of an unspoiled Travis, whom she proceeded to spoil.

Loneliness, lust, and self-doubt are the three key ingredients to a
climate for creative activity, as I told the *Paris Review*'s Barbara Phillips,
and the weeks following Travis's departure from the Halfmoon were like

a spawning of those three elements to prepare the spores in the leaf litter of my life for the mushrooming of the many fictions that sprang up out of my imagination that spring, beginning with the much-anthologized short story "I Draw a Snake upon Your Back," the first of the several pieces in what would become my second published book, not a second novel but the collection *The Names of Seeking Games*.

Travis had not been gone three days when I sat myself down at my desk and began writing the story, not in Georgian but in English—or, more accurately, I wrote the first page in my familiar, comfortable Georgian but was reminded thereby of how I'd had tirelessly to translate *Georgie Boy* from the Georgian with the "help" of Daniel Lyam Montross and his old unabridged dictionary, which still remained at my elbow; and, opening it, I felt that his spirit was with me again. To test it, to see if he was "still there," I translated that first page into English on the spot, having only a little difficulty finding one word I wanted, *altruism;* then, having found it and replaced the Georgian equivalent, I crumpled and tossed the Georgian original page and resolved thenceforward to do all my writing in the same uncomfortable but expressive style with which I essay these memoirs.

"Thanks, Dan," I said aloud, the first words I'd spoken since I'd bade Travis Coe farewell. Morris, more accustomed to the silence he'd enjoyed since I stopped crying, jerked his head up from his nap and stared at me. "I wasn't talking to you, Morris Cat," I said. But he didn't return his cheek to his paws: he continued to stare deeply into my eyes, almost as if he had never seen me before . . . or, I think, as if I had never seen him before and was just now, in the desperation of my loneliness, recognizing him for who he was. Could a "spirit" such as Daniel Lyam Montross, I wondered, take possession of the body of an animal? Would a spirit want to inhabit a living creature such as an old cat more comfortably than an inanimate object like an unabridged dictionary? "Or maybe I was talking to you," I said to Morris. "Are you really Dan, Morris?"

Any owner of cats knows that they are indifferent to human speech. Some of the less intelligent cats will appear to respond to their names by coming when called (truly intelligent cats never respond in any way to human speech), but the baby talk with which many humans address their cats (the person who asks "Does snuzzums wanta eat brekky *now?*" should realize that the cat's answer of *"Now!"* is just a reflex mewing) will cause only an aggravated tail twitch or ear lowering in the more stupid cats and will produce no response whatever in bright cats.

So I was not surprised that Morris's cool, leonine face only regarded me dispassionately and impersonally, even insouciantly, albeit with a glimmer in his slanted eyes that could only have been a wise human's. But then . . . then, I swear, he reached out with a paw and plopped it down on the opened page of the unabridged dictionary where I had been looking up *altruism.* He left his paw on the page long enough for me to peer closely to see the word he was indicating, his foreclaw resting upon it: *always.* Then, with the faintest trace of a smile (or did I just imagine the smile?), he removed his paw.

"*Always,* Dan?" I asked. "Are you saying, Morris, that you are *always* Dan?" But he betrayed not a twitch of any expression or response, just that profound but inaccessible depth of his eyes. "You know," I went on, feeling not at all silly, "I've suspected for a long time that you really *do* exist, Dan, but this is the only attempt you've made to confirm it. Would you kindly, if you *are* Dan, Morris, just nod your head? Just once? Just make the slightest little nod?"

But of course he would not, and I was left with only that *always,* which could have been purely an accident of the placement of his paw. Later, as I resumed writing my short story, I opened the dictionary to the correct page and asked Morris/Dan, "What is the backwoods *f-*word I want for a girl like Denise McWalter who's flirtatious, fast, and frisky?" I waited and silently prayed that my cat would drop his paw upon *feisty* but his only response to my continued talking was self-conscious licking of his paw and washing himself with it.

"All right, Dan," I said at length, "*be* that way. But I know you're there."

I wrote six or seven pages of the story "I Draw a Snake upon Your Back," conscious that Morris had not returned to his slumber, or that although he feigned his customary napping posture he was keeping one eye slightly open and upon me. It was perhaps my sense of his Muselike presence or inspiration, if not his actual help, that made the beginning of the story so enticing and promising, what dear friend Larry Brace would much later comment upon in his piece "Poetic Structure in the Prose of V. Kelian's 'I Draw A Snake upon Your Back,'" published in *Studies in Contemporary Fiction,* when he pointed out that the entire first section of the story is a kind of verbal foreplay matching the foreplay of the game. How surprised Larry would be when I told him that I'd written that part "under the influence" of Daniel Lyam Montross, whose life and work had come to obsess Larry totally at that point of his career.

But Morris was only so much fun, and seven pages, as I told Barbara Phillips, was more than a day's work. Later that day I was seized with a strong urge to get out of the Halfmoon for a few days, perhaps get back to Stick Around, visit Dan's grave and put some flowers on it, and—why not admit it?—see if I couldn't find the local girl named Denise McWalter, talk to her, and compare her actual self with the girl I was creating in the story, as well as verify the traces of any of the McWalter family lineage that I had once envisioned for Cathlin.

I called Sharon and asked her if she could come and get me. Oh, she'd have loved to, she said, but the thing was, she'd sold Cam, her decrepit Chevrolet, and was trying to see if she couldn't, in the process of simplifying her life, do without an automobile entirely. "Matter of fact, I got the idea from *you,*" Sharon said. "After all, you've managed to get along without a car, even now that you could own a Rolls or a Ferrari."

"I just never learned how to drive," I said into the phone, staring at Morris, whose expression suddenly somehow reminded me that once upon a time I'd been required to drive Ingraham's Blazer across the high bridge over the Mississippi River into St. Louis. As I've indicated, I suspected, even then, that Daniel Lyam Montross had "taken possession" of me during those hectic moments.

"There are driving schools," Sharon suggested. "Aren't there any in the Yellow Pages?"

No, there was no driving school in Arcata Springs, nor in Harriman, nor in Fateville. I called the local Ford dealer and said I'd like to buy their most expensive vehicle but I didn't know how to drive and wondered if they could help me. I was told that the nearest driving school was in Springfield, Missouri, a hundred miles off, and I was given their number to call, a Thompson's A-1 Driving Academy. I called and asked if they would be willing to send an instructor that far, for whatever number of lessons would be required for someone without any experience.

"It will cost you a good bit extry," they told me. How soon could we start? I asked.

The next morning there arrived at the Halfmoon a bright yellow vehicle with two steering wheels and on its roof a marquee that warned, DRIVER'S EDUCATION, to other motorists, letting them know that a neophyte was doing dumb things. The instructor was a young man, about my own age, who sat with me in the parking lot of the Halfmoon for a long talk before we started out. He gave me a manual that I would be required to read, but, because of my insistence that time was short, I could have my first lesson behind the wheel, without benefit of reading all the fundamentals of vehicular operation, maintenance, and safety. "Have you ever driven a car before, at all?" he asked.

"I once drove a Blazer over the Mississippi Interstate bridge that leads into St. Louis," I proudly declared.

"Really?" he said. "Well, then, I guess you know the difference between the brake pedal and the gas pedal."

I thought I did, but I wasn't sure. The back streets of steep Arcaty are not the best place to learn driving. Coming from mostly flat Springfield, the instructor himself had never seen streets so precipitous, and before the afternoon was over I had thoroughly terrified him. He was visibly trembling when the day's session ended, and I tipped him fifty dollars for all his trouble and dismay and fright.

He agreed to come back the following day, but he didn't. When I phoned to complain, they sent out a different instructor, a woman, who said she wouldn't "go out" with me unless I knew the fundamentals first. I'd had time to read the manual more than once, and at her questioning I was able to satisfy her that I knew how to use the parking brake to start off from an inclined position, and how to downshift an automatic drive to low, and how to pump failed brakes. Still, we wound up with the front half of the car teetering over a retaining wall high above Leatherwood Creek, and saved ourselves by climbing into the back seat and out the back doors, and had to have a wrecker come to drag the car away from the precipice.

The manager himself (or was he "principal" or "dean"?) of the academy came for my third and subsequent lessons, possibly enticed by the news of the tips I was giving his employees, or simply fearful for their safety. He asked me to call him Jim. Jim and his wife, he said, visited Arcata for a weekend every June, and he was familiar with its treacherous, tortuous roadways, and he knew when to rest his hands upon the second steering wheel on the passenger's side.

Over the next three weeks, Jim returned to the Halfmoon for a full afternoon eleven more times, and I completed the course with only one accident, when my concentration wavered as I was rounding a curve and thought I spotted Travis up ahead and ran into a ditch––but without any injury to either of us or serious damage to the training car.

If that was Travis, it was the only glimpse I'd had of him since evicting him from the Halfmoon.

II

UPON MY COMPLETION of the driving course, Jim told me it was customary for the instructor to accompany the pupil for his driver's license examination, but the state law required that the driver be tested in his or her own vehicle. I needed to purchase a vehicle, and asked Jim what he would recommend, especially for the rough back roads of the Bodarks. He suggested a Jeep. He offered, at the conclusion of my last lesson, to drive me to Springfield, where there was a Jeep dealer, as well as a number of other dealers, "in case you decide you want something different," he said.

As it turned out, I did want something different, something that cost twice as much as the finest Jeep. I saw her in a Springfield dealer's window and fell in love with her, and Jim assured me she was certainly a respectable vehicle, albeit an expensive one. A forest green Range

Rover. I called her Silvia, "of the silvan wood or forest," and she almost replaced Morris in my affections. Equipped as she was, she would get only eleven miles to the gallon of gas, and driving her was almost like driving a bus rather than a car, but she was "loaded with extras" and would go *any*where.

Jim rode with me in Silvia and gave me some tips on the special handling of her. Even the state trooper in Harriman who gave me my driver's test (which I handily passed) was impressed with Silvia. ("You've got yourself a dandy set of wheels here, lady," he said.) With my license in my purse, instead of returning immediately to Arcaty, I set out for Stick Around . . . but got only as far as the village of Parthenon before I realized that my having passed the intensive course in driver education and having passed the state driver's examination did not in any way qualify me for finding my way around. Jim had taught me nothing about map reading, or map acquiring, or even asking for directions. (Nowadays, eight-year-old Silvia, still going strong, has in her rear compartment a complete set of U.S. Geological Survey topographic survey maps, 7.5-minute series quadrangles for the entire Bodark region, but when Silvia was new she didn't even have a state highway map in her glove compartment.)

I got badly lost. On all of my many previous trips to Stick Around, I'd been driven by someone else, beginning with Ingraham, who, I now recalled, had become lost himself on that first attempt to find the place and had been required to maneuver his Blazer, four-wheel driven but vastly inferior to Silvia, on some terrible logging trails before finding his way out of the woods. Now I tried to spot any familiar landmarks, anything that I might have noticed when someone else was driving me. Being your own driver gives you a totally different view of the world.

One rough road I followed for what seemed like four or five miles south of Parthenon came to a dead end in the yard of a backwoods hovel, a squalid derelict of an old house, which appeared inhabited, at least by dogs: there were a dozen of them in the yard, and they surrounded Silvia, barking fiercely at her and even scratching her with their forepaws. I was tempted to ask directions of the owners, but I didn't dare get out of Silvia, nor did I want to subject her to any more claw marks, so I quickly reversed and drove away from there and retraced the road to its first westward turning, which led eventually into a logging trail that began, in time, to seem to me like the path on which Ingraham and I had been lost on that first trip to Stick Around. This trail, which obviously hadn't been used for years, meandered up hill and down vale all over the countryside, like the sledge paths of my homeland's Mount Layla, and as I marveled at Silvia's ability to handle the steepest incline and the muddiest bog with dispatch, I began to have a fantasy of someday taking her back home to Lisedi.

But Silvia's ability to handle the roughest terrain bred overconfidence in me, and I steered her up into a defile that was little more than the dry bed of a plunging gully, full of boulders that not even she could negotiate. Silvia lost her footing for the first time (and one of the last times) in her life, slipped, and dropped one of her rear wheels into a fissure where it had no purchase, scraping her undercarriage up on top of a rocky ledge. The drive of the front wheels, with all their power, could not pull that rear wheel out of its hole.

I got out and surveyed the situation, which appeared discouraging indeed. I opened the owner's manual, searching for a chapter called "How to Get Out of Impossible Situations," but there was none. I may have been miles from the nearest house, and the sneakers on my feet were not meant for hiking. Late afternoon was coming on, reminding me of that first trip with Ingraham—and indeed it was almost exactly four years since that trip.

I was surrounded by second- or third-growth forest, the trees not really enormous but dense, thick, unmanaged; the configuration of the woodland reminded me of the uplands east of Stick Around, and I realized I couldn't be *too* far from that glade where there was a lone grave and headstone for Daniel Lyam Montross.

"Help me, Dan!" I called aloud, desperate and forlorn. Then I realized that if indeed Dan had taken up incarnation in the person of Morris Cat, he was seventy miles away at that moment, snoozing comfortably on the cushions of my conversation pit.

. . . Or maybe he was capable of manifesting his spirit wherever I happened to be. There was no wind blowing through the woods at that moment, not even any breeze, and yet the pages of the owner's manual that I held in my hands began to flutter as if being rapidly blown or flipped by an unseen hand, until they abruptly stopped turning and remained open at a page upon which was, *Location and Operation of the Winch.* I knew that I was being led to read that page, although I hadn't the faintest idea what a "winch" was. My course in driver's education had included nothing on the use of the winch, but diagrams in the manual showed me how it was embedded in the front bumper and how to release it . . . but not what to do with the hook once it was released.

Dan must have been guiding me, because I don't see how I could have thought of this myself: By looping the hook around a sturdy tree higher up the slope and hooking it back onto its cable, and then pushing the proper button on the dash, I could slowly but surely hoist Silvia out of her hole.

"Thanks again, Dan," I said aloud as I drove on. I was careful not to overtax Silvia's abilities thereafter, and I got us back onto a trail that even had the impress of recent tire tracks on it and led eventually to a dirt road that seemed to have been at least graded and maintained. I followed that road for miles, with dark coming on, until I reached a blacktop highway. I knew there were no blacktops within any distance of Stick Around, but I followed the highway until I came to a sign, DEER, which referred not to any animals crossing the road but to the village of that name, where there was a lone store-and-service-station. I stopped and obtained, for two dollars, a state highway map that did not have Stick Around on it but did have Deer—in the extreme southern part of the county, twenty miles or so from Jasper, the county seat. "Could you tell me how to get to Stick Around?" I asked the woman who was running the store.

"Not this time of night," she replied, leaving me to wonder whether she meant that she wouldn't be able to give me directions at this time of night, or that I wouldn't be able to find it at night.

So, by a circuitous route on the meandering highways of the Bodarks, I returned that night to Arcaty, getting home just in time for bed.

"Well, Morris—or Dan, as the case may be," I said to the cat, who didn't seem any more glad to see me than he usually was—that is to say, was more or less indifferent—"I've done some seeking today, and not much finding, and I think I'm ready to do a bunch of short stories."

III

MOST OF THAT SPRING I spent seeking. Silvia took me, every day, up and down the back streets of Arcaty. My new routine would begin after breakfast in the Crystal Room, where I would usually be the only diner until the tourist season resumed in May, and then I would stop at the desk, ask Lurline for my mail or messages (she was always perfunctorily courteous but diffident, and I wondered how much she had disapproved of the time Travis had spent with me); then I would announce to her, "I'm going for a little spin," and go to the parking lot where I'd left Silvia, and I would take my lovely Range Rover for an hour or at least half an hour of exploring all the streets of Halfmoon Mountain, East Mountain, the village proper, the lower reaches of Leatherwood Creek, and the highway. Silvia and I became a familiar sight to the permanent residents of Arcaty.

Of course I was looking for Travis. In the beginning I was not even able to admit it to myself, but eventually, when I found myself fabricating imaginary conversations in which I apologized to him and invited him to return to his job as my houseboy. I realized that the sole reason for my having acquired Silvia in the first place, for having learned how to drive, was to search for him, to be more mobile for the quest. Did I detect a smirk on Lurline's mouth when I returned disheartened to the Halfmoon? More than once I was tempted to ask her if she might have any idea where he might have gone.

Finally, on one of my search excursions out of town, I found Stick Around. Or rather I arranged for help in finding it: I called Sharon and received a rather complicated but detailed description of the various forks in the road, which ones to take, what landmarks to watch for, how to know where I was, etc.; and, just to be safe, I acquired the first of the topographic survey maps in my eventually vast collection, the

Murray Quadrangle, a study of which showed me how I'd taken one single wrong turning after the time Silvia had been stuck on Henderson Mountain, where I'd been only a couple of miles from Stick Around without knowing it.

I'd been looking forward to spending a week in Stick Around, visiting with Sharon, with Lara Burns, with Diana Stoving and Day Whittacker, and, it being the morel season again, the fourth anniversary of my first week in Stick Around, I wanted to do some woods roaming in search of morels. But after what was only my first night at Sharon's, I realized that what I really wanted to hunt for was not morels but Denise McWalter . . . and possibly Fannie Coe, Travis's aunt and adoptive parent. It occurred to me that Travis might have returned home. "Do you know anybody named McWalter?" I asked Sharon. But she did not. "What about Coe?" I asked. "Are there any Coes around here?"

"Stick Around used to be full of Coes," she said. "But I think the ones that are still anywhere near here are up beyond Sidehill, a small community to the west. Vernon could tell you."

So at my first opportunity I drove Silvia up into the hills west of Stick Around and stopped to chat with Vernon Ingledew, who drew me a map: a detailed rendering of the various forks in the road, which ones to take, what landmarks to watch for, how to know where I was in my search for Sidehill and the Coe country. He marked with a black **X** the most remote holler beyond Sidehill, with a crude trail leading up into it. "That's where you'll find Fannie Coe's cabin. Along with Gran's place," he said, meaning Lara Burns's dogtrot, "it's one of the few log cabins of the Bodarks still inhabited."

I found it. My heart was beating rapidly as I pulled into the yard. There was not a pack of dogs but only one dog, an ancient sheepdog too tired to bark. I had my words ready for Travis, in case he appeared. But he did not. I got out and knocked, and a woman opened the door. She was not nearly as old as I had expected her to be. Perhaps early thirties, not much older than myself, but she had lived a hard life, a frugal life, and obviously a spinster's life, because she was "homely as sin," as Travis had described her. I felt silly asking, "Are you Fannie

Coe?" when it was obvious she was. She nodded, and I told her my name was Kat Kelly and—I had worked this out in advance—I was from the Bodarks Regional Children's Welfare Division and I would like to ask a few questions about Travis Coe.

"He don't live here no more," she said. "I aint seed him since last fall."

I knew that she was truthful. "Do you know anyone named Denise McWalter?"

"What's she got to do with it?" Fannie Coe wanted to know.

"She might know where he is," I said, "if you could just tell me where to find her."

As it turned out, the real Denise McWalter did not live in a mobile home, as I had already written in "I Draw a Snake upon Your Back," nor were her parents divorced or nearly as bad as I'd pictured them in the story, nor was Denise herself anything at all like my heroine, and her father had no family resemblance to the Clan McWalter that I had once conceived and described. Perhaps writers ought to be spared meeting any of their characters. Denise McWalter was a pleasant, polite, well-groomed, and fairly intelligent girl of fifteen who lived in a conventional and modest ranch-style house on the main highway above Sidehill. Her parents boasted that she was doing very well in school, especially in math and science, although she was making "only a 'B' " in English.

What could I say to her? First there was the problem of privacy: I didn't want to talk to her in the presence of her parents. Her father, who was a self-employed electrician, expressed a great interest in my Silvia, and I allowed him to take the Range Rover for a drive, and then I asked Denise if she'd like to ride with me for a little while, and thus I was able to get her away from her parents for not more than an hour, during which I told her I was "investigating" Travis Coe for a state agency and wanted to ask her some questions about him.

"What's he done went and done now?" she asked.

"Nothing," I said. "The question is, What had he already went and done when you knew him?"

"Nothing," she said. "He was pretty cool and sharp for his age, and he had a real mouth on him, but he never got on anybody's shit list . . . except Bobby Joe's."

"How did he get on Bobby Joe's shit list?" I asked.

"Bobby Joe is *real* jealous," she said. "I mean, he gets just crazy with jealousy if some other dude even looks at me."

"What did Travis do with you?"

The question made her blush, but she recovered and protested, "My gosh, ma'am, he was *two* whole years younger than me!"

"I know," I said, trying hard to conceal my own jealousy. Then I requested, "Tell me about the time you played I-draw-a-snake-upon-your-back."

When she was able to close her mouth after her gasp, she said, "Well, for crying out loud, somebody must have already told you everything we done!"

"Yes, somebody did," I said. "But I want to hear your side of the story."

When she finished narrating as chastely and colorlessly as she could the story of her "carrying on" with Travis, I had only one more question: "Would you tell me the names of the other games you played?"

And afterward, instead of going back to Stick Around, I returned to Arcaty, where the next morning I finished my short story "I Draw a Snake upon Your Back," and Joni Lynn Miller typed it up, and I sent it off to Liz Blaustein, who sold it shortly thereafter to *Playboy,* the same magazine that had inflamed my first American lover, Kenny Elmore.

Denise McWalter deserves almost as much credit as Travis for having provided the inspiration for the work that would keep me busy the rest of that year, the writing of the stories that would constitute my collection *The Names of Seeking Games,* including also "Come-to-Coventry," "Man-Hunting," "Kiss-Chase," "Relievo," "Gee," "Tin-Can-Tommy," "Whip," "Sardines," "Buzz-Off" (the second-most-anthologized story), "Hunt the Keg," and of course "Hide-and-Seek," as well as the three stories that were not the names of games but of cries therein: "All In, All In," "Ready or Not, Here I Come" and the collection's concluding piece, "All Hid, All Hid," which Shannon Ravenel called "the best American short story of the eighties."

IV

Once I thought I saw Travis, and it was not with Silvia's help. Having Silvia and her all-terrain mobility sometimes left me feeling lazy and flabby for having abandoned my regular habit of hiking up and down the myriad mazes of Arcaty's stairsteps. So I made a conscientious decision to leave Silvia in the parking lot while, at least once a day, I went off on foot to explore the town.

Directly below the Halfmoon on the east slope of Halfmoon Mountain is Saint Elizabeth's Catholic Church, famous because years before it had been featured in "Ripley's Believe-It-or-Not" as the only church in the world that one enters through the top of the belltower, owing to the steepness of the slope. But despite this ballyhoo, one does not actually descend the belltower to gain entrance to the church; rather, one walks down a long, gentle ramp affording a view of the church and of, directly below the ramp's parapet, the rooftop of the rectory, upon which tourists cast their spare change, like throwing coins into a wishing well. At any given time the rooftop is covered with perhaps fifty dollars in quarters, dimes, and nickels. The distance from the parapet to the rooftop is at least ten or twelve feet. Approaching it one morning, I discerned that somehow a boy, whom I took to be Travis, had leapt across this distance, landed on the roof, and was busy collecting the coins when I came along; and, spotting him, I called out, "Tray-vis!"

He disappeared instantly over the other slope of the roof, perhaps dropping to the ground from its far eaves. I ran down the ramp and attempted to find him, exploring the cramped grounds of Saint Elizabeth's, but he had disappeared. I knew at least this much: he had not left Arcaty, and he had apparently used up the hundred dollars I'd given him and was reduced to stealing change from the roof of the rectory. My heart ached anew for him, and I lost the rest of the day by redoubling my efforts to find him.

My seeking of Travis was more intense than any of the searches in any of the seeking games of my stories, although, as in each of those stories, there was a moment or two or three during which the quarry was spotted, as if to prove its existence, as if to tantalize the hunter with the elusiveness of the quarry, as if to give the game, the game of life, its zest. I became convinced, in time, that Travis was still a dweller in Arcaty, and my search for him continued long enough for me to forgive him entirely for his no longer being a virgin, and to want desperately to know him again, in all the meanings of *know*. The novelist who overcomes the chagrin he feels because the story has already been told by someone else can be content to make the hand-me-down story fetching, alluring, even unique.

But my springtime mornings in the tower of my Halfmoon penthouse were not spent brooding over Travis. Liz continued to send me galley proofs or finished copies of foreign editions of my books, and although I did not know the languages I appreciated seeing *Georgie Boy* translated into Swedish, Portuguese, Greek, Polish, and Serbian. I was especially thrilled to see the vertical columns of characters in the Japanese. Wistfully I told myself, If only it were possible to have a *Georgiy Malchik* . . . but I knew that my book would appear in Russian, if at all, only in *samizdat*: typewritten or handwritten pages of a hasty translation circulated endlessly from one eager reader to another, virgin readers all, but readers who would appreciate the experiences of the heroine and readily identify with her. I had no way of knowing that at that very moment a secretly printed edition of *Georgiy Malchik* was being pirated in Leningrad to replace the customary typewritten *samizdat* with thousands of softcover copies, one of which would find its way almost immediately into the outraged hands of Bolshakov himself.

There were two other distractions that spring, one pleasant, the other not. The disagreeable interruption came in the form of a letter from my old mentor Ingraham, who was still trying unsuccessfully, he said, to find a publisher for the nonfiction book he was writing about ghost towns. *Let us not be coy,* he said. *I have heard rumors from some of my Arcaty acquaintances that you have taken over most of the top floor of the Halfmoon, something you couldn't have done unless you are indeed V. Kelian, as I have suspected all along. I will not dwell upon how envious I am of your enormous*

success (I spend enough time in the privacy of my own resentful dignity dwelling
upon the good luck of other writers). I did truly enjoy reading Georgie Boy,
possibly the only novel I've been able to finish in many a year, and I think you
deserve every accolade that comes your way.

I have not published a book in almost a decade. The failure of my last novel
continues to puzzle its editor long after he has withdrawn from the crazy business
of publishing. It doesn't puzzle me so much as it intensifies my burning desire to
write something that cannot be ignored by the fickle public of readers.

But my ghost town project, which conceivably could do for these destitute
villages what James Agee did for destitute people in Let Us Now Praise Famous
Men, *continues to make its rounds of ever-lesser publishing houses without*
finding anyone who likes it, and even my so-called agent presumably has aban-
doned me.

I do not wish to appear to be calling in a debt, but if you feel any gratitude
whatsoever for the help I gave you in the early stages of writing Georgie Boy,
I beseech you, I beg you, please put in a good word for me to your editor.

By coincidence, I had just finished arranging the collected hardback
volumes of Ingraham's novels on a shelf in my library, and in the process
had dipped into his last-published novel, that awkwardly titled *The
Archaic Bulwarks of the Bodarks,* a comic history of Stick Around that had
been dismissed as a "spoof" (a word the great John Barth in turn
dismissed as sounding like "imperfectly suppressed flatulence") by many
reviewers when it appeared in 1975. To my surprise, Ingraham had
made no attempt to disguise or pseudonymize the Ingledew name and
had even, toward the end, mentioned Sharon, Vernon, et al., by their
actual names. But I'd read enough to convince myself that he *was* a
good writer, as undeserving of his neglect as I was perhaps undeserving
of my fame, and I *did,* as he hoped, feel some thankfulness and obligation
toward him.

So I took the trouble to write, rather than call, Wölfflin on his
behalf, with the result that Publisher Z became Ingraham's publisher
and, two years later, brought out his ghost town nonfiction, to the same
scant reviews and general disregard that his fiction had suffered. It was
widely remaindered.

The one good diversion that spring came after a phone call from Liz Blaustein informing me that Trevor Kola the Hollywood filmmaker was getting ready to plan the shooting of *Georgie Boy* and that Kola was very eager to have my views on how the film should go. Kola, Liz told me, had been exceptionally faithful to all the novels he had converted to movies, and he wanted to do everything he could to make this great best-seller into a box-office smash. But of course Liz could not put me directly in touch with him without violating the agreement that my identity and my sex be kept secret. Would I, she asked, be willing to write a letter, signed by V. Kelian, that she could forward to him? Perhaps with a treatment?

"What is a 'treatment'?" I asked.

"Just a few pages to help the development," she said. "Just write a kind of short form of the story line."

"How many pages?"

"Twenty or so. Not more than fifty. Be sure to write it in the present tense."

"Why?"

"Because that's the way it's done. It helps you visualize the picture: 'George wants Princess. Princess wants George but doesn't want to get pregnant. George must find rubbers. George steals rubbers from Bolshakov.' Et cetera. Get the idea?"

"I think," I said, and I began at once to write a treatment of the story, only mildly disturbed at having to drop everything else in order to work on it. It was easier for me to expound upon general principles for converting the novel to the screen than to write the specifics of abbreviating its story from the twelve or fourteen hours required to read it to the two hours allotted for watching it, even in the present tense, but I amazed myself by finishing the job within a week and writing a long covering letter to Mr. Kola from V. Kelian.

The result was, Liz laughingly told me, that the great Trevor Kola was insisting that he should meet and talk with V. Kelian, "on Kelian's own turf," if need be. "Wouldn't you rather just fly out to the coast?" Liz asked me.

"In drag?" I said. I had, I confess, been giving many of my idle thoughts to the contingency of having to meet or talk directly with Kola and wondering how, if need be, it could be arranged without giving away my identity. It had not occurred to me that he would want to come to the Bodarks in search of V. Kelian.

Liz sighed. "I'm thinking," she said, and there was a long moment of silence on the line. Then she said, "Hey. How about if you took a boyfriend with you and pretended to Kola that you were the interpreter for the boyfriend, Kelian, who can't speak English?"

My mind quickly examined and rejected the few males I knew: Ingraham, Day Whittacker, Vernon Ingledew, Jim the manager of the driving school, Lenny Lewin of the Esoterica Gallery (tempting but too old), Bob the porter of the Halfmoon, and even Larry Brace. "What boyfriend?" I said to Liz. "My only boyfriend is, as I told you, a twelve-year-old hillbilly named Travis Coe, and he hasn't been around for some time now."

Liz sighed again, and again there was a long silence on the line while both of us were wracking our brains. Then she said, "Well, I suppose I'll just have to tell him that the mysterious V. Kelian refuses to have any contact with anybody . . ."

"Wait," I said. "Yes, tell him that, but tell him that if he wants to come to the Halfmoon, even if Mr. Kelian refuses to see him in person, I'll be glad, as Mr. Kelian's secretary and lover, to 'relay' the discussion to him."

Silence from Liz for a long moment, and then she said, "Brilliant."

"Tell him that I'll meet his plane at Fateville, the nearest airport, and drive him the fifty miles to Arcaty. When he knows his flight, he should call the Halfmoon's desk and leave a message for 'Kat.' "

Thereafter it became part of my routine to stop by the desk at least twice a day and ask Lurline, "Any messages?"

"Nope," Lurline said, day after day. I was beginning to wonder if the very busy Trevor Kola had found another "property" that was more bankable than my novel, or if he had been disappointed to learn that V. Kelian was residing in the unknown and inaccessible Bodarks, not on Park Avenue in New York or some exotic hideaway in Costa Rica.

One day when I asked Lurline if there were any messages, she said, "Yep. It's this. You oughta take Travis back. He's hopeless wicked and caint be saved. You might as well finish up the job of ruining him."

"What?" I said. "Who's that message from?"

"Me," she said.

23

I

TRAVIS COE'S RETURN to the Halfmoon delighted and comforted me so
much that I forgot about Trevor Kola . . . Or, rather, I continued to
think about Trevor Kola only long enough to wonder at that similarity
in the sounds of their names: Travis Coe, Trevor Kola (a similarity that
would eventually grab journalists, who in turn would make allusions to
cocaine, Travis's and Trevor's apparent substance of choice, or to the
beverage "Coe-Kola.") After a tearful exchange of apologies (and, later,
I would shamelessly use Travis's words verbatim, but without the Bodarks
accent, in the so-called "Apology for Waywardness" section of the popular story "All Out Come in Free"), I took Travis to the Plaza restaurant
for dinner, and then, both of us drunk with wine and lust and the
excitement of reunion, we spent much of the rest of the evening in my
Jacuzzi until, exhausted by our erotomaniacal acrobatics in the hot water,
we tumbled into bed for a long private talk, during which he told me
all about his experience with Lurline.

Of course Lurline (whose last name I never learned) is the "Lucille
Renwick" of my prizewinning story "All Hid, All Hid," and, as Larry
Brace has shown in his essay "Formidable Heroines in the Shorter Fiction
of V. Kelian" (*Studies in Modern Literature*), she was "only a little like the
typical Kelian heroine, who has the sort of innocence that God also
protects in fools and drunks." Lurline was ultraconservatively religious,
and although I do not identify her membership specifically as with the

Jehovah's Witnesses, I give enough hints to make the affiliation unmistakable. She was required to give a tithe of her Halfmoon salary to her church and to spend time equal to a tenth of her working hours each week out on the streets, ringing doorbells and attempting to sell tracts and convert unbelievers. Travis was the only unbeliever that she had succeeded in converting, but only to the extent of helping her in the work of selling tracts.

She had taken him in when I evicted him. Twenty-two years old and a native of Arcaty, although both her parents had "moved on" in different directions, primarily westward, she had an apartment on Ojo Street, just a short distance from the Halfmoon, and it was there that Travis had been staying since I threw him out.

As anyone who has followed his rise to stardom is all too aware, Travis Coe has always been an opportunist, willing to do anything in order to survive and succeed. (I am reminded of what he said to me in our first meeting: "If you got the money, I could do anything you pay me for.") In order to have a roof over his head, Lurline's roof, he was willing to go along with her desire to convert him to her faith, to correct him (he stopped smoking cigarettes in her presence), and even, in the beginning, to banish from his mind and loins whatever lustful itches he might have acquired from Denise and Ekaterina. But gradually, inexorably, he insinuated himself into her bed, against her will but not against her pleasure. I have freely utilized their relationship in those two stories of the *Seeking Games* collection.

"She never did mind just plain ole fuckin," Travis explained. "Matter a fact, she got herself a real hankerin fer it. But she just didn't like to do all them other things you taught me. She wouldn't even let me *touch* her butthole."

Taking Travis back, I had the satisfaction that the novelist feels when she realizes that although her story is secondhand, twice told, she is giving it twists and fillips that no other novelist would have imagined. Travis came to love Silvia and confessed that he'd seen me driving her around town and was dying to go for a ride in her. I took him, and even, eventually, in deserted places, let him try his hand at the wheel.

Lurline remained on polite terms, if not cordial terms, with me and even with Travis, who continued to flirt with her each morning when he went down to get the daily flowers and paper. One morning he returned with a slip of paper in Lurline's childish scrawl: *You got a call. A Mr. Kola says pick him up at the F'ville airport at 2:00.*

"Now, listen, Travis," I said, "Here's what I want you to do . . ." and I presented him with an elegant white three-piece suit, of the sort that Tom Wolfe was beginning to wear in those days, and a white straw hat, dark glasses, a wig, and a mustache. I told him to stay in my tower bedroom and not show himself to our guest until I asked him.

Then I drove alone in Silvia to Fateville's Drake Field to pick up the famous director. He deplaned from a commuter prop craft out of Dallas, and I was able to recognize him from pictures I'd seen in newspapers and magazines: a big man, bushy black hair and heavy eyebrows, and a look (not wholly intentional, I learned) of holding in suspicion or contempt everything that came within his purview. The hills surrounding Drake Field were in the full lush greenery of late springtime, and the air was the fragrant Bodarks ozone that is found nowhere else on earth, but he sniffed it as if it came from a sewage plant, and he looked around disdainfully at his surroundings until his eyes came to rest on me, and he gave me a look as if sizing me up for the casting couch and finding me not worthy of it.

He was not alone. I don't know what I had expected, but I had planned to have him to myself for the duration of his stay in the Bodarks. He had two women with him, both of them younger than I, and he introduced them only as "Gladys" and "Jay," the former plain enough and efficient enough to be, as indeed she was, merely his hired assistant; the latter, I am sorry to say, I failed to recognize as none other than Jesslyn Fry, whose several movies I had not seen. (Since coming to America, I had scarcely been to any films at all, except for those blue movies that I saw in Pittsburgh with Ingraham.)

My failure to recognize her caused a moment of embarrassment on the drive to Arcaty, when in response to her conversational question, "How long have you known Kelian, Kat?" I replied, "A very long time. How long have you known Kola, Jay?"

"He did my last picture, of course," she said.

I turned to him. "Oh, do you paint, on the side?" I asked. And when after a moment's puzzlement all three of them laughed, I thought to correct myself: "Or take photographs?"

"Yeah, photographs, Dollface," he said. "*Lots* of photographs."

When the three of them had finished sniggering, I said to Jay, "I think I understand. You're an actress in *motion* pictures." I felt myself blushing for my ignorance.

Jay looked out the window and spoke to the Bodarks landscape. "It is *so* refreshing to discover someone who doesn't know me and therefore doesn't fawn all over me." Then she turned back to me. "I suppose you've read *Georgie Boy* yourself." It was not a question but an observation, and when I nodded, she asked, "Do you think Kelian could see me as Princess?"

Of course Jesslyn Fry is a blonde and is famous for a look of tender innocence that far surpasses my own or whatever fragility the reader perceives in Princess. Jesslyn does not resemble me, except for her large, ingenuous, curious eyes and a certain delicacy in the structure of her cheekbones and jaw. I will never forget the moment, in Silvia en route to Arcaty, passing through some hamlet called Hindsville, when the woman who had been Princess and who had written Princess's story sized up the woman who was destined to win an Academy Award for playing Princess in a motion picture and said, "Probably not. But I ought to make something clear. Mr. Kelian may not see you, period. He is extremely shy. I am under strict instructions not to let you into his presence."

"I understand that, Dollface," Trevor Kola put in, as if he truly did. "Still, we ought to be able to work it out so that if we don't see him, he can take a good look at Jay and let me know if she fits the part."

We worked it out. Once in my (or Kelian's) penthouse triplex apartment, which I think visibly impressed even Kola himself, I showed the three of them to their rooms, each to a separate one, taxing my limit of three guest rooms, and then assembled them in or around my conversation pit and, acting as servant myself, poured them the drinks of their choice (Kola had only Perrier, Gladys wanted a beer, and Jesslyn

Fry drank a Scotch and soda). Morris, whose long tenure at the Halfmoon left him if not affable at least approachable by any stranger, decided he did not like one or more of the three and, after hissing at Kola, disappeared for the duration of their stay.

The sounds of someone walking the floor overhead were distinctly audible. "Mr. Kelian knows you are here," I announced. "And he hopes you are very comfortable and that you enjoy your stay in the fabulous Bodarks. His first question to you is, Have any of you been in the Bodarks before?"

"I've been in the boondocks but not the Bodarks," Kola said, and guffawed at his own wordplay, and thereafter he would always refer to my adopted part of the country as the Boondocks. He moved to the picture window, and looked out, and sized up the sweeping view, until his eye fell upon the enormous statue. "Jesus Christ!" he exclaimed. "What is *that*?"

"Jesus Christ," I answered. "It's called the *Christ of the Bodarks* and it was erected by a fundamentalist bigot named Smith."

"What is he standing *in*?" Kola asked. "You can't see him from the knees down."

"It is just poorly proportioned, I suppose," I said. "Mr. Kelian once observed that it looked more like some kind of Bodarkadian Kewpie doll."

"What's a Kewpie doll?" Kola wanted to know, so I showed him one from my collection.

Neither I nor Travis had been prepared to serve dinner. I considered taking them to the Plaza, or even Bubba's Barbecue, but decided, for the first evening at least (and I had no idea at that point how long they intended to stay), to take them downstairs to the Crystal Room, where the menu was suitably diverse and the atmosphere, with great chandeliers and enormous windows providing the glass that gave the dining hall its name, more elegant than the rest of the hotel, which, Kola had observed, was "down at the heel."

The Crystal Room was not crowded; the few other guests scrutinized us as we were seated, and a woman came over with her menu and handed it to Jesslyn.

Jesslyn waved it away. "No, just bring me your best steak, very rare," she said.

"No, no, no," the woman said. "I don't *work* here. I just wonder if I could get your *autograph.*"

Jesslyn borrowed a pen from Kola and autographed the woman's menu. Later, two other women, a man, and a couple of teenagers would appear at our table, requesting Jesslyn's autograph on assorted scraps of paper if not their menus. I, who had never been asked for my autograph, felt somewhat curious if not envious about how it felt to receive the homage, if that was what it was.

One guest who did not approach our table but remained at his own table in the darkest corner of the large room was a small, thin man in an elegant white three-piece suit and white straw hat, wearing dark eyeglasses above a bushy mustache; he was dining alone on a cheeseburger. I faulted myself for not having told him to order something less adolescent than a cheeseburger.

I looked at Kola, Jesslyn Fry, and Gladys, each in their turn, and said, sotto voce, "Please do not look now, but Mr. Kelian is sitting over there." Kola, Jesslyn Fry, and Gladys each looked nervously at one another, as if waiting to see who would have the honor of being the first to turn slowly, inconspicuously, and cast a covert glance across the room. As if by unspoken agreement among them, this honor or duty fell upon Gladys, who coughed and very, very slowly turned her head, took a good look, dropped her mouth open, and slowly turned her head back to her boss.

"Well?" Kola said peremptorily to her. He had not dared to turn his own head.

"He's young," Gladys announced. "I think. And he looks *quite* mysterious."

Kola announced, "I think I'll take a peek." And he very slowly turned his own head until he could see the figure on the opposite side of the room. He took a quick look, blinked involuntarily, and returned his gaze to us. "Yes," he said, as if confirming not his assistant's estimate but his own unformulated one. Then he whispered to me, "If he's so shy, why is he eating in public like this?"

"He wished, as you suggested, to have a look at her." I inclined my head toward Jesslyn Fry.

Jay asked, "Do you think he'd be offended if I just, sort of, maybe sauntered over there so he could have a closer look?"

"No need for that," I said. "V. Kelian can see you very clearly." And indeed V. Kelian could.

"What does the *V* stand for, by the way?" Kola asked.

"It's like the *S* in 'Harry S Truman,' " I said.

Jay asked, "What did the *S* in 'Harry S Truman' stand for?"

"Nothing," Kola said to her. "It was just there because he needed a middle initial. He didn't have a middle name." Then Kola asked me, "Didn't Truman come from these Boondocks?"

"Not *these*," I said. "He came from a part of Missouri about two hundred miles north of here."

"I can't help noticing, Dollface," he said, "that you have an unusual accent. You're not American, are you?"

"I haven't been naturalized," I declared. "Not yet."

"So where are you from?"

"Svanetia," I said.

"Phoenicia?" he said. "Didn't the Phoenicians invent astronomy or the alphabet or something like that?"

"*Svane*tia." I pronounced it as clearly as I could.

"Where's that?"

"The Caucasus Mountains."

The mildly interested but blank look he gave me, matched by the looks of Gladys and Jesslyn, told me that none of them knew where the Caucasus Mountains were.

"Is that where Kelian is from too?" Kola asked.

I glanced across the room at Travis, who was finishing his cheeseburger and making a rather hammy acting job of wiping his big mustache delicately with his linen handkerchief. "No, he's from the Bodarks . . . or the Boondocks," I said, with a smile to acknowledge Kola's nicknaming them.

"Answer me this, if you will," Kola said. "Is he really Georgie? Was his mother a shrink?"

My smile shaded into a mysterious grin. "Who can say?"

Abruptly both Kola and his beautiful star illuminated their faces with expressions of dawning realization. Jay tried to speak, but Kola waved her silent while he asked me his next question: "So he really didn't get killed in the end, did he?" And without waiting for my reply, he continued, "Because one of the main things I need to discuss with him is *that.* I don't want my picture downbeat. I don't want Georgie to die in the end of my picture."

"It's *your* picture," I said. "Nobody has to die in one's own picture."

Jay was allowed to speak. "Don't you get it?" she asked Kola, tugging on his arm like a child trying to get her father's attention. "It just hit me. Don't you get it? Not only is that Georgie sitting right over there, but this is Princess sitting right *here.*" And although it is rude to point, she pointed her finger within touching distance of my nose.

Kola's mouth fell open. "Dollface, is that true?"

"Would you mind," I requested, "calling me something other than Dollface?"

II

KOLA AND GLADYS STAYED several nights. Jesslyn Fry had to be back on the coast the next day for a guest appearance on something called "Johnny Carson," and she took a taxicab back to the Fateville airport. Before she left, having unsuccessfully dropped a number of hints that she would truly appreciate a moment alone with V. Kelian, she said to Kola, in my presence, "Trev, you're an Oh Tour, aren't you? You don't have to have his say-so to cast me."

"Yeah, baby, I'm a real Oh Tour, but this property won't play if the man doesn't think you're Princess." I would hear Kola's mention of Oh Tour several more times before it occurred to me he was saying *auteur,* and I would not find the cinematic meaning of that "author" in Daniel Lyam Montross's dictionary. "Listen, Dolph-Kat," he said to me (the first of several times he'd address me that way before I realized he was starting to call me Dollface and interrupting himself halfway through the first name to substitute the latter), "Jay's gotta catch a plane. Could you go ask your boyfriend what he truly thinks of her?"

I already knew what my boyfriend thought of her. Late the night before, after my guests had retired to their rooms (I had expected Kola to sleep with Jay and/or Gladys but apparently he had not). Travis climbed into my bed and began to babble. "Don't ye know who that *is?* That's Jesslyn *Fry,* and she's a *real* movie star! And she's sleepin right downstairs!"

I told Travis I was beginning to get the impression that she was somebody very important. I asked him if he'd seen any of her movies, and he was able to name at least three of them that he'd seen. "Is she really good?" I asked him. He said she was terrific. Then I asked him, "Does she at all resemble the mental image you received of Princess when you were reading *Georgie Boy?*"

He had to think about that for a while. And then, bless his heart, he said, "Not as much as you do, I reckon. But I doubt you could play Princess in a movie, now, could you?"

I could not. And we both laughed over that.

To Kola I said, "Mr. Kelian wishes me to tell you that he considers Miss Fry perfectly acceptable for the role."

Jay threw her arms around me and gave me a big hug. "Oh, *thank* you!" she said. "Tell him I've *never* wanted a part more than this one! Tell him I'll make him *proud* of me! Tell him I love him!"

"I will," I said, and she kissed me, and that was the last time I saw Jesslyn Fry until she was dragged by two attendants down the hall of the Laboratory in the second scene of the film *Georgie Boy.*

After Jay left, Kola and I settled down to the first of several working sessions on the treatment that I (or Kelian) had written. "Let's take a meeting," Kola would say, and Gladys would sit at his elbow writing meticulous notes on a yellow legal pad. Kola would point out something in the treatment, raise a challenge, and send me upstairs into the penthouse to confer with "Kelian" and then report back to Kola on Kelian's opinion. In order to appear to have spent some time conferring with Kelian, I would make a game of actually talking with Travis, who was enjoying himself sprawled out on my bed reading a Jackie Collins novel,

Sinner. "Kola wants Bolshakov to be heavy," I told Travis. "But the real Bolshakov is bony, scrawny, skinny like a scarecrow."

"He seemed like a fat slob to me," Travis said, so I returned to Kola to tell him that it was all right to make Bolshakov fat.

Kola laughed. "No, I've already cast Sert Reichert in that part, and he's anything but fat."

"But you said you wanted him to be heavy . . . ?"

"*The* heavy," Kola said. " 'Heavy' as in the bad guy, the villain."

"Oh." Often in these "story conferences" I did not understand the language that Kola and Gladys used in the terminology of motion pictures. Listening to them speak to each other was like sitting in a dentist's chair eavesdropping on a technical conversation between the dentist and his hygienist. I had no inkling of the meanings of *dolly, gag, jump cut, pre-production, day player, crane, match cut, on spec, second unit, two-shot, swish pan, wipe,* or even the ubiquitous *zoom.*

Kola would say something like, "For the teaser I want a rack focus on Princess in her cell with Georgie watching her play with herself." Gladys would dutifully write this down, and then Kola would condescendingly explain to me that *teaser* refers to the opening sequences of the movie before the titles and credits or beneath them, and *rack focus* means changing the camera's focus from one person to another within the same shot. I would go upstairs and trade places with Travis and act this out with him, and he would do a remarkable job of pretending to be Georgie outside the door of my cell spying on me while I simulated masturbation.

"Yeah!" Travis would exclaim, with his eyes getting as wide as Georgie's would have been. "He wants the whole show to open with me getting bug-eyed like this."

I had no inkling, then, that the "me" he was calling himself as stand-in for Georgie would become so literally Travis Coe.

I would go back downstairs to Kola and announce, "V. thinks it will play." Kola would smack his lips in satisfaction and say to Gladys, "Flag that, then."

Gladys and I, by the way, became good friends during the course of the visit. She was an uncommonly intelligent woman, indispensable to Kola, very efficient and devoted, and she was genuinely interested in learning from me the customs of Svanetia, the character of the Svanetian landscape, and even some Svanetian recipes, which she intended to try when she got back to L.A.

I had only one uncomfortable moment with Gladys, when, as we were sitting alone together in the chess nook (we had time to relax with a few games, and she was not a bad player), she remarked, "You know, this is *your* apartment, isn't it? Not Kelian's."

"What makes you say that?" I asked, taken aback.

"Everything in it," she said, sweeping her arms, "is womanly."

All I could say was, "Kelian likes it that way."

The "story conference" went on for three working days, scene by scene, and I was beginning to have much fun, acting out with Travis the various possibilities of shooting; and for his part he took to it like a duck to water—or, to use his own expression, "This here movie play-like is easy as shootin fish in a rain barrel."

It was clear that Kola intended to "Americanize" the film in every way he could. He had already contracted to use an old Victorian warehouse in San Francisco as the Laboratory, and to use a California woman's penal institution, Frontera, for the "establishing shots" and some of the interiors of the concluding prison-camp portion. From what I could gather, there would be nothing in the movie to indicate that its scenes or people had derived from Soviet Russia.

The only serious disagreement Kola had with Kelian was over the matter of some scenes toward the end when Bolshakov and Georgie's mother are driving one car in pursuit of the car that Georgie has stolen. "But Georgie was on foot!" I protested on behalf of Kelian. "In the book, he steals a prison truck at the very end, but he never steals a car to get to the prison."

"Yeah, Dolph-Kat, I know," Kola admitted, almost as if some power greater than himself was bossing him around, "but we've got to have a car chase to keep the front office happy."

"A car chase?"

"Everybody does it, babe," Kola said.

Few experiences in my life have moved me as much as the morning, the last morning of Kola's visit, when Travis and I were in my bedroom, converted in our imaginations into the yard of the prison camp, acting out the last meeting between Princess and Georgie. Kola had hinted to me that the film should follow the novel very closely in that part of the movie, and he had asked me at breakfast, "Do you think Kelian would mind if we used the book's dialogue between Princess and Georgie, word for word, in the last shots?"

I said I was sure he would be flattered but I would run up and ask him anyway, and I jumped at the chance to "try out" with Travis that excruciatingly poignant scene that would leave millions of moviegoers fumbling for their hankies or Kleenex.

It was easy for Travis and me to hold our separate copies of the "script," in the form of the just-off-the-press paperback editions of *Georgie Boy,* which Bantam would soon leave in special display boxes in every supermarket, drugstore, and bookstore in America.

Travis threw his heart into the climactic scene and seemed to be speaking his lines more than reading them, and even his Bodarks accent seemed to vanish. The tears that he and I shed were genuine. I was seized and wracked by an emotion of much greater power than anything I had actually experienced with Dzhordzha: Art is, after all, more real than life.

And the emotional intensity of such art is greater than the most profound sexual pleasure. I would rather have done *that* with Travis than any of the Jacuzzi acrobatics we actually had done. But I knew that I could never do it again. So perhaps there was another truth: Great art happens only once.

The moment came for Georgie to reach out and hold Princess for the last time. He, Travis-who-had-become-Georgie, had dropped his copy of the paperback and didn't need it, and he gave me an indescribable look of longing—of having searched so hard to find me and, having found me, of being about to lose me forevermore.

And then his sweet freckled face and his haunted eyes were transformed by an expression of fear that wasn't in the script at all. Or, I realized, it was not craven fear so much as astonishment, discovery.

I realized that Georgie was no longer looking at Princess but at something beyond her. And I couldn't resist turning to see what it was. It was not Bolshakov but Trevor Kola, standing at the top of the stairs that led to my aerie.

He had obviously been there for a while. His arms were folded over one another and he was leaning against the wall in a posture of relaxation and contemplation, and he wore the trace of a smile, as if he'd been listening to the whole scene.

Almost automatically he said, but in a gentle voice, "Cut. Print. Perfect." And he walked up to us, gave me a hug and a kiss on my cheek, and then shook hands with Travis and threw an arm over his shoulders and said to him, "Kid, that was almost on the button. But this is a full shot and we need to see you do something with your body, like maybe shiver a little more, okay?"

"Yes, sir," Travis Coe said.

And then Kola said to me, "How do you manage to keep him forever twelve?"

III

KOLA AND GLADYS had become steadily and inexorably aware, he confessed, that I was Kelian. But he would never, he swore, reveal my secret to anyone. He apologized profusely for any incivilities or rudenesses he may have committed while he was still under the impression that I was "only Kelian's bimbo." He would not even tell Jay, when he saw her again next month, that I was actually not only Princess but also Kelian. It was a secret that only he and Gladys would know, and I could be sure that Gladys would never breathe a word of it to anyone, either.

Kola told me a little story about his "old friend" the director John Huston: how, when they were getting ready to begin shooting *The Treasure of the Sierra Madre,* Huston went down to Mexico looking for the author, B. Traven, but could find only a mysterious recluse who called himself Hal Croves and pretended to be a "go-between" for Traven. Like Kola had done with me, Huston had spent several days in Croves's company, discussing the script and planning the film, before convincing himself that Croves actually was Traven. But to the day of his death, Huston always insisted that Croves was not Traven. He insisted this to the press and Traven's biographers and anyone else, except a few of Huston's closest friends . . . including Kola.

"So," Kola said to me, "Huston hired Croves to be a technical consultant during the shooting of the picture and kept his identity as Traven a secret during production. I'm prepared to make it worth your while to come out to the coast, Kat."

I had thought about it even before Kola made the offer, and I had already reached my decision: "Thank you, but I have much work to do here."

"Your next book?" Kola asked, and when I nodded he requested, "Give me an option on it."

"It's a collection of short stories," I said. "You couldn't film it."

"Wanna bet?" he said . . . And indeed, two years later Trevor Kola made the famous and wonderful box-office hit out of an expansion of one of my stories, *All Hid, All Hid* (also starring Travis Coe).

For now, there was the problem of how Kola could, as he put it, "wrest" Travis away from me. In the presence of the wide-eyed, open-mouthed boy, Kola explained that he had already arranged with several talent agencies to conduct a major search next month for the boy actor to play Georgie, and Kola was obligated to have a look at two dozen twelve- and thirteen-year-old finalists for the part, but if I could "spare" Travis for a few days, Kola would fly him out to the coast and give him an equal chance to compete with the other kids, most of whom, of course, had several years of professional training in acting.

"He's raw," Kola said of Travis in the boy's presence. "He doesn't know his ass from his elbow about the profession, and we'll have the devil's own time cleaning up his diction. But he's a natural. He *looks* like Georgie. He *thinks* like Georgie. I believe the kid thinks he *is* Georgie, don't you, kid?"

"Yes, sir," Travis said again, which seemed to be the only words he knew to speak in the presence of Kola.

Kola's final request, before I took him and Gladys back to the airport, was to "see some real hillbillies." Travis, Kola said, was a "juvenile hick" but not a "real hillbilly." I tried to explain to Kola that the stereotyped image of rustic mountaineers had disappeared from the American scene forty years earlier, but I agreed to take them in Silvia, he and Gladys in the backseat and Travis sitting up front, out to the wilds of Stick Around country. Travis was willing to point out the cabin where he had grown up, the sight of which brought a tear to Gladys's eye and even a lump to Kola's throat, but Travis did not want to tarry. The old sheepdog I'd seen on my previous visit bestirred himself at the sight or scent of Travis, and Travis reached a hand through the car's window to pat the dog and say "Howdy, ole Prince," but then he said to me, "Let's git on out of here," just as Aunt Fannie emerged from the cabin to see what I was doing back at her place, and he turned his head so she couldn't see his face. Whatever guilt he felt for not stopping to say hello to the woman who'd raised him ("Now, she did kind of look like a hillbilly," Kola observed) was no greater than my own guilt for not pausing to introduce these people to Sharon, or Lara Burns, or Day and Diana Whittacker, some of whom may have recognized Silvia and wondered why I was not stopping. The only place I did visit, giving Silvia a workout on the mountainside, was the grave of Daniel Lyam Montross. Kola read the headstone and asked, "What's your connection with him?"

I didn't know how else to explain it than to say, "He was my mentor and lover."

Kola glanced again at the headstone. "But it says he died in 1953. You weren't even born then."

"I was born when he died, in fact," I said. And then I echoed a remark of Kola's: "But I keep him forever twelve, as a kind of phantom fiancé."

Travis rode with us to the Fateville airport and said good-bye to Kola, who promised to stay in touch by phone and arrange Travis's flight to the coast the following month. "Work on your voice," were Kola's last words to Travis.

Then I took Travis shopping in the best places in Fateville, to find a new wardrobe and luggage for his upcoming journey to Hollywood.

The boy was in a trance for days, trying without luck to imagine the adventure that awaited him and finding himself unable to stop thinking and talking about it. He couldn't function as my houseboy any longer. Strange to relate, Morris refused to have anything further to do with Travis. Morris would not even eat food that Travis opened and served for him. So I had to resume feeding Morris myself, as well as handling all the other chores that Travis neglected. The only thing Travis was still good for, I discovered, was our sexual sport in the Jacuzzi and in bed.

Did he truly understand that he was going to abandon me? Did he realize that I would feel a greater loss when he left for Hollywood than I had when he left to live with Lurline?

Yes, he did. One day, the week before he was scheduled to fly out of the Bodarks, he was gone all day, without explanation, and when he returned in the late afternoon he had another twelve-year-old boy with him.

IV

ALTHOUGH I WAS TOUCHED at his solicitude and consideration, I was shocked at his frank realism bordering on cynicism. The other boy stood bashfully with his hands in his pockets, his face openmouthed, gawking at my apartment. When I drew Travis into another room to protest, he whispered urgently, "But he aint never done it afore!" as if that somehow would make the boy more appealing to me.

" 'He *hasn't* ever done it *before*,' " I corrected him, mindful of Kola's concern for his diction.

"What I said. I don't think he even knows how to play with hisself. You'll have to learn him how."

"Travis," I said. "Oh, *Travis.*" In spite of myself, I was becoming fascinated by the idea. The other boy was not unattractive; he was simply far behind Travis in handsomeness and charm. "Where did you find him?"

"Huh?" Travis said. "Never mind where I found him. This town is full of 'em. Do you want him or not?"

"If I took him," I pointed out, "don't you understand what that would make you? A *pimp!*"

"What's a pimp?" he asked.

"A panderer!" I said.

"What's a panderer?" he asked.

"A procurer!" I said. "I don't suppose your vast reading has ever exposed you to the concept? It's a person who obtains another person to offer to a third party for sexual intrigues or prostitution." I remembered that Bolshakov had an obsession with prostitutes and spent most of his spare time simply watching them on the street, a form of silent pimping.

"What's wrong with that?" he wanted to know.

I wondered how to explain. If he didn't instantly grasp the corrupt, mercenary exploitation of pandering, his innocence was greater than I'd given him credit for. With some sarcasm, I asked, "Do you plan to watch?"

"Naw, not unless you want me to," he said.

The other boy, whose name was Billy, had supper with us, during which most of the talk concerned Travis's rather boastful account of how he was going to be flying to Hollywood soon. Billy did not want any wine; that is, he had never had any before and was "afraid to start," although Travis assured him it was "real good stuff and will loosen ye up." After supper, Travis took the remainder of the bottle of wine and retreated to his quarters, which I had recently furnished with a large-screen color television, at his request, so he could observe and imitate "real actors."

When Travis was gone, I asked the boy, "Do your parents know where you are?"

"No," he said in his tiny soft voice, "but they don't care. I just told Mom I was staying over at a friend's."

"What did Travis tell you was the reason for bringing you here?"

"He said you wanted me to get in your swimming pool with you without any clothes on."

"It's just a large tub, not a swimming pool," I said. "But would you like to do that?"

"Sounds like fun," he said.

Billy proved to be even more of a water sprite than Travis had been. Not as skinny as Travis, but still with a thoroughly undeveloped body, a body waiting to be shown all the pleasures of which the flesh is capable, Billy became a merman to my mermaid, a nixie to my nix, a Gandharva to my Apsaras, a Limnaiad to my Naiad, a kelpie to my undine. We spent so much time in my oversized Jacuzzi that the skin of our fingertips puckered. And he was truly a virgin. For me, that was as if I were the novelist who, after some minor works, suddenly thinks of a totally original story, a story that nobody has ever heard before, a story that will seize and entertain and edify anyone who reads it.

A week later Billy rode with us to the Fateville airport to send Travis off to Hollywood, and the two boys exchanged parting words:

"You lucky dog," Billy said to Travis.

"Naw, you're the real lucky one," Travis said. "Now you've got her all to yourself."

"See you in the moom pitchers," Billy said.

"You shore will," Travis said.

The next time we saw Travis, Billy and I sitting together in the Razorback Cinema in Fateville; Travis's wide-eyed, innocent face was with Jesslyn Fry's in a shifting rack focus of the teaser beneath the credit AND INTRODUCING TRAVIS COE.

Billy's education had progressed by that time, so that he knew better than the character of Georgie what Princess was doing to herself.

24

I

MORRIS AT EIGHTEEN is arthritic and slow, and the vet tells me I ought
not expect him to live much longer, but I have come to anticipate that
he may survive me. He still roams the hotel, still makes himself freely
available to guests—as if he has begun to take seriously the title of
General Manager bestowed upon him. Our actual, human general manager is the fourth or fifth—I've lost count—we've had since I've been
here, and the ownership of the Halfmoon has changed hands thrice
during the nine years of my tenure. The current owner, an outfit called
Historic Hotels, seeking to enhance business, is having tonight a much-
advertised séance for our resident quartet of ghosts and is shamelessly
capitalizing upon the success a few years ago of my off-Broadway play,
Hotel Mezzaluna, in which those ghosts converse and interact among
themselves: a Swedish carpenter who died in the construction of the
hotel, a college girl who jumped from a balcony when it was Mezzaluna
College in the 1920s, a woman cancer patient from the days in the 1930s
when it was the quack Dr. Baker's Mezzaluna Hospital, and the mysterious
"frockcoated gentleman" whose murder provides the play's plot. Dear
Trevor tried so desperately to convert *Hotel Mezzaluna* to the screen, the
fourth of my works to be filmed by him and to star Travis (who at
twenty-one played—badly, I thought—the ghost Sigbjorn, the Swedish
carpenter); Trev was hampered by the essential staginess and lack of
action in the play, as well as by competition with other recent and better

spook movies, most notably *Ghost* and *Dead Again*. Trev was also stymied by the refusal of the Halfmoon's then-management to let him actually shoot the film here, and he was required to use a hotel in Eureka, California, that bore no resemblance to the Halfmoon. I am told the film is still available on videotape, but I would just as soon not have its mangled apings of the stage play continuing to circulate and helping draw a sell-out audience for tonight's séance, which I've agreed to attend only as a favor to Jackie Randel, the Halfmoon's current sales manager, a native Bodarks lady to whom I'm indebted for several kindnesses. I have a feeling that I may even enjoy myself, having never attended a séance before and having little expectation that "Veronica," the imported British medium, will actually contact the four ghosts, not one of whom has ever manifested itself (herself, himself) to me during my many years here. But how can a dignified, proper séance be conducted in a crowded ballroom—or rather, dining room, the Crystal Room itself—with an audience of several hundred curious but skeptical snoops, many of whom, I suspect, will be here not to see the ghosts but to see the unmasked V. Kelian in his newly revealed identity as an aging but still-glamorous Svanetian princess?

When I appeared a few months ago on the cover of *Vanity Fair* with those words, V. KELIAN EXPOSED, it was almost as if one of my lives had already ended. At the time I began writing these memoirs, at Wölf-flin's urging, I had no idea that I would find myself in the position, as I am now, of having to skim over eight years of my life that I had intended to cover in detail, and it is no consolation that Nabokov himself in the prototype, *Speak, Memory,* skims over more years than that and commences his last chapter with that atypically clumsy sentence "They are passing, posthaste, posthaste, the gliding years—," although it is from him rather than from Ingraham that I slip into the comfort of this present tense. Indeed, the passing years, those not covered by this chronicle, seem illusory or illusive in the engrams of my recollection, mostly happy though they were, confirming my belief that truly memorable experiences are always unpleasant ones: I can recall that far-distant time in Pittsburgh with much greater clarity than I could tell my attentive reader just what happened to me this past winter.

It is April again, and as I approach my fortieth birthday I find myself actually anticipating the pure *poshlost* of tonight's séance because it may divert me for one evening from my essential loneliness, a condition the general human nature of which I have explored so thoroughly in my recent fictions, last year's best-selling novel *Original Flavor* and my in-press novel to appear next month, *Earthstar* (which has taken its title from the strange and lonely mushroom *Geastrum*), as well as the moderately popular nonfiction book *Dawn of the Osage,* in which I essayed to speculate upon the essential loneliness of the aboriginal inhabitants of these Bodarks. Tomorrow afternoon I'm going to grant an interview, rather belatedly it seems, to *Paris Review* for their continuing series "The Art of Fiction," and I've already told their Barbara Phillips that I'd much rather talk not about my writing habits and such as that but about the condition of loneliness, which, more than lust and self-doubt, is the essential state for successful writing. If the publication of *Louder, Engram!* brings to the Halfmoon a passel of persons seeking to ameliorate my condition, they shall be disappointed not simply because I prefer to cultivate my loneliness but because, as I am about to reveal, I will not be here when this book appears.

After the initial onslaught of fan mail following the publication of *Georgie Boy* eight years ago, adoring letters sent to V. Kelian in care of the publisher and forwarded by Publisher Z to me, I asked Dori Weintraub, their publicity person, to cease forwarding the mail, or, better yet, to selectively forward only the more interesting letters, a policy that has spared me much unnecessary reading over the years (and for which I herewith apologize to any reader who expected a personal reply from V. Kelian). But as soon as that candid *Vanity Fair* piece appeared a few months ago and the "news" of my "predilection" for young boys found its way into the popular press and the supermarket tabloids, Dori's selection of "the more interesting letters" got out of control: I began to receive actual "propositions" from a variety of bright, horny, and possibly corrupt twelve-year-olds in various parts of the country, many of them enclosing their photographs (with a few adorable nude studies) and offering to come visit me "wherever your Mezzaluna Hotel happens to be." Worse, I had letters from older men pretending to be twelve. Still worse, I began to receive a number of letters, some of them quite intelligent and almost persuasive, from older men who were convinced that their charms and their interests would "rescue" me from my "paraphilia" (as three of them put it) if only I would give them a chance to visit me at "your enchanted Mezzaluna, wherever it happens to be." To all of these charming offers, I have been constrained to answer with the same printed postcard I've been sending out for years:

> *V. Kelian deeply appreciates your interest and*
> *enthusiasm but asks you to respect a sense of privacy that can admit*
> *of no contact with the "actual world."*

Which is not strictly true. I have permitted myself, these five years since Billy's death, to continue certain habits of contact: Travis Coe phones me occasionally, usually to talk about his latest film or affair with one or another of the stars or starlets of the fantastic "actual world" of entertainment, and two years ago he flew me to his ranch in Wyoming because he wanted to see if the Wind River Mountains would make me homesick for Svanetia (they did). Travis is one of only four people with my unlisted phone number, the other three being Sharon, Liz, and Trev. Sharon has been for the past five years the wife of Larry Brace, and they live rather happily ever after in that lovely old building of Stick Around that once was Lara Burns's house and store and post office, just down the road a ways from the dogtrot log cabin where, yes, Lara Burns herself still lives and still has her populous A Cat Arena. Sharon and Larry have converted the actual post-office boxes of the old abandoned post office into the ornate headboard of their waterbed—an idea they picked up from Ingraham, who sleeps with his Kay beneath a similar set of post-office boxes taken from Limestone, a town south of Stick Around, in the same county. Ingraham's whimsical novel *The Termites of Stick Around,* a fable or allegory that played fast and loose with certain actual experiences of Sharon and Larry before their marriage, almost sold well, for an Ingraham novel, and I understand he has commenced his novel about Vernon's gubernatorial campaign. Vernon Ingledew was too distracted by his political ambitions, or his philosophical studies, or a metaphysical combination of both, to notice that his tenant of the old Jacob Ingledew house, Larry Brace, was, in the depths of alcoholism and struggle with a difficult literary analysis of Daniel Lyam Montross, allowing the house to go to ruin and even contributing to its demise during his bouts of drunkenness by firing his pistol at the termites he imagined were infesting it (a situation adroitly rendered in Ingraham's fable).

The house actually is not termite ridden, I've been assured by the team of restorationists who are busy expensively resuscitating the old place to the original condition in which Governor Jacob Ingledew erected it. Vernon alone knows the identity of the new owner of the house, who bought what's left of it from him for if not a song, a promise not to sing. I have told no one of my intention to move shortly from the Halfmoon, and ~~Wölfflin~~ (Wölfflin's successor) is under strict instructions to excise *this* paragraph from my memoirs in the event that I actually do move into the Ingledew house, which was once Stick Around's modest hotel and thus is but one generic remove from the hotel in which I've spent the last decade, although I don't expect to have the services and amenities there that I've enjoyed here. I expect, if all goes well, to move everything from my triplex, including Morris, if he's willing (and if he's not, he'll let me know), into the old house as soon as the head restorationist, Clifford Stone, gives me the go-ahead, perhaps this month or early next, and to live there alone forevermore, without servants, without guests, without a houseboy. I may thus come to resemble in my old age the woman who inhabited it for all the years of her old age until her death, the woman whom, Ingraham keeps assuring us, we cannot name.

I see that I a moment ago struck through Wölfflin's name, and I should attempt to explain, since, although Wölfflin will no longer be my editor when this work is readied for publication, I owe it to Wölfflin that this work exists at all. My readers know that I am not a vain person, that I have always hidden behind my anonymity or the pseudonymity of V. Kelian without regard for personal fame or adulation. Dear Pete Tchaikovsky, whose somewhat soupy First Piano Concerto continues to give me orgasms despite its bathos, once predicted that people would try to penetrate the intimate world of his feelings and thoughts, "everything that all my life I have so carefully hidden from the touch of the crowd." When Wölfflin first proposed the writing of this memoir, I objected strenuously on three counts: one, that like Tchaikovsky I want to keep myself hidden from the touch of the crowd; two, that I lack the requisite self-regard or self-promotion to pull off an autobiographical work (I still subscribe to Ingraham's distinction between penises and neckties); and three, as I expressed it in a very simple but crucial question to Wölfflin:

"But what if Bolshakov himself should read my memoir and thus come to know my present whereabouts?"

"We can handle that," Wölfflin assured me. "We'll simply not publish your memoir until after you've finally and safely gone home to Svanetia."

All these years, I'd made no secret to my intimates, even Billy (of whom I inquired shortly before his tragic death of his possible interest in accompanying me), that I wanted to go home. After I wrote *Lamshged; or, The Shady Side of the Mountain,* the collection of short stories with a Svanetian setting, I was so overcome with homesickness and *toska* that I actually bought an airplane ticket to Tbilisi and applied for a passport, but I was informed by the State Department that it was not advisable I return there at that particular time, especially in view of my having just been naturalized as an American citizen.

Then, when to the astonishment of the world the entire Soviet Union came crumbling down around Gorbachev's heels, my old friend and comrade-in-arms Zviady Gamsakhurdia rose to power in my native Georgia and personally wrote to me, in care of my publishers, calling me— or V. Kelian—a Georgian national literary hero and inviting me to return triumphantly to the land of my birth and see it freed at last from communism. Late last year, I actually closed up my triplex temporarily, arranged for Morris to return to his at-large feeding and roaming within the Halfmoon, and flew to New York to meet my Kennedy connection with a flight to Tbilisi via Athens, when the news came in that dear Zviady was in trouble: a junta of his Georgian opponents, accusing him of behaving like a dictator and jailing his critics—ironically, the same treatment he and I had suffered as critics of the Communist regime— had seized control from him in a civil war that left over a hundred

Georgians dead. I waited to see if those loyal to Zviady might eventually win out, but they did not, and from New York I spoke to Zviady himself by telephone at his temporary exile in Armenia and was advised that it would be dangerous for me to return.

Thwarted and unhappy, I decided that as long as I was in New York, I might as well pay a visit to Liz and to Wölfflin, my agent and my editor. But my editor, I discovered, was in the hospital, recovering from a "nervous breakdown." I visited Wölfflin there anyway and learned the distressing reason for my editor's problems.

"I was hoping I wouldn't have to tell you about it," Wölfflin said, "but since you're here, I can't avoid it. Please don't blame yourself."

It seems that just a short time before, Wölfflin, returning from an editorial conference, was accosted in the private office by a man brandishing a heavy pistol, a Beretta automatic with a silencer screwed into its barrel. From the descriptions of the man that occur throughout *Georgie Boy*, Wölfflin recognized him as the original Dr. V. T. Bolshakov, and told the man as much, and advised him to put away his weapon or face possible arrest and imprisonment.

The man laughed ("Insanely, I thought," Wölfflin told me) and shook his head, saying, "No, I intend to become as hard to find as your Kati/Kelian has been all these years. Nobody will find me. I can no longer work in the Soviet Union. There *is* no Soviet Union. I can no longer attend psychiatric conferences anywhere. Everywhere I have gone these past seven years, people have asked me if I am Bolshakov. Ha! How would you like it if everywhere you went people asked you if you were Wölfflin and, when you admitted that you were, heaped scorn and contumely upon you?"

"Is that why you are waving that pistol at me?" Wölfflin wanted to know.

"No, I am waving the pistol at you because you are going to tell me where Yekaterina Vladimirovna has been hiding all these years. I am waving the pistol at you to let you know that I shall kill you if you do not."

"She no longer goes by that name," Wölfflin confessed.

"Of course not!" Bolshakov yelled. "Any fool knows that she is V.

Kelian. Any fool knows that V. Kelian's lively stage entertainment, *Hotel Mezzaluna,* which I myself had occasion to sit through here in New York a few years ago, takes place in an enchanted but decaying resort hotel on a mountaintop somewhere. You are going to tell me where that mountaintop is located."

"And you intend to kill her?" Wölfflin asked. "Is that your objective?"

"Not at once," Bolshakov said. "No, I shall permit her to live a short time longer, long enough to listen to me. I have some things to tell her about what she has done to me."

"I should think that she has a very good idea of what she has done to you," Wölfflin said.

Bolshakov screamed, "AND SO DOES THE REST OF THE WORLD!"

("And he began trembling so much," my editor told me, "that I knew he couldn't hold the gun steady enough to shoot me with it. Which is why I reached for the button to summon Security." Wölfflin pulled aside the top of the hospital gown to reveal to me the bandaged shoulder. "He shot at me four times and missed the first three. Then he held the gun to my forehead.")

"TELL ME THE LOCATION OF THE *REAL* HOTEL MEZZA-LUNA!" Bolshakov demanded.

Wölfflin realized the inevitability of either telling him or dying. But at that moment the editor's secretary, having detected the popping of the pistol despite its silencer, stuck her head in the door, screamed, and immediately ran to alert the building's Security, and a guard chased Bolshakov down five flights of steps to the street, where he disappeared into the traffic of lower Fifth Avenue.

"Thank you so much for not telling him," I said to Wölfflin. "And I am so sorry that the terrible experience has done *this* to you." I indicated the hospital bed.

"He'll find you, Kat," Wölfflin warned me. "If you can't go home to Svanetia, you'd better get out of the 'Mezzaluna.' It won't take a cryptographer to discover that *Mezzaluna* means 'Halfmoon' in Italian."

Now, as I write these words, as if the meaning is dawning even upon him, Morris, my cat, abruptly perks his head up, as if he has heard something, or as if he knows something. The larger portion of his life he sleeps away, upon his favorite cushion beneath the painting I acquired at a Sotheby's auction some years ago, René Magritte's *Château de Croissant,* which depicts a castle floating in the air beneath a crescent moon, the castle almost a hybrid of the architecture of the Halfmoon and that of my native Svanetian towers. Now Morris, more impetuously than is his custom, rises up from his nap, looks around himself as if he's discovering his surroundings for the first time and finding them unfamiliar, then leaps down from his cushion and trots hastily to the stairs leading down from my aerie/study. His arthritis seems to have disappeared.

I consult the clock, which hangs beneath another favorite painting, William McNamara's *Leaping Rock,* an enormous watercolor depicting a landscape of Stick Around with a prominent geological feature, a bluff overhanging Swains Creek Valley. The clock informs me that this is not the customary time that Morris goes downstairs for his feeding. (I interrupt my writing here and go down to my kitchen and discover that indeed he is not dining at his dish but has apparently exited the apartment through his Cat-Port in my door.)

This simple detail of my daily life seems so fraught with portent that I cannot return to the writing of this memoir but rather, after reflecting upon the place where I left off (Wölfflin recently retired, for good, from publishing, and I, having expected for so many years that Bolshakov could show up at any minute, long ago gave up expecting to be surprised by him) and deciding to call it a day, I leave my writing desk, expecting to pick up tomorrow morning with a report on tonight's séance, and prepare to leave the apartment, first selecting and donning my disguise, so sentimentally similar to that of Cathlin McWalter in Pittsburgh: red wig, huge hat, sunglasses, much jewelry. Then I lock my apartment and go downstairs, and farther downstairs, not taking the elevator, because I need the exercise, to the lobby, where I begin my incognito search for Morris.

In the lobby, among other guests, there is a woman who looks almost like myself: huge floppy hat, red hair (or wig), dark sunglasses. As women will, we cast arch looks at each other, as if comparing jewelry, much of which we both are wearing.

Then I turn and approach Jackie Randel, the sales manager. "Pssst, Jackie, it's me, Kat," I say to her, and I give her a moment to recognize me in the shades and flaming hair. "Have you seen Morris?"

"Why, yes," she says, whispering in her Bodarks voice, so as not to give me away to anyone else in the lobby. She points. "As a matter of fact, he just jumped up on the mantel over there. I've never seen him do that before."

And there sits Morris, perched precariously on the narrow marble mantelpiece that trims the long-unused free-standing fireplace in the Halfmoon's lobby. I move to him. I am unable to discern any omen or portent in his behavior, beyond the originality of it. "Morris," I say, "what are you doing up there?" Of course he does not answer, and I wonder if he can recognize me in my disguise. He does, however, from his perch above my eye level, look deeply into my sunglass-hidden eyes, and I recall again how there have been times I've suspected him of being "inhabited" by some spirit, perhaps even Dan Montross's.

And then he stretches himself upward with unaccustomed agility and raises his paw and places it briefly upon the marble slab impaneled above the mantelpiece, where the Halfmoon's original builder had engraved some homely verses in ornate Victorian letters. This builder, one Powell Clayton, an ex-governor of the state, who in fact had succeeded Jacob Ingledew as governor during the period of Reconstruction after the Civil War, had supposedly composed these lines himself:

> Although upon a summer day,
> You'll lightly turn from me away,
>   When autumn leaves are scattered wide,
>   You'll often linger by my side.
>   But when the snow the earth doth cover,
>   Then you will be my ardent lover.

II

ALL MY YEARS IN THE HALFMOON, I have been aware of the existence of this inscription but have scarcely bothered to read it before, and I am not able to convince myself now that Morris wants me to read it. If he does, what does he want me to think the verses mean? . . . Is he trying to predict our future together in Stick Around? Is he telling me, for example, that come some winter and a snow, he will cease being Morris the feline and magically turn into the twelve-year-old Danny Montross? Or is he making some distant echo or allusion to those lines of "Danny Boy"—*But I'll come back, when summer's in the meadow, or when the valley's hushed and white with snow . . . ?*

"Excuse me again, Jackie," I say, "but would you happen to know the circumstances or significance of those verses carved over the mantel?"

She looks at me as if to question how the significance could have escaped someone intelligent. "Don't you see?" she says. "It's just the fireplace talking. What do you call it? *Pathetic fallacy?* The fireplace is just telling the guests that they will appreciate it most during the wintertime."

"Oh," I say, abashed that I didn't catch it. I laugh lightly in embarrassment and remark, "But the fireplace hasn't been operative for many years."

"Neither has Morris," she observes. "But both seem to be trying to tell you something."

I wander down the end of the lobby to the Crystal Room, where people are arranging the tables and chairs in a crescent facing the podium in preparation for tonight's séance. Morris follows me, having leapt down after his futile attempt to communicate with me by means of a long, cold fireplace's cold marble inscription. A photographer, by the looks of him not a local man or tourist but one of those national paparazzi who have been camping out at the Halfmoon in hopes of shooting me, gives me a second glance, as if to attempt to penetrate my disguise, and I leave quickly in order to avoid another of those situations that had me flipping the bird in the pages of a recent *Time* magazine.

I stroll outside, Morris continuing to follow me—and all cat owners know that cats do not follow people as dogs do; it is one of the main differences between canine and feline. Silvia, my Range Rover, rests, long unused these past months of her eighth year, in the Halfmoon's parking lot alongside a red-white-and-blue van from Fateville's Channel 7 television station. I am tempted to take Silvia and flee to Stick Around to observe the progress on my house, to watch Clifford Stone and his restorationists make love to it with their scrapers, their sandpaper, their paint remover, and their fancy wallpapering equipment. But I cannot leave Arcaty.

It is a beautiful day. Although sunny, almost balmy, it is not quite warm enough to bring the Halfmoon's guests out to the swimming pool, which is ready for the season but not occupied; the lifeguard's high chair is empty, as empty as it was on that damp November day so many years gone when Billy came out here to fall or jump into this water. Powerlessly I am drawn to the pool's side, and Morris does not stop until his foreclaws have come to grip the pool's edge. My attention is diverted from the awful water and the memory of what happened there by the uncustomary presence beside me of this old peculiar yellow cat whom my novelist's imagination keeps trying to turn into Dan.

My novelist's imagination killed Billy but did it veritably, not imaginatively. One time, I thoughtlessly blurted to him that he was not the equal of Travis Coe, that he was like a novel reader who couldn't understand what he was reading and therefore couldn't be deeply moved by it (although the analogy may have been lost on him: Billy never read anything, not even magazines). Not once in the year and a half of our relationship did he ever seem to experience the face-wrenching, shoulder-quivering, buttock-lunging ejaculations that Travis had. Billy was docile, polite, eager to please, and industrious to a fault, compared with Travis's laziness, but Billy seemed always only mildly aroused or impassioned by our lovemaking, as if he were . . . I hesitate to continue the analogy, but there it is: as if he were the reader of novels who is never caught up in them, who can never suspend disbelief, who is too timid or jaded or leery to surrender himself to the pleasure.

When Billy was already turned fourteen and the novelty of his companionship as well as the charm of his physical attractiveness were both evaporating, I told him of my plan to visit my native Svanetia (of which I had regaled him with many stories, often trying out on him those that I would publish in *Lamshged; or, The Shady Side of the Mountain*) and I gave him a choice: He could either go with me on the trip, or we would end our relationship.

"I'll have to ask my mother," he said. I was taken aback, because during the time I had known him he had rarely mentioned either of his parents; indeed, he had no father, as I was to learn when it was his mother's "boyfriend" who came to the Halfmoon to claim the body after the inquest. Billy did have a house, or cottage, on one of the most craggy precipices of Halfmoon Mountain, and I had picked him up there in Silvia several times, but I had never even seen, let alone met, his mother. She was, I gathered, a busy woman who took little interest in Billy's whereabouts and often permitted him to "stay over with a friend," his common excuse for spending the night with me.

"You're not going to tell her about me?" I said to him in response.

"Oh, she sorta knows, anyhow," he said.

I pestered him for an explanation of just what his mother knew, and he was able to reassure me that his mother didn't know about our sexual relationship but knew that Billy often visited a "rich lady on the top floor of the Halfmoon who gave spending money in return for errands and other stuff."

All he had to do, he said, was tell his mother that the rich lady wanted him to take a trip to Europe with her for a couple of weeks or so. "She'd be glad to get rid of me for a while," he said to me, of his mother.

But that may have been too much as far as the woman was concerned, because she wouldn't consent to the notion, and Billy was heartbroken, for he truly had been building up his anticipation of flying to Georgia and Svanetia. I couldn't console him, and I mistakenly thought that the best thing to do, as I had done with Travis, was to "pay him off"— more handsomely than the severance pay I'd given Travis, by three times the amount.

He stared at the money offering with disdain. "Don't you want me anymore?" he asked. "Don't you want to see me again when you get back from Svanetia?"

"I'm going to be awfully busy when I get back," I declared. "I'm going to write a stage play about the four ghosts who inhabit the Halfmoon."

"I could help," he offered. "I could play like I was one of the ghosts and say some stuff."

I smiled, touched at the offer and the thought, but I said, "Billy, I wish for you much happiness. I wish for you that you will stay out of trouble, perhaps go back to school, be a good boy."

He screwed up his face. "Haven't I been a good boy?" he whined. "Haven't I sorta made you *happy?*"

The county coroner was never able to determine conclusively that Billy had deliberately drowned himself in this swimming pool. It was highly possible, the Halfmoon's management suggested, that he had slipped on the wet tiles (it had been raining) and fallen in. I stare down at this water, and I speak aloud to the old cat who is also staring at it. "Morris, it wasn't an accident, was it?"

Morris slowly turns his old head and looks up at me. "Noo," he says. It could be simply a feline utterance, but it strikes me more as the way a Bodarks man would render a negative.

"I'm going on down the hill a ways," I tell him. "You go on back inside, if you want." Like my apartment door itself, the large French doors on the east side of the Halfmoon's lobby have a Cat-Port cut into the bottom pane of glass, expressly for Morris's convenience, with even steps, like a stile, leading up and down for his arthritic egress and ingress. Morris could easily go back to the lobby and the adulation of the hotel's guests, if he wanted, or he could return to the apartment. But he doesn't want. He wants to follow me.

Cat owners know that even those cats who uncustomarily do follow their masters for brief stretches will not stray far beyond the known delimits of their domestic domain. No cat wants to leave the boundaries of its known world, and I am certain that Morris, in the entire course of his life, except for the few occasions I'd taken him (reluctantly and complainingly on his part) for a ride in Silvia, has never been beyond the property line of the Halfmoon.

"Go home, Morris!" I snap at him as he continues to follow me down the steep slope that drops off the eastern side of the Halfmoon's front yard. But he will neither turn nor slow his determined dogging (or unwonted catting) of my heels.

The descent of a spiderweb of stone steps, concrete steps, iron steps, and wooden steps takes us, in time, to the significant place where the newly restored Victorian gazebo marks Halfmoon Spring; it's a copper-pagoda-roofed gingerbread Gothic structure that has been one of my favorite resting places on my hikes. It is within easy sight of the Arcata Springs Public Library, where I first laid eyes on Travis and where there are now three whole shelves of my books in their domestic and foreign editions, donated by the author in grateful recognition of all the research I've done in that old building.

I sit in the gazebo. Morris sits on the bench beside me, but far enough away that he can look up into my eyes without getting a crick in his neck. "Well, Morris," I say. "You have wandered a long way from home. What have you got to say for yourself, dear cat?"

"It is time, dear Kat," he says, "that you face the real reason Billy drowned himself." It is the sort of thing I might say to myself, and thus I am reluctant to believe, at first, that he has actually spoken. He certainly has not moved his lips. He doesn't have lips. But the words, I convince myself, came from his mouth.

The suggestion itself appalls me so much that I find it difficult to reflect upon this strange circumstance of his speaking not in *mews* and *ows* and *mees* and *noos* but in human speech. "I am a tired and frightened woman approaching middle age," I declare, "and I refuse to allow myself to believe that my loneliness is making me hear you speak to me."

"You're certainly frightened," he says, "and this hike has tired you. But you are a good sight short of even approaching middle age. And it isn't your loneliness that lets you hear me. It's my impatience. Do you think I've had it easy, being silent all these years?"

I laugh, but nervously. "Hush, Morris," I say. "I refuse to believe that you are talking. It won't wash, not even in one of my novels."

"This isn't your novel," he says.

"Oh?" I say. Then, "No, you're right, it isn't a novel, it's a memoir."

"At the moment, it isn't even your memoir. You aren't writing, are you? Didn't you set aside your pencil to follow me downstairs?"

"Then who is writing this?"

"I am," he says.

"In *my* voice? In this present tense, in *my* first person?"

"Keep your person, sweet Kat. You won't have it much longer."

I shudder at this suggestion of an approaching ending. Endings are hideous. In the writing of each of my books, the ending has gone too fast and too painfully for me, like . . . like Billy's premature and weak ejaculations. "Morris," I say, addressing him thus because I am not going to admit, even to myself in my deluded state, that this cat is actually Dan, "why don't you tell me why Billy killed himself?"

A tourist couple strolling on Spring Street pause and turn to stare briefly at me. Are they wondering at this weird "local character" with red hair and dark shades talking to herself? Or can they actually hear the talking cat?

The talking cat says to me, "You tried to get Billy to do something that you could never ask of Islamber, Dzhordzha, or Kenny, and that even Travis could bring himself to do only once."

The cat's reminder brings back the recent voice of Travis, mature, without a trace of his old Bodark accent, who, when I teasingly reminisced on the telephone about that one rare occasion, jokingly declared, "And look at me now! The chicks call me the best 'face man' in Hollywood!"

"Are you going to lecture me with analogies," I ask Morris, "on how the novelist demands the oral gratification of all his readers?"

The cat grins. "No," he says, "make yourself comfortable and I'm going to tell you a story."

III

EKATERINA YOU WERE, and you were not at all. You were from a land far away, once upon a time and upon no time at all, where stories always begin, "There was, and there was not at all . . . ," as if to confute truth or affirm invention, in celebration of the imagination's freedom to transcend the stubborn facts of "reality": *you were, and still are, Ekaterina: all of this is real, and not a word of it is true: you escaped the clutches of a sadist named Bolshakov (a real name) who could not separate truth from fiction, and you came to America. . . .*

All afternoon the cat talks. There are a few more pedestrians on the sidewalk of Spring Street who pause to observe this woman listening— or appearing to listen—to an old yellow cat who does not move his lips, who in fact doesn't even have any lips, just that cute bowed dimple beneath his harelip.

The cat tells me his story of my story: my coming to America, my months in Pittsburgh, Knox Ogden, Kenny, Ingraham. I have told this story in more objective form, with little reference to any "ghosts," in Chapters Fifteen and Sixteen of this memoir, and I invite my reader to refer to it. I am enchanted with the cat's fanciful conception of Daniel Lyam Montross as a sort of ghost-with-a-résumé, and I am so intent on the story that I scarcely notice that among the scant traffic on Spring Street there is an old gray Jeep that has passed me more than once.

I become convinced it is indeed the cat, not my wild imagination, when Morris tells me things about Pittsburgh that I did not know: for example, why did Kenny never ask, as both Travis and Billy were to do, to see me undress? *The answer,* Morris/Dan tells me, *and I'm sorry you've had to wait this long to learn the particulars from me, was simply that he did not need to ask.* And then he tells me about that peephole that Kenny had in the broom closet—spying upon me! I am blushing, but I am also eager to hear the rest of this cat's story, and even more eager to get back to my writing desk and revise certain parts of this memoir. I'll do it first thing tomorrow . . . But no, the woman from *Paris Review* is coming to interview me.

It is near on to suppertime when Morris says, *Dusk was fallen. The long day was over. My bag of tricks was empty, but I had you here . . . almost. You needed time to think about it, but both I. and I were confident you'd stay, because, you see, you had absolutely nowhere else to go.*

Riding down to the yellow house in I.'s Blazer, going off to meet his friends, who would become your friends too, you informed him, "I love the little serendipities of life, but this coincidence I like best: in Svanetian, Lisedi, *the name of the town I came from, means 'to remain, to stay more, to stick around.' ''*

I wait. The cat appears to have quit talking. A little girl, broken away from her strolling parents on the sidewalk, rushes into the gazebo, stares down at the trickle of Halfmoon Spring, shuts her eyes, and throws a penny into the water. "I hope your wish comes true," I say to her, and she smiles bashfully and runs back to her parents, who walk on. The old gray Jeep passes me slowly once again, and I try to detect its driver, to see if he could by any chance be Bolshakov, but he is not driving slowly enough for me to have a good look at him. I return my gaze to my cat and wait. Morris says nothing. Finally, I decide that his story is concluded, and I remark, "That was lovely. Truly. I have only a few questions. First, if indeed you are Dan Montross, or his spirit, why did you leave the Bodarks to journey all that way through time and space to Pittsburgh in search of *me?* Or was I just the accidental subject of your attentions and affections?"

Morris says nothing.

"Can't answer that one, huh?" I challenge him. "Then tell me this: Have you obliterated Anangka? Are you in full control of my destiny now?"

The cat, who was so loquacious all afternoon, has become mute. But do I detect a slight shaking of his head? Cats do not shake their heads. They toss them, or vigorously nod them when they're washing themselves, but they don't shake them.

"Did you," I ask of the cat, with a mounting sense of futility, "arrange for Ingraham to enter the story simply in order to bring me here to the Bodarks?"

Cats are self-conscious creatures, and if you talk to one intensely enough, he will begin licking himself in embarrassment. This is what Morris now does, although the nodding of his head as he does so could be an affirmative answer to my question.

"How do you suppose Ingraham would feel," I demand, "if he knew that his whole purpose in life was simply to bring me to the Bodarks? Answer me that. Or has the cat got your tongue?"

But the cat has his own tongue, and he will not respond.

"Morris," I upbraid him. "At least tell me what you meant by pointing to that inscription over the fireplace earlier today, that business about being my ardent lover 'when the snow the earth doth cover.'" When my continued questions draw no further response from the old cat, I ask in desperation, "If you are Dan, what do you want of me?" And when he doesn't answer, I entreat, "Are you waiting for me to join you in the 'spirit world'? Do you want me to die?"

The old gray Jeep has now come to a stop beside a parking meter across the street, and a tall man exits from it and places a coin in the parking meter, then crosses the street to the gazebo, glances at Morris, and says to me, "Is that you, Ekaterina? Are you reduced, in your dotage, to talking to cats?"

IV

I HAVEN'T SEEN HIM FOR YEARS. It is Ingraham. I am a bit put out by his question and his feeble but mocking laughter. *"Ot!"* I say, "or *Och*, as the case may be." He appears not to hear me. I make a sign language, a pantomime of wishing to write something, and he hands me his ballpoint and a few of his note cards. I write, *What are you doing here?*

"I heard about the séance they're having tonight," he says, "and I thought I'd like to go. I've never been to a séance before. Are you going?"

I nod and write, *I've never been to one either. And I'm* scared.

"Oh, I shouldn't think there's anything to be afraid of," he says.

Not about the séance itself. I don't think any of the Halfmoon's—or the Mezzaluna's—ghosts will actually be conjured. If they were, I'd be as delighted to meet them as I would have been to meet Lawren Carnegie or Knox Ogden or Dan Montross when we were in Pittsburgh.

He is patient while I write, as if he really has nothing better to do. He reads the card twice, frowning, then asks, "How do you know that Dan Montross—or his ghost—was in Pittsburgh?"

I smile and write, *He told me.* I am tempted to write for him the whole story just as I've heard it from Morris, if for no other reason than to convince him that Morris has been talking to me, but I am afraid that Ingraham might steal the story and appropriate it for some future fiction of his, beating me to it.

"So," he says, "in your dotage you talk to both your cat and the ghost of Montross."

Or maybe they are the same, I write. Ingraham stares at my cat, then hesitantly reaches out and attempts to stroke Morris's back. Morris shies away from his touch. My cat gives me one more look, as if a final look, and then, despite the arthritis that has often left him almost unable to drag himself from floor to floor of the Halfmoon, he bounds out of the gazebo and scampers up the hill toward home. I smile at a memory and write, *The last time you took notice of Morris was when we were leaving the Halfmoon after that BOW convention—when you were still pretending that I was Cathlin McWalter—and when I said good-bye to Morris and told him I'd be back, you said, "How come you can talk to the damned cat, but not to me?"*

"Was that"—he gestures in the direction Morris has disappeared —"the *same* cat? He must be ancient."

In finger language I count eighteen, for Morris's years.

We reminisce, Ingraham and I, about that long-ago springtime of my first coming to the Bodarks. I refresh his memory of the wonderful speech he gave to the BOW, equating the genuine writer's addiction with the genuine drinker's addiction, the precepts of which often came back to me during my struggles to become a writer. Ingraham says that he no longer drinks at all these days—"Except a glass of wine on special occasions. And I think I've become dull and uninteresting. I'm not any fun anymore."

We make idle chitchat about our current lives, our current projects: I fill a card or two with a synopsis of *Dawn of the Osage,* pointing out that perhaps it is a kind of prehistory of the Stick Around country, and thus an ultimate fulfillment of Ingraham's old wish that I write about Stick Around, which, as it turns out, he himself has resumed doing in full force, even to the extent of writing about some of the Osages who were there when the white men, the first Ingledews, arrived. Ingraham and I, two craftsmen trading shop talk as the afternoon wanes, exchange information and observations on the customs and beliefs of the Osages. I consider inviting him up to see my Halfmoon digs, which he has never seen. I consider inviting him to have supper there with me. Finally, choosing my words carefully, upon a fresh new card, I do, and when he expresses delight in his acceptance, I write, *What can I fix you for supper?* I am mindful of using *fix* in the colloquial, Bodarkadian sense.

He removes from the pocket of his windbreaker some sheets of paper, unfolds them, consults them. "Let's see," he says, "and begins quoting: ". . . *that lovely suite of rooms on the top floor of the Moonbeam Hotel, with my own futuristic kitchen, where I could whip up one of those chicken dishes that grace the pages of* Cathlin's Quick Chick Cookbook . . ."

I recognize what he is reading; two hours or so earlier this afternoon my cat Morris quoted the entire document to me as part of his narrative of my life in Pittsburgh. *You still have my obituary!* I write.

"No, this is only a Xerox. The original I have donated to Special Collections at the university, along with a few other souvenirs of my association with the famous V. Kelian. Well, could your futuristic kitchen perhaps handle a Svanetian version of chicken and dumplings?"

I laugh and write, *I'll try.*

He hands the sheets of paper to me, as if making me a present of them. "Notice the date, if you will," he suggests.

During Morris's quoting of the document, I already noticed the date, April 24, 2021, and I have already for one sweet moment sighed and reflected to myself, *Well, at least I have almost thirty more years to live.* But when Morris (or Dan, if you please) quoted my obituary back to me, I had observed that today, April 22, is just the day before the day of the month I'm supposed to die, and that has not helped my frame of mind. As if reading my thoughts, Ingraham observes, "There are so many things in your obituary that 'came true.' The Moonbeam is the Halfmoon, of course. And you do have a twelve-year-old houseboy, I presume."

I shake my head. *Not anymore,* I scribble, *not for the last five years.*

"Do you mean he's seventeen now?"

No, I mean I haven't had a servant for five years.

"Despite your enormous wealth?" he asks, and I feel the question is rhetorical and deserves no answer. "Well, do you still drink too much vodka? Do you take twelve-mile hikes each day? Are you writing a book about the mushrooms of the Bodarks?"

To each of these questions I shake my head. *Don't try to frighten me further,* I write. *There is much in this obituary that was purely fanciful and will not come true.*

"I notice you're not even smoking anymore," he observes. "Are you by any chance writing a memoir called *Louder, Engram!?*"

As I was when Morris quoted it, I am amazed that I actually used that title in that long-ago imaginary obituary, and I scan the pages he has given me, in search of it, and sure enough, there it is: *So who are the suspects? I'm a writer, after all, and I can't give away endings, and this isn't the ending. You haven't heard the last of me. But my devoted readers who are familiar with my memoirs,* Louder, Engram! *will recall that I spent some years in my early twenties incarcerated . . .*

"And how about this?" Ingraham's long finger points to another place in the obituary, where I wrote, *Do you think I might have been done in by some person driven mad by envy of my riches? (Even Professor Ingraham himself?) Then why didn't he or she murder me thirty-five years ago, when my first novel,* Geordie Lad, *catapulted me to fame?*

I hold out my hand for a fresh card upon which to write, and he gives it to me, and I write, *If you are going to kill me, why didn't you do it when* Georgie Boy *was such a success?*

"I was tempted, then," he says, smiling, "but this obituary made me a suspect, didn't it?"

I scribble hurriedly, *Let's not joke, dear friend and mentor. Often these days I am overcome with a premonition of an early death.*

His long finger slides down the page I hold in my hand until it comes to the penultimate paragraph: *I'm not going to tell you, yet, who killed me. But I can say this much: Bolshakov is actually at large. He is out there, even in the vicinity of the Moonbeam Hotel . . .*

"He is, isn't he?" Ingraham says, and I wonder how he knows. When

I nod, Ingraham's face softens in sympathy or concern and he says, "I shouldn't be showing you this document at a time like this, if you are preoccupied with an early death. But your last three books, I couldn't help noticing, have an obsession with death."

Oh? I write. *Have you read my last three books?*

"I have read everything you have written, dear Kat," he confesses. "Even your stories in *Playboy*."

I am greatly flattered, especially in view of his disinclination to read anything that has been printed. And I confess, on a new card, *Then it won't bother me to admit that I've read everything of yours, even the termite novel and your latest,* Oratorio in the Arboretum.

"Which came out the same season as your *Original Flavor* but sold a fraction of the copies yours did," he observes with a covetous leer. "That title of yours, by the way, I took to be an allusion to your return to the 'flavor' of *Georgie Boy* after your experimentation with so many different flavors. And also a return to your exploration of the ways that death is transcended."

Yes, I write, admitting it, *I stopped just short of stealing your device of using the future tense in the end. I was* dying *to use the future tense, but that it is your own personal device, with which you have ended all your books.*

"I am happy you noticed," he says, making a slight bow. "But that shouldn't have stopped you. I don't own the patent on the future tense."

But the reader would know I purloined it from you.

"What reader?" he demands. "Your millions of readers have never heard of me. If you use the future tense, probably any reader of any of my books would think I purloined it from *you*."

All right, then. I will *use the future tense.*

"You *will*," he concedes.

Then here we are together, I write, using the present tense for the last time, *in the Halfmoon Spring gazebo, one of my favorite places in Arcaty, just a stone's throw from the public library, and probably we are sitting at the same spot where once sat Osage Indians. Perhaps someday the town fathers of Arcaty will affix a bronze plaque to this bench: HERE SAT INGRAHAM AND V. KELIAN TALKING ABOUT DEATH AND INDIANS AND THE WRITING OF NOVELS.*

Ingraham will read this and laugh, but then he will say, "Allow me to make a minor correction in tense. The plaque will read: HERE WILL SIT V. KELIAN AND INGRAHAM FOREVER TALKING ABOUT DEATH AND INDIANS AND THE WRITING OF NOVELS."

"That will do," I will say aloud, and he will hear me. "And that way, neither of us will ever die."

25

I

INGRAHAM WILL ALSO SIT beside me in the Crystal Room during the séance, which, true to the stuff of memoirs rather than novels, will not be even noteworthy, let alone suspenseful or climactic. I will wish myself able to report that it was uncomfortably fraught with peril or surprise or at least revelation, but in fact I will be reminded that the last time Ingraham and I sat together in this room was the day of his speech to BOW comparing drinking and writing, which was much more entertaining than this séance will have been. Veronica, the medium, will seem almost drunk herself, but we will determine that it is some sort of self-induced trance, not intoxication, and I will comment on a card to Ingraham that perhaps there is not only a link between drinking and writing but also a link between the truly creative state and the state of spiritualistic trance: the writer summons entities who materialize from the Other Side of imagination and become temporary "presences."

But no ghosts will walk. Or even, although we will be invited by Veronica to listen carefully, talk. The audience of perhaps three hundred crowding the Crystal Room will observe an expectant silence for a half hour's worth of Veronica's "trance talk," her lubricious attempt to contact her "guide," or spirit from the Other Side, and, when that fails, her attempt to turn the meeting over to her "control," the spirit on the Other Side apparently in charge of granting permissions to the departed souls who wish to make contact with us the living. After a while, when nothing extraordinary occurs and the audience begins to grow restless, Veronica will mumble an excuse to the effect that there may be "hostile, disbelieving" persons present who have been preventing the contact from taking place. (I will reflect, and even attempt to remark on a card to Ingraham, that since I have been using the future tense, which gives the user considerable control over events, I have been unconsciously preventing anything significant from happening. Ingraham will read my card with a wry smile; he will think carefully about that, and he will whisper to me, "That will very well conceivably be the case.")

There will be only one incident worth reporting. Toward the end, Morris will wander into the Crystal Room, as he will often have done throughout his long life, and he will glance around him as if to wonder why there are people packing the place wall-to-wall, and then he will saunter slowly, hampered by his arthritis, toward the podium where Veronica sits. I will find that my breathing has stopped in anticipation, because I will have convinced myself by this time that Morris indeed is inhabited by some presence from the Other Side. Veronica will glance down at him with obvious discomfiture; spiritualists are always uneasy in the presence of cats. He will stare up at her for a long moment, with that penetrating, solemn, all-wise gaze that most cats possess to some degree and Morris possesses in abundance. I will strain my ears to catch any repetition of the sounds that Morris made to me all that afternoon. But he will be as mute as ever. Then he will turn his gaze from her to me and will seem to look at me sadly, or with longing. He will then exit slowly through the door to the kitchen. The audience, either amused by the presence of a pet at a serious séance or convinced that Morris was the only materialization during the event, will laugh, and the laughter will signal the end of the session.

Afterward, the photographers, the television cameramen, the reporters will surround me and Ingraham, and they will insist I confess my identity. But I will not. "This is a far cry from the Mezzaluna, don't you think?" one of them will pester, but I will shrug my shoulders, and I will take Ingraham's arm and lead him quickly out of the Crystal Room, with the media people in hot pursuit, and when we reach the elevator Ingraham will have the sense and the heft to bar any of them from getting on with us.

At my door, Ingraham will give me a quick, light kiss on the cheek and he will say, "I'd better hit the road, to get back to Fateville."

I will have a card ready for him, which I will already have written while in the Crystal Room: ~~Do~~ Did you by any chance see anybody in ~~here~~ the Crystal Room who resembled Bolshakov?

"I'm sorry," Ingraham will say, "but unfortunately my mental image of Bolshakov has been contaminated by having seen the movie of *Georgie Boy* more than once. Bolshakov to me no longer resembles the Bolshakov of the book, or the man I met briefly in Pittsburgh, or even that innocent Dr. MacLean we met that one morning in the Crystal Room, but rather the actor Sert Reichert, with his sinister eyes, the evil widow's peak in his slicked-down hairline, and his nasty leer. Did Bolshakov look anything at all like Sert Reichert?"

I will shake my head. Then I will seize Ingraham by both his arms as if to draw him to me, and I will exaggerate the movements of my lips the better for him to read them: "Stay with me!"

"Pardon?" He will not have heard me.

Since he will not be able to hear me anyway, I will feel free to babble whatever comes into my head: "Spend the night with me! Sleep with me if you wish! Nestle your grown man's tallywhacker into the folds of my little girl's gillyclicker that has never had a grown man before!"

He will offer me his ballpoint and cards. "Could you write any of this down?"

I will shake my head, and I will go on babbling. "When you were twelve you lusted after grown women and it has haunted all of your books! Let us pretend for one night that you are twelve again! I will take away your virginity!"

"I'm sorry, Kat. Why are you doing this? You know I can't hear a word you're saying."

"Read my lips! I cannot be alone tonight! It has been *years* since last

I had a boy! Be a boy again for me tonight! Let me undress you! Let me show you what to do with your thingie!"

Even if he hasn't caught a word, he will have sensed the distress and the longing and the loneliness in my tone, and he will usher me through my door and will close the door behind us. "I think you may be needing a stiff one," he will say.

"Yes! Yes! Let me make it stiff for us!"

But he will be at my bar, mixing drinks. *That* kind of stiffness: straight vodka for me and, despite his having been on the wagon for many years, an uncustomary bourbon for himself. "Look what you're doing to me," he will observe, offering a toast. "But cheers anyhow."

I will gulp my vodka and, emboldened, will write on a card, *You have always wanted me, haven't you?*

Reading it, he will smile. "Of course I have."

I will write, *Do you want me now?*

"Don't tease me, Kat. You know you can't violate your own pre-dilections."

I could try! I will write. Anything to get him to stay the night with me.

"I'm a married man," he will say, "not one of your boys."

I will sigh. I will think, and I will think, and I will think, desperately trying for some way to get him to stay. I will write, *Okay, if we are fated never to be lovers, then we must be sister and brother, and you must swear brotherhood. We must have the Svanetian ceremony of sworn kinship.*

He will glance at his watch. "How long will this take?"

A little while, I will write, and I will calculate how long I will be able to keep him with the ceremony. I will need several cards to explain the ceremony to him: it is really very simple, but it is solemn; it requires the pledging of oaths to each other, and, most importantly, it requires that we mingle our blood: we must make tiny cuts in the little fingers of our right hands and hold those cuts together tightly while our blood mingles and we say our words.

"I'm an old hand at pricking my little finger," he will say, "because as a diabetic I have to monitor my blood sugar regularly. But I don't know about mingling our blood. Have you been tested for HIV? I don't want to die of AIDS."

I have had no sex for five years! I will write, and I will finish off my glass and add, *Except what I can give myself!*

We will swear brotherhood and sisterhood, there in my conversation pit, performing the simple ceremony, using a single-edged razor blade, mingling our blood, taking the vows. "That wasn't so bad," he will observe when we have finished and are wrapping little Band-Aids on our pinkies.

I will write, *Now we are brother and sister. We must always be willing to receive each other at any time. I must be willing to lend you money whenever you need it, in whatever amount. I must never cheat you, nor deceive you. If either one of us dies, the other must either arrange the funeral or speak the obsequies. I want you to bury me at Stick Around.*

He will be taken aback. "But the Stick Around cemetery is strictly for natives. Not even Eli Willard is buried there. Not even Daniel Lyam Montross is buried there."

I don't need the cemetery, I will write. *Bury me in the woods near mushrooms, near Daniel, anywhere. You must promise. Promise me.*

He will laugh, but nervously. "You'll probably outlive me. But if you don't, I'll see to it you get yourself buried at Stick Around." As an afterthought, he'll add, "Do you still want to have us play Tchaikovsky's First Piano Concerto?"

I will be charmed that he has remembered. But it was, after all, in my obituary. I will nod my head. Then, at a loss for a way of keeping him longer, especially because he has not been inclined to refill his drink, I will lead him and his unfinished drink to the chess nook and show him my superlative Bombay inlaid mother-of-pearl chess table, with its Dieppe pieces in position, waiting but thoroughly covered with the dust of years, the years that have gone since last Billy and I attempted to play there.

"A game, huh?" Ingraham will say. He will glance at his watch once more and say, "I really shouldn't, but I can't resist." He will sit himself down there at the black side, although I will have been prepared to offer him the white side.

We will play. I will be badly out of practice; and his practice, he will explain, will have been limited to playing his own computer, a program called Chessmaster 2100, a sort of masturbation. He has not played a human for years. But the computer will have kept his sense of the game alive, whereas my own will have atrophied. Aloud, because he will not be able to hear me anyway, I will curse myself for my mistakes: castling too soon, forcing him to kill off both our queens. Steadily he will take my pawns, leaving me at a material disadvantage, and then he will have two horses to my one. Thinking of these horses, I will remember the old Bodark custom of ride-and-tie, and how Ingraham and I once upon a time did it. I will realize that I am doomed on this board. Neither of us will drink much; his one glass of bourbon, my one of vodka, will get us through the game.

But the game will drag on. I will be glad for that, in a way. It will keep him with me. I will be able to see where the game is leading: into a stalemate, if I am not careful. I will be able to see where the night is going: into my bed, if I can arrange it and steel myself. I will be able— for I will be controlling the future tense, will I not?—to know what will inevitably happen to prevent me from ever knowing the experience of sex with a grown man: the ultimate, inexorable, foregone arrival of the Visitor.

We will find ourselves with equal pieces: each having one rook, one bishop, one knight. Steadily we will remove these from each other until I am left with a bishop, he with a rook, which is trying to protect a pawn seeking queendom, but futilely, because of my bishop's aim on her. Ingraham will look at his watch yet again. "I'm really going to catch hell from my wife," he will say. We will be in the seventy-third move of our endgame.

I will resign myself (not resigning the game, which is almost stalemated) to Ingraham's eventual departure. The future tense will be able to keep him for only so long. I will be tempted to ask for his cards and to write upon them a final message of some sort, a proper word of thanks, perhaps, a good-bye, a farewell, a reminder of our responsibilities to each other in sworn brotherhood, some acceptable ending for him, who hates endings and cannot write them.

But at the moment I will begin to write upon the card, the long-expected knock will come at my door. At the instant of the sound, the firm, determined rapping, I will know who it is. Instead of writing what I will have intended on the card, I will write, *There is someone at the door. I know it is Bolshakov.*

Ingraham will jerk his head around nervously, as if attempting to hear the sound of the knocking. "How do you know?" he will ask, as if suspecting me of having arranged it. In a way, I will reflect, I will have arranged it, for I will have been handling the future tense, will I have not?

All these years, of course, I have been expecting him.

"Well, let me get it," he will offer boldly. "It may just be some drunk tourist or a reporter."

He will go to the door. Afraid, I will not follow, but I will know that Ingraham cannot handle any conversation with Bolshakov. I will have to do that myself. I will listen. I will hear the two men's voices. I will not hear their words. Ingraham's voice will raise in both volume and pitch, as if he is arguing with the man.

The man will be armed, of course. When I see dear Ingraham walking backward, coming back into the room one step behind the other, I will know that a Beretta automatic with a long silencer screwed into its barrel is aiming at his stomach. I will see the silencer moving laterally past the door, and then the Beretta itself, and then the hand holding it. And then the trench coat.

II

"*NA BODARKS UDIVITELNO KHOROSHO, Yekaterina,*" he will say to me in Russian, as if making pleasant conversation: "It is wonderful in the Bodarks." "*Chudnaya gostinitsa*" ("A wonderful hotel"). He will look around himself as if admiring my apartment, and he will seem almost unmindful of the weapon he will be brandishing, and he will go on making chitchat, pleasantries about the setting, the weather, the spring night. Although I have told myself a thousand times that he will appear one day, I will still find that I am not totally prepared for it: my adrenaline will be roaring, my heart thumping against my breast, my head reeling. He has aged, I will notice: his hair will be much grayer, his face not quite so babyish, his shoulders stooped. Even his trench coat, I will observe, will no longer be the neat, clean thing he always wore; it will distinctly remind me of the grungy trench coat Ingraham himself once wore: seedy, grimy, threadbare, a complete lack of neatness that Bolshakov should never bring himself to permit.

It will have been years since last I heard Russian, and, though it is a language that I know by heart, I will refuse to speak it. In English, I will ask him kindly to speak English.

He will incline his head toward Ingraham and say, still in Russian, "I do not wish to be understood."

"He can't understand you anyway," I will point out, in English. "He's deaf."

My mentor and my tormentor will stare at each other, the former defiantly, warily, and contemptuously, the latter with careful observation; and then the latter will address the former, speaking English for the first time: "Ah, yes. I did not recognize you. The professor from Pittsburgh. He of the BODARK plates. Do you know how long it took me to figure out the reference of *Bodark?*"

"If you want him to know what you're saying, you're going to have to write it down," I will tell him.

"I don't want him to know what I'm saying. I do not care. But I want him to observe what I am going to do." He will snap open the physician's gladstone bag that he is carrying, and he will bring out of it a length of rope or strong cord. Carefully, keeping his weapon trained upon Ingraham and me, he will seize one of the ladder-backed Mount Judea folk chairs that are placed against my foyer walls, and he will set it up facing my conversation pit, and he will say to Ingraham, "Please sit," and he will gesture for him to be seated in the chair. Ingraham will not comply, perhaps because he hasn't heard. Our adversary will demonstrate the pistol and its silencer, popping off a round that will puncture my precious Magritte painting, leaving a hole in the crescent moon. Ingraham, who as an art historian will have, earlier this evening, expressed enormous admiration for that painting, will wince as if he himself has been shot, and he will glare at the intruder with loathing. "SIT!" he will be told again, loudly enough for him to hear. He will sit, and Bolshakov will bind his hands behind him to the slats of the chair.

The chair will face the conversation pit. "Now, Yekaterina," he will say, "you will make yourself comfortable upon those cushions, first removing all of your garments."

I will shake my head. "You may as well shoot me now," I will tell him. "I do not intend to participate in whatever diabolical 'foreplay' you have contrived to amuse yourself before the killing."

He will laugh, or he will make that sound all too painfully familiar to me, as if something were caught in his throat while he is making an effort at expressing mirth or sadistic glee. "You seem to have prepared yourself for your punishment," he will remark. "You seem to have expected that my retribution would catch up with you." He will open the gladstone bag again and draw out a prepared hypodermic syringe. "But I assure you that the 'foreplay' I have in mind for you will not only stimulate your novelist's insatiable lust for the outlandish, the fantastic, but it will also, after all these years, prepare you to accept yourself as you really are before the moment of your death. Let me have your arm."

"Shoot me!" I will snap at him. "Not with the needle! With the gun! Kill me and get it over with!"

"This mild drug"—he will hold up the hand with the needle—"will only remove some of your inhibitions. It will not knock you out, nor even"—that demoniac coughing chuckle again—"nor even make you my slave. Your arm." And he will seize my arm and jab in the needle before I can hit him. Before his face feels the full brunt of the backhanded slap that I will throw at him, he will have injected the contents of the syringe into my arm. "There!" he will exclaim, stepping back from me and rubbing the smart from the slap I have given him on his face. "That didn't hurt either of us. Now why don't you accept my suggestion and make yourself comfortable? Please remove everything you are wearing."

Whatever the drug he will have given me, it will quickly be taking effect. I will no longer have the will to struggle against him. "Melancholy man!" I will whine at him. "You are the personification of evil!" But I will find myself unbuttoning my dress and stepping out of it. I will find myself divesting myself of all my garments, just as he will have bade me, until I am standing revealed bare to both men. I will be able to detect in the gaze of Ingraham, who has never seen me naked before, a certain admiration for my body, an art historian's appreciation of classical nudity.

"No," Bolshakov will say. "Despite how you tried so desperately to render me in your novel, I am not evil. You should have allowed your readers to see me neither as an evil man nor as a genius, but as someone who for all my prejudices was simply trying to do my best but who happened—in your case—to be wrong." Once again the man will fish around in his bulging doctor's kit and he will bring out, this time, an artificial penis, a convincingly lifelike instrument of flesh-colored rubber attached to cloth straps. He will lay his pistol aside on a cushion of the conversation pit, substituting his focus from one erect device to the other, and I will no longer have the will or the inclination even to think about attempting to seize the pistol and turn it on him. I will only wonder, momentarily, if Bolshakov's sinister career as a psychiatrist and flagrant womanizer has left him impotent, and if he will be required to use this dildo in order to rape me. "Now I intend an experiment," he will intone didactically, not unmindful of his captive audience, Ingraham, "to demonstrate that one of my theories, at least, was correct. You will recall how I attempted so unsuccessfully, as part of your therapy, to help you understand that in reality, as opposed to the unreality or surreality of your fabricated world, you are only a little girl wanting to grow up and acquire a penis. Remember how I tried to use the *matryoshka* dolls to show you? You are that smallest, innermost of the diminishing dolls, the little girl, wanting to break outward and assume the form of the boy doll. I cannot give you the form and shape of the boy, but I am going to give you the possession of this penis."

He will affix the penis to my groin, attaching the straps behind my buttocks. Despite the numbing of the drug he will have given me, I will find myself enormously amused by the sight of the erect "member" that I will have acquired. Or will it not be amusement so much as delight? Will I discover that I want this prick?

"Now," he will say, slowly unfastening the belt of his trousers, "here comes the part that you will like most. I am sure that in your most intense and private fantasies, over the years, you have dwelt often upon this daydream, and now you can do it! You are going to fuck me. You are going to penetrate me with your penis to your full and complete satisfaction, and perhaps even mine, if I am successful in pretending for your sake that I am female. And then, once you have finished fucking me, you are going to fuck your friend, the professor there."

While Bolshakov is undressing himself, I will glance at Ingraham, who of course will have no awareness of these things that Bolshakov has been saying and so will not understand what he will soon be required to watch and eventually to do. But Ingraham will know that something awful or incredible is about to happen, and he will look at me sadly, or with longing. I will recognize or recall the look: it will be the very same look that was the last look I had from my cat and friend, Morris.

Almost as if my thought of him will make him materialize again (and I will, after all, be exerting, despite the drug, continued control of the future tense), Morris will enter through his Cat-Port. The aged and feeble cat will stand there surveying this strange scene: the two men in his mistress's apartment, the one man bound to a chair, the other stepping out of boxer shorts patterned with red hearts. Bolshakov, if he will have noticed the cat at all, will pay him no mind. Morris will stand for only another moment, appearing to study the scene, and then he will exit, in the direction of the music room.

The naked Bolshakov will stretch himself out supine upon the cushions of the conversation pit, hiking up his knees and holding out his arms to me. "I am yours, dear boy," he will say to me. "Or would you rather have me turn over on my stomach?"

Mingled in my mind with powerlessness to disobey him will still be caginess, craft: perhaps if I obey him and follow through on this perverted charade, he will be sufficiently diverted not to notice that I am reaching for the pistol lying upon the near cushion. But then I will marvel at this conflict in myself: Would I rather use the penis than the pistol upon him? I will attempt to examine this conflict, to think about it.

"Wait," he will say. "I have forgotten something." He will again go to his doctor's bag and will bring out a tube of lubricating jelly, and he will smear it almost lovingly upon my penis, as if the penis is indeed part of me. "Now," he will say, lying back down. "Quickly. Fuck me!"

I will tell myself that it is the drug, not my own will, that is making me do his bidding. I will find myself between his legs, attempting to insert the artificial penis. He will have to guide me with his hand.

At the moment of my entrance, the apartment will flood with the booming baritone of long-dead Nelson Eddy:

Ah! sweet mystery of life, at last I've found thee!

Whence will come this song? I will recall that I indeed possess in my vast collection of music an old 33⅓ LP of the Victor Herbert operetta *Naughty Marietta,* but I would have been hard pressed to locate the album myself in the cabinets filled with records and compact disks. How could Morris possibly have found it, dragged it out, placed it upon the turntable, and started the machine running? Or will there have been some human other than we three in the apartment? My mind will be momentarily stunned out of its drugged submission.

Even Ingraham, deaf though he is, will recognize the music, and he will lend his atrocious off-key accompaniment to the lyrics of the unknown Rida Johnson Young:

Ah! I know at last the secret of it all!
All the longing, seeking, striving, waiting,
yearning . . .

"What is this?!" Bolshakov will demand, staring at Ingraham as if Ingraham were lip-synching Nelson Eddy's dulcet tones. "SILENCE!" Bolshakov will yell at Ingraham, and then, realizing that Ingraham cannot be producing the full orchestral accompaniment in waltz time, he will hastily withdraw his rectum from my dildo and scramble to his feet, picking up his pistol. "*Who* turned on the music?!" he will demand of me.

The burning hopes, the joy and idle tears that
fall . . . !

"Sometimes it just comes on by itself," I will tell him. "Would you like to see my music system?" I will make the suggestion in hopes that in the acceptance of it Bolshakov will allow me to discover for myself if indeed it is a rheumatoid tomcat who has turned on the music system.

Ingraham, despite whatever fear and anxiety he himself will be feeling (and surely Bolshakov will intend to shoot him ultimately as well), will go on attempting unsuccessfully to harmonize his terrible bass with the great baritone:

For 'tis love, and love alone, the world is seeking!

Ingraham's customarily dour face will be so jubilant that I will think that perhaps Ingraham, in the face of his mortality, has finally himself at last penetrated the sweet mystery of life, whatever that is.

Both naked, Bolshakov and I will step into the music room, where we will find, as I will have expected, that no cat has placed any record upon the Ortofon's turntable. Indeed, there will be no record on the turntable, nor any sign that the amplifier is actually turned on, nor any actual electronic activity at all in the Harman Kardon mechanisms of the room. But out of the corner of my eye I will notice an old yellow feline dragging himself stealthily out of the room, toward the chair in which Ingraham is bound. And still the music will wash over us:

'Tis the answer, 'tis the end and all of living!
For it is love alone that rules for aye!

Sadly, Bolshakov will remark, "The same appalling sounds came from my automobile's radio when I was attempting, those years long gone, to follow you out of Pittsburgh."

"There *are* ghosts in this hotel, you know," I will comment.

"Yes, I suffered to sit through your *Mezzaluna*," he will say, "but there was no ghostly music in your play." He will pause to admire my elaborate Harman Kardon stereophonic system and to run his hands over the walnut wood cabinets of the components. "If we *must* have musical accompaniment for our lovemaking, let us have something that we can listen to."

I will be aware that in the other room, the cat is standing on its hind legs behind Ingraham's chair, attempting to reach the cords that bind Ingraham's hands. "What would you like?" I will ask him. "My collection is enormous."

"How about Ravel's *Bolero?*" he will request.

A trite suggestion, but I will put it on for him, deliberately dawdling while searching for it, finding it, and putting it on the turntable, in order to give Morris more time to do whatever it is that he will be trying to do.

Then, as the exotic, pounding strains of the *Bolero* succeed in drowning out the Victor Herbert, Bolshakov and I will return to the conversation pit to pick up where we have left off. Morris will no longer be anywhere around. I will wonder if he has given up whatever attempt he will have been making to free Ingraham.

Bolshakov, taking notice of haggard Ingraham, will request of me, "Tell him, on one of your cards, to watch carefully what you are about to do to me, because his turn will come next."

I will perhaps be playing my last card to Ingraham, which will say, *He really wants to get fucked, and he thinks that I will fuck you next. Has Morris freed your hands? Simply nod your head if he has.* I will hold this card so that Ingraham can read it, and he will smile and give his head the slightest nod.

Then Bolshakov will lay aside his pistol once more and recline in expectation of my mounting him.

I will mount him.

Oh, there will have been so many times when Travis or Billy, no less than Islamber or Dzhordzha or Kenny or one of the many others, lay supine beneath me while I rode upon him from above. But it will have been, always, them inside of me. Now it will be me inside of him.

And my only profound regret will be that perhaps I shall never live to describe the whole experience, even in the future tense.

But the American master of the future tense, Ingraham, will have left the chair where he was bound and will be heading for the cushion where lies the pistol of Bolshakov.

He will reach the pistol, and he will seize it!

Beloved Ingraham, my sworn brother, will point the pistol at Bolshakov and say, "All right, this disgusting spectacle has continued long enough."

"I tied you!" Bolshakov will screech. "How did you get loose?"

One time Ingraham confessed to me that often when he cannot hear someone he successfully guesses what among the infinite possibilities the person has actually spoken. This will be one of those times. "Nelson Eddy untied me," Ingraham will say. "Now get up and put on your clothes. Kat, you phone for the police—or the sheriff or whoever this town has."

Bolshakov will utter a string of Russian obscenities, but he will rise up and reach for his trousers. He will make as if to step his feet into them but will then—as I gasp in foreknowledge of his intention—toss the trousers into Ingraham's face, momentarily blocking his vision, and then he will lunge at Ingraham and seize with both hands the hand holding the gun and will attempt to twist the weapon from Ingraham's grasp. The gun will go off. The two men will wrestle for possession of it, and I will find myself in my kitchen, desperately searching for some weapon: a knife or a bludgeon—for the drug may have left me submissive but it will not have rendered me incapable of thinking of aggressive maneuvers.

Ingraham and Bolshakov will be on the floor together, embracing in almost a parody of sex but fighting over possession of the pistol. I will find myself standing over them with a copper teakettle, the only thing I will have been able to think of as a weapon. I will be swinging the teakettle by its handle, waiting for a chance to bean Bolshakov with it. But the two men will be shifting position so rapidly in their struggle that I will not be able to get a good aim at Bolshakov's skull, and I will fear hitting Ingraham instead by mistake.

The contest between the two men will not be exactly equal: Ingraham, fifty-seven years of age, will be the bigger, the heavier, ostensibly the

stronger; but scrawny Bolshakov will have had, as a former KGB operative, annual training sessions in physical combat and the martial arts,
and he will, alas, be in much better condition than Ingraham. I will fault
myself for not having phoned for help immediately, but I will tell myself
there has been no time.

There will be no time, and before I will have been able to intercede
in any way, my tormentor will overpower my mentor and will regain
possession of the weapon, with which Bolshakov will assassinate Ingraham
at close range, firing three shots into his breast.

I will scream and hope that help will come.

"Drop your silly teakettle, Yekaterina," Bolshakov will say, standing
over the blood-spurting body of the Bard of the Bodarks. He will point
the weapon at me. Panting desperately for breath, he will gasp, "Now
it appears that I am going to have to shoot you also, without having
consummated our relationship as I had intended." He will aim the pistol
in the direction of my heart, and he will conclude, "Oh, there was so
much I wanted to say to you first! There was so much that you needed
to know! But now it is too late! Take with you to hell the eternal memory
of how your fictions destroyed my life!"

At the instant he pulls the trigger, from somewhere in the air—the
top of a highboy, the top of a door frame—a ball of yellow fur will
drop down on Bolshakov's head, and sharp claws will pierce both sides
of Bolshakov's neck, and Bolshakov will scream in pain as he feels his
jugular punctured, and his fired shot will enter the ceiling. With his free
hand he will swat frantically at the cat clinging to his neck, but Morris,
with incredible strength, will sink his claws even deeper into Bolshakov's
neck, and Bolshakov will fall to his knees, and I will bring the teakettle
crashing down atop his head, careful to avoid hitting the cat too. Morris
will release him and scamper away. I will hit Bolshakov again with the
teakettle. And again. I will be tempted to pick up the pistol and shoot
him with it, but I will realize that I am not capable of killing, even
without the drug.

I will find myself standing dazed with a hideously battered teakettle
in my hand, its bottom and sides mashed and dented by Bolshakov's
skull. Bolshakov will be totally unconscious. Ingraham will still retain

the last vestige of his consciousness: his eyes glazed and rolling heavenward, his hand clutching his breast as if to stop the pouring out of his life's blood. I will drop down and kneel beside him. He will be beyond medical help.

He will attempt to focus his eyes upon me and will utter a word, which I will not be able to hear. I will incline my ear to his mouth. "Louder, Ingraham," I will beg.

He will repeat himself, the one word audible: "Sister."

I will rest my cheek against his cheek, and I will begin weeping. "Brother," I will say.

He will close his tortured eyes, but he will not be quite dead. He will say one thing more: "Bury me in the woods of Stick Around."

"Stick around," I will say, and only afterward, after they have taken his body away, will I realize that I will not have simply confirmed his final two words but will have spoken them as a futile entreaty, as futile as the entreaty that the namer of the town originally made.

III

THE REST—AND I WILL HAVE TO plagiarize in my haste—will be a little flattish and faded. After the officers have come and done all of their business—the sheriff's officers first, who will manacle and revive the assassin, handling him roughly, restoring him to consciousness enough so that I can spit in his face and hear his final words to me, "Aha, Yekaterina! That was your substitute for the semen you could not give me!"—after the sheriff himself has questioned me about what transpired and why—after the sheriff's photographer has snapped the body from all angles—after the coroner's men have taken it away—and after, finally, the wicked drug Bolshakov gave me has worn off, leaving me . . . I will almost write, *myself again,* but I shall never be myself again, nor shall I ever write again—leaving me too wakeful to get through the long night, I will haul out my bottle of Stolichnaya and I will sit for a long time beside the telephone, wanting to call Sharon or somebody, even Travis, perhaps (it will still be before midnight on the coast, whereas Sharon will have been in bed asleep beside her Larry for a long time now). I will sit, continually refilling my glass with vodka, and at last my cat, my savior, will reappear, and I will decide to talk to him.

The next morning, *this* morning, late, approaching noon, the first thing I will remember will be that I have an appointment today to be interviewed by the *Paris Review*. I will be tempted to phone to cancel the appointment. But probably the interviewer will already be on her way, arriving at any minute.

The second thing I will remember—and I will be mindful that I am deliberately not remembering what will have happened in this apartment the night before—will be the dreamlike conversation I will have had with Morris. It will seem that for some time I will have thanked him for having saved my life but will have received no word of acknowledgment from him in return. It will seem that I will have consumed, even for me, an inordinate amount of vodka, and that I will have begun to pour out to Morris my feelings for Ingraham, the depths of my sadness, my sense of responsibility, my sense of guilt: If I had not persuaded him to stick around the night before he might very well still have been living even as I will be speaking. It will seem that Morris has listened patiently, sympathetically, mournfully, but has said nothing in reply.

I will not be able to recall if the words I eventually hear from Morris are actually spoken by him or are only dreamt by me in whatever semblance of sleep I will finally attain. Will I actually succeed in sleeping? The state of shock in which I will have remained will not keep me continually awake so much as the fear that the preview of death that every sleep actually is will terrify me too much to allow myself to enter it. Will Morris know of my terror of sleep's preparation for dying? It will seem to me that he will ultimately begin to speak, lecturing me about the differences between sleep and death, the one's uncontrolled plunge into disjointed events, the other's beautifully orchestrated travel through the harmony of time; the one's fitful sense of being subjected to puzzling phenomena, the other's excellent knowing of the final union of personal will and cosmic purpose. It will seem that Morris will have reminded me of his—or of Dan's (or will they not be the same?)— earlier commentary about the error in my obituary: The condition of death is not an isolation or a loneliness but their antithesis, like a "surprise birthday party, only with, if you can possibly imagine it, the entire departed population of earth in attendance. The lifeless are free to pick and choose which of those billions they may communicate with, but *all* of them are there, almost like a multitude of angels dancing on the head of a pin. So death, angel, is unimaginably not solitary but social."

"Did you call me 'angel' last night?" I will ask Morris. "Or early this morning?" But he will only commence washing himself in that way that self-conscious cats respond to spoken questions.

I will pour myself a slug of vodka, preparing myself for the interview. I will tell myself that I ought to eat something, but I will have no appetite. My phone will ring, and I will rush to it, hoping it's somebody social: Sharon or Travis or Liz. It *will* be somebody social: Jackie Randel, downstairs, letting me know that there are many media people on the phone and in the lobby, trying to get information about the previous night's event, trying to get permission to interview me. Strangely, I will think that she is referring to the séance, for I will still not be permitting myself to remember the *other* event. Chatting with her on the phone, I will finish off my glass and refill it.

"Please don't let anyone come up here," I will request of her. "Except the person from *Paris Review*. That has nothing to do with last night."

"The *Paris Review* person is here," Jackie will inform me, "and has been here for an hour, waiting with the others."

"Well, send her up," I will acquiesce. "Tell her to knock two shorts and a long, so I'll know it's her."

Waiting, I will stand at my window, and I will realize how uninteresting the view has become. A panorama from a peak loses its show through habit. The view falls away but so does the thrill. A summit leads only down. Not even that jumbo chunk of *poshlost,* Christ with his cement arms outstretched, can uplift me. I've got a long way to descend.

Somewhere out there, eastward, lies Stick Around, and I will find myself forced to think at last of my murdered mentor and his final wish, and I will realize that I will have to go, soon, to that village to attend his funeral and add my rock to the cairn that marks his hillside grave.

Thinking of cairns, I will picture Svanetia and the royal graveyard beside Saint George's church at Etseri, where I ought to be buried among my kin, although most real Svanetians seem to have preferred being buried in isolated cairns on the mountainsides. Death may be social and unimaginably gregarious, as Dan suggests, but our remains can only be interred in absolute solitude.

It will occur to me that Ingraham must have been fated to meet me and swear brotherhood so that I could honor his final request. Who fated him? Is Anangka still with me?

"Anangka?" I will call aloud, and I will address her in my native tongue: "*Im, imte, imetchu,* Anangka?"

But of course there will be no answer.

And yet, having spoken my own language again for the first time in ages, I will suddenly be seized with an idea, an ambition: to write a great Americanization of the Georgian epic, Rustavelli's *Knight in the Tiger's Skin.* I will set it in the Bodarks, in the history of Stick Around, in tribute to Ingraham, and I will call it *The Knight in the Panther's Skin,* since the old Bodarkers called their mountain lion a panther.

Whatever, a *feline.* "Morris!" I will call out for him. "I've got a new book idea!"

And I will think of stopping, right after Ingraham's funeral, at Lara Burns's cabin, to visit her A Cat Arena and to sit and

Waiting, I will stand at my window, and I will realize how uninteresting the view has become. A panorama from a peak loses its ~~appeal~~ show through habit. The view falls away but so does the thrill. A summit leads only down. Not even [that jumbo chunk of Poshlost] ~~the~~ cement Christ with ~~its~~ his arms outstretched, can uplift [I've got] me. ~~There is~~ a long way to descend.

Somewhere ~~out~~ there, eastward lies Stick Around, and I will find myself forced to think at last of my murdered mentor and his final wish, and I will realize that I will have to go, soon, to that village to attend his funeral and add my rock to the cairn that marks his hillside grave.

Thinking of cairns ~~such~~, I will picture Svanetia and the royal [beside St. George's church] graveyard at K'hourashi ETSERI, where I ought to be buried among my kin, although most Svanetians seem to have preferred being buried in isolated cairns on the mountainsides. [and unimaginably gregarious.] Death may be social, as Dan suggests, but our remains can be interred (only) in absolute solitude.

It will occur to me that Ingraham must have been [fated] ~~destined~~ to meet me and swear brotherhood so that I could honor his final request. Who ~~fated~~ him? Is Anangka still with me?

"Anangka?" I will call aloud, and I will address her in my native tongue: "Im, imte, imetchu, Anangka?"

But of course there will be no answer. And yet, having spoken my own language again for the first time in ages, I will suddenly be seized with an idea, an ambition: to write a great Americanization of the Georgian epic, Rustavelli's Knight in the Tiger's Skin. I will set it in the Bodarks, in the history of Stick Around, in ~~honor of~~ tribute to Ingraham, and I will call it The Knight in the Panther's Skin, since the old Bodarkers called their mountain lion a panther.

Whatever, a feline. "Morris!" I will call out for him. "I've got a new book idea!"

[Lara Burns's] And I will think of stopping [night] after the funeral, at ~~Latha Bourns~~ Ingraham's cabin, to visit her A Cut Arena and to sit and

The last manuscript page from V. Kelian's
Louder, Engram.

V. Kelian

the ART of FICTION cxxxviii

V. Kelian is the pseudonym of Ekaterina Vladimirovna Dadeshkeliani, who was born on May 27, 1953, at Lisedi, a remote village in the Caucasus Mountains of Georgia. Her father, Vladimir Alexandrovich Dadeshkeliani, would have been the ruling prince of Svanetia had not that principality, along with all of Georgia, been communized by the Soviet Union in 1922. Kelian would have become ruling princess if she had chosen to return to Svanetia after it regained its sovereignty following the collapse of the Soviet Union and the restoration of Georgian independence.

She majored in botany at Tbilisi University and received the equivalent of a doctorate in mycology at the University of Leningrad. A distinguished mycologist, she has published a number of scientific papers on mushrooms and is the discoverer of the rare Bodarks species Mutinus ekaterinus, *which is named after her.*

While teaching botany at her alma mater in Tbilisi in 1976, she was arrested at a human rights protest along with several other Georgian dissidents, including Zviad Ghamsa-khurdia (who later became president of independent Georgia). She spent three years in detention in Soviet Russia, both at Moscow's Serbsky Psychiatric Institute and at the strict regime prison for women in Ishimbay. Her experiences formed the basis for her first novel, Georgie Boy, *which she began writing while teaching at the University of Pittsburgh and which became an international success, both critical and financial, selling mil-lions of copies in both hardcover and paperback worldwide. The triumph of this book and of the movie version of it, filmed by Trevor Kola (the first film of the noted actor Travis Coe), made it possible for Vladimirovna to lease and refurbish the top floors of an ancient Bodarks resort hotel, which became the setting for her stage play,* The Hotel Mezzaluna.

Her other works include two collections of short stories, The Names of Seeking Games *and* Lamshged; or, The Shady Side of the Mountain, *the former set in the Bodarks, the latter the only one of her books with a Svanetian setting. Her novel* Original Flavor *was also a best-seller, and the review of it was a* Time *magazine cover story. Her major nonfiction study of American Indians,* Dawn of the Osage, *was a critical but not a popular success. Posthumously will be published her last novel,* Earthstar, *and an unfinished memoir,* Louder, Engram!

She died on Svanetian Saint George's Day, the death day of Shakespeare and Cervantes, and the birthday of her idol, Nabokov, and was buried on a hillside in a remote area of the Bodarks.

The interview was conducted in less than favorable circum-stances: only the night before, a dear friend of Kelian's had been murdered in her spacious triplex apartment on the top floors of one wing of the fortresslike Halfmoon Hotel, atop a mountain in Arcata Springs, where she had lived and worked for the past decade. The staff of the hotel had made a token gesture of tidying up after the incident, but there were still bloodstains all over the carpet. Kelian, a stunningly beautiful woman who spoke softly, with only a trace of an accent that somehow seemed more Bodarkadian than Svanetian, suggested that the interview ought to be conducted in her library, which had not been disturbed or bloodied during the foul play.

Noting the interviewer's allergy to cats, Kelian graciously removed her pet, a male tabby of marmalade color and many years, and latched the door to the animal's Cat-Port so that he could not return during the course of the interview, which took place over the duration of the afternoon. Unlike many interviews in this series, the transcription is taken directly from the tape, without any editing by the subject.

INTERVIEWER

Is this a bad time for you? I could return another day.

V. KELIAN

We may as well get it over with. Do you mind if I drink?

INTERVIEWER

Not at all. Do you mind if I ask you some questions about last night's crime?

KELIAN

I'd really rather you didn't. It has no bearing on my work.

INTERVIEWER

But wasn't the victim a fellow novelist?

KELIAN

Of such minor regard that he once confessed to me he had long ago despaired of being asked to do a *Paris Review* interview himself.

INTERVIEWER

Indeed. But he was your teacher and mentor, was he not? Wasn't he responsible for bringing you to the Bodarks so many years ago?

KELIAN

Oh? You knew him, then?

INTERVIEWER

Most of us in the Bodarks at least know of him.

KELIAN

You are from the Bodarks? I did not know that.

INTERVIEWER

Yes. Like yourself, I originated elsewhere but chose this part of the country for its . . . But forgive me, I am antic-ipating your answers. One of my first questions for you is, What made you choose the Bodarks? I should think these hills do not really resemble your native Svanetia, which is extremely mountainous and rugged.

KELIAN

The resemblance is more spiritual than topographic. I came here as part of an accident of destiny. All of my life I have been aware of being guided—sometimes com-manded—by forces or fates outside my own control.

INTERVIEWER

One might argue that your books themselves were thus composed not wholly by yourself but by those fates or forces?

KELIAN

No, my books are the only things in my life over which I have exercised absolute control. That is why I write, perhaps why any novelist writes: to have some sense of being in charge, of being capable, of being complete master of one's own vessel.

INTERVIEWER

And yet, in the history of your well-known paraphilia for twelve-year-old boys, did you not consider yourself in utter control of those youths as well?

KELIAN

Shall we not delve into my personal life?

INTERVIEWER

How can you separate your personal life from your fiction, when your fiction is replete with the manifestation of that paraphilia?

KELIAN

My fiction is invented and belongs to the public. My life is real and belongs to myself.

INTERVIEWER

Your critics have charged that all of your books are romans à clef, that you are incapable of concocting a purely imaginative plot or a character who is not closely based upon someone you've known.

KELIAN

Ha! So the characters in *Hotel Mezzaluna* are real, are they? A bunch of ghosts?

INTERVIEWER

I was going to ask you about that. Isn't it true that even your four "ghosts" in that "play for voices" are taken directly from actual historical ghosts who have been seen or heard by actual persons in this actual hotel?

KELIAN

If you'd attended the séance that was held here last night, you would've discovered that those ghosts do not exist, or at least they will not manifest themselves.

INTERVIEWER

I *did* attend the séance, and I saw you there with your friend, the late, lamented novelist. Have you considered any connection between that *séance,* which is defined as "a sitting for summoning spirits," and the sudden appearance of a long-departed spirit from your past, the Bolshakov person who was arrested for the murder?

KELIAN

Say, what is this? I thought you were supposed to be asking me questions about my working habits and what I write with and what hours I keep. I don't mind revealing that I make a monthly pilgrimage to the local Wal-Mart, where I stock up with, among other things, several packages of common Number Two lead pencils, which I do not sharpen endlessly, like Hemingway, but prefer writing with dulled, upon Wal-Mart's yellow legal pads of the long variety. I rise fairly early each morning, around seven o'clock, with a wake-up call from the desk . . . although this morning I was understandably permitted to sleep late, or to try to. After a sauna and shower—I no longer use my Jacuzzi, out of negative sentimental reasons—I usually breakfast downstairs in the Crystal Room, varying my menu from cereal one day to poached eggs with bacon the next . . . although this morning, understandably, I did not breakfast at all and in fact have had not had lunch either. Would you care for a bite?

INTERVIEWER

No, thank you, I've eaten. But don't let me stop you from eating something.

KELIAN

I'm not hungry, but if you don't mind I'll refill my drink . . . Now, would you like to ask me something about what advice I have for the young writer or whether I read my critics or what talismans I use to conjure up the magic of my art?

INTERVIEWER

Your great obligations to Nabokov are obvious, by your own admission, and I'm sure you've noticed how your life is sort of an inversion of his most famous novel, although there is not that much similarity between yourself and the notorious double Humbert. But just as Monsieur Humbert was genuinely in love with his Lolita, or Dolores, haven't you ever found yourself similarly in love with one of your boys?

KELIAN (after a long pause of thinking)

Only one.

INTERVIEWER

Dzhordzha himself? Islamber? Kenny? Or perhaps Jason, Travis, Billy . . . ?

KELIAN

How did you know of all those boys? I didn't mention *all* of them in that *Vanity Fair* piece, did I?

INTERVIEWER

I have prepared myself very thoroughly for this interview. Do you mind telling me which one it was?

KELIAN

If you must know, Travis.

INTERVIEWER

Why him more than Billy?

KELIAN

Intelligence, for one thing. You are going to ask me, now or later, to spell out for you the metaphor of the hebephiliac's seduction of the innocent, virginal youth as akin to the novelist's seduction of the innocent, virginal reader, a theme that I have been attempting with limited success to explore in my work-in-progress, my memoir, *Louder, Engram!*—its very title a shameless allusion to Nabokov's *Speak, Memory.* I am not at all confident that I shall finish the book, which has often struck me as a dreadful exercise in self-indulgence. But I have been asking myself many questions about the relationship between my lust for virginal boys and my obsession with, shall we say, virginal readers.

INTERVIEWER

Do you honestly know why it is so important to you that your boy be a virgin?

KELIAN

If he is not, it is as if the novelist discovers that someone else has already told his story. And perhaps done it better. Do you know, since you like to refer to my critics, that Pryce-Smythe wrote of my *Original Flavor,* "I feel after reading this book as if my celibacy has been ended by a master seducer."

INTERVIEWER

You must be particularly gratified that so many of your short stories have been published in such magazines as *Playboy,* where, undoubtedly, they fell into the hands of ardent young masturbators.

KELIAN

What can I say? Yes, I am. I would even confess that I have often fantasized the image of some adorable twelve-year-old lad behind the locked door of his bathroom, teaching himself how to masturbate after reading a story of mine.

INTERVIEWER

But do you think it likely he would be using your story in preference to the full-color photographs, the gatefolds?

KELIAN

A moment ago I spoke of intelligence as my reason for having loved Travis. The intelligent twelve-year-old has the wisdom both to *want* the seduction and to *appreciate* every nuance of it. The intelligent twelve-year-old is not going to be irrationally disturbed or corrupted by the initiation into sex. The intelligent boy would actually prefer the mental imagery of the story to the raw visual imagery of the cheesecake photograph.

INTERVIEWER

So you are saying that Billy was stupid?

KELIAN

If you must seize upon that particular boy, he had a number of problems, of which lack of intelligence was only one.

INTERVIEWER

You claim that you try to improve upon reality, or escape from actuality in your fictions. If you were inventing yourself as a character in a novel about, let us say, a famous novelist living in an old resort hotel in the Bodarks, wouldn't you select for the character an avocation less obvious than mushrooming? I mean, after all, the idea that mushrooms remind you of young boys' penises . . .

KELIAN

Quite frankly I have never met a mushroom the equal of a boy's urgent thing. Nor eaten one. But yes, you are right: If I wrote a novel about myself, I'd make my avocation—or my vocation, since after all I do think of writing as my avocation—the playing of the piano.

INTERVIEWER

Your fondness for concerti is well known. You have even been known to express the hope that Tchaikovsky's First Piano Concerto will be played at your funeral.

KELIAN

Did I say that publicly? Well, yes, in lieu of any spoken obsequies, I'd love to have that unabashedly romantic con-

certo played at my funeral. It can say more about me than
any words.

INTERVIEWER

Do you think often about your funeral?

KELIAN

You do not know how close I came to being killed myself
last night. I have a sense that my death could occur at any
moment. But no, I don't expect a full symphony orchestra
with a famous pianist to gather in my honor at Stick Around
and play that concerto. An old phonograph will do. The
last interviewer who asked me that question then suggested
that it would be more appropriate if I arranged to have my
ashes shipped home to Svanetia and flung to the winds
from the top of Mount Layla. A touching idea, surely, but
not one in keeping with my attachment to the Bodarks.

INTERVIEWER

Just *why* are you so attached to the Bodarks?

KELIAN

Have you ever heard of Daniel Lyam Montross?

INTERVIEWER

The name is only vaguely familiar.

KELIAN

Too bad. He deserves to be much better known. I am
going to write an idyll about him one of these days. And
as I say, I consider myself an idyllist, not a novelist. I should
explain that I have never "met" Dan Montross myself—he
died before I was born, barely—and yet he has been the
single most important person in my life.

INTERVIEWER

More important than any of your boys?

KELIAN

I will return in a minute, after opening a new bottle of vodka . . . There now. Where were we? Yes, all the boys were only diversions: playmates in the games of love and life. Dan has been more than that, and, just as Christians believe that their savior has promised them eternal life, I believe that Dan has promised me immortality in the elegiac but bucolic woodlands of the Bodarks. I don't suppose, however, that this is the sort of thing that all the aspiring writers who read these *Paris Review* interviews really want to hear, is it?

INTERVIEWER

No, they'd rather not hear your plans for the afterlife. They'd rather vicariously experience how you deal with the delicious disadvantages of your present fame.

KELIAN

Fame? "I am an obscure, doubly obscure, novelist with an unpronounceable name."

INTERVIEWER

Do I detect quotes around that statement?

KELIAN

You don't recognize it? Those were Nabokov's famous last words to the *Paris Review*.

INTERVIEWER

Oh, yes.

KELIAN

Say, are you really from the *Paris Review?*

INTERVIEWER

Of course.

KELIAN

Would you mind if I asked to see some credentials?

INTERVIEWER
Credentials? What can I show you? I don't have a membership card or anything like that.

KELIAN
A letter of authorization? Anything?

INTERVIEWER
Well, what about *this?*

KELIAN
Christ, that is a pistol. Put it back in your purse.

INTERVIEWER
Not until I've used it for the purpose I intended.

KELIAN
Which is . . . ?

INTERVIEWER
Why, to kill you, of course. By your own admission, you've seen this coming. You expected me.

KELIAN
Who are you?

INTERVIEWER
My name is Barbara Phillips. Doesn't the name Phillips mean anything to you?

KELIAN
It's a very common name. Have I ever met you before? Did you send me a manuscript to read? Phillips? I get an awful lot of unwelcome manuscripts in the mail, as if somehow I had the power to make them publishable, which they aren't. I'm sorry if I didn't respond to your manuscript.

INTERVIEWER

I am a writer, yes, but you haven't read anything of mine or been sent anything of mine to read. I have spent too much of my adult life trying to be a writer, often to the neglect of everything else. Especially to the neglect of my son, William.

KELIAN

Getting published is often simply a matter of lucky breaks and of knowing the right people. I could help you find a sympathetic editor for your stuff, if you'd let me.

INTERVIEWER

You really don't notice anything outside yourself, do you? Now you are even getting drunk, so that you can't fully appreciate why you are being shot.

KELIAN

I am getting drunk because I had a terrifying experience last night, and now you are trying to give me another one. I think one horror is enough for one day. Unless this is still night . . . and you are simply one of my nightmares. I have noticed, by the way, that this appears to be more or less in the present tense, whereas I had distinctly shifted into the future tense in what I was creating.

INTERVIEWER

I ought to be your worst nightmare. But I am sure it never even occurred to you that I existed. Did you ever even think to ask Billy if his mother had any suspicion of what he was doing with you?

KELIAN

You—? You are Billy's *mother?*

INTERVIEWER

It never occurred to you that he had one, did it?

KELIAN

No. I mean, *yes,* certainly. We often spoke of you. But he assured me that you didn't care what he was doing.

INTERVIEWER

I didn't, at least not at the time he was first being debauched by you. And then, later, when I did find out about it, my reaction was not shock, or even a proper mother's protectiveness, but rather a novelist's curiosity. I thought I could convert the story of you and Billy into a novel.

KELIAN

Did you?

INTERVIEWER

I tried. For three years I tried, but then my novelist's curiosity was utterly obliterated by my grief as a failed parent. I have been unable to feel anything but guilt. No, I'll correct that: guilt and anger. Over my abject failure as a good mother and over your ruining of my son.

KELIAN

Do you hear that desperate caterwauling? My cat wants in. Do you mind if I let my cat in?

INTERVIEWER

Let's not disturb the poor thing with the sight of our gory bodies.

KELIAN

Our bodies?

INTERVIEWER

Yes, don't you understand? I am going to kill you for your indecency, and then I am going to kill myself for my negligence.

KELIAN

Your tape recorder is still running. Do I have time for some last words?

INTERVIEWER

I'm afraid not. Haven't you said enough?

—**Barbara Phillips**

On a Book Entitled Louder, Engram!

DID EKATERINA ACTUALLY DIE? When I accepted the invitation from her publisher to edit these memoirs, it was with the clear understanding that I would not be able to communicate with the author. At the time of her supposed assassination, I was in Paris researching a project involving the medical profession's habits of prevarication, which had consumed me for so long that I had not even been aware of *Vanity Fair*'s exposé of the true identity of V. Kelian.

Thus, whatever surprise I may have felt at the news of her death was overmatched by my astonishment at the discovery of the identity of V. Kelian, whose first novel I reviewed so warmly in the pages of *The New York Review of Books* and whose subsequent books I consumed (and reviewed) with almost equal admiration. Indeed, my immediate reaction to her death was to search for a copy of that first novel and reread it in light of the knowledge that its author was female. In Paris, I could find only a used paperback of *Le Garçon Georges,* but that sufficed to satisfy my rethinking of the novel and my *arrière-pensée* that Ekaterina's achievement in having identified so thoroughly with a twelve-year-old boy was not so much the result of having lived through an actual affair of the kind *Georgie Boy* depicts as it was a triumph of the empathetic imagination. For the longest time, I could only believe that Ekaterina simply wanted to imagine that she had been murdered.

I was still in Paris, putting the finishing touches on my book *Why*

Doctors Lie when that autumn's now-notorious issue of *Paris Review* appeared, with the sensational interview of "V. Kelian" wherein the interviewer performs the actual killing that many interviewers can only hope to perform symbolically. (That literary quarterly, by the way, despite its title, is not published in Paris and actually has nothing to do with that city, wherein sheer coincidence alone happened to find me at the time the issue came out.) The decision to append that *Paris Review* interview to the present volume was one for which I assume sole responsibility, feeling that it makes a kind of necessary coda to the essentially unfinished story of Ekaterina's life. I have, however, felt constrained to omit the note by the *Paris Review* editors in which they rather coyly and disingenuously apologize for having commissioned Barbara Phillips to do the interview without knowing that she had an exceptional ax to grind or crime to commit. ("Of the one hundred and thirty-seven distinguished authors interviewed in these pages over the years, not one had ever been literally murdered.")

The substance of the interview itself, when first I read it, did not greatly interest me; only one item captivated my attention: the mention of the Tchaikovsky First Piano Concerto, which I had, in my review of *Georgie Boy,* guessed—correctly, it would seem—had mightily influenced the life and prose of the writer. I became seized with a simple wish to find out if that music had actually been played during Ekaterina's funeral . . . if any sort of services had actually been held . . . if Ekaterina had actually died.

But I was also somewhat uneasy about the italicized prefatory remarks to the interview, which, assuming Barbara Phillips was their author, must have been written *after* the supposed interview and shootings took place, but could not have been written by Barbara Phillips if she had killed herself after killing Ekaterina. Could they have? I wrote to the editors of *Paris Review* to clarify this point but thus far have received no reply. The newspapers *did* say of the tragedy that it *was* a homicide-suicide by Barbara Phillips.

My obsession to learn the truth was fueled and consummated through a stroke of fate that left me forever afterward a believer in Anangka, as Ekaterina was wont to render the Greek personification of Fate, sweet

Ananke (the word means "necessity" in Greek): My university forwarded to me a letter from her publisher inviting me to read, evaluate, edit, and if need be annotate the manuscript of *Louder, Engram!* The invitation had been prompted by some references within the manuscript to myself, including, I was abashed to discover, Ekaterina's wish to include the entire text of my original review of *Georgie Boy.* (Despite my insistence on its removal from these pages—no quirk of false modesty on my part—I have been persuaded to let the review stand uncut.)

As soon as my work on the doctor book permitted, I began a close, attentive, indeed enthralled reading of Ekaterina's uncompleted auto-biography in holograph photocopy. I armed myself with a stack of books too numerous to bibliograph here—but I ought to mention three: Doug-las W. Freshfield's two-volume *Exploration of the Caucasus* (London and New York: Edward Arnold, 1896), with, despite its age, excellent pho-togravures by Vittorio Sella of the Suanetian (sic) landscape and people; Clive Phillipps-Wolley's quaint but condescending two-volume *Savage Svânetia* (London: Richard Bentley & Son, 1883), with some amazing wood engravings; and, of our own century, Alexander Kuznetzov's *Look Down, Svanetia* (as its title would translate from Russian; Moscow: Molodaya Gvardeya, 1971) with amateurish but candid snapshot photos. My leisure hours were filled with an honest attempt to read Rustavelli's *Knight in the Tiger's Skin* and the various books by David Marshall Lang on Georgian history and culture. In one of those bookstalls on a Left Bank *quai,* Anangka led me to a yellowed issue of the American monthly *National Geographic* (July 1942), which contains an article, "Roaming Russia's Caucasus," by Rolf Singer, who discusses Svanetia (pp. 96 ff.) and gives proof, if any were needed, that its ex-ruler was one "Prince Dadish Kiliani," as Singer spells it, thinking Dadish the given name; I was able to determine that he was referring to our Ekaterina's great-uncle.

Finished with my first reading of Ekaterina's manuscript, I was embarrassingly slow to ask myself the question that has already occurred to the intelligent reader of this memoir: How could Ekaterina have referred to the interview as a *fait accompli* in several earlier parts of her story? (Cf. pp. 236, 255, 264, and 267). In other words, if she actually died at the conclusion of the interview, how could she have referred *back* to the interview in the past tense in at least five earlier parts of the manuscript? Even given her flagrant toying and frolicking with time and grammatical tenses (an indulgent habit she picked up from her mentor "Ingraham"), wherein we are often lost in time between past and future, there is simply no way that she could have anticipated what happened to her during Barbara Phillips's interview . . . unless she was *planning* it as part of the work of art's creative structure.

(Incidentally, in the history of American fiction there was a very minor writer, a dime-novelist named Prentiss Ingraham [1843–1904], who wrote over six hundred novels, two hundred of which were devoted to William "Buffalo Bill" Cody; but the "Ingraham" of Ekaterina can scarcely be considered even to allude to the actual writer Prentiss Ingraham.)

When I returned to this country last summer (my sabbatical was ended and I had fall classes coming up), I had time only for a very hurried trip, my first, to the "Bodarks," that lost secret heart of America. My ultimate goal was to find some concrete evidence, such as a tombstone, to prove that Ekaterina no longer exists. But I also wanted to see with my own eyes the "Halfmoon Hotel" in charming "Arcata Springs." In fact, I spent a couple of nights in that limestone mountaintop lodge . . . and no ghosts walked. Through the unflagging courtesy of Jackie Randel (one of several people whose actual names Ekaterina does not conceal in her memoir), I was permitted to tour the late novelist's spacious suite of rooms on the hotel's top floors. The rooms are still awaiting a new tenant. There are the faintest ghosts of bloodstains on the carpet, but Jackie Randel herself was not certain whether the blood donor was Ekaterina, Barbara Phillips, "Ingraham," Bolshakov . . . or all four. I asked her if she had herself seen Ekaterina's dead body. She confessed to a certain squeamishness that had kept her outside the door while the officers, coroner, et al. were within.

While I was viewing that penthouse with its stark confrontation by the gauche cement giant *Christ of the Bodarks,* I was gently accosted, or simply examined, by a slow, heavy yellow cat, whom I recognized at once and without much surprise. Morris, of course! Approaching twenty

years of age, he was still the "General Manager" of the hotel, according
to Jackie Randel. He was still the favorite of guests, who were asked
not to fondle him because of his advanced arthritis. So I did not pick
him up. But I returned his scrutiny of me sufficiently to convince myself
that he was no longer—if he had ever been—inhabited by the spirit of
Daniel Lyam Montross. Ekaterina really did possess, I need not tell the
reader of this memoir, a fantastic imagination.

But she often in her memoir is starkly truthful without embellishment, embroidery, or deception. As but one example, she does not
exaggerate her own difficulties in reaching that mountain-locked, mysterious Arcadian ghost village that she, out of deference to her mentor
"Ingraham," has chosen to call here "Stick Around." I had rented a self-
drive car at the "Fateville" airport, which easily got me to "Arcata
Springs" with time en route to admire the same scenery she had shown
to the great Trevor Kola. But that car, a small Avis Chrysler, was not
able to get me to Stick Around. Although I'd taken the trouble to reread
the manuscript with special notice of the descriptions of the route
southward from the still-living village of "Acropolis" (as she disguises it
early on) or Parthenon (as it is actually called, and as she calls it toward
the end, dropping her disguises), I became, as she had done, as "Ingraham"
himself had done, hopelessly lost. After two hours of driving, or attempting to drive, that small Chrysler into the most nearly impassable
byroads, I gave up, found a farmhouse where I inquired directions, and
was informed that I was "way off." The owners of the farmhouse knew,
however, the Ingledews, and they offered me their phone and the number
of Sharon Ingledew Brace. Her husband, Lawrence Brace, answered and
offered to drive over and get me in a vehicle that I recognized, as soon
as I saw her, as Silvia, who, Brace said, Ekaterina had bequeathed to
him. He became, for the rest of my brief stay in Bodarkadia, my invaluable
escort, and his generous assistance made the balance of my visit worthwhile. I am very grateful.

Subsequently, Lawrence Brace presented me with a copy of the still-
unfinished typescript of the critical study he has been preparing for seven
years, provisionally called *Benedictions and Maledictions: The Life and Work*

of Daniel Lyam Montross, which, when it is published, may shed additional light on the mysterious relationship that existed between Ekaterina and the dead poet whom she never met.

During the brief tour that Larry (in Silvia) gave me of what little remains of the village of "Stick Around," not even a conventional ghost town of the sort one pictures in western mining operations or cowboy sagas, I was especially cognizant of the restoration that had recently been performed on the verandahed two-story Victorian that had been the Governor Jacob Ingledew House and later the little village's one sleepy hotel. I asked Larry to stop. I asked him who lived there now. No one, he said, although he himself had lived there for a couple of years before he married Sharon. But obviously, I pointed out, somebody has fixed it up carefully. Who owns it? I asked. Vernon Ingledew, Larry informed me. A line of Ekaterina's text came back to me: *Vernon alone knows the identity of the new owner of the house, who bought what's left of it from him for, if not a song, a promise not to sing.* Where can I find him? I asked. Larry replied, with a condescending smile for my ignorance, "In the governor's mansion, of course." I studied the house carefully but in vain for any signs that its occupant, if it was occupied, might be a woman. I asked if I could go in, but Larry told me Vernon had the only key. "Is there anything else you'd like to see?" he asked, and I replied that I'd hoped to be shown Ekaterina's final resting place.

Larry drove me up the mountain as far as Silvia could reach. Then we walked for perhaps a quarter of a mile through weeds and woods in the late-afternoon heat of August, I carrying in my arms a green-wax-paper-wrapped bundle of three dozen red roses that I had purchased at a florist's in "Harriman" in good faith, having persuaded myself, at that point, that I conceivably might come to believe that Ekaterina was dead. We came to a sloping forest glade in a grove of red cedars where there was a single tombstone.

"That's Montross," Larry said, gazing upon the lone memorial with the sad affection of a scholar who has devoted seven years of his life to one man's story. There was no tombstone for Ekaterina.

"Where is hers?" I asked.

He pointed toward the deep woods. "Farther along," he said. He said, or rather, asked rhetorically, "Don't you know that she really had no claim to be buried beside him?"

We went deeper into the woods up the mountain, and came in time to, sure enough, a modest marble marker beside a cairn of stones, freshly stacked. Bodark people are not buried beneath cairns; Svanetians are. The small tombstone bore the engraved letters of her name, dates, and the simple inscription, NOBODY HAS TO DIE IN THE END OF ONE'S OWN PICTURE, which, I realized after only a moment's thought, was a direct quotation from Ekaterina, spoken to Trevor Kola when she was attempting to reassure him that there was nothing wrong with keeping Georgie alive in the end of the film *Georgie Boy.*

Smiling, I asked Larry, "Who chose to put these words on the stone?"

"Why, *she* did, of course," he replied. And then he, noticing the way I was looking around as if searching for something or someone, asked, "What are you looking for?"

"Where is 'Ingraham'?"

Larry gestured, sweeping his arm as if to encompass all the woods, or all the world. "Oh, he's buried much farther up the mountain, in a remote glen by a waterfall. I've never been there myself, so I couldn't take you to it."

"Ah yes," I said, and said nothing more. I unwrapped my three dozen red roses and arranged them carefully upon Ekaterina's cairn. Red roses are of course the expression of love, and Larry understood without my telling him the essential reason for my love, which, I hope, has found its way into the heart of every male reader of her memoir: We want to believe, all of us men, that we are grown-up and manly, but the simple, sometimes embarrassing truth is that none of us have ever stopped being twelve years old.

I am always twelve. And Ekaterina always lives. You who want to believe that Ekaterina did not die, forgive me my tears, and join in them.

It has been my privilege, and my pleasure, to prepare this work for publication. My job has not been an unmitigated joy: I had to fight with Ekaterina's publisher to preserve her desired title, which they felt was too allusive and punning (and they proposed such alternatives as *Princess* with a *Pen* or *Good-bye to the Old World* or the direct and colorless *My Story: The Life of V. Kelian*). I had to resist their determined efforts to remove all of her references to the whole vast and sometimes corrupt machinery of the "publishing world." Their argument that this was "inside stuff" of little interest to the general reader struck me as transparently self-protective and overly sensitive. My obligation has been to be as faithful as possible to the spirit of Ekaterina . . . wherever it is.

My private sufferings, the insect pests that reminded me that not only death but ticks too are in Bodarkadia, should not be anybody's concern, but I cite them as part of the price of bringing this task to completion: My legs were covered with chigger bites before I could leave "Stick Around," and I lost the first two weeks of the fall semester bedridden with Lyme disease, the ravages of the bacteria *Borrelia burgdorferi* infested in me by the bite of a tiny tick who was waiting for me in the woods or weeds near Ekaterina's grave or that of—I think of the punning irony of his middle name—Daniel Lyam Montross.

In the silence of the forest that hot, still August afternoon (there was not a mushroom anywhere in sight), with dusk falling and Larry urging that we should start back, I sought to catch any sound of the Tchaikovsky First Piano Concerto, any portion of the strains of the elegiac, haunting mood of that musical trail through an uncharted pastoral woodland. Larry mentioned that indeed the burial of Ekaterina had included the playing, on a portable battery-operated phonograph, of the RCA Victor record of Van Cliburn performing that work for the piano, with orchestra. I had been mildly disappointed to discover that the concluding pages of *Louder, Engram!*, unlike the magnificent finale of *Georgie Boy*, were not written in prose that paralleled the Tchaikovsky concerto. Or, if they were, I realized, I had better try again to "hear" them. There are no orgasms in the end of this work . . . unless, as Montross expresses it himself on the last page of his *Dream of a Small but Unlost Town*, the supreme orgasm, unknown and unimagined by us still living, is the moment of death. "I'm singing the short song of my last instant's ecstasy."

Frivolity and ecstasy are the twin poles between which we humans play, said Huizinga in his *Homo Ludens*, "Playful Man," and the elusive Tchaikovsky I was trying so hard to hear in that moment at Ekaterina's grave was not "playing," but it was *there* as certainly as Ekaterina herself was, and I realized that perhaps I *could* hear at least some of those snatches of the old folk tunes and popular waltzes rearranged for the keyboard and orchestra that had left poor Peter Ilyich open to charges of plagiarism as surely as Yekaterina Vladimirovna will be open, with this book, to charges of having borrowed too freely from Nabokov and from "Ingraham" and from who-knows-what hoards of Georgian and Svanetian folklore, ritual, and custom. I began to understand something very important about Ekaterina's favorite music as well as Ekaterina's final book: Both have as their true subject not frivolity, not ecstasy, not the yearnings and seekings, the losings and findings, of the human spirit, but art itself. "Art is, after all, more real than life," said V. Kelian. The Tchaikovsky is *about* music, about the making of music, about the possibilities and the limitations of the piano in relation to the other instruments of the orchestra; it is, to use the jargon of contemporary criticism, "self-referential," "self-conscious," or "self-reflexive" music. It is involuted around itself.

And so, of course, is *Louder, Engram!* It exists to remind us that our Ekaterina was, she certainly *was,* and she was not at all.